George Washington

Official Letters to the Honourable American Congress

Written during the war between the United colonies and Great Britain. Vol. 1

George Washington

Official Letters to the Honourable American Congress
Written during the war between the United colonies and Great Britain. Vol. 1

ISBN/EAN: 9783337412029

Printed in Europe, USA, Canada, Australia, Japan

Cover: Foto ©Andreas Hilbeck / pixelio.de

More available books at **www.hansebooks.com**

OFFICIAL LETTERS

TO THE HONOURABLE

AMERICAN CONGRESS,

WRITTEN DURING THE WAR BETWEEN THE

UNITED COLONIES AND GREAT BRITAIN,

BY HIS EXCELLENCY

GEORGE WASHINGTON,

COMMANDER IN CHIEF OF THE
CONTINENTAL FORCES,

NOW

PRESIDENT OF THE UNITED STATES.

Copied, by Special Permission, from the Original Papers preserved
in the Office of the Secretary of State, Philadelphia.

VOL. I.

Second Boston Edition.

Boston:
Printed by Manning & Loring,
For S. HALL, W. SPOTSWOOD, J. WHITE,
THOMAS & ANDREWS, D. WEST,
E. LARKIN, W. P. BLAKE,
and J. WEST.

1796.

ADVERTISEMENT.

RESPECTING the source from which the following Letters have been drawn, and the grounds on which the reader is expected to rest his belief of their authenticity, it may be sufficient to inform him, that permission was obtained from the proper authority, to transcribe, from the original papers preserved in the Secretary of State's office in Philadelphia, these and sundry other authentic documents relating to the contest between the colonies and the mother country, viz. Letters from the Commanders of the continental forces, and other persons employed in the public service,—intercepted Letters from British Officers and other adherents to the royal cause,—Communications from the Governors, Conventions, and Committees, of the several American States,—Dispatches from Agents and Commissioners,—Instructions,—Reports of Committees of Congress,—parts of the secret Journals hitherto unpublished,—and various other pieces elucidative of the events which led to and finally established American Independence.

That permission was granted early in the year 1792, and immediate advantage was
taken

taken of the indulgence; though, from various circumftances, of little confequence to the reader to know, the publication has been fo long delayed. Even at this late period, the editor contents himfelf with laying before the public but a part of the collection,—intending, if thefe volumes meet with a favourable reception, to continue the publication, and prefent his readers with a variety of interefting pieces penned by the leaders and principal agents in the American Revolution, and tending to throw light on many important tranfactions that have hitherto been either enveloped in total darknefs, or, at beft, but obfcurely perceived, and imperfectly underftood.

Some parts of thefe letters may perhaps appear too full of minutiæ to intereft that clafs of readers, who, unaccuftomed to enter into the inveftigation of caufes or confequences, delight only in recitals of battles, fieges, and other ftriking occurrences which conftitute the more prominent features of hiftory. But, to the reafoning philofophic reader, who wifhes to explore the fecret fprings of action,—to trace events to their remote and latent caufes,—to difcover and examine the fubordinate and collateral circumftances (oft trifling in appearance, and generally overlooked by the vulgar eye) which, in the ftruggles of contending nations give a preponderancy to the one or the other fcale,—thofe minute details will, it

is

is prefumed, be far from unacceptable, as furnifhing him with that fpecies of informa-tion, upon which alone he can venture to ground a decifive opinion, and which he might elfewhere feek in vain.

The inclofures, frequently referred to in thefe volumes, would ftill further contribute to fet every circumftance in a clearer and ftronger light; and it was the editor's origi-nal intention that they fhould have accompa-nied the letters to which they refpectively belong. Obftacles, however, *at prefent* infur-mountable, ftand in the way of their imme-diate publication: but, when thefe are re-moved, the papers alluded to fhall make their appearance in form of an Appendix,—fuch parts of them at leaft, as are of a curious and interefting nature.

Meanwhile the reader will obferve, that it was deemed as yet premature to publifh cer-tain paffages of thefe letters: fome omiffions have of courfe taken place, which are every where pointed out by afterifks, and which will be fupplied at a proper feafon, probably not far diftant. On the other hand, in per-haps half a dozen inftances a fingle word has been hazarded on conjecture, to fill up a chafm, where either the original or the copy happened to be torn or defaced; in which cafes, the fupplemental words are inclofed within crotchets and printed in Italic. A few entire letters, moreover, as appears by refer-ence made to them in fubfequent ones, are

A 2

here

here wanted to complete the chain of correfpondence. Thefe the editor can give no
account of, as the originals appear to have
been loft from the files of office.

About a dozen letters, written by the general's fecretary,* are here inferted ;—a few
from the general himfelf to the board of war,
or committee of Congrefs,—one to the prefident of the New-York Convention, and one
to R. Morris, efquire, in the department of
finance. Thefe it was thought improper to
omit : nor did it feem worth while, on account of a few exceptions, to make any alteration in the general title of the book.

* Mr. R. H. Harrifon.

OFFICIAL LETTERS

FROM

GENERAL WASHINGTON

TO

CONGRESS.

To the Honourable Members of the Continental Congress, at Philadelphia.

GENTLEMEN,   *New-York, June 24, 1775.*

THE rain on Friday afternoon and Saturday,—the advice of several gentlemen of the Jerseys and this city, by no means to cross Hudson's river at the lower ferry—and some other circumstances, too trivial to mention, prevented my arrival at this place, until the afternoon of this day.

In the morning, after giving general Schuyler such orders, as, from the result of my inquiry into matters here, appear necessary, I shall set out on my journey to the camp at Boston, and shall proceed with all the dispatch in my power. Powder is so essential an article, that I cannot help again repeating the necessity of a supply. The camp at Boston, from the best account I can get from thence, is but very poorly supplied. At this place, they have scarce any. How they are provided at general Wooster's camp, I have not been able yet to learn.

Governor Tryon is arrived, and general Schuyler directed to advise you of the line of conduct he moves in. I fear it will not be very favourable to the American cause.

I have only to add, that I am, with great respect and regard, gentlemen, your most obedient and obliged humble servant, G. WASHINGTON.

To

To JOHN HANCOCK, *esquire, President of Congress.*

New-York, Sunday, 24th June, 1775, 5 o'clock, P. M.
SIR,

UPON my arrival here this afternoon, I was informed that an express was in town, from the provincial camp in Massachusetts-Bay; and having seen, among the papers in his possession, a letter directed to you as President of the Congress, I have taken the liberty to open it. I was induced to take that liberty by several gentlemen of New-York who were anxious to know the particulars of the affair of the seventeenth instant, and agreeable to the orders of many members of the Congress, who judged it necessary that I should avail myself of the best information in the course of my journey.

You will find, Sir, by that letter, a great want of powder in the provincial army, which I sincerely hope the Congress will supply as speedily and as effectually as in their power. One thousand pounds in weight were sent to the camp at Cambridge, three days ago, from this city; which has left this place almost destitute of that necessary article; there being at this time, from the best information, not more than four barrels of powder in the city of New-York.

I propose to set off for the provincial camp to-morrow, and will use all possible dispatch to join the forces there.

Please to make my compliments to the gentlemen of the Congress; and believe me to be, Sir, your obliged friend, and humble servant,   G. W.

[N. B. *All the subsequent letters, not otherwise expressly directed, are addressed to the President of Congress for the time being.*]

SIR,   *Camp at Cambridge, July 10, 1775.*

I ARRIVED safe at this place on the third instant, after a journey attended with a good deal of fatigue, and retarded by necessary attentions to the successive civilities which accompanied me in my whole route.

Upon

Upon my arrival, I immediately vifited the feveral pofts occupied by our troops ; and as foon as the weather permitted, reconnoitred thofe of the enemy.   I found the latter ftrongly intrenched on Bunker's-hill, about a mile from Charleftown, and advanced about half a mile from the place of the late action, with their centries extended about one hundred and fifty yards on this fide of the narroweft part of the neck leading from this place to Charleftown.   Three floating batteries lie in Myftic river near their camp, and one twenty-gun fhip below the ferry place between Bofton and Charleftown.   They have alfo a battery on Copfe-hill, on the Bofton fide, which much annoyed our troops in the late attack.   Upon the neck, they have alfo deeply intrenched and fortified.   Their advanced guards, till laft Saturday morning, occupied Brown's houfes, about a mile from Roxbury meeting-houfe, and twenty roods from their lines : but, at that time, a party from general Thomas's camp furprifed the guard, drove them in, and burned the houfes.   The bulk of their army, commanded by general Howe, lies on Bunker's-hill, and the remainder on Roxbury-neck, except the light horfe, and a few men in the town of Bofton.

On our fide, we have thrown up intrenchments on Winter and Profpect hills, the enemy's camp in full view, at the diftance of little more than a mile.   Such intermediate points as would admit a landing, I have fince my arrival taken care to ftrengthen, down to Sewal's Farm, where a ftrong intrenchment has been thrown up.   At Roxbury, general Thomas has thrown up a ftrong work on the hill, about two hundred yards above the meeting-houfe ; which, with the brokennefs of the ground, and a great number of rocks, has made that pafs very fecure.   The troops raifed in New-Hampfhire, with a regiment from Rhode-Ifland, occupy Winter-hill : a part of thofe from Connecticut, under general Putnam, are on Profpect-hill.   The troops in this town are entirely of the Maffachufetts : the remainder of the Rhode-Ifland men are at Sewal's Farm.   Two regiments of Connecticut, and nine of the Maffachufetts, are at Roxbury.   The refidue of the army, to the number of about feven hundred, are pofted in feveral fmall towns along the coaft, to prevent the depredations of the enemy.
Upon

Upon the whole, I think myself authorised to say, that, considering the great extent of line and the nature of the ground, we are as well secured, as could be expected in so short a time, and under the disadvantages we labour. These consist in a want of engineers to construct proper works and direct the men, a want of tools, and a sufficient number of men to man the works in case of an attack. You will observe, by the proceedings of the council of war which I have the honour to inclose, that it is our unanimous opinion, to hold and defend these works as long as possible.

The discouragement it would give the men, and its contrary effects on the ministerial troops, thus to abandon our encampment in their face, formed with so much labour,—added to the certain destruction of a considerable and valuable extent of country, and our uncertainty of finding a place in all respects so capable of making a stand,—are leading reasons for this determination. At the same time we are very sensible of the difficulties which attend the defence of lines of so great extent, and the dangers which may ensue from such a division of the army.

My earnest wish to comply with the instructions of the Congress, in making an early and complete return of the state of the army, has led into an involuntary delay of addressing you; which has given me much concern. Having given orders for this purpose immediately on my arrival,—and unapprised of the imperfect obedience which had been paid to those of the like nature from general Ward, I was led from day to day to expect they would come in, and therefore detained the messenger. They are not now so complete as I could wish : but much allowance is to be made for inexperience in forms, and a liberty which had been taken (not given) on this subject. These reasons, I flatter myself, will no longer exist ; and of consequence, more regularity and exactness will in future prevail. This, with a necessary attention to the lines, the movements of the ministerial troops, and our immediate security, must be my apology, which I beg you to lay before Congress with the utmost duty and respect.

We labour under great disadvantages for want of tents : for, though they have been helped out by a collection of now useless sails from the sea-port towns, the number is far

short

short of our necessities.   The colleges and houses of this town are necessarily occupied by the troops; which affords another reason for keeping our present situation.   But I most sincerely wish the whole army was properly provided to take the field, as I am well assured, that (besides greater expedition and activity in case of alarm) it would highly conduce to health and discipline.   As materials are not to be had here, I would beg leave to recommend the procuring a farther supply from Philadelphia, as soon as possible.

I should be extremely deficient in gratitude as well as justice, if I did not take the first opportunity to acknowledge the readiness and attention, which the provincial Congress and different committees have shewn, to make every thing as convenient and agreeable as possible. But there is a vital and inherent principle of delay, incompatible with military service, in transacting business through such numerous and different channels. I esteem it therefore my duty to represent the inconvenience which must unavoidably ensue from a dependence on a number of persons for supplies; and submit it to the consideration of Congress, whether the public service will not be best promoted by appointing a commissary-general for these purposes. We have a striking instance of the preference of such a mode, in the establishment of Connecticut, as their troops are extremely well provided under the direction of Mr. Trumbull, and he has at different times assisted others with various articles. Should my sentiments happily coincide with those of your honours on this subject, I beg leave to recommend Mr. Trumbull as a very proper person for this department. In the arrangement of troops collected under such circumstances, and upon the spur of immediate necessity, several appointments are omitted, which appear to be indispensably necessary for the good government of the army—particularly a quarter-master-general, a commissary of musters, and a commissary of artillery. These I must earnestly recommend to the notice and provision of the Congress.

I find myself already much embarrassed, for want of a military chest. These embarrassments will increase every day: I must therefore request that money may be forwarded as soon as possible. The want of this most necessary article will (I fear) produce great inconveniences, if not prevented

vented by an early attention.   I find the army in general, and the troops raifed in Maffachufetts in particular, very deficient in neceffary clothing.   Upon inquiry, there appears no probability of obtaining any fupplies in this quarter : and, on the beft confideration of this matter I am able to form, I am of opinion that a number of hunting fhirts (not lefs than ten thoufand) would in a great degree remove this difficulty, in the cheapeft and quickeft manner. I know nothing, in a fpeculative view, more trivial, yet, if put in practice, would have a happier tendency to unite the men, and abolifh thofe provincial diftinctions which lead to jealoufy and diffatisfaction.

In a former part of this letter, I mentioned the want of engineers.   I can hardly exprefs the difappointment I have experienced on this fubject,—the fkill of thofe we have being very imperfect, and confined to the mere manual exercife of cannon ; whereas the war in which we are engaged requires a knowledge, comprehending the duties of the field, and fortification.   If any perfons thus qualified are to be found in the fouthern colonies, it would be of great public fervice to forward them with all expedition.

Upon the article of ammunition, I muft re-echo the former complaints on this fubject.   We are fo exceedingly deftitute, that our artillery will be of little ufe, without a fupply both large and feafonable.   What we have muft be referved for the fmall arms, and that managed with the utmoft frugality.   *   *   *

The ftate of the army you will find afcertained with tolerable precifion in the returns which accompany this letter.   Upon finding the number of men to fall fo far fhort of the eftablifhment, and below all expectation, I immediately called a council of the general officers, whofe opinion (as to the mode of filling up the regiments, and providing for the prefent exigency) I have the honour of inclofing, together with the beft judgment we are able to form of the minifterial troops.   From the number of boys, deferters and negroes, that have been enlifted in the troops of this province, I entertain fome doubts whether the number required can be raifed here : and all the general officers agree that no dependence can be put on the
militia,

militia, for a continuance in camp, or regularity and difcipline during the short time they may stay. This unhappy and devoted province has been so long in a state of anarchy, and the yoke * * * * * been laid so heavily on it, that great allowances are to be made for troops raised under such circumstances. The deficiency of numbers, discipline, and stores, can only lead to this conclusion, that their spirit has exceeded their strength. But at the same time I would humbly submit to the consideration of Congress the propriety of making some further provision of men from the other colonies. If these regiments should be completed to their establishment, the difmission of those unfit for duty on account of their age and character would occasion a considerable reduction ; and, at all events, they have been enlisted upon such terms, that they may be disbanded when other troops arrive. But should my apprehensions be realized, and the regiments here be not filled up, the public cause would suffer by an absolute dependence upon so doubtful an event, unless some provision is made against such a disappointment.

It requires no military skill, to judge of the difficulty of introducing proper discipline and subordination into an army while we have the enemy in view, and are in daily expectation of an attack : but it is of so much importance, that every effort will be made, which time and circumstances will admit. In the mean time I have a sincere pleasure in observing that there are materials for a good army—a great number of able-bodied men, active, zealous in the cause, and of unquestionable courage.

I am now, Sir, to acknowledge the receipt of your favour of the twenty-eighth, inclosing the resolutions of Congress, of the twenty-seventh ultimo, and a copy of a letter from the committee of Albany ; to all which I shall pay due attention.

Generals Gates and Sullivan have both arrived in good health.

My best abilities are at all times devoted to the service of my country : but I feel the weight, importance, and variety of my present duties too sensibly, not to wish a more immediate and frequent communication with the Congress. I fear it may often happen in the course of our present operations, that I shall need that assistance and direction from them, which time and distance will not allow me to receive.

Since writing the above, I have also to acknowledge your favour of the fourth instant by Fessenden, and the receipt of the commissions, and articles of war. The former are yet eight hundred short of the number required. This deficiency you will please to supply as soon as you conveniently can. Among the other returns, I have also sent one of our killed, wounded, and missing, in the late action; but have been able to procure no certain account of the loss of the ministerial troops. My best intelligence fixes it at above five hundred killed, and six or seven hundred wounded: but it is no more than conjecture,—the utmost pains being taken on their side to conceal it. I have the honour to be, &c,　　　　　　　　　　G. W.

P. S. Having ordered the commanding officer to give me the earliest intelligence of every motion of the enemy by land or water, discernible from the heights of his camp, I this instant, as I was closing my letter, received the inclosed from the brigade major. The design of this manœuvre I know not;—perhaps it may be to make a descent somewhere along the coast;—it may be for New-York; or it may be practised as a deception on us. I thought it not improper however to mention the matter to you: I have done the same to the commanding officer at New-York; and I shall let it be known to the committee of safety here, so that intelligence may be communicated, as they shall think best, along the sea-coast of this government.

SIR,　　　　　　　　　　*Camp at Cambridge, July* 14, 1775.

SINCE I did myself the honour of addressing you on the tenth instant, nothing material has happened in the camp. From some authentic and late advices of the state of the ministerial troops, and the great inconvenience of calling in the militia in the midst of harvest, I have been induced for the present to wave it:—but in the mean time recruiting parties have been sent throughout this province,

to

to fill up the regiments to the eſtabliſhment of the provincial Congreſs. At the ſame time that I received theſe advices, I alſo obtained a liſt of the officers of the enemy killed and wounded in the late battle at Charleſtown, which I take this opportunity to incloſe.

The great ſcarcity of freſh proviſions in their army has led me to take every precaution to prevent a ſupply : for this purpoſe, I have ordered all the cattle and ſheep to be drawn from the low grounds and farms within their reach. A detachment from general Thomas's camp, on Wedneſday night, went over to Long-Iſland, and brought from thence twenty cattle and a number of ſheep, with about fifteen labourers who had been put on by a Mr. Ray Thomas, to cut the hay, &c. By ſome accident, they omitted burning the hay, and returned the next day at noon to complete it ; which they effected, amidſt the firing of the ſhipping, with the loſs of one man killed and another wounded.

Laſt evening alſo a party of the Connecticut-men ſtrolled down on the marſh at Roxbury, and fired upon a centry ; which drew on a heavy fire from the enemy's lines and floating batteries, but attended with no other effect than the loſs of one killed by a ſhot from the enemy's lines. In the mean time, we are, on both ſides, continuing our works : but there has been no other movement than what I have noticed above. I ſhall endeavour to give a regular and particular account of all tranſactions as they occur, which you will pleaſe to lay before the honourable Congreſs. I have the honour to be, &c.

G. W.

SIR, *Camp at Cambridge, July 21, 1775.*

SINCE I did myſelf the honour of addreſſing you the fourteenth inſtant, I have received advice from governor Trumbull, that the aſſembly of Connecticut had voted, and that they are now raiſing, two regiments of ſeven hundred men each, in conſequence of an application from the provincial Congreſs of Maſſachuſetts-Bay. The Rhode-Iſland aſſembly has alſo made an augmentation for

this·

this purpose. These reinforcements, with the riflemen who are daily expected, and such recruits as may come in to fill up the regiments here, will, I apprehend, compose an army sufficiently strong to oppose any force which may be brought against us at present. I am very sensible that the heavy expense, necessarily attendant upon this campaign, will call for the utmost frugality and care, and would therefore, if possible, avoid enlisting one unnecessary man. As this is the first certain account of the destination of these new-raised troops, I thought proper to communicate my sentiments as early as possible, left the Congress should act upon my letter of the tenth, and raise troops in the southern colonies, which, in my present judgment, may be dispensed with.

For these eight days past, there have been no movements in either camp, of any consequence. On our side, we have continued the works without any intermission; and they are now so far advanced as to leave us little to apprehend on that score. On the side of the enemy, they have also been very industrious in finishing their lines, both on Bunker's-hill and Roxbury-neck. In this interval also, their transports have arrived from New-York; and they have been employed in landing and stationing their men. I have been able to collect no certain account of the numbers arrived : but the inclosed letter, wrote (though not signed) by Mr. Sheriff Lee, and delivered me by captain Darby, (who went express with an account of the Lexington battle) will enable us to form a pretty accurate judgment. The increase of tents and men in the town of Boston is very obvious; but all my accounts from thence agree that there is a great mortality, occasioned by the want of vegetables and fresh meat; and that their loss in the late battle at Charlestown (from the few recoveries of their wounded) is greater than at first supposed. The condition of the inhabitants detained in Boston is very distressing : they are equally destitute of the comfort of fresh provisions; and many of them are so reduced in their circumstances, as to be unable to supply themselves with salt. Such fish as the soldiery leave is their principal support. Added to all this, such suspicion and jealousy prevails, that
they

they can scarcely speak, or even look, without exposing themselves to some species of military execution.

I have not been able, from any intelligence I have received, to form any certain judgment of the future operations of the enemy. Sometimes I have suspected an intention of detaching a part of their army to some part of the coast, as they have been building a number of flat-bottomed boats, capable of holding two hundred men each. But, from their works, and the language held at Boston, there is reason to think they expect the attack from us, and are principally engaged in preparing themselves against it. I have ordered all the whale-boats along the coast to be collected: and some of them are employed every night to watch the motions of the enemy by water, so as to guard as much as possible against any surprise. * * *

Next to the more immediate and pressing duties of putting our lines in as secure a state as possible, attending to the movements of the enemy, and gaining intelligence,—my great concern is to establish order, regularity and discipline, without which our numbers would embarrass us, and, in case of action, general confusion must infallibly ensue. In order to this, I propose to divide the army into three divisions :—at the head of each will be a general officer :—these divisions to be again subdivided into brigades, under their respective brigadiers. But the difficulty arising from the arrangement of the general officers, and waiting the farther proceedings of the Congress on this subject, has much retarded my progress in this most necessary work. I should be very happy to receive their final commands, as any determination would enable me to proceed in my plan. * * *

In addition to the officers mentioned in mine of the tenth instant, I would humbly propose that some provision should be made for a judge-advocate, and provost-marshal. The necessity of the first appointment was so great, that I was obliged to nominate a Mr. Tudor, who was well recommended to me, and now executes the office under an expectation of receiving captain's pay—an allowance (in my opinion) scarcely adequate to the service, in new-raised troops, where there are court-martials every day. However, as that is the proportion in the regular army, and he is contented, there will be no neceffity of an addition.

I muft alfo renew my requeft as to money, and the appointment of a pay-mafter. I have forbore urging matters of this nature, from my knowledge of the many important concerns which engage the attention of the Congrefs : but as I find my difficulties thicken every day, I make no doubt, fuitable regard will be paid to a neceffity of this kind. The inconvenience of borrowing fuch fums as are conftantly requifite muft be too plain for me to enlarge upon, and is a fituation from which I fhould be very happy to be relieved.

Upon the experience I have had, and the beft confideration of the appointment of the feveral offices of commiffary-general, mufter-mafter-general, quarter-mafter-general, pay-mafter-general, and commiffary of artillery, I am clearly of opinion that they not only conduce to order, difpatch and difcipline, but that it is a meafure of economy. The delay, the wafte, and unpunifhable neglect of duty, arifing from thefe offices being in commiffion in feveral hands, evidently fhew that the public expenfe muft be finally enhanced. I have experienced the want of thefe officers, in completing the returns of men, ammunition, and ftores. The latter are yet imperfect, from the number of hands in which they are difperfed. I have inclofed the laft weekly return, which is more accurate than the former; and hope in a little time we fhall be perfectly regular in this as well as feveral other neceffary branches of duty.

I have made inquiry into the eftablifhment of the hofpital, and find it in a very unfettled condition. There is no principal director, nor any fubordination among the furgeons: of confequence, difputes and contention have arifen, and muft continue until it is reduced to fome fyftem. I could wifh it was immediately taken into confideration, as the lives and health of both officers and men fo much depend upon a due regulation of this department. I have been particularly attentive to the leaft fymptoms of the fmall pox; and hitherto we have been fo fortunate as to have every perfon removed fo foon, as not only to prevent any communication, but any alarm or apprehenfion it might

give

give in the camp.   We shall continue the utmost vigilance against this most dangerous enemy.

In an army properly organized, there are sundry offices of an inferior kind, such as waggon-master, master-carpenter, &c. but I doubt whether my powers are sufficiently extensive for such appointments.   If it is thought proper to repose such a trust in me, I shall be governed, in the discharge of it, by a strict regard to economy and the public interest.

My instructions from the honourable Congress direct that no troops are to be disbanded without their express direction, nor to be recruited to more than double the number of the enemy.   Upon this subject I beg leave to represent, that, unless the regiments in this province are more successful in recruiting than I have reason to expect, a reduction of some of them will be highly necessary, as the public is put to the whole expense of an establishment of officers, while the real strength of the regiment (which consists in the rank and file) is defective.   In case of such a reduction, doubtless some of the privates and all the officers would return home : but many of the former would go into the remaining regiments ; and having had some experience, would fill them up with useful men.   I so plainly perceive the expense of this campaign will exceed any calculation hitherto made, that I am particularly anxious to strike off every unnecessary charge.   You will therefore, Sir, be pleased to favour me with explicit directions from the Congress, on the mode of this reduction (if it shall appear necessary) that no time may be lost when such necessity appears.

Yesterday we had an account that the light-house was on fire :—by whom, and under what orders, I have not yet learned : but we have reason to believe it has been done by our irregulars.

You will please to present me to the Congress, with the utmost duty and respect ; and believe me to be, &c.

G. W.

P. S. Captain Darby's stay in England was so short, that he brings no other information than what the inclosed letter, and the news-papers which will accompany this, contain.   General Gage's dispatches had not arrived ; and

the

the miniftry affected to difbelieve the whole account, treat-
ing it as a fiction, or at moft, an affair of little confequence.
The fall of ftocks was very inconfiderable.

SIR,   *Camp at Cambridge, July 21, 1775, 5 o'clock, P. M.*

SINCE clofing the letters which accompany this, I
have received an account of the deftruction of the light-
houfe ; a copy of which I have the honour to inclofe,—
and of again affuring you that I am, with great refpect, &c.
              G. W.

P. S. I have alfo received a more authentic account of
the lofs of the enemy in the late battle, than any yet received. Dr. Winfhip, who lodged in the fame houfe with
an officer of the marines, affures me they had exactly one
thoufand and forty-three killed and wounded,—of whom
three hundred fell on the field, or died within a few hours.
Many of the wounded are fince dead.

SIR,   *Camp at Cambridge, July 27, 1775.*

NOTHING material has occurred in either camp,
fince I had the honour of addreffing you on the twenty-firft
inftant by exprefs : but on Tuefday, three men-of-war and
nine tranfports failed out of Bofton harbour, and ftood a
courfe about E. S. E.

One Groves, who came out of Bofton the fame evening,
informed the officer at one of the out-pofts, that the tranfports had on board fix hundred men, and were bound to
Block-Ifland, Fifher's-Ifland, and Long-Ifland, to plunder
them, and bring off what cattle they may find. The fellow
returned again into Bofton under fuch fufpicious circumftances, that it has led me to doubt the truth of his intelligence.

A deferter, who came in afterwards, informs me that it
was given out in their camp, that they were either gone for
Indians or frefh provifions ; and that each tranfport had
but twenty men on board. Upon this intelligence, I immediately wrote to governor Cooke of Rhode-Ifland, and
                          to

to general Wooſter, that they might take proper precautions for removing the cattle off thoſe iſlands and the coaſts, and to prevent any ſurpriſe. As we are cqnfirmed, by every account, in the ſcarcity of freſh proviſions in the enemy's camp, and particularly by this deſerter, it is very probable this voyage may be only intended for a ſupply : but as it may poſſibly be otherwiſe, I thought it beſt to tranſmit the intelligence to the honourable Congreſs, that they may forward it to the ſouthward, or take ſuch other ſteps as they may judge proper.

Since writing the above, three more deſerters have come out,—which makes four in twenty-four hours. Their accounts correſpond with thoſe of the firſt who came out, and which I have related above. I have the honour to be, &c. G. W.

SIR, *Camp at Cambridge, Aug. 4, 1775.*

I AM to acknowledge the receipt of your favour of the twenty-fourth July, accompanied by two hundred and eighty-four commiſſions, which are yet much ſhort of the neceſſary number. I am much honoured by the confidence repoſed in me, of appointing the ſeveral officers recommended in mine of the tenth ultimo; and ſhall endeavour to ſelect ſuch perſons as are beſt qualified to fill theſe important poſts. * * * *

In the renewal of theſe commiſſions, ſome difficulties occur, in which I ſhould be glad to know the pleaſure of the honourable Congreſs. The general officers of the Maſſachuſetts have regiments; thoſe of Connecticut have both regiments and companies; and the other field officers have companies each. From Rhode-Iſland, the general officer has no regiment, but the field officers have companies : but I do not find that they have or expect pay under more than one commiſſion. Should the commiſſions, now to be delivered, purſue theſe different eſtabliſhments, there will be a diſtinction between general and field officers of the ſame rank. In order to put New-Hampſhire, Maſſachuſetts, and Rhode-Iſland, upon a line with Connecticut, it would be neceſſary to diſmiſs a number

ber of officers, in poffeffion of commiffions, without any fault of theirs.   On the other hand, to bring the Connecticut generals and field officers to the fame fcale with the others, will add to the number of officers, and may be deemed inconfiftent with the terms on which they entered into the fervice, although you add nothing to the expenfe, except in the article of provifions. ' Upon the whole, it is a cafe which I would wifh the honourable Congrefs to confider and determine.

Colonel Gridley of this province, who is at the head of the artillery, has the rank of major-general from the provincial Congrefs.   Will it be proper to renew his commiffion here in the fame manner ?—It is proper here to remark, that, in this cafe, he will take rank of all the brigadiers-general, and even the majors-general, whofe commiffions are fubfequent in date : and this can anfwer no good purpofe, but may be productive of many bad confequences.

Thefe are matters of fome importance : but I am embarraffed with a difficulty of a fuperior kind.   The eftimate, made in Congrefs, fuppofed all the regiments to be formed upon one eftablifhment : but they are different in different provinces, and even vary in the fame province, in fome particulars.   In Maffachufetts, fome regiments have ten companies, others eleven : the eftablifhment of the former is five hundred and ninety men, officers included ; of the latter, fix hundred and forty-nine.   The eftablifhment of Rhode-Ifland and New-Hampfhire is five hundred and ninety to a regiment, officers included :—Connecticut has a thoufand men to a regiment.   Should the Maffachufetts regiments be completed, with the new levies from Rhode-Ifland and Connecticut, and the riflemen, the number will exceed twenty-two thoufand.   If they fhould not be completed,—as each regiment is fully officered, there will be a heavy expenfe to the public, without an adequate fervice.   The reduction of fome of them feems to be neceffary, and yet is a matter of much delicacy, as we are fituated.   I moft earneftly requeft it may be taken into immediate confideration, and the time and mode of doing it pointed out by the honourable Congrefs.   By an eftimate I have made from the general return,—when the new levies arrive, and the regiments are completed, there will

be

be twenty-four thousand four hundred and fifty men on the pay and provision of the United Colonies. Some of the recruiting officers, who have been out on that service, have returned with very little success; so that we may safely conclude, the number of two thousand and sixty-four, now wanting to complete, will rather increase than diminish. There are the regiment of artillery, confisting of four hundred and ninety-three men, and one under colonel Sergeant (who has not received any commission, although he had orders to raise a regiment, from the provincial Congress here) which are not included in the above estimate. This last regiment confists of two hundred and thirty-four men by the last return; but a company has since joined.

By adverting to the general return, which I have the honour of inclosing (Nº 1) it will be seen what regiments are most deficient.

If the Congress does not choose to point out the particular regiments, but the provinces in which the reduction is to be made, the several Congresses and Assemblies may be the proper channel to conduct this business, which I would also conceive the most advisable, from their better acquaintance with the merits, terms, and time of service, of the respective officers. Reducing some regiments, and, with the privates thereof, filling up others, would certainly be the best method of accomplishing this work if it were practicable: but the experiment is dangerous, as the Maffachusetts-men, under the privilege of choosing their own officers, do not conceive themselves bound, if those officers are disbanded.

As general Gage is making preparations for winter by contracting for quantities of coal, it will suggest to us the propriety of extending our views to that season. I have directed that such huts as have been lately made of boards should be done in such a manner, that, if necessary, they may serve for covering during the winter. But I need not enlarge upon the variety of necessities, such as clothing, fuel, &c. (both exceedingly scarce, and difficult to be procured) which that season must bring with it, if the army or any considerable part of it is to remain embodied.

From the inactivity of the enemy since the arrival of their whole reinforcement, their continual addition to their
lines,——

lines,—and many other circumſtances,—I am inclined to think, that, finding us ſo well prepared to receive them, the plan of operations is varied, and they mean, by regular approaches, to bombard us out of our preſent line of defence, or are waiting in expectation that the colonies muſt ſink under the weight of the expenſe, or the proſpect of a winter campaign ſo diſcourage our troops, as to break up our army. If they have not ſome ſuch expectations, the iſſue of which they are determined to wait, I cannot account for the delay, when their ſtrength is leſſened every day by ſickneſs, deſertions, and little ſkirmiſhes.

Of theſe laſt we have had only two worthy of notice. Having ſome reaſon to ſuſpect they were extending their lines at Charleſtown, I, laſt Saturday evening, ordered ſome of the riflemen down, to make a diſcovery, or bring off a priſoner. They were accidentally diſcovered ſooner than they expected, by the guard coming to relieve, and obliged to fire upon them. We have reaſon to believe they killed ſeveral. They brought in two priſoners, whoſe account (confirmed by ſome other circumſtances) removed my ſuſpicions in part. Since that time, we have, on each ſide, drawn in our centries, and there have been ſcattering fires along the line. This evening we have heard of three captains who have been taken off by the riflemen, and one killed by a cannon-ſhot from Roxbury, beſides ſeveral privates : but as the intelligence is not direct, I only mention it as a report which deſerves credit. The other happened at the light-houſe. A number of workmen having been ſent down to repair it, with a guard of twenty-two marines and a ſubaltern,—major Tupper, laſt Monday morning about two o'clock, landed there with about three hundred men, attacked them, killed the officer and four privates ; but being detained by the tide, in his return he was attacked by ſeveral boats ; but he happily got through with the loſs of one man killed, and another wounded. The remainder of the miniſterial troops (three of whom are badly wounded) he brought off priſoners, with ten tories, all of whom are on their way to Springfield-jail. The riflemen, in theſe ſkirmjſhes, loſt one man, who (we hear) is a priſoner in Boſton-jail. The enemy, in return, endeavoured to ſurpriſe our guard at Roxbury : but they, being

appriſed

apprifed of it by a deferter, had time to prepare for it : but
by fome negligence or mifconduct in the officer of the guard,
they burned the George tavern on the neck ; and have
every day fince been cannonading us from their lines, both
at Roxbury and Charleftown, but with no other effect
than the lofs of two men.   On our part, except ftraggling
fires from the fmall arms about the lines, which we endeavour to reftrain, we have made little or no return.

Our fituation in the article of powder, is much more
alarming than I had the moft diftant idea of.   Having defired a return to be made out (on my arrival) of the ammunition, I found three hundred and three barrels and a
half of powder mentioned as in the ftore : but on ordering
a new fupply of cartridges yefterday, I was informed, to
my very great aftonifhment, that there was no more than
thirty-fix barrels of the Maffachufetts ftore, which, with
the ftock of Rhode-Ifland, New-Hampfhire, and Connecticut, makes nine thoufand nine hundred and thirty-feven
pounds,—not more than nine rounds to a man.   As there
had been no confumption of powder fince, that could in
any degree account for fuch a deficiency, I was very particular in my inquiries, and found that the committee of
fupplies, not being fufficiently acquainted with the nature
of a return, or mifapprehending my requeft, fent in an account of all the ammunition which had been collected by
the province ; fo that the report included not only what
was in hand, but what had been fpent.

Upon difcovering this miftake, I immediately went up
to confer with the fpeaker of the houfe of reprefentatives,
upon fome meafures to obtain a fupply from the neighbouring townfhips, in fuch a manner as might prevent our poverty being known ; as it is a fecret of too great confequence to be divulged in the general court, fome individu-
al of which might perhaps indifcreetly fuffer it to efcape
him, fo as to find its way to the enemy,—the confequences
of which are terrible even in idea.   I fhall alfo write to the
governors of Rhode-Ifland and Connecticut, and the committee of fafety in New-Hampfhire, on this fubject, urging,
in the moft forcible terms, the neceffity of an immediate
fupply, if in their power.   I need not enlarge on our melancholy fituation : it is fufficient that the exiftence of the

army and the salvation of the country depends upon something being done for our relief, both speedy and effectual, and that our situation be kept a profound secret.

In the inclosures, N° 2 and 3, I send the allowance of provisions, &c. made by the provinces of Connecticut and Massachusetts. The mode and quantity are different from what has fallen within my experience, and, I am confident, must prove very wasteful and expensive. If any alteration can be safely made (which I much doubt) there might be a great saving to the public.

A gentleman of my family, assisted by a deserter who has some skill in fortification, has by my direction sketched out two draughts of our respective lines at Charlestown and Roxbury, which, with the explanations, will convey some idea of our situation, and, I hope, prove acceptable to the members of the honourable Congress. They are the inclosures, N° 4 and 5.

Since I had the honour of addressing you last, I have been applied to, by a committee of the general court, for a detachment of the army, to protect the inhabitants of the eastern parts of this province from some apprehended depredations on their coasts. I could have wished to have complied with their request : but, after due consideration, and consulting the general officers, together with those members of Congress who are here, I thought it my duty to excuse myself. The application and my answer are the inclosures, N° 6 and 7, which I hope will be approved by the honourable Congress.

Since I began this letter, the original (of which the inclosure N° 8 is a copy) fell into my hands. As the writer is a person of some note in Boston, and it contains some advices of importance not mentioned by others, I thought proper to forward it as I received it. By comparing the hand-writing with another letter, it appears the writer is one Belcher Noyes, a person probably known to some of the gentlemen, delegates from this province, who can determine, from his principles and character, what credit is due to him.

The army is now formed into three grand divisions, under the command of the generals Ward, Lee, and Putnam ; each division into two brigades, consisting of about six regiments each, commanded by generals Thomas and Spencer at Roxbury,—Heath at Cambridge,—Sullivan and Greene at Winter-hill. By this you will please to observe, there is a deficiency of one brigadier-general (occasioned by Mr. Pomroy's not acting under his commission) which I beg may be filled up as soon as possible. I observe the honourable Congress have also favoured me with the appointment of three brigade-majors. I presume they have or intend to appoint the rest soon, as they cannot be unacquainted that one is necessary to each brigade ; and in a new raised army, it will be an office of great duty and service.

General Gage has at length liberated the people of Boston, who land in numbers at Chelsea every day. The terms on which the passes are granted, as to money, effects and provisions, correspond with Mr. Noyes's letter.

We have several reports that general Gage is dismantling Castle-William, and bringing all the cannon up to town : but, upon a very particular inquiry, accounts are so various, that I cannot ascertain the truth of it. * * *

On the first instant, a chief of the Caghnewaga tribe, who lives about six miles from Montreal, came in here, accompanied by a colonel Bayley of Cohofs. His accounts of the temper and disposition of the Indians are very favourable. He says they have been strongly solicited by governor Carleton to engage against us ; but his nation is totally averse ;—that threats, as well as entreaties, have been used without effect ;—that the Canadians are well disposed to the English colonies ; and, if any expedition is meditated against Canada, the Indians in that quarter will give all their assistance. I have endeavoured to cherish these favourable dispositions, and have recommended to him to cultivate them on his return. What I have said, I enforced with a present, which I understood would be agreeable to him: and as he is represented to be a man of weight and consequence in his own tribe, I flatter myself his visit will have a good effect. His accounts of general Carleton's force and situation at St. John's correspond with what we have already had from that quarter.

The accession of Georgia to the measures of the Congress is a happy event, and must give a sincere pleasure to every friend of America.

August

August 5.———We have accounts this morning of two explosions at the Castle ; so that its destruction may now be supposed certain.

I have this morning been alarmed with an information that two gentlemen from Philadelphia, (Mr. Hitchbourn and captain White) with letters for general Lee and myself, have been taken by captain Ayscough at Rhode-Island, the letters intercepted and sent forward to Boston,—with the bearers as prisoners ; that the captain exulted much in the discoveries he had made : and my informer (who was also in the boat, but released) understood them to be letters of consequence.   I have therefore dispatched the express immediately back, though I had before resolved to detain him till Feffenden's return.   I shall be anxious till I am relieved from the suspense I am in, as to the contents of of those letters.

It is exceedingly unfortunate that gentlemen should choose to travel the only road on which there is danger. Let the event of this be what it will, I hope it will serve as a general caution against trusting any letters that way in future.

Nothing of consequence has occurred in camp these two days.   The inhabitants of Boston continue coming out at Chelsea, but under a new restriction, that no *men* shall come out without special license, which is refused to all mechanics, since the tory labourers were taken at the lighthouse.   I have the honour to be, &c.   G. W.

———

[*The following letter bears no date, but appears to have been written on or about the twenty-sixth of August, 1775.*]

SIR,

THE inclosed letter came under such a direction and circumstances, as led me to suppose it contained some interesting advices, either respecting a supply of powder, or the clothing lately taken at Philadelphia ; I therefore took the liberty of breaking the seal, for which I hope the service and my motives will apologize.

As

As the filling up the place of vacant brigadier-general will probably be of the firſt buſineſs of the honourable Congreſs, I flatter myſelf it will not be deemed aſſuming, to mention the names of two gentlemen, whoſe former ſervices, rank and age, may be thought worthy of attention on this occaſion. The former is colonel John Armſtrong, of Pennſylvania : he ſerved during the laſt war, in moſt of the campaigns to the ſouthward; was honoured with the command of the Pennſylvania forces, and his general military conduct and ſpirit much approved by all who ſerved with him : beſides which, his character was diſtinguiſhed by an enterpriſe againſt the Indians, which he planned with great judgment, and executed with equal courage and ſucceſs. It was not till lately that I had reaſon to believe he would enter again on public ſervice ; and it is now wholly unſolicited and unknown on his part. The other gentleman is colonel Fry, of Maſſachuſetts-Bay. He entered into the ſervice as early as 1745, and roſe through the different military ranks, in the ſucceeding wars, to that of colonel, until laſt June, when he was appointed a major-general by the Congreſs of this province. From theſe circumſtances, together with the favourable report made to me of him, I preſume he ſuſtained the character of a good officer, though I do not find it diſtinguiſhed by any peculiar ſervice.

Either of theſe gentlemen, or any other whom the honourable Congreſs ſhall pleaſe to favour with this appointment, will be received by me with the utmoſt deference and reſpect.

The late adjournment having made it impracticable to know the pleaſure of the Congreſs as to the appointment of brigade-majors, beyond the number of three which they were pleaſed to leave to me,—and the ſervice not admitting of farther delay,—I have continued the other three ; which I hope their honours will not diſapprove. Theſe latter were recommended by the reſpective corps to which they belong, as the propereſt perſons for theſe offices until farther direction, and have diſcharged the duty ever ſince. They are the majors Box, Scammel, and Samuel Brewer.

C 2

Laſt

Laſt Saturday night we took poſſeſſion of a hill conſiderably advanced beyond our former lines ; which brought on a very heavy cannonade from Bunker's-hill, and afterwards a bombardment, which has been ſince kept up with little ſpirit on their part, or damage on ours. The work having been continued ever ſince, is now ſo advanced, and the men ſo well covered, as to leave us under no apprehenſions of much farther loſs. In this affair, we had killed—one adjutant, one volunteer, and two privates. The ſcarcity of ammunition does not admit of our availing ourſelves of the ſituation, as we otherwiſe might do : but this evil, I hope, will ſoon be remedied, as I have been informed of the arrival of a large quantity at New-York, ſome at New-London, and more hourly expected at different places. I need not add to what I have already ſaid on this ſubject. Our late ſupply was very ſeaſonable, but far ſhort of our neceſſities.

The late adjournment of the honourable Congreſs having been made before my letter of the fourth inſtant was received. I muſt now beg leave to recall their attention to thoſe parts of it which reſpect the proviſion for the winter, the reduction of the troops, the double commiſſions under different eſtabliſhments, and colonel Gridley's appointment of major-general ; in all which, I hope to be honoured with their commands as ſoon as poſſible.

The advocate-general has ſent me a memorial reſpecting his ſervice, which I have the honour to incloſe ; (Nº 1) and from the variety and multiplicity of duty in a new army, as well as his regular ſervice and attendance, I am induced to recommend him to the farther notice of the honourable Congreſs.

The treatment of our officers, priſoners, at Boſton, induced me to write to general Gage on that ſubject. His anſwer and my reply I have the honour to lay before the Congreſs, in the incloſures Nº 2, 3, 4 ; ſince which I have heard nothing from him.

I remain, with the greateſt reſpect and regard, &c.

G. W.

To

To the honourable PETER VANBRUGH LIV-
INGSTON, *esquire, President of the Provincial Convention, New-York.*

SIR,   *Camp at Cambridge, August* 30, 1775.

    * * * MR. Livingston and some other gentlemen
from your city brought us the acceptable news of the safe
arrival of a large quantity of powder, and five hundred
stand of arms. Our situation is such as requires your
immediate assistance and supply in that article. We have
lately taken possession of a hill considerably advanced towards the enemy; but our poverty prevents our availing
ourselves of any advantage of situation. I must therefore
most earnestly entreat that measures may be taken to forward to this camp, in the most safe and expeditious manner, whatever ammunition can be spared from the immediate
and necessary defence of the province. The value of
whatever may be sent in consequence of this request will
be paid by order from hence when delivered, or negociat-
ed with the honourable continental Congress, at Philadelphia, as may be agreed with the proprietors. I only request that no time may be lost through any such difficulties,
as our situation is so critical, and the exigence so great.
The mode of conveyance I must leave with the provincial Congress, or the committee of the city. I doubt not
they will take every precaution to make it safe and expeditious. I have the honour to be, &c.   G. W.

SIR,   *Camp at Cambridge, Sept.* 7, 1775.

    I DO myself the honour of addressing you in conse-
quence of an application from the commissary-general, who
is, by my direction, taking all proper precautions on the
approach of winter. I desired him to commit to writing
such proposals as his experience and knowledge of the
country might entitle him to make ; which he has done in
the paper which I have the honour to inclose. The difficulty of procuring a sufficient quantity of salt, which I objected
to him, he has fully obviated, by assuring me that there is
so much now actually in store, in this and the neighbouring
towns, as will remove all possibility of a disappointment.
                                   I propose

I propose to do myself the honour of writing, in a few days, fully and particularly on several heads, to which I must now refer. In the mean time, I have only to inform the honourable Congress, that I have received a small supply of seven thousand pounds of powder this week from Rhode-Island, and in a few days expect seven tons of lead, and five hundred stand of arms, a part of the same importation ; and to request that more money may be forwarded with all expedition, the military chest being nearly exhausted.

I am, with the greatest respect, &c.　　G. W.

SIR,　　*Camp at Cambridge, Sept. 21, 1775.*

I HAVE been in daily expectation of being favoured with the commands of the honourable Congress, on the subject of my two last letters. The season now advances so fast that I cannot any longer defer laying before them such farther measures as require their immediate attention, and in which I wait their direction.

The mode in which the present army has been collected has occasioned some difficulty in procuring the subscription of both officers and soldiers to the continental articles of war. Their principal objection has been, that it might subject them to a longer service than that for which they engaged under their several provincial establishments. It is in vain to attempt to reason away the prejudices of a whole army : * * * I have therefore forbore pressing them, as I did not experience any such inconvenience from their adherence to their former rules, as would warrant the risk of entering into a contest upon it : more especially as the restraints, necessary for the establishment of essential discipline and subordination, indisposed their minds to every change, and made it both duty and policy to introduce as little novelty as possible. With the present army, I fear such a subscription is impracticable : but the difficulty will cease with this army.

The Connecticut and Rhode-Island troops stand engaged to the first of December only ; and none longer than the first of January. A dissolution of the present army
therefore

therefore will take place, unlefs fome early provifion is made againft fuch an event. Moft of the general officers are of opinion the greater part of them may be re-enlifted for the winter, or another campaign, with the indulgence of a furlough to vifit their friends, which may be regulated fo as not to endanger the fervice. How far it may be proper to form the new army entirely out of the old, for another campaign, rather than from the contingents of the feveral provinces, is a queftion which involves in it too many confiderations of policy and prudence, for me to undertake to decide. It appears to be impoffible to draw it from any other fource than the old army, for this winter ; and, as the pay is ample, I hope a fufficient number will engage in the fervice for that time at leaft. But there are various opinions of the temper of the men on the fubject ; and there may be great hazard in deferring the trial fo long.

In the continental eftablifhment, no provifion has been made for the pay of artificers, diftinct from that of the common foldiers ; whereas, under the provincial, fuch as found their own tools were allowed one fhilling per diem advance, and particular artizans, more. The pay of the artillery alfo now differs from that of the province ; the men have lefs, the officers more ; and, for fome ranks, no provifion is made, as the Congrefs will pleafe to obferve by the lift which I have the honour to inclofe. (N° 1.) Thefe particulars, though feemingly inconfiderable, are the fource of much complaint and diffatisfaction, which I endeavour to compofe in the beft manner I am able.

By the returns of the rifle companies, and that battalion, they appear to exceed their eftablifhment very confiderably. I doubt my authority to pay thefe extra men without the direction of the Congrefs : but it would be deemed a great hardfhip wholly to refufe them, as they have been encouraged to come.

The neceffities of the troops having required pay, I directed that thofe of the Maffachufetts fhould receive for one month, upon their being muftered, and returning a proper roll : but a claim was immediately made for pay by lunar months ; and feveral regiments have declined taking up their warrants on this account. As this practice was entirely new to me, though faid to be warranted by former

ufage,

ufage, here the matter now waits the determination of the honourable Congrefs.   I find, in Connecticut and Rhode-Ifland, this point was fettled by calendar months : in Maf-fachufetts, though mentioned in the Congrefs, it was left undetermined ; which is alfo the cafe of New-Hampfhire.

The inclofure, N° 2, is a petition from the fubalterns, refpecting their pay.   Where there are only two of thefe in a company, I have confidered one as an enfign, and or-dered him pay as fuch, as in the Connecticut forces.   I muft beg leave to recommend this petition to the favour of the Congrefs ; as I am of opinion the allowance is inadequate to their rank and fervice, and is one great fource of that familiarity between the officers and men, which is fo incom-patible with fubordination and difcipline.   Many valuable officers of thofe ranks, finding themfelves unable to fupport the character and appearance of officers, (I am informed) will retire as foon as the term of fervice is expired, if there is no alteration.

For the better regulation of duty, I found it neceffary to fettle the rank of the officers, and to number the regiments ; and, as I had not received the commands of the Congrefs on the fubject, and the exigence of the fervice forbade any farther delay, the general officers were confidered as having no regiments ; an alteration, which, I underftand, is not pleafing to fome of them, but appeared to me and others to be proper, when it was confidered, that, by this means, the whole army is put upon one footing, and all particular at-tachments diffolved.

Among many other confiderations which the approach of winter will demand, that of clothing appears to be one of the moft important.   So far as regards the prefervation of the army from cold, they may be deemed in a ftate of nakednefs.   Many of the men have been without blankets the whole campaign : and thofe, which have been in ufe during the fummer, are fo much worn as to be of little fer-vice.   In order to make a fuitable provifion in thefe articles, and at the fame time to guard the public againft impofition and expenfe, it feems neceffary to determine the mode of continuing the army : for, fhould thefe troops be clothed under their prefent engagement, and, at the expiration of

the

the term of fervice, decline renewing it, a fet of unprovided men may be fent to fupply their places.

I cannot fuppofe it to be unknown to the 'honourable Congrefs, that, in all armies, it is an eftablifhed practice to make an allowance to officers, of provifions and forage, proportionate to their rank.   As fuch an allowance formed no part of the continental eftablifhment, I have hitherto forbore-to iffue the orders for that purpofe : but, as it is a received opinion of fuch members of the Congrefs as I have had an opportunity of confulting, as well as throughout the army, that it muft be deemed a matter of courfe and implied in the eftablifhment of the army, I have directed the following proportion of rations, being the fame allowed in the American armies laft war :——Major-general, fifteen ; brigadier-general, twelve ; colonel, fix ; lieutenant-colonel, five ; major, four ; captain, three ; fubaltern, two ; ftaff, two.

If thefe fhould not be approved by the honourable Congrefs, they will pleafe to fignify their pleafure, as to the alterations they would have made in the whole or in part.

I am now to inform the honourable Congrefs, that, encouraged by the repeated declarations of the Canadians and Indians, and urged by their requefts, I have detached colonel Arnold with a thoufand men, to penetrate into Canada by way of Kennebeck river, and, if poffible, to make himfelf mafter of Quebec.   By this manœuvre, I propofed either to divert Carleton from St. John's, which would leave a free paffage to general Schuyler ;—or, if this did not take effect, Quebec, in its prefent defencelefs ftate, muft fall into his hands an eafy prey.   I made all poffible inquiry, as to the diftance, the fafety of the route, and the danger of the feafon being too far advanced ; but found nothing in either to deter me from proceeding, more efpecially as it met with very general approbation from all whom I confulted upon it. But, that nothing might be omitted, to enable me to judge of its propriety and probable confequences, I communicated it by exprefs to general Schuyler, who approved of it in fuch terms, that I refolved to put it in immediate execution.   They have now left this place feven days ; and, if favoured with a good wind, I hope foon to hear of their being fafe in Kennebeck river.   For the fatisfaction of the

Congrefs.

Congrefs, I here inclofe a copy of the propofed route. (N° 3.)   I alfo do myfelf the honour of inclofing a manifefto, which I caufed to be printed here, and of which colonel Arnold has taken a fuitable number with him.   This is the inclofure, N° 4.   I have alfo forwarded a copy of his inftructions (N° 5)—from all which I hope the Congrefs will have a clear view of the motives, plan, and intended execution of this enterprife, and that I fhall be fo happy as to meet with their approbation in it.

I was the more induced to make this detachment, as it is my clear opinion, from a careful obfervation of the movements of the enemy, corroborated by all the intelligence we receive by deferters and others, (of the former of whom we have fome every day) that the enemy have no intention to come out, until they are reinforced.   They have been wholly employed for fome time paft in procuring materials for barracks, fuel, and making other preparations for winter. Thefe circumftances, with the conftant additions to their works which are apparently defenfive, have led to the above conclufion, and enabled me to fpare this body of men where I hope they will be ufefully and fuccefsfully employed.

The ftate of inactivity, in which this army has lain for fome time, by no means correfponds with my wifhes, by fome decifive ftroke to relieve my country from the heavy expenfe its fubfiftence muft create.   After frequently recconnoitring the fituation of the enemy in the town of Bofton, collecting all poffible intelligence, and digefting the whole, a furprife did not appear to me wholly impracticable, though hazardous.   I communicated it to the general officers fome days before I called them to a council, that they might be prepared with their opinions.   The refult I have the honour of inclofing. (N° 6.)   I cannot fay that I have wholly laid it afide : but new events may occafion new meafures.   Of this I hope the honourable Congrefs can need no affurance, that there is not a man in America who more earneftly wifhes fuch a termination of the campaign, as to make the army no longer neceffary.

The feafon advances fo faft, that I have given orders to prepare barracks and other accommodations for the winter. The great fcarcity of tow-cloth in this country, I fear, will totally difappoint us in our expectations of procuring hunting-fhirts.

ing-fhirts.   Governor Cooke informs me, few or none are
to be had in Rhode-Ifland ; and governor Trumbull gives
me little encouragement to expect many from Connecticut.

I have filled up the office of quarter-mafter-general, which
the Congrefs was pleafed to leave to me, by the appointment of major Mifflin, which I hope and believe will be
univerfally acceptable.

It gives me great pain to be obliged to folicit the attention of the honourable Congrefs to the ftate of this army, in
terms which imply the flighteft apprehenfion of being neglected.   But my fituation is inexpreffibly diftreffing, to fee
the winter faft approaching upon a naked army ; the time of
their fervice within a few weeks of expiring ; and no provifion yet made for fuch important events.   Added to
thefe, the military cheft is totally exhaufted : the pay-mafter has not a fingle dollar in hand : the commiffary-general
affures me he has ftrained his credit, for the fubfiftence of
the army, to the utmoft.   The quarter-mafter-general is
precifely in the fame fituation ; and the greater part of the
troops are in a ftate not far from mutiny, upon the deduction
from their ftated allowance.   I know not to whom I am to
impute this failure : but I am of opinion, if the evil is not
immediately remedied, and more punctuality obferved in
future, the army muft abfolutely break up.   I hoped I had
fo fully expreffed myfelf on this fubject, (both by letter,
and to thofe members of the Congrefs who honoured the
camp with a vifit) that no difappointment could poffibly
happen : I therefore hourly expected advice from the pay-
mafter that he had received a frefh fupply, in addition to
the hundred and feventy-two thoufand dollars delivered him
in Auguft ; and thought myfelf warranted to affure the
public creditors that in a few days they fhould be fatisfied.
But the delay has brought matters to fuch a crifis, as ad-
mits of no farther uncertain expectation.   I have therefore
fent off this exprefs, with orders to make all poffible difpatch.   It is my moft earneft requeft that he may be returned with all poffible expedition, unlefs the honourable
Congrefs have already forwarded what is fo indifpenfably
neceffary.

I have the honour to be, &c.   G. W.

SIR,   *Camp at Cambridge, Sept. 30, 1775.*

THE reverend Mr. Kirkland, the bearer of this, having been introduced to the honourable Congrefs, can need no particular recommendation from me.   But as he now wifhes to have the affairs of his miffion and public employ put upon fome fuitable footing, I cannot but intimate my fenfe of the importance of his ftation, and the great advantages which have and may refult to the United Colonies, from his fituation being made refpectable.

All accounts agree that much of the favourable difpofition fhewn by the Indians, may be afcribed to his labour and influence.   He has accompanied a chief of the Oneidas to this camp, which I have endeavoured to make agreeable to him, both by civility and fome fmall prefents.   Mr. Kirkland being alfo in fome neceffity for money to bear his travelling charges and other expenfes, I have fupplied him with thirty-two pounds lawful money.

I cannot but congratulate the honourable Congrefs on the happy temper of the Canadians and Indians, our accounts of which are now fully confirmed by fome intercepted letters from officers in Canada, to general Gage and others in Bofton, which were found on board the veffel lately taken, going into Bofton with a donation of cattle and other frefh provifions for the minifterial army.

I have the honour to be, &c.   G. W.

SIR,   *Camp at Cambridge, Oct. 5, 1775.*

I WAS honoured with your favour of the twenty-fixth ultimo, late the night before laft ; and a meeting of the general officers having been called upon a bufinefs which will make a confiderable part of this letter, I took the opportunity of laying before them thofe parts of yours which refpect the continuance and new-modelling of the army, the fuel, clothing, and other preparations for the enfuing winter. They have taken two or three days to confider ; and, as foon as I am poffeffed of their opinions, I fhall lofe no time in tranfmitting the refult, not only on the above fubjects, but the number of troops neceffary to be kept up.

I have

I have alfo directed the commiffary-general and the quarter-mafter-general to prepare eftimates of the expenfe of their departments for a certain given number of men, from which a judgment may be made, when the number of men to be kept in pay is determined :—all which I fhall do myfelf the honour to lay before the Congrefs, as foon as they are ready.

I have now a painful though a neceffary duty to perform, refpecting Dr. Church, director-general of the hofpital. About a week ago, Mr. fecretary Ward, of Providence, fent up to me one Wainwood, an inhabitant of Newport, with a letter directed to major Cane, in Bofton, in [*occult*] characters, which he faid had been left with Wainwood fome time ago, by a woman who was kept by Dr. Church. She had before preffed Wainwood to take her to captain Wallace, Mr. Dudley the collector, or George Rome ; which he declined. She then gave him the letter, with a ftrict charge to deliver it to either of thofe gentlemen. He, fufpecting fome improper correfpondence, kept the letter, and after fome time opened it ; but, not being able to read it, laid it up, where it remained until he received an obfcure letter from the woman, expreffing an anxiety after the original letter. He then communicated the whole matter to Mr. Ward, who fent him up with the papers to me. I immediately fecured the woman : but for a long time fhe was proof againft every threat and perfuafion to difcover the author. However, at length fhe was brought to a confeffion, and named Dr. Church. I then immediately fecured him and all his papers. Upon his firft examination, he readily acknowledged the letter, faid it was defigned for his brother Fleming, and, when deciphered, would be found to contain nothing criminal. He acknowledged his never having communicated the correfpondence to any perfon here but the girl, and made many proteftations of the purity of his intentions. Having found a perfon capable of deciphering the letter, I in the mean time had all his papers fearched, but found nothing criminal among them : but it appeared on inquiry, that a confidant had been among the papers before my meffenger arrived. I then called the general officers together for their advice, the refult of which you will find in the inclofure, N° 1. The deciphered letter is the inclofure,

fure, N° 2. The army and country are exceedingly irritated : and upon a free difcuffion of the nature, circumftances, and confequence of this matter, it has been unanimoufly agreed to lay it before the honourable Congrefs for their fpecial advice and direction ; at the fame time fuggefting to their confideration, whether an alteration of the twenty-eighth article of war may not be neceffary.

As I fhall referve all farther remarks upon the ftate of the army till my next, I fhall now beg leave to requeft the determination of Congrefs, as to the property and difpofal of fuch veffels and cargoes as are defigned for the fupply of the enemy, and may fall into our hands. There has been an event of this kind at Portfmouth, (as by the inclofure, N° 3) in which I have directed the cargo to be brought hither for the ufe of the army, referving the fettlement of any claims of capture to the decifion of Congrefs.

As there are many unfortunate individuals whofe property has been confifcated by the enemy, I would humbly fuggeft to the confideration of Congrefs the humanity of applying, in part or in the whole, fuch captures to the relief of thofe fufferers, after compenfating any expenfe of the captors, and for their activity and fpirit. I am the more induced to requeft this determination may be fpeedy, as I have directed three veffels to be equipped in order to cut off the fupplies ; and, from the number of veffels hourly arriving, it may become an object of fome importance. In the difpofal of thefe captures, for the encouragement of the officers and men, I have allowed them one third of the cargoes, except military ftores, which, with the veffels, are to be referved for the public ufe. I hope my plan, as well as the execution, will be favoured with the approbation of Congrefs.

One Mr. Fifk, an intelligent perfon, came out of Bofton on the third inft. and gives us the following advices :—that a fleet, confifting of a fixty-four, and twenty-gun fhip, two floops of eighteen guns, and two tranfports with fix hundred men, were to fail from Bofton as yefterday ; that they took on board two mortars, four howitzers, and other artillery calculated for the bombardment of a town :—their deftination was kept a profound fecret :—that an exprefs floop of war, which left England the eighth of Auguft, arrived

four

four days ago ;—that general Gage is recalled, and laſt Sunday reſigned his command to general Howe ;—that lord Percy, colonel Smith, and other officers who were at Lexington, are ordered home with Gage ;—that ſix ſhips of the line and two cutters were coming out under Sir Peter Dennis ;—that five regiments and a thouſand marines are ordered out, and may be expected in three or four weeks : —no proſpect of accommodation ; but the miniſtry determined to puſh the war to the utmoſt.

I have an expreſs from colonel Arnold, and herewith ſend a copy of his letter and an incloſure, N° 4 and 5.— I am happy in finding he meets with no diſcouragement. The claim of the rifle officers, to be independent of all the ſuperior officers except colonel Arnold, is without any countenance or authority from me, as I have ſignified in my laſt diſpatch both to colonel Arnold and captain Morgan. The captain of the brig from Quebec for Boſton informs me that there is no ſuſpicion of any ſuch expedition ; and that, if Carleton is not drove from St. John's, ſo as to be obliged to throw himſelf into Quebec, it muſt fall into our hands, as it is left without a regular ſoldier, and many of the inhabitants are moſt favourably diſpoſed to the American cauſe ;—and that there is the largeſt ſtock of ammunition ever collected in America.

In the above veſſel ſome letters were alſo found, from an officer at Quebec, to general Gage and major Sheriff at Boſton, containing ſuch an account of the temper of the Canadians, as cannot but afford the higheſt ſatisfaction. I have thought it beſt to forward them : they are the incloſures, N° 6 and 7.

I am, with the greateſt reſpect, &c.   G. W.

SIR,   *Camp at Cambridge, Oct. 12, 1775.*

I AM honoured with your ſeveral favours of the twenty-ſixth and thirtieth of September, and fifth of October, the contents of which I ſhall beg leave to notice in their reſpective order.

Previous to the direction of Congreſs to conſult the general officers on the beſt mode of continuing and providing

for the army during the winter, I had defired them to turn
their thoughts upon thefe fubjects, and to favour me with
the refult, by a particular day, in writing.   In this interval,
the appointment of Dr. Franklin, Mr. Lynch, and colonel
Harrifon, was communicated,—an event which has given
me the higheft fatisfaction, as the fubject was too weighty
and complex for a difcuffion by letter.   This appointment
made any conclufion here unneceffary, as it is not probable
any fuch arrangement would be agreed on, as would not be
altered in fome refpects, upon a full and free conference.
This good effect will arife from the ftep already taken, that
every officer will be prepared to give his fentiments upon
thefe important fubjects.

The eftimates of the commiffary and quarter-mafter-
general I have now the honour of inclofing.   The firft is
N° 1, the other N° 2.

With refpect to the reduction of the pay of the men,
which may enter into the confideration of their fupport,
it is the unanimous opinion of the general officers, that it
cannot be touched with fafety at prefent. * * *

Upon the prefumption of there being a vacancy in the
direction of the hofpital, lieutenant-colonel Hand, formerly a furgeon in the eighteenth regiment, or royal Irifh, and
Dr. Fofter, late of Charleftown, and one of the furgeons
of the hofpital under Dr. Church, are candidates for that
office.   I do not pretend to be acquainted with their refpective merits, and therefore have given them no farther
expectation, than that they fhould be mentioned as candidates for the department.   I therefore need only to add
upon this fubject, that the affairs of the hofpital require
that the appointment fhould be made as foon as poffible.

Before I was honoured with your favour of the fifth inftant, I had given orders for the equipment of fome armed
veffels, to intercept the enemy's fupplies of provifions and
ammunition.   One of them was on a cruife between Cape
Anne and Cape Cod, when the exprefs arrived.   The
others will be fit for the fea in a few days, under the command of officers of the continental army, who are well recommended, as perfons acquainted with the fea, and capable of fuch a fervice.   Two of thefe will be immediately
difpatched

difpatched on this duty, and every particular, mentioned in your favour of the fifth inftant, literally complied with.

That the honourable Congrefs may have a more complete idea of the plan on which thefe veffels are equipped, I inclofe a copy of the inftructions given to the captains now out (N° 4). Thefe, with the additional inftruction directed, will be given to the captains who go into the mouth of St. Laurence's river. As both officers and men moft cheerfully engage in the fervice on the terms mentioned in thefe inftructions, I fear that the propofed increafe will create fome difficulty, by making a difference between men engaged on fimilar fervice. I have therefore not yet communicated this part of the plan, but referved an extra bounty as a reward for extraordinary activity. There are no armed veffels in this province ; and governor Cooke informs me the enterprife can receive no affiftance from him, as one of the armed veffels of Rhode-Ifland is on a long cruife, and the other unfit for the fervice. Nothing fhall be omitted to fecure fuccefs. A fortunate capture of an ordnance fhip would give new life to the camp, and an immediate turn to the iffue of this campaign.

Our laft accouts from colonel Arnold are very favourable : he was proceeding with all expedition ; and I flatter myfelf (making all allowances) he will be at Quebec the twentieth inftant, where a gentleman from Canada (Mr. * * *) affures me he will meet with no refiftance.

In the quarter-mafter's eftimate, there are fome articles omitted, of which he informs me he cannot pretend to furnifh a computation,—fuch as cartage, tools, &c. for which fome general allowance muft be made.

From the various accounts received from Europe, there may be reafon to expect troops will be landed at New-York, or fome other middle colony. I fhould be glad to know the pleafure of the Congrefs, whether, upon fuch an event, it would be expected that a part of this army fhould be detached, or the internal force of fuch colony and its neighbourhood be deemed fufficient ; or whether, in fuch cafe, I am to wait the particular direction of Congrefs.

The fleet, mentioned in my laft, has been feen ftanding N. N. E. ; fo that we apprehend it is intended for fome

part

part of this province, or New-Hampfhire, or poffibly Quebec.

The lateft and beft accounts we have from the enemy are, that they are engaged in their new work acrofs the fouth end of Bofton, preparing their barracks, &c. for winter :—that it is propofed to keep from five hundred to a thoufand men on Bunker's hill all winter, who are to be relieved once a week ;—the reft to be drawn into Bofton.

A perfon who has lately been a fervant to major Conolly (a tool of lord Dunmore's) has given an account of a fcheme to diftrefs the fouthern provinces, which appeared to me of fufficient confequence to be immediately tranfmitted. I have therefore got it attefted, and do myfelf the honour of inclofing it, Nº 5.

The new levies from Connecticut have lately marched into camp, and are a body of as good troops as any we have : fo that we have now the fame ftrength as before the detachment made under colonel Arnold.

I am, with the moft refpectful fentiments to the honourable Congrefs, and yourfelf, Sir, your moft obedient, &c.

G. W.

————————

SIR,   *Camp at Cambridge, Octo. 24, 1775.*

MY conjecture of the deftination of the late fquadron from Bofton, in my laft, has been unhappily verified by an outrage, exceeding, in barbarity and cruelty, every hoftile act practifed among civilized nations. I have inclofed the account given me by Mr. Jones, a gentleman of the town of Falmouth, of the deftruction of that increafing and flourifhing village. He is a very great fufferer, and informs me that the time allowed for the removal of effects was fo fmall, that valuable property of all kinds, and to a great amount, has been deftroyed. The orders fhewn by the captain for this horrid procedure (by which it appears the fame defolation is meditated upon all the towns on the coaft) made it my duty to communicate it as quickly and extenfively as poffible. As Portfmouth was the next place to which he propofed to go, general Sullivan was permitted to go up, and give them his affiftance and advice to ward off the blow. I flatter myfelf the like event will not happen

there,

there, as they have a fortification of some strength, and a vessel has arrived at a place called Sheepscot, with fifteen hundred pounds of powder.

The gentlemen of the Congress have nearly finished their business : but as they write by this opportunity, I must beg leave to refer you to their letter, for what concerns their commission.

We have had no occurrence of any consequence in the camp since I had the honour of addressing you last ; but expect every hour to hear that Newport has shared the fate of unhappy Falmouth.

I have the honour to be, &c.   G. W.

———————

SIR,   *Camp at Cambridge, Octo.* 30, 1775.

THE information, which the gentlemen who have lately gone from hence can give the Congress, of the state and situation of the army, would have made a letter unnecessary, if I did not suppose there would be some anxiety to know the intentions of the army on the subject of the re-enlistment.

Agreeably to the advice of those gentlemen, and my own opinion, I immediately began by directing all such officers as proposed to continue, to signify their intentions as soon as possible. A great number of the returns are come in, from which I find that a very great proportion of the officers of the rank of captains, and under, will retire ;—from present appearances, I may say, half,—but at least, one third. It is with some concern also that I observe, that many of the officers who retire discourage the continuance of the men, and, I fear, will communicate the infection to them. Some have advised, that those officers who decline the service should be immediately dismissed : but this would be very dangerous and inconvenient. I confess I have great anxieties upon the subject, though I still hope the pay and terms are so advantageous, that interest, and, I hope also, a regard to their country, will retain a greater proportion of the privates than their officers. In so important a matter, I shall esteem it my indispensable duty, not only to act with all possible prudence.

dence, but to give the moſt early and conſtant advice of my progreſs.

A ſupply of clothing, equal to our neceſſities, would greatly contribute to the encouragement and ſatisfaction of the men.   In every point of view, it is ſo important, that I beg leave to call the attention of the Congreſs to it in a particular manner.

A ſergeant has juſt come in from Bunker's-hill, but brings no important news.

I have the honour to be, &c.   G. W.

SIR,   *Cambridge, Nov. 2, 1775.*

I COULD not ſuffer Mr. Randolph to quit this camp without bearing ſome teſtimony of my duty to the Congreſs ; although his ſudden departure (occaſioned by the death of his worthy relative, whoſe loſs, as a good citizen and valuable member of ſociety, is much to be regretted) does not allow me time to be particular.

The incloſed return ſhews, at one view, what reliance we have upon the officers of this army, and how deficient we are like to be in ſubaltern officers.   A few days more will enable me to inform the Congreſs what they have to expect from the ſoldiery, as I ſhall iſſue recruiting orders for this purpoſe ſo ſoon as the officers are appointed,— which will be done this day,—having ſent for the general officers, to conſult them in the choice.

I muſt beg leave to recall the attention of the Congreſs to the appointment of a brigadier-general,—an officer as neceſſary to a brigade as a colonel is to a regiment, and will be exceedingly wanted in the new arrangement.

The proclamations and aſſociation, herewith incloſed, came to my hands on Monday laſt.   I thought it my duty to ſend them to you.   Nothing of moment has happened ſince my laſt.

With reſpectful compliments to the members of Congreſs, I have the honour to be, &c.   G. W.

Cambridge,

SIR,   *Cambridge, Nov.* 8, 1775.

THE immediate occasion of my giving the Congress the trouble of a letter at this time is to inform them, that, in consequence of their order signified in your letter of the twentieth ultimo, I laid myself under a solemn tie of secrefy to captain M'Pherson, and proceeded to examine his plan for the destruction of the fleet in the harbour of Boston, with all that care and attention which the importance of it deserved, and my judgment could lead to. But not being happy enough to coincide in opinion with that gentleman, and finding that his scheme would involve greater expense, than (under my doubts of its success) I thought myself justified in giving into, I prevailed upon him to communicate his plan to three gentlemen of the artillery in this army, well acquainted in the knowledge and practice of gunnery. By them he has been convinced, that, inasmuch as he set out upon wrong principles, the scheme would prove abortive. Unwilling however to relinquish his favourite project of reducing the naval force of Great-Britain, he is very desirous of building a number of row-gallies for this purpose. But as the Congress alone are competent to the adoption of this measure, I have advised him (although he offered to go on with the building of them at his own expense, till the Congress should decide) to repair immediately to Philadelphia with his proposals ; where, if they should be agreed to, or vessels of superior force, agreeably to the wishes of most others, should be resolved on, he may set instantly about them, with all the materials upon the spot :—here, they are to collect. To him therefore I refer for further information on this head.

A vessel, said to be from Philadelphia and bound to Boston, with a hundred and twenty pipes of wine (a hundred and eighteen of which are secured) stranded at a place called Eastham, in a gale of wind on the second instant :—another from Boston to Halifax, with dry goods, &c. (amounting, per invoice, to about two hundred and forty pounds lawful) got disabled in the same gale, near Beverly. These cargoes, with the papers, I have ordered to this place,—the vessels to be taken care of till further orders. I have also an account of the taking of a wood sloop bound to Boston,

and

and carried into Portſmouth by one of our armed veſſels; —particulars not yet come to hand;—and this inſtant, of two others, from Nova-Scotia to Boſton, with hay, wood, live ſtock, &c. by another of our armed ſchooners.—Theſe are in Plymouth.

Theſe accidents and captures point out the neceſſity of eſtabliſhing proper courts without loſs of time, for the deciſion of property, and the legality of ſeizures; otherwiſe I may be involved in inextricable difficulties.

Our priſoners, by the reduction of Fort Chamblee (on which happy event I moſt ſincerely congratulate the Congreſs) being conſiderably augmented, and likely to be increaſed, I ſubmit it to the wiſdom of Congreſs, whether ſome convenient inland towns, remote from the poſt-roads, ought not to be aſſigned them; the manner of their treatment, ſubſiſtence, &c. defined; and a commiſſary or agent appointed, to ſee that juſtice is done both to them and the public, proper accounts rendered, &c. Without a mode of this ſort is adopted, I fear there will be ſad confuſion hereafter, as there are great complaints at preſent.

I reckoned without my hoſt, when I informed the Congreſs in my laſt, that I ſhould in a day or two be able to acquaint them of the diſpoſition of the ſoldiery towards a new enliſtment. I have been in conſultation with the generals of this army ever ſince Thurſday laſt, endeavouring to eſtabliſh new corps of officers; but find ſo many doubts and difficulties to reconcile, that I cannot ſay when they are to end, or what may be the conſequences; as there appears to be ſuch an unwillingneſs in the officers of one government mixing in the ſame regiment with thoſe of another; and, without it, many muſt be diſmiſſed who are willing to ſerve, notwithſtanding we are deficient on the whole.

The council of officers are unanimouſly of opinion that the command of the artillery ſhould no longer continue in colonel * * *; and knowing of no perſon better qualified to ſupply his place, or whoſe appointment will give more general ſatisfaction, have taken the liberty of recommending Henry Knox, eſquire, to the conſideration of Congreſs, thinking it indiſpenſably neceſſary at the ſame time that this regiment ſhould conſiſt of two lieutenant-colonels, two majors, and twelve companies, agreeably to the

plan

plan and estimate handed in ; which, differing from the last establishment, I should be glad to be instructed on.

The commissary-general not being returned, will apologize, I hope, for my silence respecting a requisition of the expense of his clerks, &c. which I was to have obtained together with others, and forwarded.

I have heard nothing of colonel Arnold since the thirteenth ultimo. His letter of, and journal to, that date, will convey all the information I am able to give of him. I think he must be in Quebec. If any mischance had happened to him, he would, as directed, have forwarded an express. No account yet of the armed vessels sent to St. Laurence. I think they will meet the stores inward or outward bound.

Captain Symons, in the Cerberus lately sent from Boston to Falmouth, hath published the inclosed declaration at that place ; and it is suspected he intends to make some kind of a lodgment there. I wrote immediately to Colonel Finnie of this army, who went up there upon the last alarm, to spirit up the people and oppose it at all events. Falmouth is about a hundred and thirty miles from this camp.

I have the honour to be, &c. G. W.

P. S. I send a general return of the troops, and manifests of the cargoes and vessels taken at Plymouth.

———

SIR, *Cambridge, Nov. 11, 1775.*

* * * INCLOSED you have a copy of an act, passed this session, by the honourable council and house of representatives of this province. It respects such captures as may be made by vessels fitted out by the province, or by individuals thereof. As the armed vessels, fitted out at the continental expense, do not come under this law, I would have it submitted to the consideration of Congress, to point out a more summary way of proceeding, to determine the property and mode of condemnation of such prizes as have been or hereafter may be made, than is specified in this act.

Should not a court be established by authority of Congress, to take cognizance of prizes made by the continental vessels ? Whatever the mode is which they are pleased to

adopt, there is an abfolute neceffity of its being fpeedily determined on : for I cannot fpare time from military affairs,
to give proper attention to thefe matters.

The inhabitants of Plymouth have taken a floop, laden
with provifions, &c. from Halifax, bound to Bofton : and
the inhabitants of Beverly have, under cover of one of the
armed fchooners, taken a veffel from Ireland, laden with
beef, pork, butter, &c. for the fame place. The latter
brings papers and letters of a very interefting nature, which
are in the hands of the honourable council, who informed
me they will tranfmit them to you by this conveyance,
To the contents of thefe papers and letters I muft beg leave
to refer you and the honourable Congrefs, who will now
fee the abfolute neceffity there is of exerting all their wifdom, to withftand the mighty efforts of our enemies.

The trouble I have in the arrangement of the army is really inconceivable. Many of the officers fent in their names
to ferve, in expectation of promotion : others ftood aloof
* * * ; whilft a number who had declined have again fent
in their names, to ferve. So great has the confufion, arifing from thefe and many other perplexing circumftances,
been, that I found it abfolutely impoffible to fix this very interefting bufinefs exactly on the plan refolved on in the conference, though I have kept up to the fpirit, as near as the
nature and neceffity of the cafe would admit of : the difficulty with the foldiers is as great, indeed more fo, if poffible,
than with the officers. They will not enlift, until they
know their colonel, lieutenant-colonel, major, captain, &c. ;
fo that it was neceffary to fix the officers the firft thing ;
which is, at laft, in fome manner done ; and I have given
out enlifting orders.

You, Sir, can much eafier judge, than I can exprefs,
the anxiety of mind I muft labour under on the occafion,
efpecially at this time, when we may expect the enemy
will begin to act on the arrival of their reinforcement,
part of which is already come, and the remainder daily
dropping in.

I have other diftreffes of a very alarming nature. The
arms of our foldiery are fo exceeding bad, that I affure
you, Sir, I cannot place a proper confidence in them.
Our powder is wafting faft, notwithftanding the ftricteft
care,

care, economy and attention are paid to it. The long feries of wet weather we have had, renders the greater part of what has been ferved out to the men of no ufe. Yefterday I had a proof of it, as a party of the enemy, about four or five hundred, taking the advantage of a high tide, landed at Leechmore's point: we were alarmed, and of courfe ordered every man to examine his cartouch-box, when the melancholy truth appeared; and we were obliged to furnifh the greater part of them with frefh ammunition.

The damage done at the point was the taking of a man who watched a few horfes and cows: ten of the latter they carried off. Colonel Thompfon marched down with his regiment of riflemen, and was joined by colonel Woodbridge, with a part of his and a part of Patterfon's regiment, who gallantly waded through the water, and foon obliged the enemy to embark under cover of a man-of-war, a floating battery, and the fire of a battery on Charleftown neck. We have two of our men dangeroufly wounded by grape-fhot from the man-of-war; and, by a flag fent out this day, we are informed the enemy loft two of their men.

I have the honour to be, &c. G. W.

SIR, *Cambridge, Nov.* 19, 1775.

I RECEIVED your favours of the feventh and tenth inftant, with the refolves of the honourable Congrefs, to which I will pay all due attention. As foon as two capable perfons can be found, I will difpatch them to Nova-Scotia, on the fervice refolved on in Congrefs.

The refolve to raife two battalions of marines will (if practicable in this army) entirely derange what has been done. It is therein mentioned, " one colonel for the two battalions :"—of courfe, a colonel muft be difmiffed. One of the many difficulties which attended the new arrangement, was in reconciling the different interefts, and judging of the merits of the different colonels. In the difmiffion of this one, the fame difficulties will occur. The officers and men muft be acquainted with maritime

affairs;

affairs ; to comply with which, they muſt be picked out
of the whole army,—one from this corps, one from another,—ſo as to break through the whole ſyſtem, which
has coſt us ſo much time, anxiety and pains, to bring into
any tolerable form.   Notwithſtanding any difficulties
which will ariſe, you may be aſſured, Sir, that I will uſe
every endeavour to comply with their reſolve.

I beg leave to ſubmit it to the conſideration of Congreſs (if theſe two battalions can be formed out of this
army) whether this is a time to weaken our lines, by employing any of the forces appointed to defend them, on
any other ſervice.   The gentlemen who were here from
the Congreſs know their vaſt extent : they muſt know
that we ſhall have occaſion for our whole force for that
purpoſe ; more ſo now than at any paſt time, as we may
expect the enemy will take the advantage of the firſt hard
weather, and attempt to make an impreſſion ſomewhere.
That this is their intention, we have many reaſons to ſuſpect.

We have had, in the laſt week, ſix deſerters, and took
two ſtraggling priſoners.   They all agree that two companies, with a train of artillery and one of the regiments from
Ireland, were arrived at Boſton ;—that freſh ammunition
and flints have been ſerved out ;—that the grenadiers and
light infantry had orders to hold themſelves in readineſs at
a moment's warning.

As there is every appearance that this conteſt will not
be ſoon decided, and of courſe that there muſt be an augmentation of the continental army, would it not be eligible
to raiſe two battalions of marines in New-York and Philadelphia, where there muſt be numbers of ſailors now unem-
ployed ?—This however is matter of opinion, which I mention with all due deference to the ſuperior judgment of the
Congreſs.

Incloſed you have copies of two letters,—one from
colonel Arnold,—the other from colonel * * *.   I can
form no judgment on the latter's conduct, until I ſee him.
Notwithſtanding the great defection, I do not deſpair of
colonel Arnold's ſucceſs.   He will have, in all probability, many more difficulties to encounter than if he had been
a fortnight ſooner ; as it is likely that governor Carleton

will,

will, with what forces he can collect after the surrender of the rest of Canada, throw himself into Quebec, and there make his last effort. There is no late account from captains Broughton and Sillman, sent to the river St. Laurence. The other cruisers have been chiefly confined to harbour, by the badness of the weather. The same reason has caused great delay in building of our barracks; which, with a most mortifying scarcity of fire-wood, discourages the men from enlisting. The last, I am afraid, is an insuperable obstacle. I have applied to the honourable house of representatives of this province, who were pleased to appoint a committee to negociate this business: and notwithstanding all the pains they have and are taking, they find it impossible to supply our necessities. The want of a sufficient number of teams I understand to be the chief impediment.

I got returns this day from eleven colonels, of the numbers enlisted in their regiments. The whole amount is nine hundred and sixty-six men. There must be some other stimulus besides love for their country, to make men fond of the service. It would be a great encouragement, and no additional expense to the continent, were they to receive pay for the months of October and November; also a month's pay advance. The present state of the military chest will not admit of this. The sooner it is enabled to do so, the better.

The commissary-general is daily expected in camp. I cannot send you the estimate of the clerks in his department, until he arrives.

I sincerely congratulate you upon the success of your arms, in the surrender of St. John's, which I hope is a happy presage of the reduction of the rest of Canada.

I have the honour to be, &c.   G. W.

SIR,   *Cambridge, November* 28, 1775.

I HAD the honour of writing to you on the nineteenth instant. I have now to inform you that Henry Knox, esquire, is gone to New-York, with orders to forward to this place what cannon and ordnance stores can be there procured. From thence he will proceed to general Schuyler on the fame bufinefs, as you will fee by the inclofed copy of inftructions which I have given him.   It would give me much fatisfaction, that this gentleman, or any other whom you may think qualified, was appointed to the command of the artillery regiment.   In my letter to you, of the eighth inftant, I have expreffed myfelf fully on this fubject, which I beg leave to recommend to your immediate attention ; as the formation of that corps will be at a ftand, until I am honoured with your inftructions thereon. * * * *

There are two perfons engaged to go to Nova-Scotia, on the bufinefs recommended in your laft.   By the beft information we have from thence, the ftores, &c. have been withdrawn fome time.   Should this not be the cafe, it is next to an impoffibility to attempt any thing there, in the prefent unfettled and precarious ftate of the army. * * *

From what I can collect by my inquiries amongft the officers, it will be impoffible to get the men to enlift for the continuance of the war ; which will be an infuperable obftruction to the formation of the two battalions of marines on the plan refolved on in Congrefs.   As it can make no difference, I propofe to proceed on the new arrangement of the army, and, when completed, inquire out fuch officers and men as are beft qualified for that fervice, and endeavour to form thefe two battalions out of the whole. This appears to me the beft method, and will, I hope, meet the approbation of Congrefs.

As it will be very difficult for the men to work when the hard froft fets in, I have thought it neceffary (though of little ufe at prefent) to take poffeffion of Coble-hill, for the benefit of any future operations.   It was effected, without the leaft oppofition from the enemy, the twenty-third inftant.   Their inactivity on this occafion is what I cannot account for ;—it is probable they are meditating a blow fomewhere.

About three hundred men, women and children of the poor inhabitants of Bofton, came out to Point-Shirley laft Friday.   They have brought their houfehold furniture, but are unprovided of every other neceffary of life.   I have recommended them to the attention of the
                                        committee

committee of the honourable council of this province, now sitting at Watertown.

The number enlisted since my last are two thousand four hundred and fifty men. * * * * Our situation is truly alarming : and of this general Howe is well apprised, it being the common topic of conversation when the people left Boston last Friday. No doubt, when he is reinforced, he will avail himself of the information.

I am making the best disposition I can for our defence, having thrown up, besides the work on Coble-hill, several redoubts, half-moons, &c. along the bay : and I fear I shall be under the necessity of calling in the militia and minute-men of the country to my assistance : I say, I fear it,—because, by what I can learn from the officers in the army, belonging to this colony, it will be next to an impossibility to keep them under any degree of discipline, and that it will be very difficult to prevail on them to remain a moment longer than they choose themselves. It is a mortifying reflection, to be reduced to this dilemma. There has been nothing wanting on my part, to infuse a proper spirit amongst the officers, that they may exert their influence with the soldiery. You see, by a fortnight's recruiting amongst men with arms in their hands, how little has been the success.

As the small-pox is now in Boston, I have used the precaution of prohibiting such as lately came out from coming near our camp. General Burgoyne, I am informed, will soon embark for England. I think the risk too great to write you by post, whilst it continues to pass through New-York. It is certain that a post has been intercepted the beginning of last month, as they sent out several letters from Boston with the post-mark of Baltimore on them. This goes by captain Joseph Blewer, who promises to deliver it carefully unto you.

You doubtless will have heard, before this reaches, of general Montgomery's having got possession of Montréal. I congratulate you thereon. He has troubles with his troops, as well as I have. All I can learn of colonel Arnold is, that he is near Quebec. I hope Montgomery will be able to proceed to his assistance. I shall be very uneasy until I hear they are joined.

My

My beſt reſpects attend the gentlemen in Congreſs: and believe me, Sir, your moſt obedient, &c.

G. W.

SIR,   *Cambridge, Novem.* 30, 1775.

I HAD the honour to write to you the twenty-eighth inſtant, by captain Joſeph Blewer.   Laſt evening I received the agreeable account of the ſchooner Lee, commanded by captain Manly, having taken and carried into Cape-Anne a large brigantine, bound from London to Boſton, laden with military ſtores, the inventory of which I have the pleaſure to incloſe you.   Cape-Anne is a very open harbour, and acceſſible to large ſhips; which made me immediately ſend off colonel Glover and Mr. Palfrey, with orders to raiſe the minute-men and militia of that part of the country, to have the cargo landed without loſs of time, and guarded up to this camp.   This, I hope, they will be able to effect, before it is known to the enemy what port ſhe is carried into.   I ſincerely congratulate you on this very great acquiſition; and am, Sir, your moſt humble, &c.   G. W.

Manly has alſo taken a ſloop in the miniſterial ſervice; and captain Adams, in the ſchooner Warren, has taken a ſchooner laden with potatoes and turnips, bound to Boſton, and carried her into Portſmouth.

SIR,   *Cambridge, Dec.* 4, 1775.

I HAD the honour of writing to you the thirtieth ultimo, incloſing an inventory of the military ſtores taken on board the brig Nancy by captain Manly of the armed ſchooner Lee.   I have now to inform you that he has ſince ſent into Beverly a ſhip named the Concord, James Lowrie, maſter, from Greenock in Scotland, bound to Boſton.   She has on board dry goods and coals, to the value of three thouſand ſix hundred and ſix pounds, nine ſhillings and ſeven pence ſterling, ſhipped by Crawford, Anderſon, and Co. and conſigned to James Anderſon, merchant in Boſton.   It is mentioned in the letters found

on

on board, that this cargo was for the ufe of the army: but, on a ftrict examination, I find it is really the property of the fhippers and the perfon to whom configned. Pray what is to be done with this fhip and cargo? and what with the brigantine which brought the military ftores?—It was agreed, in the conference laft October, *"that all veffels employed merely as tranfports, and unarmed, with their crews, be fet at liberty, upon giving fecurity to return to Europe; but that this indulgence be not extended longer than till the firft of April next."* In the fhippers' letter, they mention:. "You muft procure a certificate from the general and admiral, of the Concord's being in the government fervice, fuch as the Glafgow packet brought with her, which was of great fervice, procured a liberty to arm her, which was refufed us;. alfo gave her a preference for fome recruits that went out in her." In another part of the letter, they fay: "Captain Lowrie will deliver you the contract for the coals: we gave it to him, as it perhaps might be of ufe, as a certificate of his fhip being employed in the government fervice." Every letter on board breathes nothing but enmity to this country:. and a vaft number of them there are.

It is fome time fince I recommended to the Congrefs that they would inftitute a court for the trial of prizes made by the continental armed veffels; which I hope they have ere now taken into their confideration: otherwife I fhould again take the liberty of urging it in the moft preffing manner.

The conduct of a great number of the Connecticut troops has laid me under the neceffity of calling in a body of the militia, much fooner than I apprehended there would be an occafion for fuch a ftep. I was afraid fome time ago that they would incline to go home, when the time of their enliftment expired. I called upon the officers of the feveral regiments, to know whether they could prevail on the men to remain until the firft of January, or till a fufficient number of other forces could be raifed to fupply their place. I fuppofe they were deceived themfelves: I know they deceived me by affurances that I need be under no apprehenfion on that fcore, for the men would not leave the lines. Laft Friday fhewed how much they were miftaken, as the major part of the troops of that colony were

going

going away with their arms and ammunition. We have however by threats, perfuafion, and the activity of the people of the country who fent back many of them that had fet out, prevailed upon the moft part to ftay. There are about eighty of them miffing.

I have called in three thoufand men from this province ; and general Sullivan, who lately returned from the province of New-Hampfhire, having informed me that a number of men were there ready at the fhorteft notice, I have demanded two thoufand from that province. Thefe two bodies, I expect, will be in by the tenth inftant, to make up the deficiency of the Connecticut-men whom I have promifed to difmifs on that day, as well as the numbers to whom I was obliged to grant furloughs before any would enlift. As the fame defection is much to be apprehended when the time of the Maffachufetts-Bay, New-Hampfhire, and Rhode-Ifland forces is expired, I beg the attention of Congrefs to this important affair.

I am informed that it has been the cuftom of thefe provinces in the laft war, for the legiflative power to order every town to provide a certain quota of men for the campaign. This or fome other mode fhould be at prefent adopted, as I am fatisfied the men cannot be had without. This the Congrefs will pleafe to take into their immediate confideration. My fufpicions on this head I fhall alfo communicate to the governors Trumbull and Cooke, alfo to the New-Hampfhire convention.

The number enlifted in the laft week are about thirteen hundred men. By this you fee how flow this important work goes on. * * *

An exprefs is juft come in from general Schuyler, with letters from colonel Arnold and general Montgomery, copies of which I have the honour to inclofe you. Upon the whole, I think affairs carry a pleafing afpect in that quarter. The reduction of Quebec is an object of fuch great importance, that I doubt not the Congrefs will give every affiftance in their power for the accomplifhing it this winter.

By the laft accounts from the armed fchooners fent to the river St. Laurence, I fear we have but little to expect from them : they were falling fhort of provifion, and men-

tion

tion that they would be obliged to return ; which at this time is particularly unfortunate, as, if they chose a proper ſtation, all the veſſels coming down that river muſt fall into their hands. The plague, trouble and vexation I have had with the crews of all the armed veſſels, is inexpreſſible. I do believe there is not on earth a more diſorderly ſet : every time they come into port, we hear of nothing but mutinous complaints. Manly's ſucceſs has lately, and but lately, quieted his people. The crews of the Waſhington and Harriſon have actually deſerted them ; ſo that I have been under the neceſſity of ordering the agent to lay the latter up, and get hands for the other on the beſt terms he could.

The houſe of repreſentatives and the honourable board have ſent me a vote of theirs relative to the harbour of Cape-Cod, which you have herewith. I ſhall ſend an officer thither to examine what can be done for its defence, though I do not think I ſhall be able to give them ſuch aſſiſtance as may be requiſite ; for I have at preſent neither men, powder, nor cannon to ſpare. The great want of powder is what the attention of Congreſs ſhould be particularly applied to. I dare not attempt any thing offenſive, let the temptation or advantage be ever ſo great, as I have not more of that moſt eſſential article than will be abſolutely neceſſary to defend our lines, ſhould the enemy attempt to attack them.

By recent information from Boſton, general Howe is going to ſend out a number of the inhabitants, in order, it is thought, to make more room for his expected reinforcements. There is one part of the information I can hardly give credit to :—a ſailor ſays that a number of thoſe coming out have been inoculated, with deſign of ſpreading the ſmall-pox through this country and camp. I have communicated this to the general court ; and recommended their attention thereto.

They are arming one of the tranſports in Boſton, with which they mean to decoy ſome of our armed veſſels. As we are appriſed of their deſign, I hope they will be diſappointed.

My beſt reſpects wait on the gentlemen in Congreſs, and I am, Sir, your moſt humble, &c. G. W.

P. S.

P. S. I was mifinformed when I mentioned that one regiment had arrived at Bofton: a few companies of the feventeenth and artillery are all that are yet come. Near three hundred perfons are landed on Point-Shirley from Bofton.

SIR,   *Cambridge, Decem. 7, 1775.*

I WROTE you, the fourth inftant, by exprefs, to which I beg you will be referred. My fears, that Broughton and Sillman would not effect any good purpofe, were too well founded. They are returned, and brought with them three of the principal inhabitants from the ifland of St. John's. * * * They brought the governor's commiffion, the province feal, &c. &c. As the captains acted without any warrant for fuch conduct, I have thought it but juftice to difcharge thefe gentlemen, whofe families were left in the utmoft diftrefs.

I am credibly informed that James Anderfon, the confignee and part owner of the fhip Concord and cargo, is not only unfriendly to American liberty, but actually in arms againft us,—being captain of the Scotch company at Bofton. Whether your being acquainted with this circumftance, or not, will operate againft the veffel and cargo, I will not take upon me to fay: but there are many articles on board, fo abfolutely neceffary for the army, that, whether fhe is made a prize or not, we muft have them.

I have the honour to be, &c.   G. W.

SIR,   *Cambridge, Decem. 11, 1775.*

* * * THE numbers enlifted laft week are   men. If they go on at this flow rate, it will be a long time before this army is complete. I have wrote to the governors of Connecticut and Rhode-Ifland, alfo to the convention of New-Hampfhire, on this fubject. A copy of my letter to them I have the honour to inclofe herewith.

A letter

A letter to the fame purport I fent to the legiflature of this province.

The militia are coming in faft. I am much pleafed with the alacrity which the good people of this province, as well as thofe of New-Hampfhire, have fhewn upon this occafion. I expect the whole will be in this day and to-morrow, when what remains of the Connecticut [*troops,*] who have not enlifted, will have liberty to go to their fire-fides.

The commiffary-general is ftill by his indifpofition de-tained from camp. He committed an error, when mak-ing out the ration-lift : for he was then ferving out (and has continued fo to do) fix ounces per man per week of butter, though it is not included in the lift approved of by Congrefs. I do not think it would be expedient to put a ftop thereto ; as every thing, that would have a tendency to give the foldiery room for complaint, muft be avoided.

The information I received that the enemy intended fpreading the fmall-pox amongft us, I could not fuppofe them capable of. I now muft give fome credit to it, as it has made its appearance on feveral of thofe who laft came out of Bofton. Every neceffary precaution has been taken to prevent its being communicated to this army ; and the general court will take care that it does not fpread through the country.

I have not heard that any more troops are arrived at Bofton ; which is a lucky circumftance, as the Connecticut troops, I now find, are for the moft part gone off. The houfes in Bofton are leffening every day : they are pulled down, either for fire-wood, or to prevent the effects of fire, fhould we attempt a bombardment or an attack upon the town. Coble-hill is ftrongly fortified, without any interruption from the enemy. * * * This is what at prefent occurs ; from, Sir, your moft obedient, &c.

G. W.

P. S. The weekly returns of enliftments not being yet received for more than ten regiments, amounting to feven hundred and twenty-five men, I cannot fill up the blank in this letter : but this, added to the former, makes in the whole five thoufand two hundred and fifty-three.

Vol. 1.   F   *Cambridge,*

I RECEIVED your favour of the second inftant with the feveral refolves of Congrefs therein inclofed.   The refolves relative to captures made by continental armed veffels only want a court eftablifhed for trial, to make them complete.   This, I hope, will be foon done, as I have taken the liberty to urge it often to the Congrefs.

I am fomewhat at a lofs to know whether I am to raife the two battalions of marines here, or not.   As the delay can be attended with but little inconvenience, I will wait a farther explanation from Congrefs, before I take any fteps therein.

I am much pleafed that the money will be forwarded with all poffible expedition, as it is much wanting; alfo that Conolly and his affociates are taken.   It has been a very fortunate difcovery.   I make no doubt but that the Congrefs will take every neceffary meafure to difpoffefs lord Dunmore of his hold in Virginia : the fooner fteps are taken for that purpofe, the more probability there will be of their being effectual.   *   *   *   *

I will make application to general Howe, and propofe an exchange for Mr. Ethan Allen.   I am much afraid I fhall have a like propofal to make for captain Martindale, of the armed brigantine Wafhington, and his men, which, it is reported, was taken a few days paft by a man-of-war, and carried into Bofton.   We cannot expect to be always fuccefsful.

You will doubtlefs hear of the barbarity of captain Wallace on Conanicut ifland, ere this reaches your hands.

About a hundred and fifty more of the poor inhabitants are come out of Bofton.   The fmall-pox rages all over the town : fuch of the military as had it not before are now under inoculation.   This, I apprehend, is a weapon of defence they are ufing againft us.   What confirms me in this opinion, is, that I have information that they are tearing up the pavement, to be provided againft a bombardment.

I wrote you this day by Meffrs. Pennel and De Pliarné, who will lay before the Congrefs, or a committee there-

of,

of, proposals for furnishing the continent with arms and
ammunition. I refer you to themselves for further particulars.

I have the honour to be, &c.   G. W.

———

Chelsea, Decem. 16, 1775.

OBSERVATIONS OF THE DAY.

LAST evening, eight men came in a boat from
Boston, to our guard at the ferry,—six of them captains
of vessels. They brought the following account :

Yesterday, one large mortar was carried over to Bunker's hill :—the troops filling water, carrying it on board
the transports :—provisions scarce,—not more than sufficient for six weeks. One regiment of foot, and three
companies of the light-horse, sail for Halifax this day.

Dorchester, Dec. 16, 1775.

Sailed out of Boston harbour this morning, eight large
and two small vessels, taken to be tenders ;—by their firing, appeared to be going a voyage out to sea.

Mr. Joshua Pico came last night from Boston. He
confirms the information that the regiment of foot, and
some companies of light-horse, were preparing to embark
for Halifax.

SIR,   Cambridge, Decem. 16, 1775.

THE information, contained in the above, coming
so many different ways, corroborated by several vessels
having sailed this day from Boston,—I thought it my
duty to transmit it to you. Though Halifax is the place
given out for their destination, it is possible they may be
bound elsewhere. I shall communicate this intelligence
to governors Cooke and Trumbull, and to the convention
of New-York, for their government.

I remain, Sir, your most obedient, &c.   G. W.

Cambridge,

SIR,   *Cambridge, Decem.* 19, 1775.

CAPTAIN Manly, of the Lee armed fchooner, took and fent into Beverly the floop Betfey, A. Atkinfon, mafter.   She is an armed veffel, difpatched by lord Dunmore, with Indian corn, potatoes, and oats, for the army in Bofton.   The packets of letters found on board, I have the honour to fend you with this by captain James Chambers, they being of fo much importance that I do not think it would be prudent to truft them by a common exprefs.

As lord Dunmore's fchemes are fully laid open in thefe letters, I need not point out to the Congrefs the neceffity there is of a vigorous exertion being adopted by them, to difpoffefs his lordfhip of the ftrong hold he has got in Virginia.   I do not mean to dictate: but I am fure they will pardon me for giving them freely my opinion, which is, that the fate of America a good deal depends on his being obliged to evacuate Norfolk this winter, or not.

I have Kirkland well fecured, and think I will fend him to you for examination.   By moft of the letters relative to him, he is a dangerous fellow.   John Stewart's letters and papers are of a very interefting nature.   Governor Tonyn's and many other letters from Auguftine fhew the weaknefs of the place; at the fame time, of what vaft confequence it would be for us to poffefs ourfelves of it, and the great quantity of ammunition contained in the forts.   Indeed thefe papers are of fo great confequence, that I think this but little inferior to any prize our famous Manly has taken.

We now work at our eafe on Leechmore's hill.   On difcovering our party there yefterday morning, the fhip which lay oppofite began a cannonade, to which Mount Horam added fome fhells.   One of our men was wounded.   We fired a few fhot from two eighteen pounders which are placed on Coble-hill, and foon obliged the fhip to fhift her ftation.   She now lies in the ferry-way: and, except a few fhells from the mount in Bofton, (which do no execution) we have no interruption in profecuting our works, which will in a very fhort time be completed.

When

When that is done,—when we have powder to fport with,—I think, if the Congrefs refolve on the execution of the propofal made relative to the town of Bofton, it can be done.

I have fent a letter in this day to general Howe, of which a copy goes herewith. My reafon for pointing out brigadier-general Prefcot as the object who is to fuffer Mr. Allen's fate, is, that, by letters from general Schuyler, and copies of letters from general Montgomery to Schuyler, I am given to underftand that Prefcot is the caufe of Allen's fufferings. I thought it beft to be decifive on the occafion, as did the generals whom I confulted thereon.

The returns of men enlifted fince my laft amount to about eighteen hundred, making in the whole feven thonfand one hundred and forty. The militia that are come in, both from this province and New-Hampfhire, are very fine-looking men, and go through their duty with great alacrity. The difpatch made, both by the people in marching and by the legiflative powers in complying with my requifition, has given me infinite fatisfaction.

Your letter of the eighth inftant, with the explanatory refolve refpecting my calling forth the militia and minutemen, is come to hand ; to which I fhall pay all due attention. You have removed all the difficulties which I laboured under, about the two battalions of marines. I fha!! obey the orders of Congrefs in looking out for proper officers to command that corps. I make no doubt but, when the money arrives to pay off the arrears and the month's advance, that it will be a great encouragement for the men to enlift.

Inclofed is a letter I lately received from Mr. James Lovell. His cafe is truly pitiable. I wifh fome mode could be fallen upon to relieve him from the cruel fituation he is now in. I am fenfible of the impropriety of exchanging a foldier for a citizen : but there is fomething fo cruelly diftrefling in regard to this gentleman, that I dare fay you will take it under your confideration.

I am, with great refpect, &c.   ~ G. W.

        Cambridge,

S I R,	*Cambridge, Dec. 25, 1775.*

I HAD the honour to addrefs myfelf to you on the nineteenth inftant, fince which I have received undoubted information that the genuine inftructions given to Conolly have not reached your hands ; that they are very artfully concealed in the tree of his faddle, and covered with canvafs fo nicely that they are fcarcely difcernible ; that thofe which were found upon him were intended to deceive, if he was caught. You will moft certainly have his faddle taken to pieces, in order to difcover this deep-laid plot.

Inclofed is a copy of general Howe's letter in anfwer to the one I wrote him the eighteenth inftant. The conduct I am to obferve towards brigadier Prefcot in confequence of thefe letters, the Congrefs will oblige me by determining for me.

The gentlemen by whom you fent the money are arrived. The fum they brought, though large, is not fufficient to anfwer the demands of the army, which at this time are remarkably heavy : there is three month's pay due, one month's advance, two dollars for each blanket,—the arms, that are left by thofe who are difmiffed, to be paid for,—befides the demands which are on the commiffary and quarter-mafter generals. You will therefore fee the neceffity of another remittance, which I beg may be as foon as you conveniently can.

I will take the opportunity of the return of thefe gentlemen, to fend colonel Kirkland to you for examination, and that you may difpofe of him as to you may feem proper.

A committee from the general court of this province called on me the other day, informing me that they were in great want of ordnance for the defence of the colony ; that, if what belonged to them, now in ufe here, was kept for the continent, they would be under the neceffity of providing themfelves with others : of courfe, what is kept muft be paid for. There are many of the cannon of very little ufe : fuch of them as are good, I cannot at prefent part with : perhaps when I receive the fupply

from

from New-York and Canada, it may be in my power to
spare them.

Mr. Wadsworth has sent in his report respecting Cape-
Cod harbour, a copy of which you will receive herewith;
also a letter from a Mr. Jacob Bailey, put into my hands
by colonel Little. It contains some things that may not
be unworthy the confideration of Congrefs.

We have made good progrefs in the works on Leechmore's point. They would have been finifhed ere this,
but for the feverity of the weather, which prevents our people from working.

I received a letter from governor Cooke, which expreffes the fears of the people of Rhode-Ifland, left the fhips,
which we had information were failed, with fome troops
on board, were deftined for Newport. I fent major-general Lee there, to point out to them fuch defence as he
may think the place capable of. I fincerely wifh he may
be able to do it with effect, as that place, in its prefent
ftate, is an afylum for fuch as are difaffected to American
liberty.

Our returns of enliftments, to this day, amount to eight
thoufand five hundred men.

I have the honour to be, &c. G. W.

P. S. Inclofed is an eftimate of the demands of the
army.

SIR, *Cambridge, Decem.* 31, 1775.

I WROTE to you the twenty-fifth inftant; fince
which I am not honoured with any of your favours.
The eftimate I then inclofed you was calculated to pay
the troops, &c. up to the firft of January. That cannot
be done for want of funds in the pay-mafter-general's
hands; which caufes a great murmuring amongft thofe
who are going off. The monthly expenfes of this army
amount to near two hundred and feventy-five thoufand
dollars, which I take the liberty of recommending to the
obfervation of Congrefs, that their future remittances may
be governed thereby.

It

It sometimes happens that persons would wish to deposit money in the hands of the pay-master-general, for his bills on the treasury at Philadelphia. He has hitherto declined such offers, not having authority from Congress to draw. Would it not be proper to give this power? If it should be approved of, you will please to point out the mode that the Congress would choose to have it done in.

The clothing sent to the quarter-master-general is not sufficient to put half our army into regimentals; nor is there a possibility of getting any quantity here. I have wrote to general Schuyler, that I wish what was lodged at Albany could be spared for these troops, as general Montgomery would clothe the men under his command at Montréal. If this can be done, it will be of infinite service; and no time should be lost in forwarding them to this camp.

In forming the regiments for the new establishment, I thought it but justice to appoint the officers, detached under colonel Arnold, to commissions in them. Their absence at present is of very great detriment to the service, especially in recruiting: I would therefore wish, if the Congress intend raising troops in or for Canada, that they could be taken in there. The sooner I have their opinion of this matter, the better, that, if they can be commissioned in Canada, I may appoint officers here to replace them.

Inclosed you have a copy of a representation sent to me by the legislative body of this province respecting four companies stationed at Braintree, Weymouth, and Hingham. As they were never regimented, and were doing duty at a distance from the rest of the army, I did not know whether to consider them as a part of it; nor do I think myself authorised to direct payment for them without the approbation of Congress.

It has been represented to me that the free negroes who have served in this army are very much dissatisfied at being discarded. As it is to be apprehended that they may seek employ in the ministerial army, I have presumed to depart from the resolution respecting them, and have given license for their being enlisted. If this is disapproved of by Congress, I will put a stop to it. * * * I must

* * * I muſt remark that the pay of the aſſiſtant engineers is ſo very ſmall, that we cannot expeſt men of ſcience will engage in it. Thoſe gentlemen who are in that ſtation, remained under the expeſtation that an additional allowance would be made them by the reſpeſtive provinces in which they were appointed, to that allowed by the Congreſs.

Captain Freeman arrived this day at camp from Canada. He left Quebec the twenty-fourth ultimo, in conſequence of general Carleton's proclamation which I have the honour to ſend you herewith. He ſaw colonel Arnold the twenty-ſixth, and ſays that he was joined at Point-á-tremble by general Montgomery, the firſt inſtant;—that they were about two thouſand ſtrong, and were making every preparation for attacking Quebec; that general Carleton had with him about twelve hundred men, the majority of whom are ſailors;—that it was his opinion the French would give up the place if they get the ſame conditions granted to the inhabitants of Montréal. * * *

Captains Semple and Harbeſon take under their care Mr. Kirkland. * * * Captain Mathews and Mr. Robinſon will accompany them. The two latter were taken priſoners by lord Dunmore, who was ſending them to Boſton, from whence there is little doubt but they would be forwarded to England, to which place I am credibly informed captain Martindale and the crew of the Waſhington are ſent; alſo colonel Allen, and the priſoners taken with him in Canada. This may account for general Howe's ſilence on the ſubjeſt of an exchange of priſoners mentioned in my letter to him.

General Lee is juſt returned from his excurſion to Rhode-Iſland:—he has pointed out the beſt method the iſland would admit of for its defence; he has endeavoured all in his power to make friends of thoſe that were our enemies. You have, incloſed, a ſpecimen of his abilities in that way, for your peruſal. I am of opinion that, if the ſame plan was purſued through every province, it would have a very good effeſt.

I have long had it on my mind to mention to Congreſs, that frequent applications had been made to me reſpeſting the chaplains' pay, which is too ſmall to encourage men

of

of abilities. Some of them, who have left their flocks, are obliged to pay the parson acting for them more than they receive. I need not point out the great utility of gentlemen whose lives and conversation are unexceptionable, being employed for that service in this army. There are two ways of making it worth the attention of such: one is an advancement of their pay; the other, that one chaplain be appointed to two regiments. This last, I think, may be done without inconvenience. I beg leave to recommend this matter to Congress, whose sentiments hereon I shall impatiently expect.

Upon a farther conversation with captain Freeman, he is of opinion that general Montgomery has with him near three thousand men, including colonel Arnold's. He says that lord Pitt had received repeated orders from his father to return home; in consequence of which, he had embarked, some time in October, with a captain Green who was master of a vessel belonging to Philadelphia.

By a number of salutes in Boston harbour yesterday, I fancy admiral Shuldham is arrived. Two large ships were seen coming in.

Our enlistments now amount to nine thousand six hundred and fifty.

Those gentlemen who were made prisoners by lord Dunmore, being left destitute of money and necessaries, I have advanced them a hundred pounds lawful money belonging to the public, for which I have taken captain Mathews's draughts on the treasury of Virginia, which goes inclosed.

I have the honour to be, &c.   G. W.

P. S. You have, inclosed, the returns of the army.

SIR,   *Cambridge, January 4, 1776.*

SINCE my last of the thirty-first ultimo, I have been honoured with your favour of the twenty-second, inclosing sundry resolves, which shall, in matters they respect, be made the rule of my conduct.

The resolution relative to the troops in Boston, I beg the favour of you, Sir, to assure Congress shall be attempted ed to be put in execution the firſt moment I ſee a probability of ſucceſs, and in ſuch a way as a council of officers ſhall think moſt likely to produce it : but if this ſhould not happen as ſoon as you may expect or my wiſhes prompt to, I requeſt that Congreſs will be pleaſed to advert to my ſituation, and do me the juſtice to believe, that circumſtances, and not want of inclination, are the cauſe of delay.

It is not in the pages of hiſtory perhaps to furniſh a caſe like ours :——to maintain a poſt within muſket-ſhot of the enemy, for ſix months together, without*   , and at the ſame time to diſband one army, and recruit another within that diſtance of twenty-odd Britiſh regiments,—is more, probably, than ever was attempted.   But if we ſucceed as well in the laſt, as we have heretofore in the firſt, I ſhall think it the moſt fortunate event of my whole life.

By a very intelligent gentleman, a Mr. Hutchinſon, from Boſton, I learn, that it was admiral Shuldham that came into the harbour on Saturday laſt ; that two of the five regiments from Cork are arrived at Halifax ; two others have ſailed for Quebec ; but what was become of them could not be told :—and the other (the fifty-fifth) has juſt got into Boſton.   Certain it is alſo, that the greateſt part of the ſeventeenth regiment is arrived there.   Whether we are to conclude from hence that more than five regiments have been ſent out, or that the companies of the ſeventeenth, arrived at Boſton, are part of the regiments deſtined for Halifax and Quebec, I know not.

We alſo learn from this gentleman and others, that the troops, embarked for Halifax (as mentioned in my letter of the ſixteenth) were really deſigned for that place, but recalled from Nantaſket road, upon advice being received of the above regiments there.   I am alſo informed of a fleet now getting ready under the convoy of the Scarborough and Fowey men-of-war,—conſiſting of five tranſports and two bomb veſſels, with about three hundred marines, and ſeveral flat-bottomed boats.   It is whiſpered that they are deſigned for Newport, but generally thought

in

---

* Left blank in the original to guard againſt the danger of miſcarriage.   Read, "*without powder.*"

in Bofton that it is meant for Long-Ifland: and it is probable it will be followed by more troops, as the other tranfports are taking in water,—to lie, as others fay, in Nantafket road, to be out of the ice. A large quantity of bifcuit is alfo baking.

As the real defign cannot with certainty be known, I fubmit it, with all due deference, to the fuperior judgment of Congrefs, whether it would not be confiflent with prudence to have fome of the Jerfey troops thrown into New-York, to prevent an evil which would be almoft irremediable, fhould it happen,—I mean, the landing of troops at that place, or upon Long-Ifland near it.

As it is poffible you may not yet have received his majefty's " *moft gracious* " fpeech, I do myfelf the honour to inclofe one of many, which were fent out of Bofton yefterday. It is full of * * *, and explicitly holds forth his royal will to be, that vigorous meafures muft be purfued to deprive us of our * * *. Thefe meafures, whatever they be, I hope will be oppofed by more vigorous ones, and rendered unavailing and fruitlefs, though fanctioned and authorifed by the name of majefty,—a name, which ought to promote the bleffings of his people, and not their oppreffion.

I am, Sir, &c.   G. W.

<hr>

SIR,   *Cambridge, Jan.* 11, 1776.

EVERY account I have out of Bofton confirms the embarkation of troops mentioned in my laft, which, from the feafon of the year and other circumftances, muft be deftined for fome expedition to the fouthward of this. I have therefore thought it prudent to fend major-general Lee to New-York. I have given him letters recommendatory to governor Trumbull, and to the committee of fafety at New-York. I have good hopes that in Connecticut he will get many volunteers, who (I have fome reafon to think) will accompany him on this expedition, without more expenfe to the continent than their maintenance. But fhould it be otherwife, and that they fhould expect pay, I think it is a trifling confideration, when put

in

in competition with the importance of the object, which is
to put the city of New-York, with such parts of the North-
river and Long-Island as to him shall seem proper, in that
state of defence, which the season of the year and circumstances will admit of,—so as, if possible, to prevent the
enemy from forming a lodgment in that government,
which, I am afraid, contains too many persons disaffected
to the cause of liberty and America. I have also wrote
to lord Stirling to give him all the assistance that he can
with the troops under his command in the continental service, provided it does not interfere with any orders he may
receive from Congress relative to them.

I hope the Congress will approve of my conduct in sending general Lee upon this expedition :—I am sure I mean
it well ; as experience teaches us that it is much easier to
prevent an enemy from posting themselves, than it is to
dislodge them after they have got possession.

The evening of the eighth instant, a party of our men,
under the command of major Knoulton, were ordered to
go and burn some houses which lay at the foot of Bunker's-
hill, and at the head of Charlestown. They were also ordered to bring off the guard, which, we expected, consist-
ed of an officer and thirty men. They crossed the mill-
dam about half after eight o'clock, and gallantly executed
their business,—having burned eight houses, and brought
with them a sergeant and four privates of the tenth regiment. There was but one man more there, who making
some resistance, they were obliged to dispatch. The gun
that killed him was the only one discharged by our men,
though several hundred were fired by the enemy from
within their works, but in so confused a manner, that not
one of our people was hurt.

Our enlistments go on very heavily.

I am, with great respect, &c.   C. W.

SIR,   *Cambridge, Jan.* 14, 1776.

I AM exceedingly sorry that I am under the necessity of applying to you, and calling the attention of Congress to the state of our arms, which is truly alarming.
VOL. I.   G   Upon

Upon the diffolution of the old army, I was apprehenfive that the new would be deficient in this inftance : and, that the want might be as inconfiderable as poffible, I gave it out in orders, that the arms of fuch men as did not re-enlift (or fuch of them as were good) fhould be retained at the prices which fhould be affixed by perfons appointed to in-fpect and value them : and, that we might be fure of them, I added that there would be a ftoppage of pay for the months of November and December, from thofe who fhould carry their firelocks away without their being firft examined. I hoped, by thefe precautions, to have procured a confider-a'le number : but, Sir, I find with much concern, that from the badnefs of the arms, and the difobedience of too many in bearing them off without a previous infpection,— very few were collected.   Neither are we to expect that many will be brought in by the new recruits, the officers, who are out enlifting, having reported that few men who have arms will engage in the feryice ; and that they are under the difagreeable alternative of taking men without arms, or of getting none.   Unhappy fituation, and much to be deplored !—efpecially when we have every reafon to convince us, that we have to contend with a formidable army, well provided of every neceffary ; and that there will be a moft vigorous exertion of minifterial vengeance againft us, as foon as they think themfelves in a condition for it.   I hope it is in the power of Congrefs to afford us relief ;—if it is not, what muft, what can be done ?

Our treafury is almoft exhaufted, and the demands againft it very confiderable.   A conftant fupply of money, to anfwer every claim and exigency, would much promote the good of the feryice.   In the common affairs of life, it is ufeful : in war, it is abfolutely neceffary and effential. I would beg leave, too, to remind you of the tents, and of their importance,—hoping that, if an opportunity has offered, you have procured them.   I fear that our army will not be raifed to the new eftablifhment in any reafona-ble time, if ever : the enlifting goes on fo very flow, that it almoft feems at an end.

In my letter of the fourth inftant, I wrote you that I had received certain intelligence from a Mr. Hutchinfon and others, that two of the five regiments from Cork were

arrived

arrived at Halifax, one at Bofton, and the two others had
failed for Quebec, and had not been heard of. I am
now affured (as a matter to be relied on) by four captains
of fhips, who left England about the fecond of November,
and who appear to be men of veracity, that the whole
of thefe regiments, (except the two companies that arrived
at Bofton fome time ago) when they failed, were at
Milford Haven, where they had been obliged to put in,
by a violent ftorm, the nineteenth of October ; that they
would not be able to leave it for a confiderable time, as
they were under the neceffity of repairing their veffels,
and getting fome new ones taken up. Such is the uncertainty and contradiction in what I now hear, that it is
not poffible to know what to believe or difbelieve.

I wrote to the general court yefterday, and to the convention of New-Hampfhire, immediately upon feeing the
great deficiency in our arms,—praying that they would intereft themfelves in the matter, and furnifh me with all in
their power. Whether I fhall get any, or what quantity,
I cannot determine, not having received their anfwers.
The fame application will be made to the governments of
Connecticut and Rhode-Ifland.

I do myfelf the honour to fend you fundry newfpapers
I received from the above-mentioned captains, as they may
be later than any you have feen, and contain fome interefting intelligence.

I have the honour to be, &c.   G. W.

SIR,   *Cambridge, Jan.* 19, 1776.

TAKING it for granted that general Schuyler has
not only informed you of the fall of the brave and much-
to-be-lamented general Montgomery, but of the fituation
of our affairs in Canada, (as related by general Woofter,
colonel Arnold, colonel Campbell, and others) I fhall not
take up much more of your time on this fubject, than is
neceffary to inclofe you a copy of his letter to me, with
the refult thereon, as appears by the council of war
which I immediately fummoned on the occafion, even the

which Mr. Adams, by my particular defire, was good
enough to attend.

It may appear ftrange, Sir, as I had not men to fpare
from thefe lines, that I fhould prefume (without firft fending to Congrefs, and obtaining an exprefs direction)
to recommend to the governments of Maffachufetts, Connecticut and New-Hampfhire, to raife each a regiment, on
the continental account, for this fervice. I wifh moft ardently that the urgency of the cafe would have admitted
of the delay. I wifh alfo that the purport of general Schuyler's letter had not, unavoidably as it were, laid me under
an indifpenfable obligation to do it :—for having informed
you in his letter (a copy of which he inclofed me) of his
dependence on this quarter, for men, I thought you
might alfo have fome reliance on my exertions. This
confideration, added to my fears of the fatal confequences
of delay,—to an information of your having defigned three
thoufand men for Canada,—to a belief, founded chiefly
on general Schuyler's letters, that few or none of them
were raifed,—and to my apprehenfions for New-York,
which led me to think that no troops could be fpared from
that quarter,—induced me to lofe not a moment's time in
throwing in a force there ; being well affured that general
Carleton will improve to the utmoft the advantages gained,
leaving no artifices untried, to fix the Canadians and Indians (who, we find, are too well difpofed to take part
with the ftrongeft) in his intereft.

If thefe reafons are not fufficient to juftify my conduct
in the opinion of Congrefs,—if the meafure contravenes
any refolution of theirs, they will pleafe to countermand
the levying and marching of the regiments as foon as poffible, and do me the juftice to believe that my intentions
were good, if my judgment has erred.

The Congrefs will pleafe alfo to obferve, that the meafure of fupporting our pofts in Canada appeared of fuch exceeding great importance, that the general officers (agreeing with me in fentiment, and unwilling to lay any burden
which can poffibly be avoided,—although it may turn out
ill-timed piece of parfimony) have refolved that the
had regiments for Canada fhall be part of the thirteen
and others, ents which were requefted to reinforce this
army.—

army,—as appears by the minutes of another council of war, held on the sixteenth instant. I shall (being much hurried and fatigued) add no more in this letter, than my duty to Congress, and that I have the honour to be, &c.   G. W.

P. S.   I inclose you a copy of my letter to the governments of Massachusetts, Connecticut and New-Hampshire; also a copy of a resolution of this colony in answer to an application of mine for arms.

Since writing the above, I have been informed by a message from the general court of Massachusetts, that they have resolved upon the raising of a regiment for Canada, and appointed the field officers for it in the western parts of this government.   I am also informed by express from governor Trumbull, that he and his council of safety had agreed upon the raising of a regiment for the same purpose; which was anticipating my application to that government.

If commissions (and they are applied for) are to be given by Congress to the three regiments going to Canada, you will please to have them forwarded, as I have none by me for that purpose.

Cambridge, Jan. 24, 1776.

S I R,

THE commissary-general being at length [*recovered*] from a long and painful illness, I have it in my power to comply with the requisition of Congress in forwarding an estimate of the expense attending his office, as also that of the quarter-master-general.

You will please to observe that the commissary, by his account of the matter, has entered into no special agreement with any of the persons he has found occasion to employ, (as those to whose names sums are annexed, are of their own fixing) but left it to Congress to ascertain their wages.   I shall say nothing therefore on this head, farther than relates to the proposition of Mr. * * *, to be allowed one eighth for his trouble and the delivery of the other seven eighths of provisions, which to me appears exorbitant in the extreme, however conformable it may be to even the and ufuage : I therefore think that reafonable ftipends had better be fixed upon. Both the quarter-mafter and com-miffary-generals affure me, that they do not employ a fingle perfon ufelefsly : and as I have too good an opinion of them to think they would deceive me, I believe them.

I fhall take the liberty, in this place, of recommending the expediency, indeed the abfolute neceffity, of appoint-ing fit and proper perfons to fettle the accounts of this army. To do it with precifion, requires time, care, and at-tention : the longer it is left undone, the more intricate they will be, the more liable to error, and difficult to ex-plain and rectify;—as alfo the perfons in whofe hands they are (if difpofed to take undue advantage) will be lefs fubject to detection. I have been as attentive as the nature of my office would admit of, in granting warrants for mon-ey on the pay-mafter : but it would be abfolutely impoffi-ble for me to go into an examination of all the accounts incident to this army, and the vouchers appertaining to them, without devoting fo large a portion of my time to the bufinefs, as might not only prove injurious, but fatal to it in other refpects. This ought, in my humble opinion, to be the particular bufinefs of a felect committee of Con-grefs, or one appointed by them, who, once in three months at furtheft, fhould make a fettlement with the officers in the different departments.

Having met with no encouragement from the govern-ments of Maffachufetts and New-Hampfhire, from my application for arms, and expecting no better from Con-necticut and Rhode-Ifland, I have, as the laft expedient, fent one or two officers from each regiment into the country, with money, to try if they can buy. In what manner they fucceed, Congrefs fhall be informed as foon as they return.

Congrefs, in my laft, would difcover my motives for ftrengthening thefe lines with the militia : but whether, as the weather turns out exceedingly mild, infomuch as to promife nothing favourable from ice,—and no appearance of powder,—I fhall be able to attempt any thing decifive, time only can determine. No man upon earth wifhes more ardently to deftroy the neft in Bofton, than I do :— and others would be willing to go greater lengths than I

shall,

ſhall, to accompliſh it, if it ſhall be thought adviſeable.   But if we have neither powder to bombard with, nor ice to paſs on, we ſhall be in no better ſituation than we have been in all the year:—we ſhall be worſe, becauſe their works are ſtronger.

I have accounts from Boſton, which I think may be relied on, that general Clinton, with about four or five hundred men, hath left that place within theſe four days. Whether this is part of the detachment which was making up (as mentioned in my letter of the fourth inſtant, and then at Nantaſket) or not, is not in my power to ſay. If it is deſigned for New-York or Long-Iſland as ſome think, throwing a body of troops there may prove a fortunate circumſtance. If they go farther ſouth agreeable to the conjectures of others, I hope there will be men to receive them.

Notwithſtanding the poſitive aſſertions of the four captains from Portſmouth, noticed in my letter of the fourteenth, I am now convinced from ſeveral corroborating circumſtances,—the accounts of deſerters, and of a lieutenant Hill, of lord Percy's regiment, who left Ireland the fifth of November, and was taken by a privateer from Newbury-port,—that the ſeventeenth and fifty-fifth regiments are arrived at Boſton, and other troops at Halifax, agreeable to the information of Hutchinſon and others. Lieutenant Hill ſays that the tranſports of two regiments only were forced into Milford Haven.

Congreſs will think me a little remiſs, I fear, when I inform them that I have done nothing yet towards raiſing the battalion of marines: but I hope to ſtand exculpated from blame, when they hear the reaſon, which was, that already having twenty-ſix incomplete regiments, I thought it would be adding to an expenſe, already great, in officers, to ſet two entire corps of officers on foot, when perhaps we ſhould not add ten men a week by it to our preſent numbers.   In this opinion the general officers have concurred, which induced me to ſuſpend the matter a little longer.   Our enliſtments, for the two laſt weeks, have not amounted to a thouſand men, and are diminiſhing. The regiment for Canada (it is thought) will ſoon be filled, as

the

the men are to choose all but their field officers, who are appointed by the court.

On Sunday evening, thirteen of the Caghnewaga Indians arrived here on a visit. I shall take care that they be so entertained during their stay, that they may return impressed with sentiments of friendship for us, and also of our great strength. One of them is colonel Louis, who honoured me with a visit once before.

I have the honour to be, &c.   G. W.

SIR,   *Cambridge, Jan.* 30, 1776.

YOUR favours of the sixth and twentieth instant I received yesterday, with the several resolves of Congress alluded to; for which I return you my thanks.

Knowing the great importance Canada will be of to us in the present interesting contest, and the relief our friends there stand in need of, I should be happy, were it in my power to detach a battalion from this camp: but it cannot be done. On the nineteenth instant, I had the honour to write to you, which will fully convey the resolutions of a council of war, and the sentiments of the general officers here, as to the propriety and expediency of sending troops from these lines, for the defence of which we have been and now are obliged to call in the militia; —to which I beg leave to refer you. You may rest assured that my endeavours and exertions shall not be wanting, to stimulate the governments of Connecticut and New-Hampshire to raise and forward reinforcements as fast as possible; nor in any other instance that will promote the expedition.

I shall, in obedience to the order of Congress, though interdicted by general Howe, propose an exchange of governor Skene for Mr. Lovell and family, and shall be happy to have an opportunity of putting this deserving man (who has distinguished his fidelity and regard to his country to be too great for persecution and cruelty to overcome) in any post agreeable to his wishes and inclination.

I do

I do not know that there is any particular rank annexed to the office of aide-de-camp. Generally they are captains, and rank as fuch: but higher rank is often given on account of particular merit and particular circumftances. Aides to the king have the rank of colonels. Whether any diftinction fhould be made between thofe of your commander in chief and the other generals, I really know not: I think there ought.

You may rely that Conolly had inftructions concealed in his faddle. Mr. * * * who was one of lord Dunmore's family, and another gentleman who wifhes his name not to be mentioned, faw them cafed in tin, put in the tree, and covered over. He probably has exchanged his faddle, or withdrew the papers when it was mended, as you conjecture. Thofe that have been difcovered are fufficiently bad; but I doubt not of the others being worfe, and containing more diabolical and extenfive plans. I hope he will be taken proper care of, and meet with rewards equal to his merits.

I fhall appoint officers in the places of thofe who are in Canada, as I am fully perfuaded they will wifh to continue there, for making our conqueft complete in that quarter. I wifh their bravery and valour may be attended with the fmiles of fortune.

It gives me great pleafure to hear of the meafures Congrefs are taking for manufacturing powder. I hope their endeavours will be crowned with fuccefs. I too well know and regret the want of it. It is fcarcely poffible to defcribe the difadvantages an army muft labour under, when not provided with a fufficient fupply of this neceffary. It may feem ftrange, that, after having received about eleven tons, added to about five tons which I found here, and no general action has happened, we fhould be fo deficient in this article, and require more. But you will pleafe to confider, that, befides its being in its nature fubject to wafte, and (whilft the men lay in bad tents) unavoidably damaged by fevere and heavy rains (which could not have been prevented, unlefs it had been entirely withdrawn from the men, and an attack hazarded againft us without ammunition in their hands)—the armed veffels, our own occafional firings, and fome fmall fupplies I have

been

been obliged to afford the sea-port towns threatened with destruction,—to which may be added the supply to the militia, and going off of the old troops,—have occasioned, and ever will, a large consumption of it, and waste, in spite of all the care in the world. The king's troops never have less than sixty rounds a man in their possession, independent of their stores. To supply an army of twenty thousand men in this manner, would take near four hundred barrels, allowing nothing for stores, artillery, &c. I have been always afraid to place more than twelve or fifteen rounds at a time in the hands of our men, lest, any accident happening to it, we should be left destitute, and be undone. I have been thus particular, not only to shew our poverty, but to exculpate myself from even a suspicion of unnecessary waste.

I shall inform the pay-master-general of the resolution of Congress respecting his draughts, and the mode and account of them.

The companies at Chelsea and Malden are and have always been regimented. It was not my intention to replace with continental troops the independent companies at Hingham, Weymouth and Braintree. These places are exposed, but not more than Cape-Ann, Beverly, Salem, Marblehead, &c. &c. &c.

Is it the intention of Congress that the officers of the army should pay postage? They are not exempted by the resolve of the ninth instant.

The Congress will be pleased, I have no doubt, to recollect that the five hundred thousand dollars, now coming, are but little more than enough to bring us up to the first day of this month; that to-morrow will be the last of it; and, by their resolves, the troops are to be paid monthly.

I wish it was in my power to furnish Congress with such a general as they desire, to send to Canada. Since the unhappy reverse of our affairs in that quarter, general Schuyler has informed me, that, though he had thoughts of declining the service before, he would now act. My letter of the eleventh will inform them of general Lee's being at New-York. He will be ready to obey their orders, should they incline to send him : but, if I am not greatly deceived, he or some other spirited able officer will be wanted there

in

in the fpring, if not fooner; as we have undoubted intelligence that general Clinton has failed with fome troops.
The reports of their number are various, from between four
and five hundred to nineteen companies of grenadiers and
light-infantry.   It is alfo imagined that the regiments,
which were to fail the firft of December, are intended for
that place or Virginia.   General Putnam is a moft valuable
man, and a fine executive officer : but I do not know how
he would conduct in a feparate department.   He is a young-
er major-general than Mr. Schuyler, who, as I have obferved, having determined to continue in the fervice, will,
I expect, repair into Canada.   A copy of my letter to him
on this and other fubjects, I inclofe you, as it will explain
my motives for not ftopping the regiments from thefe governments.

When captain Cockran arrives, I will give him every
affiftance in my power, in obedience to the orders of Congrefs : but I fear it will be the means of lay up our own
veffels, as thefe people will not bear the diftinction.
Should this be the confequence, it will be highly preju-
dicial to us, as we fometimes pick up their provifion-veffels,
and may continue to diftrefs them in this way.

Laft week captain Manly took a fhip and a brig bound
to Bofton from Whitehaven, with coals chiefly, and fome
potatoes, for the army.   I have, for his great vigilance
and induftry, appointed him commodore of our little fquadron ; and he now hoifts his flag on board the fchooner
Hancock.

I congratulate you upon the recovery of Smith, and am
exceedingly glad to hear of the meafures Congrefs are taking for the general defence of the continent.   The clouds
thicken faft : where they will burft, I know not : but we
fhould be armed at all points.

I have not fucceeded in my applications to thefe governments for arms.   They have returned for anfwer, that
they cannot furnifh any.   Whether I fhall be more lucky
in the laft refource left me in this quarter, I cannot determine, having not received returns from the officers fent out
to purchafe of the people.   I greatly fear that but very
few will be procured in this way, as they are exceedingly
fcarce, and but a fmall part of what there are, fit for fervice.

vice. When they make their report, you shall be informed.

The quarter-master-general has just received from general Schuyler clothing for the soldiery, amounting to about seventeen hundred pounds York currency. It has come very seasonably, as they are in great want, and will contribute a little to their relief.

Since writing the above, I saw Mr. * * *, and mentioning that nothing had been found in the tree of Conolly's saddle, he told me there had been a mistake in the matter; that the instructions were artfully concealed on the two pieces of wood which are on the mail-pillion of his portmanteau-saddle; that, by order of lord Dunmore, he saw them contrived for the purpose, the papers put in, and first covered with tin, and over that with a waxed canvass cloth. He is so exceedingly pointed and clear in his information, that I have no doubt of its being true. I could wish them to be discovered, as I think they contain some curious and extraordinary plans.

In my letter of the twenty-fourth instant I mentioned the arrival of thirteen of our Caghnewaga friends. They honoured me with a talk to-day, as did three of the tribes of the St. John's and Pasmiquoddi Indians;—copies of which I beg leave to inclose you. I shall write to general Schuyler respecting the tender of service made by the former, and not to call for their assistance, unless he shall at any time want it, or be under the necessity of doing it to prevent their taking the side of our enemies.

I had the honour of writing you on the nineteenth of November, and then I informed you of having engaged two persons to go to Nova-Scotia on the business recommended in your letter of the tenth; and also that the state of the army would not then admit of a sufficient force being sent, for carrying into execution the views of Congress respecting the dock-yards, &c.——I would now beg leave to mention, that, if the persons, sent for information, should report favourably of the expediency and practicability of the measure, it will not be in my power to detach any men from these lines : the situation of our affairs will not allow it. I think it would be adviseable to raise them in the eastern parts of this government. If it is attempted, it must

.be

be by people from the country.   A colonel * * * and a captain * * * have been with me :—they think the men neceſſary may be eaſily engaged there, and the meaſure practicable : provided there are not more than two hundred British troops at Halifax, they are willing and ready to embark in the matter, upon the terms mentioned in their plan, which I incloſe you.   I would wiſh you to advert to the conſiderations inducing them to the expedition, as I am not without apprehenſion, ſhould it be undertaken upon their plan, that the innocent and guilty will be involved in one common ruin.   I preſume they do not expect to receive more than the five or ten thouſand pounds mentioned in their ſcheme, and to be at every expenſe.   If we had men to ſpare, it might be undertaken for leſs than either, I conceive.   Perhaps, if Congreſs do not adopt their propoſition, they will undertake to raiſe men for that particular purpoſe, who may be diſbanded as ſoon as it is effected, and upon the ſame terms that are allowed the continental troops in general.   Whatever may be the determination of Congreſs upon the ſubject, you will pleaſe to communicate it to me immediately : for the ſeaſon moſt favourable for the enterpriſe is advancing faſt : and we may expect in the ſpring, that there will be more troops there, and the meaſure be more difficult to execute.

I have the honour to be, &c.   G. W.

SIR,   *Cambridge, Feb.* 9, 1776.

THE purport of this letter will be directed to a ſingle object: through you, I mean to lay it before Congreſs; and, at the ſame time that I beg their ſerious attention to the ſubject, to aſk pardon for intruding an opinion, not only unaſked, but, in ſome meaſure, repugnant to their reſolves.

The diſadvantages attending the limited enliſtment of troops are too apparent to thoſe who are eye-witneſſes of them, to render any animadverſions neceſſary : but to gentlemen at a diſtance, whoſe attention is engroſſed by a thouſand important objects, the caſe may be otherwiſe.

That this cauſe precipitated the fate of the brave and much-to-be-lamented general Montgomery, and brought on the defeat which followed thereupon, I have not the moſt diſtant doubt : for, had he not been apprehenſive of the troops leaving him at ſo important a criſis, but continued the blockade of Quebec, a capitulation (from the beſt accounts I have been able to collect) muſt inevitably have followed.   And that we were not at one time obliged to diſpute theſe lines under diſadvantageous circumſtances (proceeding from the ſame cauſe, to wit, the troops diſbanding of themſelves before the militia could be got in) is to me a matter of wonder and aſtoniſhment : and proves that general Howe was either unacquainted with our ſituation, or reſtrained by his inſtructions from putting any thing to a hazard till his reinforcements ſhould arrive.

The inſtance of general Montgomery—(I mention it becauſe it is a ſtriking one ; for a number of others might be adduced)—proves, that inſtead of having men to take advantage of circumſtances, you are in a manner compelled, right or wrong, to make circumſtances yield to a ſecondary conſideration.   Since the firſt of December, I have been deviſing every means in my power to ſecure theſe encampments ; and, though I am ſenſible that we never have, ſince that period, been able to act upon the offenſive, and at times not in a condition to defend, yet the coſt of marching home one ſet of men,—bringing in another,—the havoc and waſte occaſioned by the firſt,—the repairs neceſſary for the ſecond, with a thouſand incidental charges and inconveniences which have ariſen, and which it is ſcarce poſſible either to recollect or deſcribe—amount to near as much, as the keeping up a reſpectable body of troops the whole time, ready for any emergency, would have done.   To this may be added, that you never can have a well-diſciplined army. To bring men well acquainted with the duties of a ſoldier, requires time.   To bring them under proper diſcipline and ſubordination, not only requires time, but is a work of great difficulty, and, in this army where there is ſo little diſtinction between the officers and ſoldiers, requires an uncommon degree of attention.   To expect then the ſame ſervice from raw and undiſciplined recruits as from veteran ſoldiers, is to expect what never did and perhaps never will happen.   Men who are familiarized to danger meet it without ſhrinking ; whereas thoſe who have never ſeen ſervice

often

often apprehend danger where no danger is. Three things prompt men to a regular difcharge of their duty in time of action—natural bravery, hope of reward, and fear of punifhment. The two firft are common to the untutored and the difciplined foldier : but the latter moft obvioufly diftinguifhes the one from the other. A coward, when taught to believe, that, if he breaks his ranks and abandons his colours, he will be punifhed with death by his own party—will take his chance againft the enemy : but a man who thinks little of the one, and is fearful of the other, acts from prefent feelings, regardlefs of confequences.

Again, men of a day's ftanding will not look forward ; and from experience we find, that, as the time approaches for their difcharge, they grow carelefs of their arms, ammunition, camp utenfils, &c. Nay, even the barracks themfelves have felt uncommon marks of wanton depredation, and lay us under frefh trouble and additional expenfe in providing for every frefh fet, when we find it next to impoffible to procure fuch articles as are abfolutely neceffary in the firft inftance. To this may be added the feafoning which new recruits muft have to a camp, and the lefs confequent thereupon. But this is not all. Men, engaged for a fhort limited time only, have the officers too much in their power : for, to obtain a degree of popularity in order to induce a fecond enliftment, a kind of familiarity takes place, which brings on a relaxation of difcipline, unlicenfed furloughs, and other indulgences incompatible with order and good government ; by which means, the latter part of the time for which the foldier was engaged is fpent in undoing what you were aiming to inculcate in the firft.

To go into an enumeration of all the evils we have experienced in this late great change of the army, and the expenfes incidental to it—to fay nothing of the hazard we have run, and muft run, between the difcharging of one army and enliftment of another, unlefs an enormous expenfe of militia is incurred—would greatly exceed the bounds of a letter. What I have already taken the liberty of faying will ferve to convey a general idea of the matter; and therefore I fhall, with all due deference, take the freedom to give it as my opinion, that, if the Congrefs have any reafon to believe that there will be occafion for

troops

troops another year, and confequently of another enliftment, they would fave money, and have infinitely better
troops, if they were, even at a bounty of twenty, thirty, or
more dollars, to engage the men already enlifted (till January next) and fuch others as may be wanted to complete
the eftablifhment, for and during the war. I will not undertake to fay that the men can be had upon thefe terms :
but I am fatisfied that it will never do to let the matter
alone, as it was laft year, till the time of fervice was near
expiring. The hazard is too great in the firft place :—in
the next, the trouble and perplexity of difbanding one army and raifing another at the fame inftant, and in fuch a
critical fituation as the laft was, is fcarcely in the power of
words to defcribe, and fuch as no man, who has experienced it once, will ever undergo again.

If Congrefs fhould differ from me in fentiment upon this
point, I have only to beg that they will do me the juftice
to believe, that I have nothing more in view than what to
me appears neceffary to advance the public weal, .although
in the firft inftance it will be attended with a capital expenfe ;—and that I have the honour to be, &c.

G. W.

SIR,   *Cambridge, Feb.* 9, 1776.
IN compliance with the refolves of Congrefs, I have
applied to general Howe for the exchange of Mr. Lovell.
A copy of my letter, and his anfwer thereto, you have
inclofed.

Captain Watters and captain Tucker, who command
two of the armed fchooners, have taken and fent into
Glocefter a large brigantine, laden with wood, a hundred
and fifty butts for water, and forty fuits of bedding, bound
from La Have in Nova-Scotia, for Bofton. She is one of
the tranfports in the minifterial fervice. The captain fays
that he was at Halifax the feventeenth of January, and
that general Maffey was arrived there with two regiments
from Ireland.

The different prizes were all libelled immediately on the
receipt of the refolves of Congrefs pointing out the mode ; but
none of them yet brought to trial, owing to a difference between

tween the law paffed in this province, and the refolutions of Congrefs. The general court are making an amendment to their law, by which the difficulties that now occur will be removed, as I underftand it is to be made conformable to your refolves. The unavoidable delay attending the bringing the captures to trial is grievoufly complained of by the mafters of thefe veffels, as well as the captors. Many of the former have applied for liberty to go away without waiting the decifion—which I have granted them.

I beg leave to recall the atten.ion of Congrefs to their appointing a commiffary in thefe parts, to attend the providing of neceffaries for the prifoners who are difperfed in thefe provinces. Complaints are made by fome of them, that they are in want of bedding and many other things. As I underftand that Mr. Franks has undertaken that bufinefs, I wifh he was ordered to fend a deputy immediately to fee that the prifoners get what is allowed them by Congrefs ; alfo to fupply the officers with money as they may have occafion. It would fave me much time and much trouble.

There are yet but few companies of the militia come in. This delay will, I am much afraid, fruftrate the intention of their being called upon, as the feafon is flipping faft away when they may be of fervice.

The demands of the army were fo very preffing before your laft remittance came to hand, that I was under the neceffity of borrowing twenty-five thoufand pounds lawful money from this province. They very cheerfully lent it, and paffed a vote for as much more, if required. I have not repaid the fum borrowed, as I may ftand in need of it before the arrival of another fupply, which the demands of the commiffary-general, quarter-mafter-general, and paying off the arrearages, will very foon require.

Your efteemed favour of the twenty-ninth ultimo is juft come to hand. It makes me very happy to find my conduct hath met the approbation of Congrefs. I am entirely of your opinion, that, fhould an accommodation take place, the terms will be fevere or favourable in proportion to our ability to refift, and that we ought to be on a refpectable footing to receive their armaments in the fpring. But how far we fhall be provided with the means, is a matter I profefs not to know, under my prefent unhappy want of arms, ammunition, and, I may add, men—as our regiments are very incomplete. The recruiting goes on very flow, and will, I apprehend, be more fo, if for other fervice the men receive a bounty, and none is given here.

I have tried every method I could think of, to procure arms for our men. They really are not to be had in thefe governments (belonging to the public;) and if fome method is not fallen upon, in the fouthern governments, to fupply us, we fhall be in a diftreffed fituation for want of them. There are near two thoufand men now in camp without firelocks. I have wrote to the committee of New-York this day, requefting them to fend me thofe arms which were taken from the difaffected in that government. The Congrefs interefting themfelves, in this requeft will doubtlefs have a good effect. I have fent officers into the country, with money to purchafe arms in the different towns. Some have returned, and brought in a few:— many are ftill out:—what their fuccefs will be, I cannot determine.

I was in great hopes that the expreffes, refolved to be eftablifhed between this place and Philadelphia, would ere now have been fixed. It would, in my opinion, rather fave than increafe the expenfe; as many horfes are deftroyed by one man coming the whole way. It will certainly be more expeditious, and fafer, than writing by the poft or private hands, which I am often under the neceffity of doing.

I am, with great refpect, &c.   G. W.

SIR,   *Cambridge, Feb. 9, 1776.*

I BEG leave to inform you, at the requeft of the committee of pay-table of the colony of Connecticut, that I have not advanced, to any of the regiments from that government, any money except the fum of feven thoufand one hundred and feventy-two dollars and one ninth on the twentieth of November laft to major-general Putnam, for the thirty-fourth regiment under his command. I fhould have paid them in the fame manner I did the reft of the

army,

army, had I not been prevented by the colonels, who expressed their inclination to receive the whole at once upon their return home at the expiration of service, as was customary in their colony. For this reason I never included them in my estimates of money, and have made no provision for their payment, always imagining that, whatever payments the colony made them, Congress would apply to their credit in the general account against the United Colonies, or refund upon application.

I have the honour to be, &c.   G. W.

- - -

SIR,   *Cambridge, Feb. 14, 1776.*

THROUGH you, I beg leave to lay before Congress the inclosed letter from lord Drummond to general Robertson, which came to my hands a few days ago in order to be sent into Boston.

As I never heard of his lordship being vested with power to treat with Congress upon the subject of our grievances, nor of his having laid any propositions before them for an accommodation, I confess it surprised me much, and led me to form various conjectures of his motives, and intended application to general Howe and admiral Shuldham for a passport for the safe-conduct of such deputies as Congress might appoint for negociating terms of reconciliation between Great-Britain and us. Whatever his intentions are, however benevolent his designs may be, I confess that his letter has embarrassed me much; and I am not without suspicion of its meaning more than the generous purposes it professes. I should suppose, that, if the mode for negociation, which he points out, should be adopted (which I hope will never be thought of) it ought to have been fixed and settled previous to any application of this sort; and at best, that his conduct in this instance is premature and officious, and leading to consequences of a fatal and injurious nature to the rights of this country. His zeal and desire perhaps of an amicable and constitutional adjustment's taking place may have suggested and precipitated the measure. Be that as it may, I thought it of too much importance, to suffer it to go in without having the express direction of

Congress

Congrefs for that purpofe ; and that it was my indifpenfable duty to tranfmit them the original, to make fuch interpretations and inferences as they may think right.

Meffrs. Willard and Child, who were fent to Nova-Scotia in purfuance of the refolve of Congrefs, have juft returned, and made their report, which I do myfelf the honour to inclofe you. They have not anfwered the purpofes of their commiffion by any means, as they only went a little way into that country, and found their intelligence upon the information of others. You will fee the reafons they affign in excufe or juftification of their conduct, in the report itfelf.

Laft night a party of regulars, faid to be about five hundred, landed on Dorchefter neck, and burned fome of the houfes there, which were of no value to us ; nor would they have been unlefs we take poft there : they then might be of fome fervice.   A detachment went after them as foon as the fire was difcovered : but before it could arrive, they had executed their plan, and made their retreat.

Inclofed is a letter for David Franks, efquire, from Mr. Chamier in Bofton upon the fubject of victualling fuch of the king's troops as may be prifoners within the limits of his contract, which I beg the favour of you to deliver him, and that proper agents may be appointed by him, to fee that it is done. I could wifh, too, that Congrefs would fall upon fome mode for fupplying the officers with fuch money as they may really ftand in need of, and depute proper perfons for that purpofe, and furnifhing the privates with fuch clothing as may be abfolutely neceffary. I am applied to, and wearied by their repeated requefts. In fome inftances I have defired the committees to give the prifoners within their appointments what they fhould judge abfolutely neceffary for their fupport—as the only means in my power of relieving their diftrefs. But I imagine, that, if there were perfons to fuperintend this bufinefs, their wants would be better attended to, and many exorbitant charges prevented and faved to the continent ; and the whole would then be brought into a proper account.

I am, Sir, with great efteem, &c. —   G. W.

P. S.   I fend a return of the ftrength of the regiments.

Cambridge,

SIR, *Cambridge, Feb.* 18, 1776.

THE late freezing weather having formed some pretty strong ice from Dorchester point to Boston neck, and from Roxbury to the Common, thereby affording a more expanded and consequently a less dangerous approach to the town, I could not help thinking,—notwithstanding the militia were not all come in, and we had little or no powder to begin our operation by a regular cannonade or bombardment,—that a bold and resolute assault upon the troops in Boston with such men as we had (for it could not take many men to guard our own lines at a time when the enemy were attacked in all quarters): might be crowned with success : and therefore, seeing no certain prospect of a supply of powder on the one hand, and a certain dissolution of the ice on the other, I called the general officers together, for their opinion, agreeably to the resolve of Congress, of the twenty-second of December.

The result will appear in the inclosed council of war ; and, being almost unanimous, I must suppose it to be right ; although, from a thorough conviction of the necessity of attempting something against the ministerial troops before a reinforcement should arrive, and while we were favoured with the ice, I was not only ready, but willing and desirous of making the assault, under a firm hope (if the men would have stood by me) of a favourable issue, notwithstanding the enemy's advantage of ground, artillery, &c.

Perhaps the irksomeness of my situation may have given different ideas to me, than those which influenced the gentlemen I consulted, and might have inclined me to put more to the hazard than was consistent with prudence :—if it had, I am not sensible of it, as I endeavoured to give it all the consideration that a matter of such importance required. True it is, and I cannot help acknowledging, that I have many disagreeable sensations on account of my situation : for, to have the eyes of the whole continent fixed with anxious expectation of hearing of some great event,—and to be restrained in every military operation, for want of the necessary means of carrying it on,—is not very pleasing, especially as the

means

between the northern and southern United Colonies exceedingly precarious and difficult.   To prevent them from effecting their plan, is a matter of the highest importance, and will require a large and respectable army, and the most vigilant and judicious exertions.

Since I wrote by Mr. Hooper, some small parcels of powder have arrived from Connecticut, which will give us a little assistance.

On Thursday night a party of our men at Roxbury made the enemy's out-centries, consisting of a corporal and two privates, prisoners, without firing a gun or giving the least alarm.

I shall be as attentive to the enemy's motions as I can, and obtain all the intelligence in my power ; and, if I find them embark, shall in the most expeditious manner detach a part of the light troops to New-York, and repair thither myself if circumstances shall require it.   I shall be better able to judge what to do, when the matter happens.   At present I can only say that I will do every thing that shall appear proper and necessary.

Your letter of the twelfth instant, by colonel Bull, came to hand yesterday evening : and I shall, agreeable to your recommendation, pay proper notice to him.   The supply of cash came very seasonably, as our treasury was just exhausted, and nothing can be done here without it.

I have the honour to be, &c.   G. W.

P. S.   This was intended to have been sent by express : but meeting with a private opportunity, the express was countermanded.

S I R,   *Cambridge, March* 7, 1776.

ON the twenty-sixth ultimo I had the honour of addressing you, and then mentioned that we were making preparations for taking possession of Dorchester heights.   I now beg leave to inform you, that, a council of general officers having determined a previous bombardment and cannonade expedient and proper, in order to harass the enemy and divert their attention from that quarter—on Saturday, Sunday, and Monday nights last, we carried

them

them on from our pofts at Coble-hill, Leechmore's-point,
and Lam's-dam.   Whether they did the enemy any confiderable and what injury, I have not yet heard, but have
the pleafure to acquaint you that they greatly facilitated
our fchemes, and would have been attended with fuccefs
equal to our moft fanguine expectations, had it not been
for the unlucky burfting of two thirteen, and three ten-inch
mortars, among which was the brafs one taken in the ordnance brig.   To what caufe to attribute this misfortune, I
know not—whether to any defect in them, or to the inexperience of the bombardiers.   But to return—on Monday
evening, as foon as our firing commenced, a confiderable
detachment of our men, under the command of brigadier-
general Thomas, croffed the neck, and took poffeffion of
the two hills, without the leaft interruption or annoyance
from the enemy ; and by their great activity and induftry,
before the morning, advanced the works fo far as to be fecure againft their fhot.   They are now going on with fuch
expedition, that in a little time I hope they will be complete, and enable our troops ftationed there to make a vigorous and obftinate ftand.   During the whole cannonade,
which was inceffant the laft two nights, we were fortunate
enough to lofe but two men—one, a lieutenant, by a cannon ball's taking off his thigh—the other, a private, by the
explofion of a fhell, which alfo flightly wounded four or
five more.

Our taking poffeffion of Dorchefter heights is only pre-
paratory to taking poft on Nuke-hill, and the points oppofite the fouth end of Bofton.   It was abfolutely neceffary
that they fhould be previoufly fortified, in order to cover
and command them.   As foon as the works on the former
are finifhed and complete, meafures will be immediately
adopted for fecuring the latter, and making them as ftrong
and defenfible as we can.   Their contiguity to the enemy
will make them of much importance, and of great fervice
to us.

As mortars are effential, and indifpenfably neceffary for
carrying on our operations, and for the profecution of our
plans, I have applied to two furnaces to have fome thirteen-
inch ones caft with all expedition imaginable, and am encouraged to hope, from the accounts I have had, that they

will be able to do it.   When they are done, and a proper
fupply of powder obtained, I flatter myfelf, from the pofts
we have juft taken and are about to take, that it will be in
our power to force the minifterial troops to an attack, or to
difpofe of them in fome way that will be of advantage to us.
I think from thefe pofts they will be fo galled and annoyed, that they muft either give us battle or quit their prefent
poffeffions.   I am refolved that nothing on my part fhall
be wanting, to effect the one or the other.

It having been the general opinion that the enemy would
attempt to diflodge our people from the hills, and force
their works as foon as they were difcovered, which probably might have brought on a general engagement,—it was
thought advifeable that the honourable council fhould be
applied to, to order in the militia from the neighbouring
and adjacent towns.   I wrote to them on the fubject,
which they moft readily complied with : and, in juftice to
the militia, I cannot but inform you that they came in at
the appointed time, and manifefted the greateft alertnefs,
and determined refólution to have acted like men engaged
in the caufe of freedom.

When the enemy firft difcovered our works in the
morning, they feemed to be in great confufion, and, from
their movements, to have intended an attack.   It is much
to be wifhed that it had been made : the event, I think,
muft have been fortunate, and nothing lefs than fuccefs
and victory on our fide, as our officers and men appeared
impatient for the appeal, and to have poffeffed the moft
animated fentiments and determined refolution.

On Tuefday evening a confiderable number of their
troops embarked on board of their tranfports, and fell
down to the caftle, where part of them landed before dark.
One or two of the veffels got a-ground, and were fired
at by our people with a field-piece, but without any damage.   What was the defign of this embarkation and landing, I have not been able to learn.   It would feem as if
they meant an attack ; for it is moft probable, that, if they
make one on our works at Dorchefter at this time, they
will firft go to the caftle, and come from thence.   If fuch
was their defign, a violent ftorm that night, and which
lafted till eight o'clock the next day, rendered the execution

eution of it impracticable.   It carried one or two of their
veffels a-fhore, which have fince got off.

In cafe the minifterial troops had made an attempt to
diflodge our men from Dorchefter hills, and the number
detached upon the eccafion had been fo great as to have
afforded a probability of a fuccefsful attack's being made
upon Bofton,—on a fignal given from Roxbury for that
purpofe, agreeable to a fettled and concerted plan, four
thoufand chofen men, who were held in readinefs, were
to have embarked at the mouth of Cambridge river, in
two divifions, the firft under the command of brigadier-
general Sullivan, the fecond under brigadier-general
Greene,—the whole to have been commanded by major-
general Putnam.   The firft divifion was to land at the
powder-houfe, and gain poffeffion of Beacon-hill and
Mount-Horam,—the fecond at Barton's point or a little
fouth of it, and, after fecuring that poft, to join the other
divifion, and force the enemy's gates and works at the
neck, for letting in the Roxbury troops.   Three floating
batteries were to have preceded, and gone in front of the
other boats, and kept up a heavy fire on that part of the
town were our men were to land.

How far our views would have fucceeded, had an opportunity offered for attempting the execution, is impoffible for me to fay ; nothing lefs than experiment could
determine with precifion.   The plan was thought to be
well digefted ; and, as far as I could judge from the cheerfulnefs and alacrity which diftinguifhed the officers and
men who were to engage in the enterprife, I had reafon
to hope for a favourable and happy iffue.

The militia who were ordered in from the adjacent
towns brought with them three days' provifion.   They
were only called upon to act under the idea of an attack's
being immediately made, and were all difcharged this
afternoon.

I beg leave to remind Congrefs that three major-generals are effential and neceffary for this army ; and that
by general Lee's being called from hence to the command
in Canada, the left divifion is without one.   I hope they
will fill up the vacancy by the appointment of another.
General Thomas is the firft brigadier, ftands fair in point

of

of reputation, and is efteemed a brave and good officer. If he is promoted, there will be a vacancy in the brigadier-generals, which it will be neceffary to fupply by the appointment of fome other gentleman that fhall be agreeable to Congrefs: but juftice requires me to mention that William Thompfon, efquire, of the rifle regiment, is the firft colonel in this department, and, as far as I have had an opportunity of judging, is a good officer and a man of courage. What I have faid of thefe two gentlemen, I conceived to be my duty, at the fame time acknowledging, whatever promotions are made will be fatisfactory to me.

March 9.——Yefterday evening, a captain Irvine, who efcaped from Bofton the night before with fix of his crew, came to head-quarters, and gave the following intelligence:—" That our bombardment and cannonade caufed a great deal of furprife and alarm in town, as many of the foldiery faid they never heard or thought we had mortars or fhells;—that feveral of the officers acknowledged they were well and properly directed; that they made much diftrefs and confufion;—that the cannon-fhot, for the greateft part, went through the houfes; and he was told that one took off the legs and arms of fix men lying in the barracks on the neck;—that a foldier, who came from the lines there on Tuefday morning, informed him that twenty men had been wounded the night before:—(it was reported that others were alfo hurt, and one of the light-horfe torn to pieces by the explofion of a fhell: this was afterwards contradicted)—that, early on Tuefday morning, admiral Shuldham, difcovering the works our people were throwing up on Dorchefter heights, immediately fent an exprefs to general Howe, to inform him that it was neceffary they fhould be attacked and diflodged from thence, or he would be under the neceffity of withdrawing the fhips from the harbour, which were under his command;—that preparations were directly made for that purpofe, as it was faid; and, from twelve to two o'clock, about three thoufand men embarked on board the tranfports, which fell down to the caftle with a defign of landing on that part of Dorchefter next to it, and attacking our works on the heights at five o'clock next morning;—

that

that lord Percy was appointed to command ;—that it was generally believed the attempt would have been made, had it not been for the violent ftorm which happened that night, as I have mentioned before ;—that he heard feveral of the privates, and one or two ferjeants, fay as they were embarking, that it would be another Bunker's-hill affair."

He further informs—" that the army is preparing to leave Bofton, and that they will do it in a day or two ;—that the tranfports neceflary for their embarkation were getting ready with the utmoft expedition ;—that there had been great movements and confufion among the troops, the night and day preceding his coming out, in hurrying down their cannon, artillery and other ftores, to the wharfs, with the utmoft precipitation ; and they were putting them on board the fhips in fuch hafte, that no account or memorandum was taken of them ;—that moft of the cannon were removed from their works, and embarked or embarking ;—that he heard a woman fay, whom he took to be an officer's wife, that fhe had feen men go under the ground at the lines on the neck, without returning ;—that the fhip he commanded was taken up, places fitted, and fitting, for officers to lodge, and feveral fhot, fhells, and cannon already on board ;—that the tories were to have the liberty of going where they pleafe, if they can get feamen to man the veffels, of whom there was a great fcarcity ;—that, on that account, many veffels could not be carried away, and would be burned ;—that many of the inhabitants apprehended the town would be deftroyed ; and that it was generally thought their deftination is Halifax."

The account given by captain Irvine, as to the embarkation, and their being about to leave the town, I believe true. There are other circumftances corroborating ; and it feems fully confirmed by a paper figned by four of the felectmen of the town, (a copy of which I have the honour to inclofe you) which was brought out yefterday evening by a flag, and delivered to colonel Learned, by major Baffet of the tenth regiment, who defired it might be delivered me as foon as poffible. I advifed with fuch of the general officers upon the occafion as I could immediately affemble ; and we determined it right (as it was not addreffed to me or any one elfe, nor authenticated by the

fignature

signature of general Howe, or any other act obliging him to a performance of the promise mentioned on his part) that I should give it no answer; at the same time, that a letter should be returned, as going from colonel Learned, signifying his having laid it before me,—with the reasons assigned for not answering it.   A copy of this is sent.

To-night I shall have a battery thrown up on Nuke-hill (Dorchester point) with a design of acting as circumstances may require; it being judged adviseable to prosecute our plans of fortification, as we intended before this information from the selectmen came.

It being agreed on all hands that there is no possibility of stopping them in case they determine to go,—I shall order look-outs to be kept upon all the head-lands, to discover their movements and course, and moreover direct commodore Manly and his little squadron to dog them, as well for the same purpose as for picking up any of their vessels that may chance to depart their convoy.   From their loading with such precipitancy, it is presumable they will not be in the best condition for sea.

If the ministerial troops evacuate the town and leave it standing, I have thoughts of taking measures for fortifying the entrance into the harbour, if it shall be thought proper, and the situation of affairs will admit of it.

Notwithstanding the report from Boston that Halifax is the place of their destination, I have no doubt but that they are going to the southward of this,—and, I apprehend, to New-York.   Many reasons lead to this opinion: it is in some measure corroborated by their sending an express ship there, which, on Wednesday week, got on shore and bilged at Cape-Cod.   The dispatches, if written, were destroyed when she was boarded.   She had a parcel of coal, and about four thousand cannon-shot, six carriage-guns, a swivel or two, and three barrels of powder.

I shall hold the riflemen and other parts of our troops in readiness to march at a moment's warning, and govern my movements by the events that happen, or such orders as I may receive from Congress, which I beg may be ample, and forwarded with all possible expedition.

On the sixth instant, a ship bound from London, with stores for the ministerial army, consisting of coal, porter,

and

and krout, fell in with our armed veffels, four of them in
company, and was carried into Portfmouth. She had
had a long paffage, and of courfe brought no papers of
a late date. The only letters of importance, or in the
leaft interefting that were found, I have inclofed.

I beg leave to mention to Congrefs that money is much
wanted. The militia from thefe governments, engaged
till the firft of April, are then to be paid : and, if we
march from hence, the expenfe will be very confiderable,
muft be defrayed, and cannot be accomplifhed without it.
The neceffity of making the earlieft remittance for thefe
purpofes is too obvious for me to add more.

When I wrote that part of this letter which is antecedent to this date, I fully expected it would have gone before now by colonel Bull, not deeming it of fufficient
importance to fend a fpecial meffenger. But he deferred
his return from time to time, and never fet off till to-day.
Thefe reafons I hope will excufe the delay, and be received as a proper apology for not tranfmitting it fooner.

I have the honour to be, &c.   G. W.

S I R,   *Cambridge, March* 13, 1776.

IN my letter of the feventh and ninth inftant which
I had the honour of addreffing you, I mentioned the intelligence I had received refpecting the embarkation of
the troops from Bofton ; and fully expected, before this,
that the town would have been entirely evacuated. Although I have been deceived, and was rather premature
in the opinion I had then formed, I have little reafon to
doubt but the event will take place in a very fhort time,
as other accounts which have come to hand fince, of
the failing of a great number of tranfports from the harbour to Nantafket-road, and many circumftances corref-
ponding therewith, feem to confirm and render it unqueftionable.

Whether the town will be deftroyed, is a matter of
much uncertainty : but it would feem, from the deftruction they are making of fundry pieces of furniture, of
many of their waggons, carts, &c. which they cannot take

with

with them as it is said, that it will not : for, if they intended it, the whole might be involved in one general ruin.

Holding it of the last importance in the present contest that we should secure New-York, and prevent the enemy from possessing it,—and conjecturing they have views of that sort, and their embarkation to be for that purpose,—I judged it necessary, under the situation of things here, to call a council of general officers to consult of such measures as might be expedient to be taken at this interesting conjuncture of affairs. A copy of the proceedings I have the honour to inclose you.

Agreeable to the opinion of the council, I shall detach the rifle regiment to-morrow, under the command of brigadier-general Sullivan, with orders to repair to New-York with all possible expedition ;—which will be succeeded, the day after, by the other five in one brigade,—they being all that it was thought adviseable to send from hence till the enemy shall have quitted the town. Immediately upon their departure, I shall send forward major-general Putnam, and follow myself with the remainder of the army as soon as I have it in my power,—leaving here such a number of men as circumstances may seem to require.

As the badness of the roads at this season will greatly retard the march of our men, I have, by advice of the general officers, wrote to governor Trumbull by this express, to use his utmost exertions for throwing a reinforcement of two thousand men into New-York, from the western parts of Connecticut,—and to the commanding officer there, to apply to the provincial convention or committee of safety of New-Jersey, for a thousand more for the same purpose, to oppose the enemy and prevent their getting possession in case they arrive before the troops from hence can get there ; of which there is a probability, unless they are impeded by contrary winds. This measure, though it may be attended with considerable expense, I flatter myself, will meet with the approbation of Congress. Past experience, and the lines in Boston and on Boston neck, point out the propriety, and suggest the necessity of keeping

ing

ing our enemies from gaining poffeffion and making a lodgement.

Should their deftination be further fouthward, or for Halifax (as reported in Bofton) for the purpofe of going into Canada,—the march of our troops to New-York will place them nearer the fcene of action, and more convenient for affording fuccours.

We have not taken poft on Nuke-hill, and fortified it, as mentioned that we fhould, in my laft. On hearing that the enemy were about to retreat and leave the town, it was thought imprudent and unadvifeable to force them with too much precipitation, that we might gain a little time, and prepare for a march. To-morrow evening we fhall take poffeffion, unlefs they are gone.

As New-York is of fuch importance, prudence and policy require that every precaution that can be devifed fhould be adopted, to fruftrate the defigns which the enemy have of poffeffing it. To this end I have ordered veffels to be provided and held ready at Norwich, for the embarkation and tranfportation of our troops thither. This I have done with a view not only of greatly expediting their arrival, (as it will fave feveral days marching) but alfo that they may be frefh and fit for intrenching and throwing up works of defence as foon as they get there, if they do not meet the enemy to contend with ;—for neither of which would they be in a proper condition after a long and fatiguing march in bad roads. If Wallace, with his fhips, fhould be apprifed of the meafure, and attempt to prevent it by. ftopping up the harbour of New-London, they can but purfue their march by land.

You will pleafe to obferve that it is the opinion of the general officers, if the enemy abandon the town, that it will be unneceffary to employ or keep any part of this army for its defence ; and that I have mentioned, on that event's happening, I fhall immediately repair to New-York with the remainder of the army not now detached, leaving only fuch a number of men here as circumftances may feem to require. What I partly allude to, is, that, as it will take a confiderable time for the removal of fuch a body of men, and the divifions muft precede each other in fuch order as to allow intermediate time fufficient for

them

them to be covered and provided for, and many things done previous to the march of the whole, for fecuring and forwarding fuch neceffaries as cannot be immediately carried, and others which it may be proper to keep here,—that directions might be received from Congrefs refpecting the fame, and as many men ordered to remain for that and other purpofes, as they may judge proper. I could wifh to have their commands upon the fubject, and in time; as I may be under fome degree of embarraffment as to their views.

Congrefs having been pleafed to appoint colonel Thompfon a brigadier-general, there is a vacancy for a colonel in the regiment he commanded, to which I would beg leave to recommend the lieutenant-colonel Hand. I fhall alfo take the liberty of recommending captain Hugh Stephenfon, of the Virginia riflemen, to fucceed colonel Hand, and to be appointed in his place as lieutenant-colonel,—there being no major to the regiment fince the promotion of major Magaw to be lieutenant-colonel of one of the Pennfylvania battalions, and who is gone from hence. He is, in my opinion, the fitteft perfon in this army for it, as well as the oldeft captain in the fervice, having diftinguifhed himfelf at the head of a rifle company all the laft war, and highly merited the approbation of his fuperior officers.

Colonel Mifflin informed me to-day of his having received tent-cloths from Mr. Barrell, of Philadelphia, to the amount of feven thoufand five hundred pounds Pennfylvania currency, and applied for a warrant for payment of it. But, as our fund is low, and many neceffary demands againft it which muft be fatisfied,—and our calls for money are and will be exceedingly great,—I could not grant it, thinking it might be convenient for payment to be made in Philadelphia, by your order on the treafury there. I have the honour to be, &c.　　　G. W.

———

SIR,　　　　　　*Head-Quarters, Cambridge, March* 19, 1776.

IT is with the greateft pleafure I inform you, that, on Sunday laft, the feventeenth inftant, about nine o'clock in
the

the forenoon, the minifterial army evacuated the town of
Bofton, and that the forces of the United Colonies are
now in actual poffeffion thereof. I beg leave to congratulate you, Sir, and the honorable Congrefs, on this happy
event, and particularly as it was effected without endanger-
ing the lives and property of the remaining unhappy inhabitants.

I have great reafon to imagine their flight was precipitated by the appearance of a work which I had ordered to be
thrown up laft Saturday night on an eminence at Dorchefter which lay neareft to Bofton neck, called Nuke-hill.

The town, although it has fuffered greatly, is not in fo
bad a ftate as I expected to find it; and I have a particular pleafure in being able to inform you, Sir, that your houfe
has received no damage worth mentioning. Your furniture
is in tolerable order, and the family pictures are all left entire and untouched. Captain Cazneau takes charge of the
whole, until he fhall receive further orders from you.

As foon as the minifterial troops had quitted the town,
I ordered a thoufand men, (who had had the fmall-pox)
under command of general Putnam, to take poffeffion of
the heights, which I fhall endeavour to fortify in fuch a manner as to prevent their return, fhould they attempt it. But,
as they are ftill in the harbour, I thought it not prudent to
march off with the main body of the army until I fhould
be fully fatisfied they had quitted the coaft. I have therefore only detached five regiments, befides the rifle battalion, to New-York, and fhall keep the remainder here till
all fufpicion of their return ceafes.

The fituation in which I found their works evidently
difcovered that their retreat was made with the greateft
precipitation. They have left their barracks and other
works of wood at Bunker's hill, &c. all ftanding, and
have deftroyed but a fmall part of their lines. They have
alfo left a number of fine pieces of cannon, which they firft
fpiked up, alfo a very large iron mortar; and, as I am informed, they have thrown another over the end of your
wharf. I have employed proper perfons to drill the cannon, and doubt not I fhall fave the moft of them.—I am
not yet able to procure an exact lift of all the ftores they
have left. As foon as it can be done, I fhall take care to

tranfmit

tranfmit it to you.—From an eftimate of what the quarter-mafter-general has already difcovered, the amount will
be twenty-five or thirty thoufand pounds.

Part of the powder mentioned in yours of the fixth inftant has already arrived. The remainder I have ordered
to be ftopped on the road, as we fhall have no occafion for
it here. The letter to general Thomas, I immediately fent
to him. He defired leave for three or four days, to fettle
fome of his private affairs ; after which, he will fet out for
his command in Canada. I am happy that my conduct in
intercepting lord Drummond's letter is approved of by
Congrefs.

I have the honour to be, &c.   G. W.

SIR,   *Cambridge, March* 24, 1776.

WHEN I had the honour to addrefs you on the
nineteenth inftant upon the evacuation of the town of Bofton by the minifterial army, I fully expected, as their retreat and embarkation were hurried and precipitate, that,
before now, they would have departed the harbour, and been
far in their paffage to the place of deftination. But, to
my furprife and difappointment, the fleet is ftill in Nantafket-road. The purpofe inducing their ftay is altogether
unknown ; nor can I fuggeft any fatisfactory reafon for it.
On Wednefday night laft, before the whole of the fleet fell
down to Nantafket, they demolifhed the caftle and houfes
belonging to it, by burning them down, and the feveral fortifications. They left a great number of the cannon, but
have rendered all of them, except a very few, entirely ufelefs, by breaking off the trunnions ; and thofe they fpiked
up : but they may be made ferviceable again :—fome are
already done.

There are feveral veffels in the docks, which were taken
by the enemy (fome with and others without cargoes,)
which different perfons claim as their property and right.
Are they to be reftored to their former owners on making
proof of their title, or to belong to the continent, as captures
made from the enemy ?—I wifh Congrefs would direct a
mode of proceeding againft them, and eftablifh a rule for
decifion :

decifion : they appear to me to be highly neceffary. In like manner, fome of the cannon which are in Bofton are faid to have come from the caftle. Suppofing them, with thofe remaining at the caftle, to have been purchafed by and provided originally at the expenfe of this province,—are they now to be confidered as belonging to it, or to the public ? I beg leave to refer the matter to the opinion of Congrefs, and pray their direction how I am to conduct refpecting them.

It having been fuggefted to me that there was confiderable property, &c. belonging to perfons who had, from the firft of the prefent unhappy conteft, manifefted an unfriendly and inveterate difpofition, in the town of Bofton, I thought it prudent to write to the honourable General Court upon the fubject, that it might be inquired after and fecured. A copy of the letter I herewith fend you, and fubmit it to Congrefs, through you, whether they will not determine how it is to be difpofed of, and as to the appropriation of the money arifing from the fale of the fame.

As foon as the town was abandoned by the enemy, I judged it advifeable to fecure the feveral heights, left they fhould attempt to return ; and, for this purpofe, have caufed a large and ftrong work to be thrown up on Fort-hill, a poft of great importance, as it commands the whole harbour, and, when fortified, if properly fupported, will greatly annoy any fleet the enemy may fend againft the town, and render the landing of their troops exceedingly difficult, if not impracticable. This work is almoft done, and in a little time will be complete : and, that the communication between the town and country may be free and open, I have ordered all the lines upon the neck to be immediately deftroyed, and the other works on the fides of the town facing the country, that the inhabitants from the latter may not be impeded, and afforded an eafy entrance, in cafe the enemy fhould gain poffeffion at any future time. Thefe matters I conceived to be within the line of my duty ; of which I advifed the General Court, and recommended to their attention fuch other meafures as they might think neceffary for fecuring the town againft the hoftile defigns of the enemy.

I have juſt got an inventory of ſtores and property belonging to the crown, which the enemy left in Boſton, at the caſtle and Bunker's-hill, which I have the honour to tranſmit you ; and ſhall give ſtrict orders that a careful attention be had to any more that may be found. I ſhall take ſuch precautions reſpecting them, that they may be ſecure, and turn to the public advantage, as much as poſſible, or circumſtances will admit of.

A Mr. Bulfinch from Boſton, who acted as clerk to Mr. * * *, having put into my hands a liſt of rations drawn the Saturday before the troops evacuated the town, I have incloſed it for your inſpection. He ſays, neither the ſtaff officers nor women are included in the liſt ; from which it appears that their number is greater than we had an idea of.

Major-general Ward and brigadier-general Frye are deſirous of leaving the ſervice ; and, for that purpoſe, have requeſted me to lay the matter before Congreſs, that they may be allowed to reſign their commiſſions. The papers containing their applications you will herewith receive. They will give you a full and more particular information upon the ſubject ; and therefore I ſhall take the liberty of referring you to them.

I would mention to Congreſs that the commiſſary of artillery ſtores has informed me, that whatever powder has been ſent to this camp has always come without any bill aſcertaining the number of caſks or quantity. This, it is probable, has proceeded from forgetfulneſs or inattention in the perſons appointed to ſend it, or the negligence of thoſe who brought it, though they have declared otherwiſe, and that they never had any. As it may in ſome meaſure prevent embezzlements, (though I do not ſuſpect any to have been made) and the commiſſary will know what and how much to receive, and be enabled to diſcover miſtakes if any ſhould happen,—I ſhould be glad if you will direct a bill of parcels to be always ſent in future.

There have been ſo many accounts from England, all agreeing that commiſſioners are coming to America, to propoſe terms for an accommodation, as they ſay,—that I am inclined to think the time of their arrival not very far off. If they come to Boſton, (which probably will be the

caſe

cafe if they come to America at all) I fhall be under much embarraffment refpecting the manner of receiving them, and the mode of treatment that ought to be ufed. I therefore pray that Congrefs will give me directions, and point out the line of conduct to be purfued—whether they are to be confidered as ambaffadors, and to have a pafs or permit for repairing through the country to Philadelphia or to any other place—or whether they are to be reftrained in any and what manner. I fhall anxioufly wait their orders, and, whatever they are, comply with them literally.

I have the honour to be, &c. G. W.

———

SIR, *Cambridge, March* 27, 1776.

. I RECEIVED your favour of the eleventh inftant by Saturday night's poft, and muft beg pardon for not acknowledging it in my laft of the twenty-fourth. The hurry I was then in occafioned the neglect, and I hope will apologize for it.

I now beg leave to inform you that I have juft received intelligence that the whole of the minifterial fleet, befides three or four fhips, got under way this evening at Nantafket-road, and were ftanding out for fea : in confequence of which, I fhall detach a brigade of fix regiments immediately from hence for New-York, under the command of brigadier-general Sullivan (brigadier-general Heath having gone with the firft) which will be fucceeded by another in a day or two ; and directly after I fhall forward the remainder of the army (except four or five regiments which will be left for taking care of the barracks and public ftores, and fortifying the town, and erecting fuch works for its defence as the honourable General Court may think neceffary)—and follow myfelf.

Apprehending that general Thomas will ftand in need of fome artillerifts in Canada, I have ordered two companies of the train to march immediately ; and two mortars, with a quantity of fhells and fhot, to be fent him. He fet out on the twenty-firft inftant.

Inclofed you have a copy of the return of ordnance ftores left in Bofton by the enemy. In it are not included
the

the cannon left at the castle, amounting to a hundred and thirty-five pieces, as reported, all of which, except a very few, they have destroyed and rendered useless, by knocking off the trunnions, and spiking up.

I beg leave to transmit you the copy of a petition from the inhabitants of Nova-Scotia, brought me by * * *, esquire, mentioned therein, who is now here with an Acadian. From this it appears they are in a distressed situation; and, from Mr. * * *'s account, are exceedingly apprehensive that they will be reduced to the disagreeable alternative of taking up arms and joining our enemies, or to flee their country, unless they can be protected against their insults and oppressions. He says that their committees think many salutary and valuable consequences would be derived from five or six hundred men being sent there, as it would not only quiet the minds of the people from the anxiety and uneasiness they are now filled with, and enable them to take a part in behalf of the Colonies, but be the means of preventing the Indians (of whom there are a good many) from taking the side of government, and the ministerial troops from getting such supplies of provisions from thence as they have done.

How far these good purposes would be answered if such a force was sent as they ask for, is impossible to determine in the present uncertain state of things. For, if the army from Boston is going to Halifax (as reported by them before their departure) that or a much more considerable force would be of no avail : if not, and they possess the friendly disposition to our cause, suggested in the petition and declared by Mr. * * *, it might be of great service, unless another body of troops should be sent thither by administration, too powerful for them to oppose. It being a matter of some importance, I judged it prudent to lay it before Congress for their consideration; and requesting their direction upon the subject, shall only add, if they determine to adopt it, that they will prescribe the number to be sent, and whether it is to be from the regiments which will be left here. I shall wait their decision, and, whatever it is, will endeavour to have it carried into execution.

I have the honour to be, &c.   G. W.

Head-Quarters,

SIR,   *Head-Quarters, Cambridge, April 1, 1776.*

THIS letter will be delivered you by * * *, esquire, the gentleman from Nova-Scotia whom I mentioned to you in mine of the twenty-seventh ultimo. He seemed desirous of waiting on the honourable Congress, in order to lay before them the state of public affairs, and situation of the inhabitants of that province. And, as it might be in his power to communicate many things personally which could not be so well done by letter, I encouraged him in his design, and have advanced him fifty dollars to defray his expenses. The Acadian accompanies him: and, as they seem to be solid judicious men, I beg leave to recommend them both to the notice of Congress;—and am most respectfully, Sir, your most obedient, &c.   G. W.

———

SIR,   *Head-Quarters, Cambridge, April 1, 1776.*

AN express arrived this morning with a letter from governor Cooke of Rhode-Island, of which the inclosed is a copy. In consequence of this important intelligence, I immediately dispatched an express after general Sullivan who is on his march to Norwich with six regiments, and ordered him to file off to Providence, if he should be so desired by governor Cooke, to whom I have wrote on the subject.

General Greene was to have marched this morning with five more regiments by way of Providence. I have ordered him to hasten his march for that place ; and hope to collect a force there sufficient to prevent the enemy from effecting their purpose.

Whether this movement be only a feint to draw our attention from their principal object, or not, is at present impossible to determine. I momently expect further intelligence from governor Cooke. If the alarm should be well grounded, I shall hasten to Providence, and make the necessary dispositions for their reception. I beg you to assure the honourable Congress I shall exert myself to the utmost to frustrate the designs of the enemy.

I am, Sir, your most obedient, &c.   G. W.

K 2

Cambridge,

SIR,   *Cambridge, April 4, 1776.*

I WAS honoured with your favours of the twenty-first and twenty-fifth ultimo, on the second instant,—the former by Mr. Hanson, &c. the latter by Feffenden. I heartily with the money had arrived fooner, that the militia might have been paid as foon as their time of fervice expired. The difappointment has given them great uneafinefs, and they are gone home much diffatisfied: nor have I been without fevere complaints from the other troops on the fame account. When I get to New-York, I hope a fufficient fum will be there, ready to pay every claim.

It is not in my power to make report of the deficiency of arms in compliance with the direction of Congrefs at this time, as fome of the regiments are at, and moft of the others on their march to New-York; nor do I know that it would anfwer any good purpofe, if it were,—having made repeated applications to the feveral affemblies and conventions upon the fubject, and conftantly received for anfwer, that they could afford no relief.

When I arrive at New-York, I fhall, in purfuance of the order of Congrefs, detach four battalions to Canada, if the fituation of affairs will admit of it: and fhall be extremely happy if they and the troops already there can effect the important end of their going.

In my letter of the firft inftant, per poft, I inclofed you a copy of a letter from governor Cooke, advifing me of the arrival of a fhip of war, &c. at and near the harbour of Newport. I have now the pleafure to inform you that the report was entirely premature, and without any foundation. You have a copy of his letter of the firft inftant to this effect. I wifh the alarm had never been given: it occafioned general Sullivan and his brigade to make an unneceffary and inconvenient diverfion from their route.

Inclofed is a copy of an account, prefented by the honourable General Court, of powder furnifhed the continental army by this colony. From the account, it appears that part of it was fupplied before the army was under my command; and therefore I know nothing of it; but have not the fmalleft doubt of the juftice of the charge.

I fhall

I fhall leave about two hundred barrels of this article with major-general Ward, out of which Congrefs will direct him to make a return, if they think proper,—and alfo re-payment of what may have been furnifhed by the other governments.

A proclamation of general Howe's, iffued a few days before his departure from town, having fallen into my hands, I have inclofed you a copy, which may probably have been the occafion of large quantities of goods being carried away, and the removal of many perfons, which otherwife would not have happened.

Colonel Warren, pay-mafter-general, finding the army likely to be removed from hence, informed me the other day that the fituation of his affairs and engagements in the bufinefs of the colony are fuch, as to prevent him from perfonally attending the army; and offered, in cafe it fhould be required, to refign. This was rather embarraffing. To me it appears indifpenfably neceffary that the pay-mafter-general, with his books, fhould be at or near head-quarters. Indeed it is ufual for the head of every department in the army, however difperfed that army may be, to be with the commanding general, keeping deputies in the fmaller departments. On the other hand, colonel Warren's merit and attachment to the caufe are fuch, that I could do nothing lefs than defire, (as fome money muft be left for the pay and contingent charges of the army which will remain here) he would wait here till Congrefs fhall be pleafed to give their fentiments upon the matter—fending in the mean time fome perfon in whom he could confide, with the money, but little of which there will be to carry, though great the demands, as nine of the regiments which have marched to New-York have only received five hundred pounds each, towards their pay for the months of February and March—and fix others, not a farthing. I hope therefore this matter will be confidered by Congrefs, and the refult tranfmitted me as foon as done.

I would alfo mention to Congrefs, that the militia regiments which were laft called upon, in making up their abftracts, charged pay—the officers, from the time they received orders to raife companies—and the privates, from

the

the time they refpectively engaged to come or were called upon, though they did not march for a confiderable
time after—fome not within three, four, to twenty days,
during all which, they remained at home about their own
private affairs, without doing any thing elfe than "preparing for the march," as they fay by way of plea. This
appeared to me fo exceedingly unreafonable, and fo contrary to juftice, that the public fhould pay for a longer time
than from the day of their march to that of their return,
that I ordered the abftracts to be made out accordingly,
and refufed to give warrants on any other terms. They
fay that the enlifting orders, which went out from their
governments, give them the pay they claim. The fact
may be that fomething in thefe may feem to authorife it :
but I muft fubmit it to Congrefs, and wifh for their decifion, whether the continent muft pay it.

I am, with great efteem, &c.   G. W.
    P. S.   I fhall fet off to-day.

SIR,   *New-York, April 15, 1776.*

I AM now to inform you that on the fourth inftant
I fet out from Cambridge, and arrived here on Saturday
laft.   I came through Providence, Norwich, and New-
London, in order to fee and expedite the embarkation of
the troops.—The third brigade, under the command of
general Greene, was at New-London when I left it, where
there was a fufficient number of tranfports to embark
them—and moft probably would have arrived here before
this, had it not been for a fevere ftorm which happened
the night they failed, which difperfed them, and, I fear,
has done them fome injury.

General Spencer, with the laft brigade, marched from
Roxbury the day I left Cambridge, and would be at New-
London, ready to embark in the return-tranfports which
brought general Sullivan's divifion to this place.   The
whole of the troops may be reafonably expected here in
the courfe of this week.   The badnefs of the roads, and
difficulty of procuring teams for bringing the ftores, baggage, &c. have greatly prolonged their arrival at this place.

I have

I have not had time, since I came, to look fully about me; but find many works of defence begun, and some finished. The troops are much difperfed—fome on Long-Ifland, others on Staten-Ifland, &c.

I have ordered four battalions from hence to Canada, and am taking meafures to have them forwarded to Albany, by water, with all poffible expedition. This will greatly expedite their arrival, and eafe the men of much fatigue. I have wrote general Schuyler of their coming, that he may have neceffary meafures taken to hurry their march to general Thomas.

I am informed by general Putnam that the militia, that were called in for the fupport of this town in cafe the minifterial army had arrived before our troops, are all dif-charged, it being unneceffary to keep them longer.

All the fhips of war, befides the Afia, moved out of this harbour on Saturday, and the Afia yefterday; fome of which are now below the Narrows, and the reft gone to fea.

Your favour of the tenth inftant, by major Sherburne, directed to general Putnam or the commanding officer here, came to hand on Saturday evening, with three boxes of money, which I fhall deliver the pay-mafter as foon as he arrives, and tranfmit you his receipt for the fame.

Having received information from hence before my departure from Cambridge, that thirty pieces of heavy cannon were wanting, and effentially neceffary for the defence of this place, in addition to thofe already here—I took the liberty of applying to admiral Hopkins, whom I faw at New-London, for that number, with the mortars and ftores he brought from Providence,—a lift of which he had tranfmitted you. He told me, that, as many were wanting for the defence of Providence river and the harbour at New-London, it was uncertain whether I could have all I wanted; but that he would fend me all that could be fpared.

I have not been able to get a return of the troops fince I came :—as foon as I do, I will fend it you.

I am, Sir, with great refpect, &c.   G. W.
New-York,

SIR,   *New-York, April* 18, 1776.

PERMIT me, through you, to convey to the honourable Congrefs the fentiments of gratitude I feel for the high honour they have done me in the public mark of approbation contained in your favour of the fecond inftant, which came to hand laft night. I beg you to affure them that it will ever be my higheft ambition to approve myfelf a faithful fervant of the public; and that, to be in any degree inftrumental in procuring to my American brethren a reftitution of their juft rights and privileges, will conftitute my chief happinefs.

Agreeable to your requeft, I have communicated, in general orders, to the officers and foldiers under my command, the thanks of Congrefs for their good behaviour in the fervice; and am happy in having fuch an opportunity of doing juftice to their merit. They were indeed, at firft, *" a band of undifciplined hufbandmen:"* but it is (under God) to their bravery and attention to their duty that I am indebted for that fuccefs which has procured me the only reward I wifh to receive—the affection and efteem of my countrymen.

The medal, intended to be prefented to me by your honourable body, I fhall carefully preferve as a memorial of their regard. I beg leave to return you, Sir, my warmeft thanks for the polite manner in which you have been pleafed to exprefs their fentiments of my conduct; and am, with fincere efteem and refpect, Sir, yours and their moft obedient and moft humble fervant,   G. W.

SIR,   *New-York, April* 19, 1776.

I HAVE this moment received a letter from general Schuyler, containing inclofures of a very important nature, copies of which, I imagine, are contained in the inclofed letter to you, which I thought it my duty immediately to forward by exprefs, that they may be laid before the honourable Congrefs, and proper meafures purfued to prevent the fatal effects which are therein apprehended. For my own part, I have done my utmoft to forward the four

regiments

regiments ordered by Congrefs: but a variety of incidents have hitherto confpired to prevent their embarkation. The men had fcarcely recovered themfelves from the fatigues of their march from Bofton, and are quite unprovided with neceffaries. The colonels of the regiments, though repeatedly called upon for that purpofe, had neglected making out the abftracts for their pay. All obftacles however are now removed.; and I hope to begin the embarkation this day. Indeed it would have been beft, in my opinion, to have fent the regiments, raifed in this province and New-Jerfey, upon that fervice, had not the peculiar circumftances under which they were raifed prevented it. By the terms of their enliftment, they are to ferve during the war, and at five dollars per month, on condition (as I am informed) that they fhall not be fent out of thofe provinces. Befides, they are very ill provided with arms, fome companies not having any. It muft be a great burden upon the continent to keep fuch a number of ufelefs men in pay: and yet, if they fhould be difmiffed, and an unexpected fupply of arms fhould arrive, it may be found very difficult to replace them.

The officers of the feveral corps that have arrived here have been fo bufily employed in fixing their men in quarters, that I have not yet been able to procure an exact return of their numbers. Some are yet behind. As foon as the whole are collected, I fhall order the proper returns, and tranfmit them to Congrefs.

You will pleafe to notice what colonel Hazen fays of the difpofition of the Indians. In my opinion, it will be impoffible to keep them in a ftate of neutrality. They muft, and, no doubt, foon will take an active part either for or againft us: and I fubmit it to the confideration of Congrefs, whether it would not be beft immediately to engage them on our fide, and to ufe our utmoft endeavours to prevent their minds being poifoned by minifterial emiffaries, which will ever be the cafe while a king's garrifon is fuffered to remain in their country. Would it not therefore be advifeable to fend a fufficient force from the back counties of Pennfylvania, to take poffeffion of the garrifons of Niagara and Detroit? This, I think, might eafily be effected, and would anfwer the moft falutary

purpofes.

purpofes.   The Seneca Indians, who have hitherto appeared friendly to us, might be ufefully employed in this
bufinefs.

I am in hopes moft of the difficulties mentioned in
colonel Hazen's letter will be obviated by the appearance
of the refpectable committee of Congrefs in Canada, and
the forces that have been and will be fent there.   The
fecurity of that country is of the utmoft importance to us.
This cannot be done fo effectually by conqueft, as by
taking ftrong hold of the affections and confidence of
the inhabitants.   It is to be lamented that any conduct of
the continental troops fhould tend to alienate their affections
from us.

The honourable Congrefs will be able to judge from
the papers fent them by general Schuyler, and the information they may receive of the defigns of the enemy, whether it is expedient to fend a further reinforcement to
Canada.   If fuch fhould be their determination, I ftand
ready to execute their orders; and am, with refpect, Sir,
your moft obedient, humble fervant,   G. W.

Inclofed is a return of the four regiments ordered to
Canada; befides which, there will be two rifle companies,
a company of artificers, and two artillery-men, all under
the command of brigadier-general Thompfon.

SIR,   *New-York, April 22, 1776.*

I WAS this day honoured with the receipt of your
favour of the twentieth inftant.   I have now the pleafure
to acquaint you that the four regiments defigned for Canada embarked yefterday with a fair wind for Albany, under the command of colonels Greaton, Patterfon, Bond,
and Poor; befides which there was a company of riflemen,
a company of artificers, and two engineers,—the whole
commanded by brigadier-general Thompfon.

I have repeatedly mentioned to the honourable Congrefs the diftrefsful fituation we are in for want of arms.
With much pains and difficulty I got moft of the regiments from the eaftward tolerably well furnifhed; but find
the York regiments very badly provided.   Colonel Ritzema's

ma's has scarcely any: and yet these men, being enlisted during the war, and at five dollars per month, ought not (in my judgment) to be discharged; as we find it almost as difficult to get men, as arms. This is a matter of some importance, which I should be glad to receive the particular opinion of Congress upon.

Mr. Baldwin is one of the assistant engineers ordered to Canada. He is indeed a very useful man in his department, but declined the service on account of his pay, which he says is inadequate to his support. In order to induce him to continue, I promised to represent his case to Congress; and would recommend an increase of his pay, and that he should have the rank of lieutenant-colonel, of which he is very deserving. I beg leave therefore to recommend him to the Congress, and that they would make provision for him accordingly.

A few days ago, application was made to me by the committee of safety for this colony, for an exchange of prisoners. For the particulars I beg leave to refer you to their letter, a copy of which you have inclosed. As there is a standing order of Congress that no sailors or soldiers shall be exchanged for citizens, I did not incline to comply with the request without the particular direction of Congress: but I have been since informed that the prisoners, mentioned in the committee's letter as citizens, are really seamen taken from private vessels, but not in arms. How far this may alter the case, or how far the reasons which induced the Congress to pass the resolve above-mentioned may still exist, must be left to their determination.

The militia, who, on my application, were ordered to this place to keep possession until I should arrive with the continental forces, were obliged to return home without their pay, as there was not then money sufficient in the treasury for that purpose, and to answer the exigencies of the army. This occasioned great uneasiness among them, and may be attended with very bad consequences in case we should have occasion for their service on any future emergency. I therefore beg the Congress would make provision for their pay, and point out particularly whether it is to be done by the commander of the continental forces,

Vol. I.Lor

or by the provincial affemblies or conventions from whence
they are fent.

As the time for which the riflemen enlifted will expire
on the firft of July next, and as the lofs of fuch a valuable
and brave body of men will be of great injury to the fervice,
I would fubmit it to the confideration of Congrefs, whether
it would not be beft to adopt fome method to induce them
to continue.   They are indeed a very ufeful corps : but I
need not mention this, as their importance is already well
known to the Congrefs.   It is neceffary they fhould pay
an early attention to this matter, as we know from paft experience that men are very flow in re-enlifting.

When I had the honour of feeing admiral Hopkins at
New-London, he reprefented to me the weak ftate of his
fleet, occafioned by ficknefs and the damage he received in
his engagement with the enemy ; and requefted I would
fpare him two hundred men to affift him in a defign he had
formed of attacking Wallace.   This I readily confented
to ; and the men are to be returned as foon as the fervice
is performed.

I wifh it was in my power at prefent to furnifh general
Lee with the companies of artillery he defires.   I have already fent two companies to Quebec ; and I have not yet
been able to procure a return of thofe that are here.   I
expect colonel Knox every moment, and fhall then be able
to determine whether any can be fpared from hence.
Blankets we are in great want of, ourfelves ; and it was
with great difficulty a few could be procured for the riflemen that were ordered for Canada.

I inclofe you Mr. Winthrop's receipt for two hundred
thoufand dollars brought fome time ago from Philadelphia
by major Sherburne, which you will pleafe to deliver to
the continental treafurers.

On my arrival here, I found that Mr. Livingfton had
been appointed by the provincial Congrefs a commiffary,
to furnifh the continental troops ftationed in this city with
provifions.   I fuppofe this was done becaufe there was no
continental commiffary then on the fpot.   Mr. Livingfton
ftill claims a right of furnifhing all the troops but thofe
lately arrived from Cambridge.   Mr. Trumbull is now
here : and, as I confider him as the principal in that office,

I fhould

I should be glad to know whether any part of the continental troops is to be furnished by any other than their commiffary-general. I muft needs fay, that to me it appears
very inconfiftent, and muft create great confufion in the
accounts as well as in the contracts. I intended to have
laid before Congrefs the amount of the rations, as fupplied
by colonel Trumbull and Mr. Livingfton; and called
upon thofe gentlemen to furnifh me with a feparate
eftimate for that purpofe. Colonel Trumbull has given
me his, by which it appears he fupplies the troops at
eight pence and one third per ration. I have not yet received any from Mr. Livingfton; but am informed his
contract is at ten pence half-penny. The difference is im-
menfe, as it will amount to no lefs than two hundred
pounds per day, for twenty thoufand men. It is indeed
to be confidered that Mr. Livingfton's contract is, including every other charge; and that to Mr. Trumbull's
muft be added ftore hire, clerks, and every other contingent expenfe. But even then it will not amount to fo
much as Mr. Livingfton's, by a penny per ration, which,
in the grofs, will be fomething very confiderable. I
thought it my duty, without prejudice or partiality, to ftate
the matter fairly to Congrefs, that they might take fuch
order upon it as to them fhall feem neceffary. I cannot
however, in juftice to Mr. Trumbull, help adding that he
has been indefatigable in fupplying the army; and I believe, from his connexions in New-England, is able to do
it on as good terms as any perfon in America.

The feveral matters contained in the foregoing, I muft
beg the early attention of Congrefs to; and that I may
be favoured with an anfwer as foon as poffible.

I have the honour to be, &c.   G. W.

SIR,   *New-York, April 23, 1776.*

IN a letter which I had the honour to receive from
Congrefs fome confiderable time ago, they were pleafed to
afk what rank aides-de-camp bore in the army? from
whence I concluded that they had adverted to the extraordinary trouble and confinement of thofe gentlemen, with
a view

a view to make them an adequate allowance. But nothing being since done or said of the matter, I take the liberty, unsolicited by, and unknown to my aides-de-camp, to inform your honourable body that their pay is not by any means equal to their trouble and confinement.

No person wishes more to save money to the public, than I do : and no person has aimed more at it. But there are some cases in which parsimony may be ill placed; and this I take to be one. Aides-de-camp are persons in whom entire confidence must be placed : it requires men of abilities to execute the duties with propriety and dispatch, where there is such a multiplicity of business, as must attend the commander-in-chief of such an army as ours : and persuaded I am, that nothing but the zeal of those gentlemen (who live with me, and act in this capacity) for the great American cause, and personal attachment to me, has induced them to undergo the trouble and confinement they have experienced since they have become members of my family.

I give in to no kind of amusements myself; and consequently those about me can have none, but are confined from morning till eve, hearing and answering the applications and letters of one and another, which will now, I expect, receive a pretty considerable addition, as the business of the northern and eastern departments (if I continue here) must, I suppose, pass through my hands. If these gentlemen had the same relaxation from duty as other officers have in their common routine, there would not be so much in it. But, to have the mind always upon the stretch—scarce ever unbent—and no hours for recreation, makes a material odds. Knowing this, and at the same time how inadequate the pay is, I can scarce find inclination to impose the necessary duties of their office upon them. To what I have here said, this further remark may be made, and is a matter of no small concernment to me, and, in its consequences, to the public :—and that is, that, while the duty is hard and the pay small, it is not to be wondered at, if there should be found a promptness in them to seek preferment, or in me to do justice to them by facilitating their views; by which means I must lose their aid when they have it most in their power to assist me.

me.   Influenced by thefe motives, I have taken the liberty
of laying the matter fully, and with all due deference, before your honourable body, not doubting its meeting with
a patient hearing.

I am, Sir, with the greateft refpect, &c.   G. W.

- - - - - - - -

SIR,   *New-York, April 23, 1776.*

THAT I might be in readinefs to take the field in
the fpring, and prepared for any fervice Congrefs fhould
think proper to fend me upon, this campaign—I defired
colonel Reed, when he left Cambridge in the fall, to get
me a fet of camp equipage, tents, and a baggage-waggon,
made at Philadelphia under his own infpection, and fent to
me.   This, he informs me, is now done, and ready to
come on.   I have therefore to beg the favour of Congrefs,
through you, to order payment of them from the treafury,
as it will fave the expenfe and hazard of a remittance from
hence, where we ftand much in need of every farthing we
have.

I have the honour to be, &c.   G. W.

- - - - - - - -

SIR,   *New-York, April 25, 1776.*

I RECEIVED by laft evening's poft a letter from
Jofhua Wentworth, efquire, of Portfmouth, whom I had
appointed agent for our little fleet in that province.   It is
dated the fifteenth inftant ; an extract from which I have
the honour of tranfcribing for your perufal.

" The third inftant, commodore Manly brought in the
brigantine Elizabeth, one of the third divifion which failed
from Nantafket, with a valuable cargo of Englifh goods,
and a few hogfheads of rum and fugar, by a Mr. J * * *,
who was paffenger, part freighter, and a very tory.   Sup-
pofe the cargo worth twenty thoufand pounds fterling.
Thofe goods are, the greater part, owned by the late inhabitants of Bofton, and by fome that were inhabitants
when the troops left it,—the refidue of this Mr. J * * *,
and others of the fame caft.   The complicate ftate of this

                                prize

prize required my immediate fetting off for Bofton, ex-pecting I might find fome directions for my government there; when I waited on general Ward, who was obliging enough to give me his opinion (but not able to direct, hav-ing received no inftructions to the point) that the veffel and cargo muft be libelled, and a dividend to the captors would follow, of all fuch goods as might be legally claim-ed by the friends to America; and thofe that were the property of them inimical, might be decreed forfeited. Upon further inquiry, I was informed a refolve paffed in Congrefs that all veffels and goods, retaken previous to a condemnation by a Britifh court of admiralty, were liable to a partial decree (by every colony judge) to the captors, not more than one-third, nor lefs than one-fourth. The prefent prize falls under this refolve: and any other, that [*makes the*] property of our internal enemies liable to a full confifcation, may be neceffary for my government: there-fore fhall be much obliged by your full direction of this capture, and a copy of the continental refolves thereon. This brigantine is owned by a Mr. Richard Hart, of this town, taken on her return from the Weft-Indies laft Oc-tober, and carried into Bofton, not condemned. The rum on board are feventeen hogfheads,—and four of fugar, not removed out of her from the time of capture. The other cargo was in general ftolen by virtue of general Howe's proclamation (which undoubtedly you have feen) appointing one C * * * B * * * fuperintendant, who, by the way, was taken in the prize, and is now confined in the Maffachufetts colony, with Mr. J * * * and fundry others, by order of the general court, to whom general Ward delivered them.

" There were a ferjeant and twelve privates of the fourth, or king's own regiment, taken prifoners on board, with the others, making fixty-three fouls. * * *

" There appeared from the pillage of this cargo by ma-ny of the paffengers, the property was in him who could fecrete the moft. For, when examining the chefts and bedding of the prifoners, I found great quantity of goods that they had collected while on board, which were taken out of ware-houfes without packing, and hove promifcu-oufly on board the veffel. Even the failors had provided

for

for their difpofal at pleafure. In fact, the deftruction of property, under cover of general Howe's proclamation, is unparelleled. * * *

" I am now difcharging the cargo, as it is in a perifhing fituation ; and, when felected, and the regular courfe purfued through the admiralty, fhall advertife agreeable to his Excellency's inftructions to general Ward, who was obliging enough to give me an abftract.

" The general court of this province, finding a difficulty in making a code of laws for the admiralty-court, did not complete that inftitution their laft feffion, when they adjourned to June ; which lapfe of time will not admit my facilitating the difpofal of the prizes under my care, fo early as I could wifh, for the fafety of part of the intereft of the Sufanna's cargo, viz. the porter, which I fear may be fpoiled by lying fo long,—it not having equal body to that commonly imported for fale ;—which induces me to defire your direction for a difpofal of that article either at private or public fale."

That, Sir, is an exact copy of part of Mr. Wentworth's letter to Mr. Moylan. I now requeft you will pleafe to direct me, in what manner I fhall inftruct the agent refpecting the complicated cargo, and whether he may be empowered to difpofe of the porter or any other articles on board the prizes under his care, which the delay of eftablifhing the court of admiralty may make liable to perifh.

I have not yet heard that there has been any trial of the prizes carried into Maffachufetts-Bay. This procraftination is attended with very bad confequences. Some of the veffels I had fitted out are now laid up, the crews being diffatisfied that they cannot get their prize-money. I have tired the Congrefs upon this fubject : but the importance of it makes me again mention, that, if a fummary way of proceeding is not refolved on, it will be impoffible to get our veffels manned. I muft alfo mention to you, Sir, that captain Manly and his crew are defirous to know when they may expect their part of the value of the ordnance ftores taken laft fall. They are anxious to know what the amount may be. As the inventory of that cargo is in the hands of Congrefs, I would humbly fubmit it

to

to them, whether a valuation thereof fhould not be made, and the captors' dividend be remitted them as foon as poffible.   It will give them fpirit, and encourage them to be alert in looking out for other prizes.

Several officers belonging to the regiments raifed in thefe middle colonies inform me that their men (notwithftanding their agreement) begin to murmur at the diftinction of pay made between them and the regiments from the eaftward.   I would be glad that the Congrefs would attend to this in time, left it may get to fuch a pitch as will make it difficult to fupprefs.   They argue that they perform the fame duty, undergo the fame fatigue, and receive five dollars, when the eaftern regiments receive fix dollars and two-thirds per month.   For my own part, I wifh they were all upon the fame footing: for, if the Britifh army will not face this way, it will be neceffary to detach a great part of our troops: in that cafe, I would, for many reafons, be forry there fhould be any diftinctions of regiments that are all in the pay of the United Colonies.

The deficiency of arms (in the New-York regiments efpecially) is very great.   If I am rightly informed, there are fcarce as many in colonel Ritzema's regiment as will arm one company.   Can the Congrefs remedy this evil ? If they can, there fhould not a moment be loft in effecting it, as our ftrength at prefent is, in reality, on paper only. Should we think of difcharging thofe men who are without arms, the remedy would be worfe than the difeafe : for, by vigorous exertions, I hope arms may be procured ; and I well know that the raifing men is exceeding difficult, efpecially to be engaged during the continuance of the war, which is the footing on which colonel Ritzema's regiment is engaged.

April 26.——I had wrote thus far before I was honoured with your favour of the twenty-third inftant.   In obedience to the order therein contained, I have directed fix regiments more for Canada, which will embark as foon as veffels and other neceffaries can be provided.   Thefe regiments will be commanded by general Sullivan.   I fhall give him inftructions to join the forces in that country under general Thomas, as foon as poffible.

With refpect to fending more troops to that country, I

am

am really at a lofs what to advife, as it is impoffible at
prefent to know the defigns of the enemy.   Should they
fend the whole force under general Howe up the river St.
Lawrence, to relieve Quebec and recover Canada, the
troops gone and now going will be infufficient to ftop their
progrefs : and fhould they think proper to fend that or an
equal force this way from Great-Britain for the purpofe of
poffeffing this city and fecuring the navigation of Hudfon's
river, the troops left here will not be fufficient to oppofe
them : and yet, for any thing we know, I think it not improbable they may attempt both,—both being of the greateft importance to them,—if they have men.

I could wifh indeed that the army in Canada fhould be
more powerfully reinforced : at the fame time I am con-
fcious that the trufting this important poft (which is now
become the grand magazine of America) to the handful
of men remaining here, is running too great a rifk.   The
fecuring this poft and Hudfon's river is to us alfo of fo
great importance, that I cannot at prefent advife the fending any more troops from hence :—on the contrary, the
general officers now here, whom I thought it my duty to
confult, think it abfolutely neceffary to increafe the army
at this place with at leaft ten thoufand men, efpecially
when it is confidered, that, from this place only, the army
in Canada muft draw its fupplies of ammunition, provifions,
and, moft probably, of men ; and that all reinforcements
can be fent from hence much eafier than from any other
place.   By the inclofed return, you will fee the ftate of
the army here, and that the number of effective men is far
fhort of what the Congrefs muft have expected.

I have found it neceffary to order colonel Dayton's
regiment from New-Jerfey to march as one of the fix to
Canada : wherefore I muft recommend it to Congrefs to
order two companies of one of the regiments ftill in Pennfylvania to march to Cape-May, which can be done much
fooner : for, had this deftination of that regiment not tak-
en place, it would have been very inconvenient to have detached two companies from it to that place ; as the march
would (according to lord Stirling's and other accounts)
have been at leaft two hundred miles from Amboy, and
they muft have paffed within twenty miles of Philadelphia,

there

there being no practicable road along the sea-coast of New-Jersey for their baggage to have passed.

Dr. Potts, who is bearer hereof, was, I understand, appointed director of the hospital for these middle colonies : but the army being removed, with the general hospital, from the eastward, does in course supersede him.   He is inclined to go to Canada, where he may be very useful, if a person is not already appointed for that department.   I would humbly beg leave to ask the Congress whether, in all these appointments, it would not be best to have but one chief, to whom all the others should be subordinate.

I have the honour to be, &c.   G. W.

———

SIR,   *New-York, April* 30, 1776.

I MEAN, through you, to do myself the honour of laying before Congress a copy of an address transmitted them some time ago by the assembly of Rhode-Island, which governor Cooke favoured me with in the month of January, at the same time requesting me to interest myself in procuring a body of forces on the continental establishment, for the defence of that colony.   I doubt not but the address and the subject of it have had the attention and consideration of Congress before now.   But if they have not decided upon the matter, I would beg leave to mention that I have made inquiry into the situation and condition of the colony, and find it to be as stated in the address ; and, with all deference to the opinion of Congress, conceive it highly necessary and expedient that they should adopt some measures for relieving their distress, and granting the aid prayed for.   The importance of it in the chain of the union,—its extensive sea-coast, affording harbours for our shipping and vessels, at the same time exposing and subjecting the inhabitants to the ravages and depredations of our enemies,—the zeal and attachment which it has shewn, and which still actuates it, towards the common cause,—their incapacity to pay a sufficient number of men for its defence, should they be able to furnish them after so many engaged in other sevices ;—these, and many other reasons which are too obvious to be mentioned, plead powerfully.

erfully for the notice and attention of Congress, and seem to me to claim their support.

Having thus stated the matter to Congress for their consideration, agreeable to my promise to governor Cooke when I had the honour of seeing him on my way here,—I shall leave it with them, not doubting but they will duly weigh its importance, and give such assistance as they may think reasonable and just. What they chiefly wish for is that the troops they have raised may be taken into continental pay, and commanding officers appointed by Congress.

I have the honour to be, &c.   G. W.

———

SIR,   *New-York, May 5, 1776.*

I AM honoured with your favour of the thirtieth ultimo, and observe what Congress have done respecting the settlement of the paymaster's accounts. This seems expedient, as he is out of office, and, I am certain, will be attended with but little if any difficulty; nothing more being necessary, than to compare the warrants with his debts, and the receipts he has given, with his credits. I wish every other settlement as easy, and that a committee was appointed to examine and audit the accounts upon which the warrants are founded, particularly those of the quarter-master and commissary generals. They are long and of high amount, consisting of a variety of charges,—of course more intricate, and will require time and an extraordinary degree of attention to adjust and liquidate in a proper manner.— Upon this subject, I did myself the honour to write you a considerable time ago.

Having had several complaints from the officers in the eastern regiments who have been and are engaged in recruiting, about the expense attending it, and for which they have never yet been allowed any thing, though the officers in these governments have, as I am informed,—I shall be glad to know whether the allowance of ten shillings, granted to the officers for every man enlisted, by the resolve of Congress in [*January*] is general and indiscriminate, or confined to the middle districts. If general, must I have

retrospect

retrofpect to the time of the refolve, and pay for the fervices fince, or only for future enliftments ?

In a letter I wrote to Congrefs the twenty-fifth of December, I inclofed one I had received from Jacob Baily,
efquire, about opening a road from Newbury to Canada.
I have received another of the fifteenth ultimo : and, from
his account and the intelligence I have from others upon
inquiry, I have no doubt of the practicability of the meafure ; and am well informed that the diftance will be confiderably fhortened, infomuch that our people going from
any part of the New-England governments eaftward of
Connecticut-river, to Canada, or returning from thence
home, will perform their march in five or fix days lefs
time than by coming or going any way now ufed. Add
to this, that the road may be fo conducted (as it is faid)
as to go to the river Miffifque, from whence the water-
carriage to St. John's is good, except forty odd miles,—
or be carried fo far to the northward, as to keep clear of
the Lakes altogether, and afford an eafy pafs into Canada
at all feafons. The advantage refulting from this route
being fo great and important, I have advanced colonel Bailey two hundred and fifty pounds to begin with, and directed him to execute his plan. No doubt it will require
a confiderable advance to accomplifh it : but that will
be foon funk. The expenfe faved, by taking off fix day's
pay and provifions from the foldiers returning to the eaftern governments at the expiration of this campaign,
will be almoft if not more than equal to the charge incurred in opening it. If not,—as in all probability there
will be often a neceffity for fending detachments of our
troops to Canada from thofe governments, and for others
to return, it will foon be repaid.

By a letter from general Schuyler, of the twenty-feventh
ultimo, I find general Thompfon and his brigade were at
Albany ;—general Sullivan with the laft (except three or
four companies of colonel Wayne's regiment, not yet come)
is embarked and gone, and probably will be foon there. I
am apprehenfive, from general Schuyler's account, that they
will not proceed with the wifhed-for expedition, owing to
a difficulty in getting teams and provender for cattle neceffary to move their baggage, and a fcarcity of batteaux at

the Lakes for so large a number, though he is taking the utmost pains to procure them.   Should they be stopped for any time, it will be exceedingly unfortunate, as their going from hence has weakened us here much, and our army in Canada will not be strengthened.

I have sent with the last brigade sixty barrels of powder, and other stores and intrenching tools, a supply being asked for ; also the chain for a boom at the narrows of Richelieu, and the three boxes of money brought by Mr. Hanson ; and have wrote to general Schuyler to have the boom fixed as soon as possible.   The commissary too has forwarded about eight hundred barrels of pork, and is in expectation of a further quantity from Connecticut, which will go on without stopping here.

As the magazine from whence the northern and eastern armies will occasionally receive supplies of powder will probably be here, and our stock is low and inconsiderable, being much reduced by the sixty barrels sent to Canada, I shall be glad to have a quantity immediately forwarded. Our stores should be great : for if the enemy make an attack upon the town, or attempt to go up the North-river, the expenditure will be very considerable.   Money too is much wanted :—the regiments that are paid have only received to the first of April, except those of Pennsylvania and Jersey which are gone to Canada : they are paid to the last of April.   By a letter from general Ward, I find his chest is just exhausted ; the money which was left with him for the payment of the five regiments at Boston and Beverly being almost expended by large draughts in favour of the commissary and quarter-master, and in fitting out the armed vessels.

I would here ask a question, to wit, whether, as Mr. Warren's commission is superseded by Mr. Palfrey's appointment, it will not be necessary to fix upon some person to pay the troops there : or are the payments to go through his hands ?—He does not incline to do any thing in the affair without the direction of Congress.

I have inclosed you a return of the last brigade detached, and also of the forces remaining here.   And as it is a matter of much importance to know the whole of our strength from time to time, and to see it at one view, for regulating our movements with propriety, I wish it were a direction from Congress to the commanding officers in the different districts to make monthly returns to the commander-in-chief of the continental army, of the state of the troops in their departments, and also of the military stores. Such direction will probably make them more attentive than they otherwise would be. I could not get a return of the army in Canada all last year.

I beg leave to lay before Congress a copy of the proceedings of a court-martial upon lieutenant * * * *, of the second regiment, and of his defence—which I should not have troubled them with, had I not conceived the court's sentence, upon the facts stated in the proceedings, of a singular nature, to be by no means adequate to the enormity of his offence, and to be of exceeding dangerous and pernicious tendency. Upon these principles I thought it my duty to transmit the proceedings to them, in order that they may form such a judgment upon the facts stated, as they may conceive right and just, and advancive of the public good. At the same time I would mention to Congress that I think it of material consequence that they should pass a resolve, cutting off the right of succession in the military line from one rank to another, which is claimed by many upon the happening of vacancies—(upon which principle this offence seems to have originated in a great measure, and the extraordinary judgment in this instance to be founded)—declaring that no succession or promotion can take place upon any vacancy, without a continental commission giving and authorising it. It is of much consequence to check and entirely suppress this opinion and claim, which is becoming too prevalent, and has an obvious tendency to introduce mutiny and disorder ;—or, if they conceive the claim good, and that it should take place, that they will declare it so, that the point may be settled and known in future.

I have the honour to be, &c.   G. W.

                       New-York, May 5, 1776.
I HAVE so often and so fully communicated my want of arms to Congress, that I should not have given
                                        them

them the trouble of receiving another letter upon this fubject at this time, but for the particular application of colonel Wayne, of Pennfylvania, who has pointed out a method by which he thinks they may be obtained.

In the hands of the committee of fafety at Philadelphia, there are, according to colonel Wayne's account, not lefs than two or three thoufand ftand of arms for provincial ufe. From hence he thinks a number might be borrowed by Congrefs, provided they are replaced with continental arms as they are brought into the magazine in that city. At a crifis fo important as this, fuch a loan might be attended with the moft fignal advantages—while the defencelefs ftate of the regiments, if no relief can be had, may be productive of fatal confequences.

To give Congrefs fome idea of our fituation with refpect to arms—(and juftice to my own character requires that it fhould be known to them, although the world at large will form their opinion of our ftrength from numbers, without attending to circumftances)—it may not be amifs to inclofe a copy of a return which I received a few days ago from the forts in the Highlands, and add, that, by a report from colonel Ritzema's regiment, of the twenty-ninth ultimo, there appeared to be only ninety-feven firelocks and feven bayonets belonging thereto; and that all the regiments from the eaftward are deficient from twenty to fifty of the former. Four of thofe companies at the fortifications in the Highlands belong to colonel Clinton's regiment: but in what condition the refidue are on account of arms, and how colonel Wynkoop's men are provided, I cannot undertake to fay, but am told, moft miferably ; as colonel Dayton's of New-Jerfey and colonel Wayne's of Pennfylvania alfo are. This, Sir, is a true though melancholy defcription of our fituation. The propriety therefore of keeping arms in ftore when men in actual pay are in want of them, and who (it is to be prefumed) will, as they ought, bear the heat and burden of the day, is fubmitted with all due deference to the fuperior judgment of others.

I cannot, by all the inquiries I have been able to make, learn what number of arms have been taken from the tories, where they lie, or how they are to be got at. The
committee

committee of safety for this colony have assured me that no exertions of theirs shall be wanting to procure arms: but our sufferings in the mean while may prove fatal, as men without are in a manner useless. I have therefore thoughts of employing an agent whose sole business it shall be to ride through the middle and interior parts of these governments, for the purpose of buying up such arms as the inhabitants may incline to sell, and are fit for use.

The designs of the enemy are too much behind the curtain for me to form any accurate opinion of their plan of operations for the summer's campaign. We are left to wander therefore in the field of conjecture: and as no place (all its consequences considered) seemed of more importance in the execution of their grand plan, than possessing themselves of Hudson's river, I thought it adviseable to remove with the continental army to this city so soon as the king's troops evacuated Boston. But if Congress, from their knowledge, information, or belief, think it best for the general good of the service that I should go to the northward or elsewhere, they are convinced, I hope, that they have nothing more to do than signify their commands.

With the greatest respect, I have the honour to be, &c.
G. W.

———

                                  New-York, May 7, 1776.

AT a quarter after seven this evening, I received by express a letter from Thomas Cushing, esquire, chairman of a committee of the honourable general court, covering one to them from the committee of Salem; copies of which I do myself the honour to lay before Congress, that they may judge of the intelligence contained therein, and direct such measures to be taken upon the occasion as they may think proper and necessary.

I would observe, that supposing captain Lee's account to be true in part, I think there must be a mistake either in the number of troops or the transport ships. If there are no more ships than what are mentioned, it is certain there cannot be so many troops. Of this, however, Con-

grefs

grefs can judge as well as myfelf; and I fubmit to them, whether, upon the whole of the circumftances, and the uncertainty of their deftination (if they were feen at all) they choofe that any forces fhall be detached from hence, as they will fee, from the returns tranfmitted yefterday, that the number of men now here is but fmall and inconfiderable, and, (what is to be regretted) no fmall part of thefe without arms. Perhaps, by dividing and fubdividing our force too much, we fhall have no one poft fufficiently guarded.

I fhall wait their direction; and, whatever their order is, fhall comply with it as foon as poffible.

I have the honour to be, &c.   G. W.

P. S. I have by the fame exprefs a letter from general Ward, containing a fimilar account to that from the Salem committee, and by way of captain Lee.

Should the commiffioners arrive that are mentioned, how are they to be received and treated?—I wifh the direction of Congrefs upon the fubject, by return of the bearer.

SIR,   *New-York, May* 11, 1776.

I AM now to acknowledge the receipt of your favours of the fourth and feventh inftant with their feveral inclofures, and am exceedingly glad, that before the refolution refpecting lieutenant-colonel Ogden came to hand, I had ordered him to join his regiment, and had quelled a difagreeable fpirit both of mutiny and defertion, which had taken place and feemed to be rifing to a great degree in confequence of it. In order to effect it, I had the regiment paraded, and ordered two more at the fame time under arms, convinced them of their error and ill conduct, and obtained a promife for their good behaviour in future. To fuch of the men as had abfconded I gave pardons, on their affurances to return to their duty again.

In my letter of the fifth inftant which I had the honour of addreffing you, I mentioned to Congrefs the refractory and mutinous conduct of lieutenant * * * *, of regiment, and laid before the of a court-martial upon him, and of his defence, with a view that such measures might be adopted as they should think adequate to his crime. I would now beg leave to inform them, that, since then, he has appeared sensible of his misconduct; and having made a written acknowledgment of his offence, and begged pardon for it, (as by the inclosed copy will appear) I thought it best to release him from his confinement, and have ordered him to join his regiment; which I hope will meet their approbation, and render any determination, as to him, unnecessary;—observing at the same time that I have endeavoured, and, I flatter myself, not ineffectually, to support their authority, and a due subordination in the army. I have found it of importance and highly expedient to yield many points in fact, without seeming to have done it—and this, to avoid bringing on a too frequent discussion of matters, which, in a political view, ought to be kept a little behind the curtain, and not be made too much the subjects of disquisition. Time only can eradicate and overcome customs and prejudices of long standing: they must be got the better of, by slow and gradual advances.

I would here take occasion to suggest to Congress (not wishing or meaning of myself to assume the smallest degree of power in any instance) the propriety and necessity of having their sentiments respecting the filling up the vacancies and issuing commissions to officers, especially to those under the rank of field officers. Had I literally complied with the directions given upon this subject when I first engaged in the service, and which I conceived to be superseded by a subsequent resolve for forming the army upon the present establishment, I must have employed one clerk for no other business than issuing warrants of appointment, and giving information to Congress for their confirmation or refusal. It being evident from the necessity of the thing, that there will be frequent changes and vacancies in office, from death and a variety of other causes, I now submit it to them, and pray their direction whether I am to pursue that mode and all the ceremonies attending it, or to be at liberty to fill up and grant commissions at once to such as may be fit and proper persons to succeed. * * *

Before

Before I have done, with the utmoſt deference and re-
ſpeſt I would beg leave to remind Congreſs of my former
letters and applications reſpecting the appointment of proper perſons to ſuperintend and take direction of ſuch priſoners as have already fallen and will fall into our hands
in the courſe of the war—being fully convinced, that, if
there were perſons appointed who would take the whole
management of them under their care, the continent would
ſave a conſiderable ſum of money by it, and the priſoners
be better treated and provided with real neceſſaries than
they now are ;—and ſhall take the liberty to add that it
appears to me a matter of much importance, and worthy
of conſideration, that particular and proper places of ſecu-
rity ſhould be fixed on and eſtabliſhed in the interior parts
of the different governments for their reception.

Such eſtabliſhments are agreeable to the practice and
uſage of the Engliſh and other nations, and are founded on
principles of neceſſity and public utility.   The advantages
which will ariſe from them are obvious and many :—I ſhall
only mention two or three.   They will tend much to
prevent eſcapes, (which are difficult to effect when the
public is once advertiſed that the priſoners are reſtrained
to a few ſtated and well-known places, and not permitted
to go from thence,) and the more ingenious among them
from diſſeminating and ſpreading their artful and pernicious intrigues and opinions throughout the country,
which would influence the weaker and wavering part of
mankind, and meet with but too favourable a hearing.
Further, it will be leſs in their power to join and aſſiſt
our enemies in caſes of invaſion, and will give us an opportunity always to know, from the returns of thoſe appointed to ſuperintend them, what number we have in poſſeſſion, the force ſufficient to check and ſuppreſs their hoſtile
views in times of emergency, and the expenſes neceſſary
for their maintenance and ſupport.   Many other reaſons
might be adduced to prove the neceſſity and expediency
of the meaſure :—I ſhall only ſubjoin one more, and then
have done on the ſubject,—which is, that many of the
towns where priſoners have been already ſent, not having
convenience for or the means of keeping them, complain
they are burdenſome ; and have become careleſs, inat-
tentive,

tentive, and altogether indifferent whether they escape or not ; and those of them that are restricted to a closer confinement (the limits of jail) are neglected, and not treated with that care and regard which Congress wish.

I have not received further intelligence of the German troops since my letter of the seventh instant, covering Mr. Cushing's dispatches. But, lest the account of their coming should be true, may it not be adviseable and good policy to raise some companies of our Germans to send among them when they arrive, for exciting a spirit of disaffection and desertion ?—If a few sensible and trusty fellows could get with them, I should think they would have great weight and influence with the common soldiery, who certainly have no enmity towards us, having received no injury nor cause of quafrel from us. The measure having occurred, and appearing to me expedient, I thought it prudent to mention it for the consideration of Congress.

Having received a letter from general Ward, advising that Congress have accepted his resignation, and praying to be relieved,—and it being necessary that a general officer should be sent to take the command of the troops at Boston, especially if the army should arrive which is talked of, and which some consider as a probable event,—I must beg leave to recommend to Congress the appointment of some brigadier-generals, not having more here (nor so many at this time) than are essential to the government and conducting the forces and the works that are carrying on. Generals Sullivan and Thompson being ordered to Canada, I cannot spare one more general officer from hence without injuring the service greatly, and leaving the army here without a sufficient number.

Having frequent applications from the committee of safety and others, about an exchange of prisoners, and not having authority to pursue any other mode in this instance, than that marked out by a resolve of Congress some considerable time ago, I hope they will pardon me when I wish them to take under consideration such parts of my letter of the twenty-second ultimo as relate to this subject ; and for their determination upon it. I shall then have it in my power to give explicit and satisfactory answers to those who shall apply.

I am, Sir, &c.

G. W.
New-York,

SIR,   *New-York, May* 15, 1776.

SINCE my laſt of the eleventh inſtant which I had the honour to addreſs you, nothing of moment or importance has occurred ; and the principal deſign of this is to communicate to Congreſs the intelligence I received laſt night from general Schuyler by a letter of the tenth, reſpecting the progreſs of our troops in getting towards Canada, not doubting of their impatience and anxiety to hear of it and of every thing relating to the expedition.   For their more particular information and ſatisfaction, I have done myſelf the pleaſure to extract the ſubſtance of his letter on this head, which is as follows :—" that general Thompſon, with the laſt of his brigade, on the morning of Tueſday ſe'nnight, embarked at Fort-George ; and, in the evening of the next day, general Sullivan arrived at Albany ; that he had ordered an additional number of carpenters to aſſiſt in building boats ; who, finiſhing eight every day, would have a hundred and ten complete by the twenty-firſt, before which he was fearful the laſt of general Sullivan's brigade could not embark ;—that they would carry thirty men each, beſides the baggage, ammution, and intrenching tools." * * *

He alſo informs, " that the ſixty barrels of powder had arrived, and would be forwarded that day ;—that the firſt regiment of general Sullivan's brigade marched that morning ; and that the intrenching tools and about ſix hundred barrels of pork were alſo gone on ;—that he cannot poſſibly ſend more than half of the three hundred thouſand dollars into Canada, (being greatly in debt on the public account, and the creditors exceedingly clamorous and importunate for payment) which ſum he hopes will be ſufficient till the Canadians agree to take our paper currency, to which they are much averſe, and of which he is exceedingly doubtful ;—that he had got the chain, and would forward it that day to general Arnold, with orders to fix it at the rapids of Richelieu."   He adds " that he had reviewed general Sullivan's brigade in preſence of about two hundred and ſixty Indians, who were greatly pleaſed with the order and regularity of the troops, and ſurpriſed at the number, which, the tories had induſtriouſ-

ly

ly propagated, confifted only of three companies, and that they were kept always walking the ftreets, to induce them to believe their number was much greater than it really was."

I have inclofed a copy of general Schuyler's inftructions to James Price, efquire, deputy commiffary-general, for the regulation of his conduct in that department, which I received laft night, and which general Schuyler requefted me to forward you. I alfo beg leave to lay before Congrefs a copy of a letter from Samuel Stringer, director of one of the hofpitals, purporting an application for an increafe of furgeons'-mates, &c. an eftimate of which is alfo inclofed; and fubmit it to them, what number muft be fent from hence or got elfewhere. It is highly probable that many more will be wanted in Canada than are already there, on account of the late augmentation of the army: but I thought it moft advifeable to make his requifition known to Congrefs, and to take their order and direction upon it. As to the medicines, I fhall fpeak to Dr. Morgan (not yet arrived) as foon as he comes, and order him to forward fuch as may be neceffary and can be poffibly fpared.

I have the honour to be, &c.   G. W.

S I R,   *New-York, May* 17, 1776.

I THIS moment received by exprefs from general Schuyler an account of the melancholy profpect and reverfe of our affairs in Canada: and prefuming that the letters which accompany this will give Congrefs full information upon the fubject, I fhall only add that general Schuyler, in purfuance of orders from the honourable commiffioners, has directed brigadier-general Sullivan to halt his brigade; as a further reinforcement (on account of the fcarcity of provifions) would not relieve, but contribute greatly to diftrefs our troops already in Canada. Before he received thefe orders, all the brigade, except Dayton's and Wayne's regiments, had left Albany: but I fuppofe he will be able to ftop their march.

By

By my letter of the fifteenth, Congrefs will perceive the quantity of pork already gone from hence : and the commiffary has affured me that he will forward a further fupply as foon as it can be poffibly collected. I had alfo directed five tons of lead to be fent to general Schuyler for the Canada expedition, before I received this unfortunate account ; which was as much as could be fpared for the prefent (our ftock being inconfiderable in proportion to the demand we may reafonably expect for it ;) and fhall do every thing in my power to relieve our affairs from their prefent diftreffed and melancholy fituation in that quarter, which occurs to me and appears neceffary.

I am alfo to acknowledge the receipt of your favours of the tenth and thirteenth inftant, with their feveral inclofures. The money, accompanying the latter, came to the paymafter's hands fafe.

I have the honour to be, &c.　　　　G. W.

SIR,　　　　　　　　　　*New-York, May* 18, 1776.

I DO myfelf the honour to tranfmit to you the inclofed letters and papers I received this morning in the ftate they now are, which contain fundry matters of intelligence of the moft interefting nature. As the confideration of them may lead to important confequences and the adoption of feveral meafures in the military line, I have thought it advifeable for general Gates to attend Congrefs—(he will follow to-morrow, and fatisfy, and explain to them fome points they may wifh to be informed of in the courfe of their deliberations)—not having an opportunity at this time to fubmit my thoughts to them upon thefe interefting accounts.

I have the honour to be, &c.　　　　G. W.

SIR,　　　　　　　　　　*New-York, May* 19, 1776.

THIS will be delivered you by general Gates who fets out to-day for Congrefs, agreeable to my letter of yefterday.

yefterday.   I have committed to him the heads of fundry matters to lay before Congrefs for their confideration, which, from the interefting intelligence contained in my laft, appear to me of the utmoft importance, and to demand their moft early and ferious attention.

Senfible that I have omitted to fet down many things neceffary, and which probably, when deliberating, they will wifh to be acquainted with,—and not conceiving myfelf at liberty to depart from my poft (though to attend them) without their previous approbation,—I have requefted general Gates to fubjoin fuch hints of his own, as he may apprehend material.   His military experience and intimate acquaintance with the fituation of our affairs will enable him to give Congrefs the fulleft fatisfaction about the meafures neceffary to be adopted at this alarming crifis ; and, with his zeal and attachment to the caufe of America, have a claim to their notice and favours.

When Congrefs fhall have come to a determination on the fubject of this letter, and fuch parts of my former letters as have not been determined on, you will be pleafed to honour me with the refult.

I am, Sir, &c.   G. W.

<hr>

S I R,   *New-York, May* 20, 1776.

YOUR favour of the fixteenth, with feveral refolutions of Congrefs therein inclofed, I had not the honour to receive till laft night.   Before the receipt, I did not think myfelf at liberty to wait on Congrefs, although I wifhed to do it ; and therefore the more readily confented to general Gates's attendance, as I knew there were many matters which could be better explained in a perfonal interview than in whole volumes of letters.   He accordingly fet out for Philadelphia yefterday morning, and muft have been too far advanced on his journey (as he propofed expedition) to be overtaken.

I fhall, if I can fettle fome matters which are in agitation with the provincial Congrefs here, follow to-morrow or next day ; and therefore, with every fentiment of regard, attachment, and gratitude to Congrefs for their kind atten-

tion

tion to the means which they think may be conducive to my health, and with particular· thanks to you for the politenefs of your invitation to your houfe, conclude, dear Sir, your moft obedient, &c.   G. W.

S I R,   *Philadelphia, June* 3, 1776.

I HAVE perufed the petition preferred by the independent corps of Bofton, and beg leave, through you, to inform Congrefs that the five regiments there are extremely deficient in arms, as are many other regiments in continental pay ; and fubmit it to their confideration, whether any part of the arms lately taken, under thefe circumftances, fhould be delivered to the gentlemen applying for them ; determining at the fame time, that whatever decifion they come to will be agreeable to me, and be literally complied with, by, Sir, your moft obedient, &c.   G. W.

S I R,   *New-York, June* 7, 1776.

I DO myfelf the honour to inform Congrefs that I arrived here vefterday afternoon about one o'clock, and found all in a ftate of peace and quiet. I had not time to view the works carrying on, and thofe ordered to be begun when I went away ; but have reafon to believe, from the report of·fuch of the general and other officers as I had the pleafure to fee, that they have been profecuted and forwarded with all poffible diligence and difpatch.

I am much concerned for the fituation of our affairs in Canada, and am fearful, ere this, it is much worfe than was firft reported at Philadelphia. The intelligence from thence, in a letter from captain Wilkinfon of the fecond regiment, to general Greene, is truly alarming. It not only confirms the account of colonel Biddle and major Sherburne's defeat, but feems to forebode general Arnold's, with the lofs of Montréal. I have inclofed a copy of the letter, which will but too well fhew that there is foundation for my apprehenfions.

On Wednesday evening I received an express from general Schuyler, with sundry papers respecting Sir John Johnston, which I have not time to copy, as the post is just going off, but will do myself the honour of transmitting you as soon as I possibly can.

Before I left Philadelphia, I employed a person to superintend the building of the gondolas which Congress had resolved on for this place. He is arrived, and all things seem to be in a proper channel for facilitating the work: but when they are done, we shall be in much want of guns, having never received any of those taken by commodore Hopkins.

Be pleased to mention me to Congress with the utmost respect; and I am, Sir, with every sentiment of regard and esteem, your and their most obedient servant,   G. W.

P. S. I this minute received your favour of the fifth instant. I am in need of commissions, and beg Congress to point out precisely the line I am to pursue in filling them up. This I mentioned in my letter of the eleventh ultimo. I am much pleased at the fortunate captures, and the generous conduct of the owners and masters, for the tender of the money to Congress.

———

S I R,   *June* 8, 1776.

IN my letter of yesterday which I had the honour of addressing you, and which was designed to have gone by post, but was prevented by his departure before the usual time, I mentioned my having received by express a letter and sundry papers from general Schuyler, respecting Sir John Johnston, copies of which I herewith transmit you for your inspection and perusal. They will shew you what measures were planned and attempted for apprehending him, and securing the Scotch Highlanders in Tryon county.

Having heard that the troops at Boston are extremely uneasy and almost mutinous for want of pay, (several months being now due) I must take the liberty to repeat a question contained in my letter of the fifth ultimo—" What mode is to be pursued respecting it ? whether is money to be sent from hence by the pay-master-general, or some person subordinate

ordinate to him to be appointed there for that purpofe ?" I expected fome direction would have been given in this inftance, long ere this, from what was contained in yours accompanying (or about the time of) the laft remittance.   I prefume it has been omitted by reafon of the multiplicity of important bufinefs before Congrefs.

In perufing the feveral refolves you honoured me with when at Philadelphia and fince my return, 1 find one allowing a chief engineer for the army in a feparate department. The fervice requiring many of them, I wifh Congrefs, if they know any perfons fkilled in this bufinefs, would appoint them.   General Schuyler has frequently applied, and fuggefted the neceffity of having fome in Canada.   I myfelf know of none.

I alfo find there is a refolve of the third of June for taking Indians into the fervice, which, if literally conftrued, confines them to that in Canada.   Is that the meaning of Congrefs, or that the commander in chief may order their fervice to any place he may think neceffary ?

In refpect to the eftablifhing expreffes between the feveral continental pofts,—who is to do it ? the refolve does not fay.   Is it expected by Congrefs that I fhould ? Whoever the work is affigned to, I think, fhould execute it with the utmoft difpatch.   The late imperfect and contradictory accounts refpecting our defeat at the Cedars, ftrongly point out the neceffity there is for it.   No intelligence is yet come from any officer in command there, (and moft probably for want of a proper channel to convey it) though this misfortune happened fo long ago.

When I had the honour of being in Congrefs, if I miftake not, I heard a refolve read, or was told of one, allowing the New-York troops the fame pay as others in the continental fervice.   This, if any fuch, I do not find ; and if there is not fuch a one, I fhall be under fome embarraffment, how to pay the militia to be provided by this province.   The refolve providing them fays they are to be paid, while in fervice, as other troops are.   But if thofe enlifted heretofore in this province are to receive according to the firft eftablifhment, it is a matter of doubt what the militia are to have.

Before

Before this comes to hand, a hand-bill, containing an account of a victory gained by general Arnold over the party that had defeated colonel Biddle and major Sherburne, will moſt probably have reached you. I have inquired into the authenticity of this fortunate report, and have found there is no dependence to be put in it; nor do I believe it deſerving of the leaſt credit. I ſhall be happy not to hear the reverſe.

I have the honour to be, &c.   G. W.

P. S. If Congreſs have come to any reſolution about an allowance to induce men to re-enliſt, you will pleaſe to favour me with it, as the time the rifle regiment is engaged for is juſt expired.

As the militia will be coming in, and they will be in much need of covering, pleaſe to have all the tents, and cloth proper for making them that can be procured, forwarded as ſoon as poſſible.

SIR,   *New-York, June* 9, 1776.

I WAS honoured yeſterday with your favour of the ſeventh, with its incloſures. When doctor Potts arrives, I ſhall order him to Canada or Lake-George, as may appear moſt proper. It is certainly neceſſary that he or doctor Stringer ſhould go to the former. The reſolve reſpecting general Wooſter's recal I will immediately tranſmit him, with directions to repair hither without delay.

The ſituation of our affairs in Canada, as reported by the honourable commiſſioners, is truly alarming; and I am ſorry that my opinion of the ill conſequences reſulting from the ſhort enliſtment of the army ſhould be but too well confirmed by the experience they have had of the want of diſcipline and order in our ſoldiery there. This induces me again to wiſh Congreſs to determine on a liberal allowance to engage the troops already in ſervice to re-enliſt for a longer period, or during the continuance of the war; nor can I forbear expreſſing my opinion of the propriety of keeping the military cheſt always ſupplied with money, as evils of the moſt intereſting nature are often produced for want of a regular payment of troops. The neglect makes them impatient and uneaſy.

I am

I am much surprised at the scarcity of provisions there, particularly of flour ; as, from several accounts I had received from thence, I was led to expect that confiderable supplies of that article could be procured there. That our misfortunes may not become greater, I have wrote to the commiffary to forward more provisions, in addition to thofe already fent.

An adjutant and quarter-mafter-general are indifpenfably neceffary, with affiftants. The money faved to the continent by their non-appointment will be but fmall and trifling, when put in competition with the lofs for want of them. Colonel Fleming, who acted in the former capacity, under general Montgomery, is now here : but his indifpofition is fuch as to render him unfit, at this time, for the poft :— it is an important one, and requires vigour and activity to difcharge the duties of it. He will be of much fervice to colonel Reed, the bufinefs of whofe office will increafe confiderably by the augmentation of the army.

It will be neceffary too, that the commiffaries in Canada, and the deputy quarter-mafter-generals, fhould have feveral affiftants and clerks : nor do I think a precife number can be fixed on, as a variety of circumftances may and muft occur, to render the number, effential for doing the bufinefs in thofe departments, greater or lefs at different times. It will be better, I apprehend, to leave it indefinite, and with power to the commanding officer to allow fuch as may be wanted.

I am ftill in the dark, how the unfortunate affair ended at the Cedars, or on what terms the furrender was made, as the laft letter from the commiffioners has reference to a former, and mentions an agreement entered into, which I have not feen : but I know of it more than I could wifh.

I have received from Providence, in confequence of Mr. Morris's order, as chairman of the fecret committee of Congrefs, two hundred and thirty-four mufkets, in part of the two hundred and forty-four directed to be fent. The inclofed copy of a letter from Mr. Brown will account for the deficiency.

I fhall be much obliged by your ordering a quantity of lead and flints to be immediately forwarded : our demands for both are and will be very preffing. There are alfo want-

ed

ed some particular and necessary medicines to complete our hospital chests, of which I will get doctor Morgan to furnish Congress with a list, when he writes or waits on them about some other matters necessary to be fixed in his department.

As general Wooster, in all probability, will be here in a little time in compliance with the resolve of Congress and my order transmitted to him, I wish to know what I am to do with him when he comes.

General Schuyler, in his letter of the thirty-first ultimo, of which I transmitted you a copy yesterday, mentions that sundry persons had a design to seize him as a tory, and probably still have, and wishes Congress to give him some public mark of their approbation, if they are convinced of his zeal and attachment to the cause of his country. Whether he intended that I should communicate his desire to them, or not, I am not certain : but, supposing that he did, I must beg leave to request that you will lay the paragraph before them, that they may do, in the instance of his requisition, whatever they may judge necessary.

I have the honour to be, &c.   G. W.

P. S. If Congress have agreed to the report of the committee for allowing the Indians fifty pounds for every prisoner they shall take at Niagara, &c. it is material I should be informed of it.   This will be a favourable opportunity for them to embrace, to gain possession of Detroit and the other posts, whilst the enemy are engaged towards Montréal, &c.

SIR,   *New-York, June* 10, 1776.

SINCE I did myself the honour of writing to you yesterday, I have had the satisfaction of seeing, and for a few minutes conversing with Mr. Chase and Mr. Carroll, from Canada. Their account of our troops and the situation of affairs in that department cannot possibly surprise you more than it has done me. But I need not touch upon a subject which you will be so well informed of from the fountain-head ; nor should I have given you the trouble of a letter by this day's post, but for the distraction
                                                    which

which feems to prevail in the commiffary's department,
as well as others in that quarter,—the neceffity of having
it under one general direction,—and the diffatisfaction of
colonel Trumbull at the allowance made him by Congrefs
as an equivalent for his trouble. With refpect to this
particular matter, I can only fay that I think he is a man
well [*calculated*] for the bufinefs, and that, where a fhilling is faved in the pay, a pound may be loft by mifman-
agement in the office ; and that his refignation at this time
(I mean this campaign) may poffibly be attended with fatal confequences. I therefore humbly fubmit to Congrefs
the propriety of handfomely rewarding thofe gentlemen
who hold fuch very important, troublefome, and hazard-
ous offices, as commiffary and quarter-mafter.

In fpeaking to the former about the fupplies neceffary
for the troops to be raifed, he informed me that the quantity of falt provifions which was fhipping from hence might
render his attempts to do it precarious ; in confequence of
which, I defired him to lay the matter before the convention of this colony, which he will do this day, but in
the mean while defired Congrefs might be informed of the
matter, which I cannot better do than in his own words
inclofed, and fubmit the confideration of it to the wifdom
of that honourable body.

To Congrefs I alfo fubmit the propriety of keeping the
two continental battalions (under the command of colonels
Shee and M'Gaw) at Philadelphia, when there is the
greateft probability of a fpeedy attack upon this place from
the king's troops. The encouragements given by governor Tryon to the difaffected, which are circulated, no one
can well tell how,—the movements of thefe kind of people, which are more eafy to perceive than defcribe,—the
confident report, which is faid to have come immediately
from governor Tryon, and brought by a frigate from Halifax, that the troops at that place were embarking for
this,—added to a thoufand incidental circumftances, trivial
in themfelves, but ftrong from comparifon,—leave not a
doubt upon my mind but that troops are hourly expected
at the Hook.

I had no doubt when I left this city for Philadelphia,
but that fome meafures would have been taken to fecure
the

the fufpected and dangerous perfons of this government before now, and left orders for the military to give every aid to the civil power.   But the fubject is delicate, and nothing is done in it.   We may therefore have internal as well as external enemies to contend with.

I have the honour to be, &c.   —   G. W.

SIR,   *Head-Quarters, New-York, June 13, 1776.*

I HAVE the honour of tranfmitting to Congrefs a letter which came by exprefs laft night from general Schuyler, inclofing a copy of a letter to him from colonel Kirkland.   I have likewife inclofed the copy of one directed to general Putnam or the commanding officer at New-York.   The reprefentations contained in thefe letters have induced me, without waiting the determination of Congrefs, to direct general Schuyler immediately to commence a treaty with the Six Nations, and to engage them in our intereft, upon the beft terms he and his colleagues in commiffion can procure: and I truft the urgency of the occafion will juftify my proceeding to the Congrefs :— the neceffity for decifion and difpatch in all our meafures, in my opinion, becomes every day more and more apparent.

The exprefs, Mr. Bennet, was overtaken at Albany by general Schuyler, who had received intelligence at Fort-George that a confiderable body of Mohawk Indians were coming down the Mohawk river under the conduct of Sir John Johnfton.   The general's extreme hurry would not allow him to write: but it feems his intention is to collect at Albany a fufficient force to oppofe Sir John.   I have given him my opinion that colonel Dayton's regiment fhould be employed in that fervice, and to fecure the poft where Fort-Stanwix formerly ftood.

In confequence of an information that feveral merchants were exporting falt pork and beef from this place, I requefted the commiffary to make application to the provincial Congrefs for a reftraint to be laid on the exportation of thofe articles, as I apprehended, not only that the enemy might receive fupplies by the capture of

our

our veffels, but that our people might fhortly experience
a fcarcity. The provincial Congrefs have accordingly
made a refolution (a copy of which is inclofed), to ftop
the exportation for fourteen days. They expect Congrefs
will in the mean time frame fome general regulations on
this head. They are unwilling (they fay) to fubject their
conftituents to partial reftraints.

I once mentioned to Congrefs that I thought a war-
office extremely neceffary, and they feemed inclined to inftitute one for our army ; but the affair feems to have been
fince dropped. Give me leave again to infift on the utility and importance of fuch an eftablifhment. The more
I reflect upon the fubject, the more I am convinced of its
neceffity, and that affairs can never be properly conducted
without it.

It is with pleafure I receive the refolve inclofed in your
favour of the eleventh inftant. One confiderable ground
of diffatisfaction in the army is thereby removed.

I have employed perfons in building the gondolas and
rafts which the Congrefs thought neceffary for the defence
of this place ; and, in conjunction with the provincial
Congrefs, have determined to fink chevaux-de-frife, one
of which is already begun.

I am, with the utmoft refpect and efteem, &c.

G. W.

SIR,   *New-York, June* 14, 1776.

I HEREWITH tranfmit you copies of a letter
from general Schuyler and its feveral inclofures, which I
received fince I had the honour of addreffing you yefterday. From thefe you will learn that general Thomas
died the fecond inftant ; and the apprehenfions of our
frontier friends in this colony, that our favage foes are
meditating an attack againft them.

I muft beg leave to refer you to a paragraph in the copy
of general Schuyler's letter to general Putnam or the commanding officer here, inclofed in mine of the thirteenth,
where he requefts a fupply of cloathing to be fent for the
army in Canada. As there is but little or no probability of
getting

getting it here, I shall be glad to know whether there will be any chance of procuring it in Philadelphia; and, if it should be sent through the hands of the quarter-master here, to what account it is to be charged.

I was last evening favoured with yours of the eleventh instant, and hope the two battalions, which Congress have ordered from Philadelphia for the defence of this place, will come provided with arms. If they do not, they will be of no service, as there are more troops here already than are armed.

From general Schuyler's letter, he has in view the taking post where Fort-Stanwix formerly stood. I wrote him I thought it prudent, previous to that, to secure a post lower down, about the falls below the German-Flats, lest the savages should possess themselves of the country, and prevent supplies of men and provisions that may be necessary to send there in future. He says he is in want of cannon and ammunition; but has expressed himself so ambiguously, that I am at a loss to know whether he meant what he has said as an application or not,—this being the only intelligence on the subject, and the first mention of his want. I have desired him to explain the matter, and, in his future requisitions for necessaries, to be more certain and explicit as to quantity and quality. In the mean time I shall send him some intrenching tools, and inquire whether there are any cannon that can be spared from hence.

I have the honour to be, &c.   G. W.

SIR,   *New-York, June* 16, 1776.

I DO myself the honour to transmit to Congress a copy of a letter covering copies of other papers, which I received yesterday evening from general Sullivan. The intelligence communicated by him is pleasing and interesting, and such as must afford the greatest satisfaction, if the conduct the Canadians have discovered since his arrival among them is ingenuous and sincere.

General Sullivan mentions his having given commissions to some of the Canadians as a measure founded in necessity, and requests my approbation of it. But not considering

myself

myfelf empowered to fay any thing upon the fubject, it may not be improper for Congrefs to give him their opinion in this inftance.

I have alfo inclofed copies of general Schuyler's letters received at the fame time. They contain accounts refpecting the Indians, variant from what was reported by Mr. Kirkland, but amounting to the fame thing,—the probability of the favages attacking our frontiers.

By laft night's poft I had information of a capture made by our armed veffels, of one of the tranfports with a company of Highlanders on board, bound to Bofton. The inclofed extract from general Ward's letter to me will give you the intelligence more particularly. There are accounts in the city mentioning other valuable prizes: but as general Ward has faid nothing of them, I fear they want authenticity.

I beg leave to mention that a further fum of money will be wanted for our military cheft by the time it can be fent. The inclofed note from the pay-mafter-general fhews the neceffity for it; and, I may add, befides his eftimate of draughts to be made, there are the claims of the eaftern troops at Bofton for three or four months' pay, not included, and now due.

Colonel M'Gaw is arrived with part of his battalion; and by Wednefday evening the whole both of his and colonel Shee's will be here, as I am told.

As it is and may be of great importance to have a communication with the Jerfeys and Long-Ifland, I have had feveral flat-bottomed boats built for the purpofe, and have thoughts of getting more for Pofaic and Hackinfac rivers, where they may be equally neceffary for tranfporting our army or part of it occafionally, or fuccours coming to or going from it.

I have the honour to be, &c.   G. W.

SIR,*New-York, June* 17, 1776.

I BEG leave to inform Congrefs that general Woofter has repaired to head-quarters in obedience to their refolve tranfmitted him; and fhall be extremely glad if
they

they will give me such further directions about him as they may conceive necessary. He is desirous of seeing his family in Connecticut, as I am informed, having been a good while from it. I shall wait their instructions as to his future employment.

I am, Sir, with sentiments of much esteem, &c.

G. W.

SIR,   *New-York, June* 20, 1776.

I AM now to acknowledge the receipt of your favours of the fourteenth and eighteenth instant, and the interesting resolves contained in them, with which have been honoured. The several matters recommended to my attention shall be particularly regarded, and the directions of Congress and your requests complied with in every instance, as far as in my power.

The instituting a war-office is certainly an event of great importance, and, in all probability, will be recorded as such in the historic page. The benefits derived from it, I flatter myself, will be considerable, though the plan upon which it is first formed may not be entirely perfect. This, like other great works, in its first edition, may not be free from error :—time will discover its defects, and experience suggest the remedy, and such further improvements as may be necessary ; but it was right to give it a beginning, in my opinion.

The recommendation to the convention of New-York for restraining and punishing disaffected persons, I am hopeful, will be attended with salutary consequences ; and the prohibition against exporting provisions appears to have been a measure founded in sound policy, lest proper supplies should be wanted, wherewith to supply our armies.

I have transmitted general Schuyler the resolves about the Indians, and the others on which he is to act : and have requested his strict attention and exertions in order to their being carried into execution with all possible dispatch.

I note your request respecting Mr. Hancock. He shall have such directions as may be necessary for conducting

his

his office ; and I am happy he will have so early a remittance for paying the troops in his department.

The silver and paper money designed for Canada will be highly serviceable, and I hope will be the means of re-establishing our credit there in some degree with the Canadians, and also encourage our men too, who have complained in this instance. When it arrives, I will send it forward under a proper guard.

I have communicated to major-general Gates the resolve of Congress for him to repair to Canada, and directed him to view Point-au-fer, that a fortress may be erected if he shall judge necessary. He is preparing for his command, and in a few days will take his departure for it. I would fain hope his arrival there will give our affairs a complexion different from what they have worn for a long time past, and that many essential benefits will result from it.

The kind attention Congress have shewn to afford the commander-in-chief here every assistance, by resolving that recommendatory letters be written to the conventions of New-Jersey, New-York, and assembly of Connecticut, to authorize him to call in the militia in case of exigency, claims my thankful acknowledgments ; and, I trust, if carried into execution, will produce many advantages in case it may be expedient at any time to call in early reinforcements. The delays incident to the ordinary mode may frequently render their aid too late, and prove exceedingly injurious.

I this evening received intelligence of the nineteenth instant from captain Pond, of the armed sloop Schuyler, of his having taken, about fifty miles from this, on the south side of Long-Island, a ship and a sloop bound to Sandy-Hook. The ship, from Glasgow, with a company of the forty-second regiment, had been taken by one of commodore Hopkins's fleet, who took the soldiers out, and ordered her to Rhode-Island ; after which, she was retaken by the Cerberus, and put under the convoy of the sloop. As captain Pond informs me, there were five commissioned officers, two ladies, and four privates on board. They are not yet arrived at head-quarters. Inclosed is an invoice of what they have on board.

General Woofter having expreffed an inclination and wifh to wait on Congrefs, I have given him permiffion, not having any occafion for him here. He fet out this morning.

I have been up to view the grounds about Kingfbridge, and find them to admit of feveral places well calculated for defence ; and, efteeming it a pafs of the utmoft importance, have ordered works to be laid out, and fhall direct part of the two battalions from Pennfylvania to fet about the execution immediately, and will add to their number feveral of the militia when they come in, to expedite them with all poffible difpatch. Their confequence, as they will keep open the communication with the country, requires the moft fpeedy completion of them.

I have the honour to be, &c.   G. W.

SIR,   *New-York, June* 21, 1776.

I WAS this morning honoured with your favour of the nineteenth inftant, with fundry refolves of Congrefs, which came to hand after I had clofed mine of the twentieth. I fhall appoint a deputy mufter-mafter-general as foon as I can fix upon a proper perfon for the office, and direct him immediately to repair to Canada.

Mr. Bennet, the bearer of this, delivered me a letter to-day from general Schuyler, inclofing the proceedings of the commiffioners of Indian affairs at a meeting at Albany in confequence of the refolution of Congrefs (as they fay) which I tranfmitted, the feventh inftant, for engaging the Indians in our fervice. The gentlemen appear to me to have widely miftaken the views of Congrefs in this inftance, and to have formed a plan for engaging fuch Indians as were not in contemplation. I cannot account upon what principles they have gone, as a part of their proceedings fhews they are about to hold a conference with the Six Nations. I fuppofe they efteemed what they have done a neceffary meafure :—a copy of which I have the honour to inclofe you.

I fhall now beg leave to lay before Congrefs a propofition made to me by captain Leary of this city, in behalf

of

of a body of men who are defirous of being employed in
the continental fervice as a troop of horfe, and at the fame
time to offer my opinion that fuch a corps may be extremely ufeful in many refpects. In a march, they may
be of the utmoft fervice in reconnoitring the enemy and
gaining intelligence, and have it in their power to render
many important benefits. The terms on which they are
willing to engage are inclofed, which appear to me mod-
erate and reafonable. I am alfo informed that another
company might readily be made up, and moft probably
upon the fame terms. I would therefore fubmit the propriety and expediency of the meafure to the confideration
of Congrefs, and wifh their opinion whether it will be
agreeable to them that both or either of them fhould be
formed and incorporated in this army, in manner as has
been propofed by captain Leary, if it can be done.

I have the honour to be, &c. G. W.

SIR, *Head-Quarters, June* 21, 1776.

THIS will be delivered to you by the chevalier de
Kirmovan and monfieur de Vermonet. They are French
gentlemen juft arrived in this place, who have made application to me to be received into the continental fervice.
They bring letters to Dr. Franklin and fome other gentlemen of the Congrefs. I fuppofe it will better appear
from thofe letters, than from any information I can give,
whether it will be proper to employ them in the capacity
they are defirous of.

I am, Sir, with the greateft efteem, &c. G. W.

SIR, *New-York, June* 23, 1776.

I HEREWITH tranfmit you an extract of a letter
from general Ward which came to hand by laft night's
poft, containing the agreeable intelligence of their having
obliged the king's fhips to leave Nantafket-road, and of
two tranfports more being taken by our armed veffels,
with two hundred and ten Highland troops on board.

I fincerely

I sincerely wish the same success had attended our arms in another quarter—but it has not. In Canada, the situation of our affairs is truly alarming. The inclosed copies of generals Schuyler, Sullivan, and Arnold's letters will inform you that general Thompson has met with a repulse at Three-Rivers, and is now a prisoner in the hands of general Burgoyne, who (these accounts say) is arrived with a considerable army. Nor do they seem to promise an end of our misfortunes here :—it is greatly to be feared that the next advices from thence will be, that our shattered, divided, and broken army (as you will see by the return) have been obliged to abandon the country, and retreat, to avoid a greater calamity,—that of being cut off or becoming prisoners. I will have done upon the subject, and leave you to draw such conclusions as you conceive from the state of facts are most likely to result, only adding my apprehensions that one of the latter events,—either that they are cut off, or become prisoners,—has already happened, if they did not retreat while they had an opportunity. General Schuyler and general Arnold seem to think it extremely probable : and if it has taken place, it will not be easy to describe all the fatal consequences that may flow from it. At least our utmost exertions will be necessary, to prevent the advantages they have gained being turned to our greater misfortunes. General Gates will certainly set out to-morrow, and would have gone before now had he not expected to receive some particular instructions from Congress, which colonel Braxton said he imagined would be given, and transmitted here.

Inclosed is a copy of a letter from general Arnold, respecting some of the Indian tribes, to general Schuyler, and of a talk had at Albany with thirteen of the Oneidas. They seemed then to entertain a friendly disposition towards us, which I wish may not be changed by the misfortunes we have sustained in Canada.

I have the honour to be, &c.　　　　　G. W.

———————

SIR,　　　　　　　　　　　*New-York, June* 27, 1776.

I THIS morning received, by express, letters from generals Schuyler and Arnold, with a copy of one from general

general Sullivan to the former, and alfo of others to general Sullivan ; of all which I do myfelf the honour to tranfmit you copies. They will give you a further account of the melancholy fituation of our affairs in Canada, and fhew that there is nothing left to fave our army there but evacuating the country.

I am hopeful general Sullivan would retreat from the Ifle-aux-noix without waiting for previous orders for that purpofe ; as, from generals Schuyler and Arnold's letters, it is much to be feared, by remaining there any confiderable time, his retreat would be cut off, or at leaft be a matter of extreme difficulty. I would obferve to Congrefs that it is not in my power to fend any carpenters from hence to build the gondolas and galleys general Arnold mentions, without taking them from a work equally neceffary (if not more fo) here, of the fame kind :—and fubmit it to them whether it may not be advifeable (as it is of great importance to us to have a number of thofe veffels on the Lake, to prevent the enemy's paffing) to withdraw the carpenters for the prefent from the frigates building up the North-river, and detach them immediately, with all that can be got at Philadelphia, for that purpofe and carrying on thofe here.

I have the pleafure to inform you of another capture made by our armed veffels, of a tranfport, on the nineteenth inftant, with a company of Highland grenadiers on board. The inclofed extract of a letter from general Ward, by laft night's poft, contains the particulars ; to which I beg leave to refer you.

I have been honoured with your favours of the twenty-firft and twenty-fifth inftant in due order, with their important inclofures, to which I fhall particularly attend. I have tranfmitted general Schuyler a copy of the refolve of Congrefs refpecting the Mohickan and Stockbridge Indians, and directed him to put an immediate ftop to the raifing the two companies.

The quarter-mafter-general has been called upon for ftopping the tents defigned for Maffachufetts-Bay, and ordered to forward them immediately. He means to write to Congrefs upon the fubject, and hopes his conduct will

not

not appear to deferve their reprehenfion. Of this they will judge from his relation of the matter.

Being extremely defirous to forward the intelligence from Canada to Congrefs, well knowing their anxiety about our affairs there, I muft defer writing upon fome other matters I want to lay before them, until the next opportunity, which I hope will be to-morrow, when I will inform them fully upon the fubject of rations, having defired the commiffary-general to furnifh me with fome things neceffary in that inftance.

I have the honour to be, &c.   G. W.

———

SIR,   *New-York, June 27, 1776.*

UPON information that major * * * was travelling through the country under fufpicious circumftances, I thought it neceffary to have him fecured. I therefore fent after him. He was taken at South-Amboy, and brought up to New-York. Upon examination, he informed me that he came from New-Hampfhire, the country of his ufual abode, where he had left his family ; and pretended he was deftined to Philadelphia on bufinefs with Congrefs.

As by his own confeffion he had croffed Hudfon's-river at New-Windfor, and was taken fo far out of his proper and direct route to Philadelphia—this confideration, added to the length of time he had taken to perform his journey,—his being found in fo fufpicious a place as Amboy,—his unneceffary ftay there on pretence of getting fome baggage from New-York, and an expectation of receiving money from a perfon here, of bad character, and in no circumftances to furnifh him out of his own ftock,—the major's reputation, and his being a half-pay officer, have increafed my jealoufies about him.

The bufinefs, which he informs me he has with Congrefs, is a fecret offer of his fervices, to the end that, in cafe it fhould be rejected, he might have his way left open to an employment in the Eaft-Indies, to which he is affigned : and in that cafe he flatters himfelf he will obtain leave of Congrefs to go to Great-Britain.

As

As he had been put upon his parole by Congrefs, I thought it would be improper to ftay his progrefs to Philadelphia, fhould he be in fact deftined thither. I therefore fend him forward, but (to prevent impofition) under the care of an officer, with letters found upon him, which, from their tenor, feem calculated to recommend him to Congrefs. I fubmit it to their confideration, whether it would not be dangerous to accept of the offer of his fervices.

I am, Sir, with the greateft refpect, &c.   G. W.

SIR,   *New-York, June 28, 1776.*

IN compliance with the requeft of Congrefs contained in your favour of the twenty-fifth inftant, and my promife of yefterday, I do myfelf the honour to inform you that the coft of a ration, according to the commiffary-general's eftimate, from the firft of July to the firft of December, will be from eight-pence to eight-pence half-penny, York currency.

Having difcharged the obligation I was under in this inftance, and finding that many applications have been made for victualling the flying camp, I would, with all poffible deference, wifh Congrefs to confider the matter well before they come to any determination upon it. Who the gentlemen are that have made offers upon this occafion, I know not : confequently my objections to their appointment cannot proceed from perfonal diflike ; nor have I it in view to ferve Mr. Trumbull, the commiffary-general, by wifhing him to have the direction of the whole fupplies for his emolument ; becaufe whatever rations are taken from him fave him the trouble of fupplying provifions to the amount, without diminifhing his pay,—that being fixed and certain :—but what influences me is a regard to the public good. I am morally certain, if the bufinefs is taken out of Mr. Trumbull's hands and put into another's, that it may and will in all probability be attended with great and many inconveniences. It is likely, during the continuance of the war between us and Great-Britain, that the army here, or part of it, and the troops compofing

compofing the flying camp, will be frequently joined, and under the neceffity of affording each other mutual aid.   If this event is probable (and moft certainly it is) the fame confufion and diforder will refult from having two commiffaries, or one commiffary and one contractor in the fame army in the fame department, as did between Mr. Trumbull and Mr. Livingfton on the coming of the former to New-York.   I cannot difcriminate the two cafes; and not forefeeing that any good confequences will flow from the meafure, but that many bad ones will,—fuch as clafhing of interefts,—a contention for ftores, carriages,— and many other caufes that might be mentioned if hurry of bufinefs would permit,—I confefs I cannot perceive the propriety of appointing a different perfon, or any but the commiffary.

I would alfo add, that few armies, if any, have been better fupplied than the troops under Mr. Trumbull's care in this inftance; which, I fhould fuppofe, ought to have confiderable weight, efpecially as we have ftrong reafons to believe that a large fhare of the misfortunes our arms have fuftained in Carlada fprang from a want of proper and neceffary fupplies of provifions.

Mr. Trumbull too (I am informed) has already made provifion in New-Jerfey for the flying camp which will be ftationed there, and employed proper perfons in that colony to tranfact the bufinefs incident to his department, in obedience to my orders, and in full confidence that it was to come under his management.

My great defire to fee the affairs of this important poft, on which fo much depends, go on in an eafy, fmooth and uninterrupted courfe, has led me to fay thus much upon the fubject, and will, I hope, (if I am unhappy enough to differ in opinion with Congrefs) plead my excufe for the liberty I have taken.

I would alfo beg leave to mention to Congrefs the neceffity there is of fome new regulations being entered into, refpecting the chaplains of this army.   They will remember that applications were made to increafe their pay, which was conceived too low for their fupport; and that it was propofed (if it could not be done for the whole) that the number fhould be leffened, and one be appointed to two regiments, with an additional allowance. This latter expedient was adopted, and, while the army continued all together at one encampment, anfwered well, or at leaft did not produce many inconveniences. But the army now being differently circumftanced from what it then was,—part here, part at Bofton, and a third part detached to Canada,—has introduced much confufion and diforder in this inftance; nor do I know how it is poffible to remedy the evil, but by affixing one to each regiment, with falaries competent to their fupport. No fhifting, no change from one regiment to another can anfwer the purpofe; and in many cafes it could never be done though the regiments fhould confent,—as where detachments are compofed of unequal numbers, or ordered from different pofts. Many more inconveniences might be pointed out: but thefe, it is prefumed, will fufficiently fhew the defect of the prefent eftablifhment, and the propriety of an alteration. What that alteration fhall be, Congrefs will pleafe to determine.

Congrefs, I doubt not, will have heard of the plot that was forming among many difaffected perfons in this city and government for aiding the king's troops upon their arrival. No regular plan feems to have been digefted: but feveral perfons have been enlifted, and fworn to join them. The matter, I am in hopes, by a timely difcovery, will be fupprefled and put a ftop to. Many citizens and others, among whom is the mayor, are now in confinement. The matter has been traced up to governor Tryon; and the mayor appears to have been a principal agent, or go-between him and the perfons concerned in it. The plot had been communicated to fome of the army, and part of my guard engaged in it. T * * * H * * *, one of them, has been tried, and, by the unanimous opinion of a court-martial, is fentenced to die,—having enlifted himfelf, and engaged others. The fentence, by the advice of the whole council of general officers, will be put in execution to-day at eleven o'clock. The others are not tried. I am hopeful this example will produce many falutary confequences, and deter others from entering into the like traiterous practices.

The

The inclofed copy of a refolve of the provincial Congrefs will fhew that fome of the difaffected on Long-Ifland have taken up arms. I have, agreeable to their requeft, fent a party after them, but have not as yet been able to apprehend them,—having concealed themfelves in different woods and moraffes.

General Gates fet out on Tuefday with a fine wind which has been fair ever fince, and would foon arrive at Albany.

I this moment received a letter from lieutenant Davifon, of the Schuyler armed floop, a copy of which I have inclofed ; to which I beg leave to refer you for the intelligence communicated by him.

I could wifh general Howe and his armament not to arrive yet, as not more than a thoufand militia have yet come in, and our whole force (including the troops at all the detached pofts, and on board the armed veffels, which are comprehended in our returns) is but fmall and inconfiderable, when compared with the extenfive lines they are to defend, and (moft probably) the army that he brings. I have no further intelligence about him than what the lieutenant mentions : but it is extremely probable his accounts and conjectures are true.

I have the honour to be, &c.　　　　　G. W.

P. S. I have inclofed a general return :—and it may be certainly depended on, that general Howe and fleet have failed from Halifax. Some of the men, on board the prizes mentioned in the lieutenant's letter, were on board the Greyhound, and faw general Howe.

———

S I R,　　　　　　　　　　*New-York, June 29, 1776.*

I was laft night honoured with your favour of the twenty-fixth inftant, and, agreeable to your requeft, fhall pay proper attention to the refolves it inclofed.

I obferve the augmentation Congrefs have refolved to make to the forces deftined for the northern department, and the bounty to be allowed fuch foldiers as will enlift for three years. I hope many good confequences will refult from thefe meafures ; and that, from the latter, a confiderable

fiderable number of men may be induced to engage in the
fervice.

I fhould efteem myfelf extremely happy to afford the
leaft affiftance to the Canada department in compliance
with the defire of Congrefs and your requifition, were it
in my power : but it is not.   The return which I tranfmitted yefterday will but too well convince Congrefs of
my incapacity in this inftance, and point out to them that
the force I now have is trifling, confidering the many and
important pofts that are neceffary, and muft be fupported,
if poffible.   But few militia have yet come in, the whole
being about twelve hundred, including the two battalions
of this city, and one company from the Jerfies.   I wifh
the delay may not be attended with difagreeable confequences, and their aid may not come too late, or when it
may not be wanted.   I have wrote, I have done every
thing I could, to call them in : but they have not come,
though I am told that they are generally willing.

The accounts communicated yefterday through lieutenant Davifon's letter are partly confirmed, and, I dare fay,
will turn out to be true on the whole.   For two or three
days paft, three or four fhips have been dropping in ; and
I juft now received an exprefs from an officer appointed
to keep a look-out on Staten-Ifland, that forty-five arrived
at the Hook to-day :—fome fay more ; and I fuppofe the
whole fleet will be in, within a day or two.   I am hopeful, before they are prepared to attack, that I fhall get
fome reinforcements.   Be that as it may, I fhall attempt
to make the beft difpofition I can of our troops, in order
to give them a proper reception, and to prevent the ruin
and deftruction they are meditating againft us.

As foon as the exprefs arrived laft night, I fent the letters for the northern colonies to the quarter-mafter-general,
with orders to forward them immediately.

When monfieur Wiebert comes, (I have not feen him
yet) I fhall employ him as Congrefs have directed.   The
terms upon which he offers his fervice feem to promife
fomething from him.   I wifh he may anfwer, and be fkilled in the bufinefs he fays he is acquainted with.

I have the honour to be, &c.   G. W.
New-York,

SIR,   *New-York, June* 30, 1776.

I HAD the pleasure of receiving your favour of the twenty-ninth early this morning, with which you have been pleased to honour me, together with the resolves for a further augmentation of our army.

The battalion of Germans, which Congress have ordered to be raised, will be a corps of much service ; and I am hopeful that such persons will be appointed officers, as will complete their enlistments with all possible expedition.

I shall communicate to colonel Stevenson and one of his field-officers what you have requested, and direct them to repair immediately to Philadelphia. It is an unlucky circumstance that the term of enlistment of these three companies, and of the rifle battalion, should expire at this time when a hot campaign is, in all probability, about to commence.

Canada, it is certain, would have been an important acquisition, and well worth the expenses incurred in the pursuit of it. But as we could not reduce it to our possession, the retreat of our army with so little loss, under such a variety of distresses, must be esteemed a most fortunate event. It is true, the accounts we have received do not fully authorise us to say that we have sustained no loss : but they hold forth a probable ground for such conclusion. I am anxious to hear it confirmed.

I have the honour of transmitting you an extract of a letter received last night from general Ward. If the scheme the privateers had in view, and the measures he had planned, have been carried into execution, the Highland corps will be tolerably well disposed of : but I fear the fortunate event has not taken place.

In general Ward's letter, was inclosed one from lieutenant-colonel Campbell, who was made prisoner with the Highland troops. I have transmitted you a copy. This will give you a full and exact account of the number of prisoners that were on board the four transports ; and will prove, beyond a possibility of doubt, that the evacuation of Boston by the British troops was a matter neither known nor expected when he received his orders. Indeed so

many

many facts had concurred before to settle the matter, that no additional proofs were neceffary.

When I had the honour of addreffing you yefterday, I had only been informed of the arrival of forty-five of the fleet in the morning. Since that, I have received authentic intelligence from fundry perfons (among them, from general Greene) that a hundred and ten fail came in before night, that were counted, and that more were feen about dufk in the offing. I have no doubt but the whole that failed from Halifax are now at the Hook.

Juft as I was about to conclude my letter, I received one from a gentleman upon the fubject of calling the five regiments from Bofton to the defence of Canada or New-York, and to have militia raifed in their lieu. I have fent you a copy, and fhall only obferve, that I know the author well: his hand-writing is quite familiar to me: he is a member of the General Court, very fenfible, of great influence, and a warm and zealous friend to the caufe of America. The expedient propofed by him is fubmitted to Congrefs.

I have the honour to be, &c. G. W.

SIR, *New-York, July* 3, 1776.

SINCE I had the honour of addreffing you, and on the fame day, feveral fhips more arrived within the Hook, making the number that came in then a hundred and ten ; and there remains no doubt of the whole of the fleet from Halifax being now here. Yefterday evening fifty of them came up the bay and anchored on the Staten-Ifland fide. Their views I cannot precifely determine ; but am extremely apprehenfive, as part of them only came, that they mean to furround the ifland, and fecure the flock upon it. I had confulted with a committee of the provincial Congrefs upon the fubject, before the arrival of the fleet ; and they appointed a perfon to fuperintend the bufinefs, and to drive the flock off. I alfo wrote to brigadier-general Heard, and directed him to the meafure left it might be neglected ; but am fearful it has not been effected.

Our reinforcement of militia is yet but small :—I cannot afcertain the amount, not having got a return. However, I truft, if the enemy make an attack, they will meet with a repulfe, as I have the pleafure to inform you that an agreeable fpirit and willingnefs for action feem to animate and pervade the whole of our troops.

As it is difficult to determine what objects the enemy may have in contemplation, and whether they may not detach fome part of their force to Amboy, and to ravage that part of the country, if not extend their views farther, I fubmit it to Congrefs whether it may not be expedient for them to repeat and prefs home their requefts to the different governments that are to provide men for the flying camp, to furnifh their quotas with all poffible difpatch. It is a matter of great importance, and will be of ferious confequence, to have the camp eftablifhed in cafe the enemy fhould be able to poffefs themfelves of this river, and cut off the fupplies of troops that might be neceffary on certain emergencies to be fent from hence.

I muft entreat your attention to an application I made fome time ago for flints. We are extremely deficient in this neceffary article, and fhall be greatly diftreffed if we cannot obtain a fupply. Of lead we have a fufficient quantity for the whole campaign, taken off the houfes here.

Efteeming it of infinite advantage to prevent the enemy from getting frefh provifions, and horfes for their waggons, artillery, &c. I gave orders to a party of our men on Staten-Ifland (fince writing to general Heard) to drive the ftock off without waiting for the affiftance or direction of the committees there, left their flow mode of tranfacting bufinefs might produce too much delay ;—and have fent this morning to know what they have done. I am this morning informed by a gentleman, that the committee of Elizabeth-Town fent their company of light-horfe on Monday to effect it, and that fome of their militia were to give their aid yefterday. He adds that he was credibly told laft night by a party of the militia coming to this place, that yefterday they faw a good deal of ftock driving off the

island,

iſland, and croſſing to the Jerſeys.   If the buſineſs is not executed before now, it will be impoſſible to do it.

I have the honour to be, &c.   G. W.

—————

SIR,   *New-York, July 4, 1776.*

THIS will be handed to you by colonel Stevenſon, whom I have ordered, with the captains of the two rifle companies from Maryland, to wait on Congreſs.   They will point out ſuch meaſures as they conceive moſt likely to advance the raiſing of the new rifle battalion, and the perſons they think worthy of promotion, that have ſerved in the three companies here, agreeable to the incloſed liſt. I am not acquainted with them myſelf, but from their report and recommendation, which I doubt not to be juſt ; and that, if Congreſs will pleaſe to inquire of them, they will mention other proper perſons for officers.

Only about forty of the three old companies have re-enliſted, whom I ſhall form into one for the preſent, and place under an officer or two, till a further and complete arrangement is made of the whole battalion.

I have the honour to be, &c.   G. W.

—————

SIR,   *New-York, July 4, 1776.*

WHEN I had the honour to addreſs you on the thirtieth ultimo, I tranſmitted a copy of a letter I had received from a gentleman, a member of the honourable General Court, [*of Maſſachuſetts*] ſuggeſting the improbability of ſuccours coming from thence in any reaſonable time, either for the defence of this place, or to reinforce our troops engaged in the Canada expedition.   I am ſorry to inform you, that, from a variety of intelligence, his apprehenſions appear to be juſt, and to be fully confirmed : nor have I reaſon to expect but that the ſupplies from the other two governments, Connecticut and New-Hampſhire, will be extremely ſlow and greatly deficient in number.

As it now ſeems beyond queſtion, and clear to demon-ſtration, that the enemy mean to direct their operations

and

and bend their moſt vigorous efforts againſt this colony, and will attempt to unite their two armies,—that under general Burgoyne, and the one arrived here,—I cannot, but think the expedient propoſed by that gentleman is exceedingly juſt ; and that the continental regiments, now in the Maſſachuſetts-Bay, ſhould be immediately called from thence, and be employed where there is the ſtrongeſt reaſon to believe their aid will be indiſpenſably neceſſary. The expediency of the meaſure I ſhall ſubmit to the conſideration of Congreſs, and will only obſerve, as my opinion, that there is not the moſt diſtant proſpect of an attempt being made, where they now are, by the enemy ; and, if there ſhould, that the militia that can be aſſembled upon the ſhorteſt notice will be more than equal to repel it. They are well armed, reſolute, and determined, and will inſtantly oppoſe any invaſion that may be made in their own colony.

I ſhall alſo take the liberty again to requeſt Congreſs to intereſt themſelves in having the militia raiſed and forwarded with all poſſible expedition, as faſt as any conſiderable number of them can be collected, that are to compoſe the flying camp. This I mentioned in my letter yeſterday, but think proper to repeat it, being more and more convinced of the neceſſity. The camp will be in the neighbourhood of Amboy : and I ſhall be glad that the conventions, or committees of ſafety, of thoſe governments from whence they come, may be requeſted to give me previous notice of their marching, that I may form ſome plan, and direct proviſion to be made for their reception.

The diſaffection of the people at that place and others not far diſtant is exceedingly great ; and, unleſs it is checked and over-awed, it may become more general, and be very alarming. The arrival of the enemy will encourage it. They, or at leaſt a part of them, are already landed on Staten Iſland, which is quite contiguous ; and about four thouſand were marching about it yeſterday, as I have been adviſed, and are leaving no arts un-eſſayed to gain the inhabitants to their ſide, who ſeem but too favourably diſpoſed. It is not unlikely that in a little time they may attempt to croſs to the Jerſey ſide, and induce many to

join

join them, either from motives of interest or fear, unless there is a force to oppose them.

As we are fully convinced that the ministerial army we shall have to oppose this campaign will be great and numerous, and well know that the utmost industry will be used, as it already has been, to excite the savages and every body of people to arms against us whom they can influence, it certainly behoves us to strain every nerve to counteract their designs. I would therefore submit it to Congress, whether (especially as our schemes for employing the western Indians do not seem to be attended with any great prospect of success, from general Schuyler's accounts) it may not be adviseable to take measures to engage those of the eastward, the St. John's, Nova-Scotia, Penobscot, &c. in our favour. I have been told that several might be got, perhaps five or six hundred or more, readily to join us. If they can, I should imagine it ought to be done. It will prevent our enemies from securing their friendship; and further, they will be of infinite service in annoying and harassing them, should they ever attempt to penetrate the country. Congress will be pleased to consider the measure : and if they determine to adopt it, I conceive it will be necessary to authorise and request the General Court of the Massachusetts-Bay to carry it into execution. Their situation and advantages will enable them to negociate a treaty and an alliance better than it can be done by any persons else.

I have been honoured with your two favours of the first instant; and, agreeable to the wishes of Congress, shall put monsieur Wiebert in the best place I can to prove his abilities in the art he professes. I shall send him up immediately to the works erecting towards Kingsbridge under the discretion of general Mifflin, whom I shall request to employ him.

I this moment received a letter from general Greene, an extract of which I have inclosed. The intelligence it contains is of the most important nature, and evinces the necessity of the most spirited and vigorous exertions on our part.

The expectation of the fleet under admiral Howe is certainly the reason the army already come have not begun

their

their hoftile operations.   When that arrives, we may look for the moft interefting events, and fuch as, in all probability, will have confiderable weight in the prefent conteft. It behoves us to be prepared in the beft manner : and I fubmit it again to Congrefs, whether the accounts given by their prifoners do not fhew the propriety of calling the feveral continental regiments from the Maffachufetts government, raifing the flying camp with all poffible difpatch, and engaging the eaftern Indians.

July 5.—General Mercer arrived here on Tuefday, and, the next morning, was ordered to Paulus-Hook to make fome arrangements of the militia as they came in, and the beft difpofition he could to prevent the enemy croffing from Staten-Ifland, if they fhould have any fuch views. The diftreffed fituation of the inhabitants of Elizabeth-Town and Newark has fince induced me, upon their application, to give up all the militia from the Jerfeys, except thofe engaged for fix months.   1 am hopeful they will be able to repel any incurfions that may be attempted.   Generals Mercer and Livingfton are concerting plans for that purpofe.   By a letter from the latter laft night, I am informed the enemy are throwing up fmall works at all the paffes on the north fide of Staten-Ifland, which it is probable they mean to fecure.

None of the Connecticut militia are yet arrived : fo that the reinforcement we have received is very inconfiderable.

A letter from general Schuyler, with fundry inclofures, (of which N° 1, 2 and 3 are exact copies) this moment came to hand, and will no doubt claim, as it ought to do, the immediate attention of Congrefs.   The evils which muft inevitably follow a difputed command, are too obvious and alarming to admit a moment's delay in your decifion thereupon : and, although I do not prefume to advife in a matter, now, of this delicacy, yet as it appears evident that the northern army has retreated to Crown-Point, and mean to act upon the defenfive only, I cannot help giving it as my opinion that one of the major-generals in that quarter would be more ufefully employed here, or in the flying camp, than there : for it becomes my duty to obferve, if another experienced officer is taken from hence in order to command the flying camp, that your

grand

grand army will be entirely ftripped of generals who have feen fervice,—b ing in a manner already deftitute of fuch.   My diftrefs on this account,—the appointment of general Whitcomb to the eaftern regiments,—a conviction in my own breaft that no troops will be fent to Bofton, and the certainty of a number coming to this place, —occafioned my poftponing, from time to time, fending any general officer from hence to the eaftward heretofore : and now I.fhall wait the fentiments of Congrefs relative to the five regiments in Maffachufetts-Bay, before I do any thing in this matter.

The commiffary-general has been with me this morning concerning the other matter contained in general Schuyler's letter refpecting the bufinefs of that department. He has, I believe, (in order to remove difficulties) recalled Mr. Avery, but feems to think it neceffary in that cafe that Mr. Livingfton fhould be left to himfelf, as he cannot be refponfible for perfons not of his own appointment.   This matter fhould alfo be clearly defined by Congrefs.   I have already given my opinion of the neceffity of thefe matters being under one general direction, in fo full and clear a manner, that I fhall not take up the time of Congrefs to repeat it in this place.

I have the honour to be, &c.   G. W.

S I R,   *New-York, July 8, 1776.*

CONGRESS having refolved to raife a regiment of Germans to counteract the defigns of our enemies, I muft beg leave to recommend to their notice John David Wilpert, now a firft-lieutenant in colonel Shee's battalion, to the office of captain in faid regiment.   I am perfonally acquainted with him, and know that he joined the Virginia forces under my command in the year 1754, and continued in fervice the whole war, during which he conducted himfelf as an active, vigilant, and brave officer. He is a German ; and his merit, as a foldier, entitles him much to the office he wifhes for.

I have the honour to be, &c.   G. W.
New-York,

S I R,   *New-York, July* 10, 1776.

I AM now to acknowledge the receipt of your two favours of the fourth and fixth inftant, which came duly to hand, with their important inclofures.

I perceive that Congrefs have been employed in deliberating on meafures of the moft interefting nature. It is certain that it is not with us to determine in many inftances what confequences will flow from our councils : but yet it behoves us to adopt fuch, as, under the fmiles of a gracious and all-kind Providence, will be moft likely to promote our happinefs. I truft the late decifive part they have taken is calculated for that end, and will fecure us that freedom and thofe privileges, which have been and are refufed us, contrary to the voice of nature and the Britifh conftitution. Agreeable to the requeft of Congrefs, I caufed "THE DECLARATION" to be proclaimed before all the army under my immediate command ; and have the pleafure to inform them that the meafure feemed to have their moft hearty affent,—the expreffions and behaviour, both of officers and men, teftifying their warmeft approbation of it. I have tranfmitted a copy to general Ward at Bofton, requefting him to have it proclaimed to the continental troops in that department.

It is with great pleafure that I hear the militia from Maryland, the Delaware government, and Pennfylvania, will be in motion every day to form the flying camp. It is of great importance, and fhould be accomplifhed with all poffible difpatch. The readinefs and alacrity with which the committee of fafety of Pennfylvania and the other conferees have acted, in order to forward the affociated militia of that State to the Jerfeys for fervice till the men to compofe the flying camp arrive, ftrongly evidence their regard to the common caufe, and that nothing on their part will be wanting to fupport it. I hope, and I doubt not, that the affociated militia, impreffed with the expediency of the meafure, will immediately carry it into execution, and furnifh in this inftance a proof of the continuance of that zeal which has fo eminently marked their conduct. I have directed the commiffary

                                                        to

to make the neceffary provifion for their reception, who will alfo fupply the army for the flying camp with rations. A proper officer will be appointed to command it.

In purfuance of the power given me by Congrefs, and the advice of my general officers, I have wrote to general Ward, and defired him forthwith to detach three of the fulleft regiments from the Maffachufetts-Bay to join the northern army,—effeeming it a matter of the greateft importance to have a fufficient force there to prevent the enemy paffing the Lake and making an impreffion in that quarter. The gondolas and galleys will be of great fervice ; and I am hopeful the carpenters you have fent from Philadelphia, and that will go from the eaftward on your application, will be able to build a fufficient number in time to anfwer every exigency.

I have requefted governor Cooke, if the duck mentioned in Mr. Greene's letter is proper for tents, to have it made up as early as poffible, and forwarded here. I have alfo defired him to fend the flints and fmall arms, as I have general Ward thofe of the latter that were taken out of the Scotch tranfports,—our deficiency in thefe neceffary articles being ftill great.

Obferving that Congrefs have particularly mentioned a bounty of ten dollars, to be paid to men of fome corps directed to be raifed in two or three inftances fince their refolve of the twenty-fixth of June, allowing fuch bounty, I have been led to doubt how that refolve is to be conftrued ; whether it is a general regulation, and extends to all men that will engage for three years,—for inftance, the foldiers of the prefent army, if they will enlift for that time. If it is, and extends to them, it will be neceffary to forward a large fum of money : many perhaps would engage.

I alfo obferve, by their refolve of the twenty-fifth of June for raifing four regiments of militia in the eaftern governments to augment the troops in the northern department, that the affemblies of thofe governments are empowered to appoint paymafters to the faid regiments. This appears to me a regulation of great ufe, and I could wifh that it was made general, and one allowed to eve-

ry

ry regiment in the ſervice. Many advantages would reſult from it.

The Connecticut militia begin to come in: but from every account the battalions will be very incomplete, owing, they ſay, to the buſy ſeaſon of the year. That government, leſt any inconvenience might reſult from their militia not being here in time, ordered three regiments of their light-horſe to my aſſiſtance, part of which have arrived. But, not having the means to ſupport them (and, if it could be done, the expenſe would be enormous) I have thanked the gentlemen for their zeal, and the attachment they have manifeſted upon this occaſion, and informed them that I cannot conſent to their keeping their horſes,—at the ſame time wiſhing them to ſtay themſelves. I am told they or part of them mean to do ſo.

General Mercer is now in the Jerſeys, for the purpoſe of receiving and ordering the militia coming for the flying camp; and I have ſent over our chief engineer to view the ground within the neighbourhood of Amboy, and to lay out ſome neceſſary works for the encampment, and ſuch as may be proper at the different paſſes in Bergen-Neck, and other places on the Jerſey ſhore oppoſite Staten-Iſland, to prevent the enemy making impreſſions, and committing depredations on the property of the inhabitants.

The intelligence we have from a few deſerters that have come over to us, and from others, is, that general Howe has between nine and ten thouſand men, who are chiefly landed on the iſland, poſted in different parts, and ſecuring the ſeveral communications from the Jerſeys with ſmall works and intrenchments, to prevent our people from paying them a viſit;—that the iſlanders have all joined them, ſeem well diſpoſed to favour their cauſe, and have agreed to take up arms in their behalf. They look for admiral Howe's arrival every day with his fleet and a large reinforcement; are in high ſpirits, and talk confidently of ſucceſs, and carrying all before them when he comes. I truſt, through divine favour and our own exertions, they will be diſappointed in their views: and, at all events, any advantages they may gain will coſt them

very

very dear. If our troops will behave well (which I hope will be the case, having every thing to contend for that freemen hold dear) they will have to wade through much blood and slaughter before they can carry any part of our works, if they carry them at all,—and, at best, be in possession of a melancholy and mournful victory. May the sacredness of our cause inspire our soldiery with sentiments of heroism, and lead them to the performance of the noblest exploits !—

With this wish, I have the honour to be, &c.

G. W.

———

SIR,   *New-York, July* 11, 1756.

I WAS honoured with your favour of the eighth instant by yesterday morning's post, with the several resolves to which you referred my attention. I shall duly regard them, and attempt their execution as far as I am able.

By virtue of the discretionary power that Congress were pleased to vest me with, and by advice of such of my general officers as I have had an opportunity of consulting, I have ordered the two remaining continental regiments in the Massachusetts-Bay to march immediately for the defence of this place, in full confidence that nothing hostile will be attempted against that State in the present campaign.

I have wrote to the General Court of Massachusetts-Bay, and transmitted a copy of the resolve for employing the eastern Indians, entreating their good offices in this instance, and their exertions to have them forthwith engaged and marched to join this army. I have desired five or six hundred of them to be enlisted for two or three years, if they will consent to it,—subject to an earlier discharge if it shall be thought necessary,—and upon the same terms as the continental troops, if better cannot be had,—though I am hopeful they may.

In my letter of yesterday, I mentioned the arrival of part of the Connecticut light-horse to assist in the defence of this place, and my objection to their horses being kept. Four or five hundred of them are now come in ; and, in justice to their zeal and laudable attachment to the cause of

their

their country, I am to inform you that they have confented to ftay as long as occafion may require, though they fhould be at the expenfe of maintaining their horfes themfelves. They have paftured them out about the neighbourhood of Kingfbridge (being unwilling to fend them away) at the rate of half a dollar per week each, meaning to leave it entirely with Congrefs either to allow or refufe it, as they fhall judge proper.   I promifed to make this reprefentation and thought it my duty ; and will only obferve that the motives which induced them at firft to fet out were good and praife-worthy, and were, to afford the moft fpeedy and early fuccour, which they apprehended would be wanted before the militia arrived. Their fervices may be extremely important,—being moft of them, if not all, men of reputation and of property.

The fubject of the inclofed copy of a letter from governor Trumbull I beg leave to fubmit to the confideration of Congrefs.   They will perceive from his reprefentation the difquieting apprehenfions that have feized on the minds of the people fince the retreat of the northern army, and how expofed the northern frontiers of New-York and New-Hampfhire are to the ravages and incurfions of the Indians. How far it may be expedient to raife the battalion he conceives neceffary to prevent the calamities and diftreffes he points out, they will determine, upon what he has faid, and the neceffity that may appear to them for the meafure ;— what I have done, being only to lay the matter before them in compliance with his wifhes.

I have alfo inclofed a memorial from the furgeons'-mates, fetting forth the inadequacy of their pay to their fervices and maintenance, and praying that it may be increafed.   I fhall obferve that they have a long time complained in this inftance, and that fome additional allowance may not be unneceffary.

As I am truly fenfible the time of Congrefs is much taken up with a variety of important matters, it is with unwillingnefs and pain I ever repeat a requeft after having once made it, or take the liberty of enforcing any opinion of mine after it is once given : but as the eftablifhing of fome office for auditing accounts is a matter of exceeding importance to the public intereft, I would beg leave once

more

more to call the attention of Congress to an appointment competent to the purpose. Two motives induce me to urge the matter; first, a conviction of the utility of the meafure—secondly, that I may ftand exculpated if hereafter it fhould appear that money has been improperly expended, and neceffaries for the army obtained upon unreafonable terms.

For me, whofe time is employed from the hour of my rifing till I retire to bed again, to go into an examination of the accounts of fuch an army as this with any degree of precifion and exactnefs, withou neglecting other matters of equal importance, is utterly impracticable. All that I have been able to do (and that, in fact, was doing nothing) was, when the commiffary, and quarter-mafter, and directorgeneral of the hofpital (for it is to thefe the great advances are made) applied for warrants,—to make them at times produce a general account of their expenditures. But this anfwers no valuable purpofe. It is the minutiæ that muft be gone into,—the propriety of each charge examined,— the vouchers looked into ;—and, with refpect to the commiffary-general, his victualling returns and expenditures of provifions fhould be compared with his purchafes : otherwife a perfon in this department, if he was inclined to be knavifh, might purchafe large quantities with the public money, and fell one half of it again for private emolument; and yet his accounts upon paper would appear fair, and be fupported with vouchers for every charge.

I do not urge this matter from a fufpicion of any unfair practices in either of the departments before mentioned ; and forry fhould I be if this conftruction was put upon it, having a high opinion of the honour and integrity of thefe gentlemen. But there fhould neverthelefs be fome control as well upon their difcretion as honefty :—to which may be added, that accounts become perplexed and confufed by long ftanding, and the errors therein not fo difcoverable as if they underwent an early revifion and examination. I am well apprifed that a treafury-office of accounts has been refolved upon, and an auditor-general for fettling all public accounts : but, with all deference and fubmiffion to the opinion of Congrefs, thefe inftitutions are not calculated to prevent the inconveniences I have men tioned; nor can they be competent to the purpofes, circumftanced as they are.

We have intelligence from a deferter that came to us, that on Wednefday morning the Afia, Chatham, and Greyhound men-of-war weighed anchor, and (it was faid) intended to pafs up the North-river above the city, to prevent the communication with the Jerfeys. They did not attempt it, nor does he know what prevented them. A prifoner belonging to the tenth regiment, taken yefterday, informs that they hourly expected admiral Howe and his fleet. He adds that a veffel has arrived from them, and the prevailing opinion is, that an attack will be made immediately on their arrival.

By a letter from general Ward, I am informed that the fmall-pox has broke out at Bofton, and infected fome of the troops. I have wrote to him to place the invalids under an officer, to remain till they are well; and to ufe every poffible precaution to prevent the troops from thence bringing the infection. The diftreffes and calamities we have already fuffered by this diforder in one part of our army, I hope, will excite his utmoft care that they may not be increafed.

I have the honour to be, &c.   G. W.

SIR,   *New-York, July 12, 1776.*

THE defign of this is to inform Congrefs, that, about half after three o'clock this evening, two of the enemy's fhips of war, one of forty and the other of twenty guns, with three tenders, weighed anchor in the bay oppofite Staten-Ifland, and, availing themfelves of a brifk and favourable breeze, with a flowing tide, ran paft our batteries up the North-river, without receiving any certain damage that I could perceive, notwithftanding a heavy and inceffant cannonade was kept up from our feveral batteries here, as well as from that at Paulus-Hook. They, on their part, returned and continued the fire as they ran by. I difpatched an exprefs to brigadier-general Mifflin, at our encampment towards the upper end of the ifland;

but

but have not heard whether they have got by, or received any damage.

The account tranfmitted by this morning's poft, refpecting the arrival of one of the fleet, feems to be confirmed. Several fhips have come in to-day : among them, one this evening, with a Saint-George's flag at her fore-top-maft-head, which we conclude to be admiral Howe, from the circumftance of the flag, and the feveral and general falutes that were paid. It is probable they will all arrive in a day or two, and immediately begin their operations.

As it will be extremely neceffary that the flying camp fhould be well provided with powder and ball, and it may be impracticable to fend fupplies from hence on account of our hurry and engagements, (befides, the communication may be uncertain) I muft beg the attention of Congrefs to this matter, and requeft that they will forward with all poffible expedition fuch a quantity of mufket-powder and lead, (if balls of different fizes cannot be had) as will be fufficient for the militia to compofe that camp.

By an exprefs this minute arrived from general Mifflin, the fhips have paffed his works.

I am, in hafte, with fentiments of great regard, &c.

G. W.

A quarter paft eight, P. M.

S I R,   *New-York, July 14, 1776.*

MY laft of Friday evening, which I had the honour of addreffing you, advifed that two of the enemy's fhips of war and three tenders had run above our batteries here and the works at the upper end of the ifland. I am now to inform you, that, yefterday forenoon, receiving intelligence from general Mifflin that they had paffed the Tappan-Sea, and were trying to proceed higher up,—by advice of R. R. Livingfton, efquire, and other gentlemen, I difpatched expreffes to general Clinton of Ulfter, and the committee of fafety for Duchefs-county, to take meafures for fecuring the paffes in the Highlands, left they might have defigns of feizing them, and have a force concealed

for

for the purpose. I wrote the evening before to the commanding officer of the two garrisons there to be vigilant and prepared against any attempts they or any disaffected persons might make against them, and to forward expresses all the way to Albany, that provision and other vessels might be secured and prevented falling into their hands.

The information given general Mifflin was rather premature, as to their having gone past the Sea. A letter from the committee of Orange-county, which came to hand this morning, says they were there yesterday, and that a regiment of their militia was under arms, to prevent their landing and making an incursion. The messenger who brought it, and to whom it refers for particulars, adds that a party of them, in two or three boats, had approached the shore, but were forced back by our people firing at them. Since the manœuvre of Friday, there have been no other movements in the fleet.

General Sullivan, in a letter of the second instant, informs me of his arrival with the army at Crown-Point, where he is fortifying and throwing up works. He adds that he has secured all the stores except three cannon left at Chamblee, which in part is made up by taking a fine twelve-pounder out of the Lake. The army is sickly,—many with the small-pox ; and he is apprehensive the militia, ordered to join them, will not escape the infection. An officer he had sent to reconnoitre had reported that he saw at Saint John's about a hundred and fifty tents,—twenty at Saint Roy's, and fifteen at Chamblee ; and works at the first were busily carrying on.

I have inclosed a general return of the army here, which will shew the whole of our strength. All the detached posts are included.

A letter from the eastward, by last night's post, to Mr. Hazard, post-master in this city, advises that two ships had been taken and carried into Cape-Ann,—one from Antigua, consigned to general Howe, with four hundred and thirty-nine puncheons of rum,—the other a Jamaica-man, with four hundred hogsheads of sugar, two hundred puncheons of rum, thirty-nine bales of cotton, pimento, fustic, &c. &c. Each mounted two guns, six-pounders.

About three o'clock this afternoon I was informed that a flag from lord Howe was coming up, and waited with

two

two of our whale-boats, until directions should be given.
I immediately convened such of the general officers as
were not upon other duty, who agreed in opinion that I
ought not to receive any letter directed to me as a private
gentleman : but if otherwise, and the officer desired to
come up to deliver the letter himself, as was suggested, he
should come under a safe-conduct. , Upon this, I directed
colonel Reed to go down and manage the affair under the
above general instruction.

On his return, he informed me, that, after the common
civilities, the officer acquainted him that he had a letter
from lord Howe to Mr. Washington, which he shewed under a superscription, " *To George Washington, esquire.*"
Colonel Reed replied there was no such person in the army, and that a letter intended for the general could not be
received under such a direction. The officer expressed
great concern,—said it was a letter rather of a civil than
military nature,—that lord Howe regretted he had not arrived sooner,—that he (lord Howe) had great powers.
The anxiety to have the letter received was very evident,
though the officer disclaimed all knowledge of its contents.
However, colonel Reed's instructions being positive, they
parted. After they had got some distance, the officer
with the flag again put about, and asked under what direction Mr. Washington chose to be addressed :—to which
colonel Reed answered, his station was well known, and
that certainly they could be at no loss how to direct to
him. The officer said they knew it and lamented it ; and
again repeated his wish that the letter could be received.
Colonel Reed told him a proper direction would obviate
all difficulties, and that this was no new matter,—this subject having been fully discussed in the course of the last year ;
of which lord Howe could not be ignorant :—upon which
they parted.

I would not upon any occasion sacrifice essentials to punc-
tilio ; but in this instance, the opinion of others concurring
with my own, I deemed it a duty to my country and my
appointment, to insist upon that respect, which, in any other than a public view, I would willingly have waved. Nor
do I doubt, but, from the supposed nature of the message,

Q 2

and the anxiety expreſſed, they will either repeat their flag, or fail upon ſome mode to communicate the import and [*contents*] of it.

I have been duly honoured with your two letters, that of the tenth by Mr. Anderſon,—and the eleventh, with its incloſures. I have directed the quarter-maſter to provide him with every thing he wants to carry his ſcheme into execution. It is an important one, and I wiſh it ſucceſs; but am doubtful that it will be better in theory than practice.

The paſſage of the ſhips of war and tenders up the river is a matter of great importance, and has excited much conjecture and ſpeculation. To me two things have occurred, as leading them to this proceeding,—firſt a deſign to ſeize on the narrow paſſes on both ſides of the river, giving almoſt the only land-communication with Albany, and of conſequence with our northern army; for which purpoſe they might have troops concealed on board, which they deemed competent of themſelves, as the defiles are narrow,—or that they would be joined by many diſaffected perſons in that quarter. Others have added a probability of their having a large quantity of arms on board, to be in readineſs to put into the hands of the tories immediately on the arrival of the fleet, or rather at the time they intend to make their attack. The ſecond is, to cut off entirely all intercourſe between this and Albany by water, and the upper country, and to prevent ſupplies of every kind going and coming.

Theſe matters are truly alarming, and of ſuch importance that I have wrote to the provincial Congreſs of New-York, and recommended to their ſerious conſideration the adoption of every poſſible expedient to guard againſt the two firſt; and have ſuggeſted the propriety of their employing the militia, or ſome part of them, in the counties in which theſe defiles are, to keep the enemy from poſſeſſing them, till further proviſion can be made; and to write to the ſeveral leading perſons on our ſide in that quarter, to be attentive to all the movements of the ſhips and the diſaffected, in order to diſcover and fruſtrate whatever pernicious ſchemes they have in view.

In

In refpect to the fecond conjecture of my own, and which feems to be generally adopted, I have the pleafure to inform Congrefs, that, if their defign is to keep the armies from provifion, the commiffary has told me upon inquiry, he has forwarded fupplies to Albany (now there, and above it) fufficient for ten thoufand men for four months ; that he has a fufficiency here for twenty thoufand men for three months, and an abundant quantity fecured in different parts of the Jerfeys for the flying camp, befides having about four thoufand barrels of flour in fome neighbouring part of Connecticut. Upon this head, there is but little occafion for any apprehenfions, at leaft for a confiderable time.

I have the honour to be, &c. G. W.

P. S. I have fent orders to the commanding officer of the Pennfylvania militia to march to Amboy, as their remaining at Trenton can be of no fervice.

SIR, *New-York, July* 15, 1776.

THIS will be handed you by Mr. Griffin, who has alfo taken upon him the charge and delivery of two packets containing fundry letters which were fent to Amboy yefterday by a flag, and forwarded to me to-day by general Mercer. The letter addreffed to governor Franklin came open to my hands.

I was this morning honoured with yours of the thirteenth inftant, with its important and neceffary inclofures ; and, in obedience to the commands of Congrefs, have tranfmitted general Howe the refolves intended for him. Thofe for general Burgoyne I inclofed and fent to general Schuyler, with directions immediately to forward them to him.

The inhuman treatment of the whole, and murder of part of our people, after their furrender and capitulation, was certainly a flagrant violation of that faith which ought to be held facred by all civilized nations, and founded in the moft favage barbarity. It highly deferved the fevereft reprobation ; and I truft the fpirited meafures Congrefs have adopted upon the occafion will prevent the like in future :

future : but if they fhould not, and the claims of humanity are difregarded, juftice and policy will require recourfe
to be had to the law of retaliation, however abhorrent
and difagrecable to our natures in cafes of torture and capital punifhments.

I have the honour to be, &c.   G. W.

———

SIR,   *New-York, July* 17, 1776.

I WAS this morning honoured with yours of the
fifteenth inftant, with fundry refolves.

I perceive the meafures Congrefs have taken to expedite the raifing of the flying camp, and providing it with
articles of the greateft ufe.   You will fee by a poftfcript
to my letter of the fourteenth, I had wrote to the commanding officer of the Pennfylvania militia, ordering them
to be marched from Trenton to Amboy, as their remaining there could not anfwer the leaft public good.   For,
having confulted with fundry gentlemen, I was informed,
if the enemy mean to direct their views towards Pennfylvania or penetrate the Jerfeys, their route will be from
near Amboy, and either by way of Brunfwic or Boundbrook,—the lower road from South-Amboy being through
a woody fandy country.   Befides, they will be then able
to throw in fuccour here, and to receive it from hence
in cafes of emergency.

The Connecticut light-horfe, mentioned in my letter
of the eleventh, notwithftanding their then promife to
continue here for the defence of this place, are now difcharged, and about to return home,—having peremptorily
refufed all kind of fatigue duty, or even to mount guard,
claiming an exemption as troopers.   Though their affiftance is much needed, and might be of effential fervice in
cafe of an attack, yet I judged it advifeable, on their application and claim of fuch indulgences, to difcharge them ;
as granting them would fet an example to others, and
might produce many ill confequences.   The number of
men included in the laft return, by this, is leffened about
five hundred.

I laft

I laft night received a letter from general Schuyler, with feveral inclofures, copies of which I have herewith tranfmitted. They will give Congrefs every information I have refpecting our northern army and the fituation of our affairs in that quarter; to which I beg leave to refer their attention. I cannot but exprefs my furprife at the fcarcity of provifion which general Schuyler mentions, after what the commiffary affured me, and which formed a part of my letter of the fourteenth. He ftill affures me of the fame. This is a diftreffing circumftance, as every article of provifion, and every thing neceffary for that department, can have no other now than a land conveyance, the water-communication from hence to Albany being entirely cut off.

Congrefs will pleafe to confider the inclofure, N° 6, about raifing fix companies out of the inhabitants about the Lakes, to prevent the incurfions of the Indians. The general officers, in their minutes of council, have determined it a matter of much importance;—and their attention to the price of goods furnifhed the foldiery may be extremely neceffary. They have complained much upon this head.

The retreat from Crown-Point feems to be confidered in oppofite views by the general and field-officers. The former (I am fatisfied) have weighed the matter well; and yet the reafons affigned by the latter againft it appear ftrong and forcible. I hope whatever is done will be for the beft. * * *

By a letter from the committee of Orange-county, received this morning, the men-of-war and tenders were yefterday at Haverfham-bay, about forty miles above this. A number of men in four barges from the tenders, attempted to land, with a view (they fuppofe) of taking fome fheep and cattle, that had been previoufly removed. A fmall number of militia that were collected obliged them to retreat, without their doing any damage with their cannon. They were founding the water up towards the Highlands; by which it is probable they will attempt to pafs with part of the fleet, if poffible.

Yefterday evening a flag came from general Howe with a letter addreffed " *To George Wafhington, efquire, &c. &c.*

&c. &c." It was not received, upon the fame principle that the one from lord Howe was refufed.

I have the honour to be, &c.　　　　　　G. W.

———

SIR,　　　　　　　　　　*New-York, July* 19, 1776.

I HAVE been duly honoured with your favours of the fixteenth and feventeenth, with the feveral refolves they contained ; to the execution of which, fo far as fhall be in my power, I will pay proper attention.

In my letter of the feventeenth I tranfmitted you a copy of one from general Schuyler, and of its feveral inclofures. I confefs the determination of the council of general officers on the feventh, to retreat from Crown-Point, furprifed me much : and the more I confider it, the more ftriking does the impropriety appear. The reafons affigned againft it by the field-officers, in their remonftrance, coincide greatly with my own ideas and thofe of the other general officers I have had an opportunity of confulting with, and feem to be of confiderable weight,— I may add, conclufive. I am not fo fully acquainted with the geography of that country and the fituation of the different pofts, as to pronounce a peremptory judgment upon the matter : but, if my ideas are right, the poffeffion of Crown-Point is effential, to give us the fuperiority and maftery upon the Lake.

That the enemy will poffefs it as foon as abandoned by us, there can be no doubt ; and if they do, whatever galleys or force we keep on the Lake will be unqueftionably in their rear. How they are to be fupported there, or what fuccour can be drawn from them there, is beyond my comprehenfion. Perhaps it is only meant that they fhall be employed on the communication between that and Ticonderoga. If this is the cafe, I fear the views of Congrefs will not be anfwered, nor the falutary effects be derived from them, that were intended.

I have mentioned my furprife to general Schuyler, and would, by the advice of the general officers here, have directed that that poft fhould be maintained, had it not been for two caufes,—an apprehenfion that the works

have

have been deftroyed, and that, if the army fhould be ordered from Ticonderoga, or the poft oppofite to it (where
I prefume they are) to re-poffefs it, they would have neither one place nor another fecure and in a defenfible ftate:
the other, left it might increafe the jealoufy and diverfity
of opinions which feem already too prevalent in that army, and eftablifh a precedent for the inferior officers to
fet up their judgments whenever they would, in oppofition to thofe of their fuperiors,—a matter of great delicacy, and that might lead to fatal confequences, if counte-
nanced;—though in the prefent inftance I could wifh their
reafoning had prevailed.

If the army has not removed, what I have faid to general Schuyler may perhaps bring on a re-confideration of
the matter; and it may not be too late to take meafures
for maintaining that poft.   But of this I have no hope.

In confequence of the refolve of Congrefs for three of
the eaftern regiments to reinforce the northern army,
I wrote to general Ward, and, by advice of my general officers, directed them to march to Norwich, and
there to embark for Albany; conceiving that two valuable purpofes might refult therefrom,—firft, that they
would fooner join the army, by purfuing this route, and
be faved from the diftrefs and fatigue that muft attend
every long march through the country at this hot and un-
comfortable feafon; and fecondly, that they might give
fuccour here, in cafe the enemy fhould make an attack
about the time of their paffing.   But the enemy having
now, with their fhips of war and tenders, cut off the
water-communication from hence to Albany, I have
wrote this day and directed them to proceed by land
acrofs the country.   If Congrefs difapprove the route, or
wifh to give any orders about them, you will pleafe to
certify me thereof, that I may take meafures accordingly.

Inclofed I have the honour to tranfmit you copies of a
letter and fundry refolutions which I received yefterday
from the convention of this State.   By them you will perceive they have been acting upon matters of great importance, and are exerting themfelves in the moft vigorous
manner to defeat the wicked defigns of the enemy, and
fuch difaffected perfons as may incline to affift and facilitate

tate their views. In compliance with their requeſt, and on account of the ſcarcity of money for carrying their ſalutary views into execution, I have agreed to lend them, out of the ſmall ſtock now in hand, (not more than ſixty thouſand dollars) twenty thouſand dollars, in part of what they want ; which they promiſe ſpeedily to re-place. Had there been money ſufficient for paying the whole of our troops and no more, I could not have done it. But as it was otherwiſe, and by no means proper to pay a part and not the whole, I could not foreſee any in-conveniences that would attend the loan ;—on the con-trary, that it might contribute in ſome degree to forward their ſchemes. I hope my conduct in this inſtance will not be diſapproved.

1 incloſed governor Trumbull a copy of their letter and of their ſeveral reſolves, to-day, by colonel Broom and Mr. Duer, two members of the convention, who are go-ing to wait on him ; but did not think myſelf at liberty to urge or requeſt his intereſt in forming the camp of ſix thouſand men, as the levies, directed by Congreſs to be furniſhed the third of June, for the defence of this place, by that government, are but little more than one third come in. At the ſame time, the propoſition I think a good one, if it could be carried into execution. In caſe the enemy ſhould attempt to effect a landing above Kingſbridge, and to cut off the communication between this city and the country, an army to hang on their rear would diſtreſs them exceedingly.

I have the honour to be, &c.   G. W.

The incloſed paper ſhould have been ſent before, but was omitted through hurry.

P. S. After I had cloſed my letter I received one from general Ward, a copy of which is herewith tranſmit-ted. I have wrote him to forward the two regiments now at Boſton, by the moſt direct road, to Ticonderoga, as ſoon as they are well, with the utmoſt expedition ; and conſider their having had the ſmall pox as a fortunate cir-cumſtance. When the three arrive which have marched for Norwich, I ſhall immediately ſend one of them on, if Congreſs ſhall judge it expedient ;—of which you will pleaſe to inform me.

New-York,

SIR,   *New-York, July* 21, 1776.

I HAVE juft time to acknowledge the receipt of your favour of the nineteenth. The interefting intelligence of the fuccefs of our arms in the fouthern department gives me the higheft fatisfaction. Permit me to join my joy to the congratulations of Congrefs upon this event. To-morrow I will write more fully.

Two o'clock, P. M.—I this moment had a report made me, that ten fhips were feen in the offing, coming in,—I fuppofe, part of admiral Howe's fleet.

I have the honour to be, &c.   G. W.

SIR,   *New-York, July* 22, 1776.

YOUR favours of the eighteenth and nineteenth, with which you have been pleafed to honour me, have been duly received, with the feveral refolves alluded to.

When the letter and declaration, from lord Howe to Mr. Franklin and the other late governors, come to be pub-lifhed, I fhould fuppofe the warmeft advocates for depend-ence on the Britifh crown muft be filent, and be convinc-ed beyond all poffibility of doubt, that all that has been faid about the commiffioners was illufory, and calculated exprefsly to deceive and unguard, not only the good peo-ple of our own country, but thofe of the Englifh nation that were averfe to the proceedings of the king and minif-try. Hence we fee the caufe why a fpecification of their powers was not given the mayor and city of London, on their addrefs requefting it. That would have been danger-ous, becaufe it would then have been manifeft that the line of conduct they were to purfue would be totally variant from that they had induftrioufly propagated, and amufed the public with. The uniting the civil and military offices in the fame perfons too, muft be conclufive to every think-ing one, that there is to be but little negociation of the civil kind.

I have inclofed for the fatisfaction of Congrefs, the fub-ftance of what paffed between myfelf and lieutenant-colo-nel Patterfon, adjutant-general, at an interview had yefter-

day in confequence of a requeft from general Howe the
day before ;—to which I beg leave to refer them for particulars.

Colonel Knox of the train having often mentioned to
me the neceflity of having a much more numerous body of
artillerifts than what there now is, in cafe the prefent conteft fhould continue longer,—and knowing the deficiency
in this inftance, and their extreme ufefulnefs,—I defired
him to commit his ideas upon the fubject to writing, in order that I might tranfmit them to Congrefs for their confideration.   Agreeable to my requeft he has done it ; and
the propriety of his plan is now fubmitted for their decifion.
It is certain that we have not more at this time than are
fufficient for the feveral extenfive pofts we now have,—
including the draughts which he fpeaks of, and which, I
prefume (not only from what he has informed me, but from
the nature of the thing) can never be qualified to render
the fame fervice as if they were regularly appointed and
formed into a corps for that particular purpofe.

I beg leave to remind Congrefs that fome time ago I
laid before them the propofals of fome perfons here for
forming a company of light-horfe ; and the prefident's anfwer, a little time after, intimated that the plan feemed to
be approved of.   As thofe who wanted to make up the
troop are frequently prefling me for an anfwer, I could
wifh to be favoured with the decifion of Congrefs upon
the fubject.

By a letter from general Schuyler, of the fourteenth
inftant, dated at Albany, he informs me, that, the day
before, fome defperate defigns of the tories in that quarter had been difcovered, the particulars of which he could
not divulge, being under an oath of fecrecy ;—however,
that fuch meafures had been taken, as to promife a pre-
vention of the intended mifchief; and that four of the
confpirators (among them, a ringleader) were apprehended about one o'clock that morning, not far from the town.
What the plot was, or who were concerned in it, is a
matter I am ignorant of as yet.

With my beft regards to Congrefs, I have the honour
to be your and their moft obedient fervant,   G. W.

P. S. Congress will please to observe what was proposed respecting the exchange of Mr. Lovell, and signify their pleasure in your next. The last week's return is also inclosed.

SIR, *New-York, July 22, 1776.*

CONGRESS having been pleased to appoint Mr. Wilpert to the command of a company in the German battalion now raising, I have directed him to repair to Philadelphia for their orders. From my acquaintance with him, I am persuaded his conduct as an officer will merit their approbation : and, thanking them for their kind attention to my recommendation of him, I have the honour to be, with sentiments of the highest respect, &c.

G. W.

SIR, *New-York, July 23, 1776.*

I WAS honoured with your favour of the twentieth by yesterday's post, since which, and my letter, nothing of moment has occurred.

The ships, mentioned in my letter of the twenty-first to have been in the offing, got in that day, and are supposed to be part of the Scotch fleet, having landed some Highlanders yesterday.

Inclosed I have the honour to transmit you copies of a letter and sundry resolutions which I received last night from the convention of this State. They will inform you of the computed number of inhabitants and stock upon Nassau-Island, and their sentiments on the impracticability of removing the latter ; and also of the measures they think necessary and likely to secure them.

I have also inclosed a letter from Mr. Faesh to lord Stirling upon the subject of a cannon-furnace for the use of the States. Congress will see his plan and proposals, and determine upon them as they shall judge proper.

I am, Sir, with every sentiment of respect, &c.

G. W.
New-York,

SIR,   *New-York, July* 23, 1776.

SINCE I had the pleasure of writing you by this morning's post, I was favoured with a letter from governor Trumbull, a copy of which is inclosed, and to which I beg leave to refer you.   In regard to the stock he mentions, I wrote to him, requesting that they might be removed from the islands on which they were, as I conceived it of great importance to distress the enemy as much as possible in the article of fresh provision.   I wish the other governments may follow his example, and have it removed from the islands belonging to them respectively.

When the ships of war and tenders went up the river, it was thought expedient that application should be made for the Connecticut row-galleys and those belonging to Rhode-Island, in order to attempt something for their destruction. As soon as they arrive we shall try to employ them in some useful way,—but in what, or how successfully, I cannot at present determine.

Congress will please to observe what Mr. Trumbull says respecting the continental regiment raising under colonel Ward.   If they incline to give any orders about their destination, you will please to communicate them by the earliest opportunity, as their march will be suspended till they are known.

The orders Mr. Trumbull has given to the officers of their cruisers, to stop provision-vessels, seem to be necessary. We have too much reason to believe that some have gone voluntarily to the enemy, and that there are many persons who would continue to furnish them with large supplies : and, however upright the intentions of others may be, it will be a matter of the utmost difficulty, if not an impossibility, for any to escape falling into their hands now, as every part of the coast (it is probable) will swarm with their ships of war and tenders.   I had proposed writing to the convention of this State upon the subject before I received his letter ; and am now more persuaded of the necessity of their taking some steps to prevent further exportations down the Sound.   In my next I shall inform them of the intelligence received from Mr. Trumbull, and recommend the matter to their attention.

I have the honour to be, &c.   G. W.

P. S.   It appears abſolutely neceſſary that the exportation of proviſion ſhould be ſtopped.   Our army is large, and otherwiſe may want.   Nor can individuals be injured, as they have a ready-money market for every thing they have to diſpoſe of in that way.

SIR,   *New-York, July* 25, 1776.

DISAGREEABLE as it is to me and unpleaſing as it may be to Congreſs to multiply officers, I find myſelf under the unavoidable neceſſity of aſking an increaſe of my aides-de-camp.   The augmentation of my command,—the increaſe of my correſpondence,—the orders to give,—the inſtructions to draw,—cut out more buſineſs than I am able to execute in time with propriety.   The buſineſs of ſo many different departments centring with me, and by me to be handed on to Congreſs for their information,—added to the intercourſe I am obliged to keep up with the adjacent States,—and incidental occurrences,—all of which require confidential and not hack writers to execute,—renders it impoſſible, in the preſent ſtate of things, for my family to diſcharge the ſeveral duties expected of me, with that preciſion and diſpatch that I could wiſh.   What will it be then, when we come into a more active ſcene, and I am called upon from twenty different places perhaps at the ſame inſtant ?

Congreſs will do me the juſtice to believe (I hope) that it is not my inclination or wiſh to run the continent to any unneceſſary expenſe ; and thoſe who better know me will not ſuſpect that ſhew and parade can have any influence on my mind in this inſtance.   A conviction of the neceſſity of it, for the regular diſcharge of the truſt repoſed in me, is the governing motive for the application ; and, as ſuch, is ſubmitted to Congreſs by, Sir, your moſt obedient, &c.   G. W.

SIR,   *New-York, July* 27, 1776.

'I WAS yeſterday morning honoured with your favour 'of the twenty-fourth inſtant with its ſeveral incloſures, to which I ſhall pay the ſtricteſt attention.

R 2

The

The confidence Congreſs are pleaſed to repoſe in my judgment demands my warmeſt acknowledgments, and they may reſt aſſured it ſhall be invariably employed, ſo far as ſhall be in my power, to promote their views and the public weal. * * *

Since my laſt, nothing material has occurred. Yeſterday evening report was made that eight ſhips were ſeen in the offing, ſtanding towards the Hook. The men-of-war and tenders are ſtill up the river. They have never attempted to paſs the Highland fortifications ; and, a day or two ago, quitted their ſtation, and fell down the river eight or ten miles. The vigilance and activity of the militia oppoſite where they were have prevented their landing and doing much injury. One poor peaſant's cot they plundered and then burnt.

I would wiſh to know whether the allowance given to officers, the ſeventeenth of January, of a dollar and one-third for every man they enliſt, Congreſs mean to extend to the officers who enliſt for the new army for three years. At firſt it may appear wrong, or rather exorbitant, ſuppoſing that many will be recruited out of the regiments now in ſervice, and under them : but the allowance will be of great uſe, as it will intereſt the officers, and call forth their exertions, which otherwiſe would be faint and languid. Indeed I am fearful, from the inquiries I have made, that their utmoſt exertions will be attended with but little ſucceſs. It is objected that the bounty of ten dollars is too low ; and argued,——" if the States, furniſhing men for five or ſix months, allow conſiderably more, why ſhould that be accepted when the term of enliſtment is to be for three years." I heartily wiſh a bounty in land had been or could be given, as was propoſed ſome time ago. I think it would be attended with ſalutary conſequences.

In conſequence of my application to governor Trumbull, he has ſent me two row-galleys ; and I expect another from him. None from governor Cooke are yet come ; nor have I heard from him on the ſubject. One is complete here. The fire-ſhips are going on under Mr. Anderſon's direction, but rather ſlowly ; and I am preparing ſome obſtructions for the channel nearly oppoſite the works at the upper end of this iſland. When all things are ready, I in-

tend

tend to try, if it fhall feem practicable, to deftroy the fhips.
and tenders above, and to employ the galleys, if they can
be of advantage.

The militia for the flying camp come in but flowly. By
a return from general Mercer yefterday, they are but little
more than three thoufand. If they were in, or can be there
fhortly, and the fituation of the enemy remains the fame, I
would make fome efforts to annoy them, keeping our pofts
here well guarded, and not putting too much to the hazard,
or in any manner to the rifk.

I have the honour to be, &c.   G. W.

SIR,   *New-York, July 29, 1776.*
YOUR favour of the twenty-fourth I received on
Saturday evening, and, agreeable to your requeft, fhall ex-
punge the preamble to the refolution fubjecting the property of fubjects to the Britifh crown to forfeiture and confifcation.

Our ftock of mufket-powder is entirely made up in cartridges. I therefore requeft that Congrefs will order four
or five tons more of that fort to be immediately forwarded ;
it being not only neceffary that we fhould have more for
that purpofe, but alfo fome ftock to remain in barrels.

Yefterday evening Hutchinfon's and Sergeant's regiments from Bofton arrived ; alfo two row-galleys from
Rhode-Ifland. I am fearful the troops have not got entirely clear of the fmall-pox. I fhall ufe every poffible
precaution to prevent the infection fpreading ; and, for that
purpofe, have ordered them to an encampment feparate and
detached from the reft.

By Saturday's report from Long-Ifland camp, five fhips,
a brig, and five fchooners, had got into the Hook ; by yefterday's, two fhips more, and a floop, were ftanding in.
What they are, I have not been able to learn.

I have tranfmitted a general return herewith, by which
Congrefs will perceive the whole of our force at the time
it was made.

I have inclofed you an account of fundry prizes, which
was tranfmitted to feveral gentlemen here by Saturday's
                                        poft.

poſt.　The two laſt prizes I did not ſee mentioned in the letters ſhewn me; and I fear the report of the ſecond proviſion-veſſel is premature.　I was alſo this minute informed that captain Biddle had taken a ſhip with ſugars for Britain, and, in bringing her in, unfortunately loſt her on Fiſher's-Iſland.

I have the honour to be, &c.　　　　G. W.

SIR,　　　　　　　　　　　　*New-York, July 30, 1776.*

I WAS this morning honoured with your two favours of yeſterday's date; and, agreeable to your requeſt, have given Mr. Palfrey liberty to negociate your claim with Mr. Brimer, and wiſh it may be ſatisfied agreeably to you.

I laſt night received a letter from general Schuyler, a copy of which I do myſelf the honour to tranſmit you. You will thereby perceive his reaſons for leaving Crown-Point, and preferring the poſt the council of officers determined to take oppoſite to Ticonderoga.　I am totally unacquainted with thoſe ſeveral poſts and the country about them, and therefore cannot determine on the validity of his obſervations, or think myſelf at liberty to give any direction in the matter.

Congreſs will pleaſe to obſerve what he ſays of their diſtreſs for money.　From hence he can have no relief, there being only about three or four thouſand dollars in the paymaſter's hands, according to his return this morning,—and all but two months pay due to the army, beſides many other demands.　I could wiſh that proper ſupplies of money could be always kept:—the want may occaſion conſequences of an alarming nature.

By a letter from him, of a prior date to the copy incloſed, he tells me that a Mr. Ryckman, who has juſt returned through the country of the Six Nations, reports that the Indians who were at Philadelphia have gone home with very favourable ideas of our ſtrength and reſources.　This he heard in many of their villages:—a lucky circumſtance if it will either gain their friendſhip or ſecure their neutrality.

In

In my letter of the twenty-seventh I informed Congress of my views and wishes to attempt something against the troops on Staten-Island. I am now to acquaint them, that, by the advice of general Mercer and other officers at Amboy, it will be impracticable to do any thing upon a large scale, for want of craft, and as the enemy have the entire command of the water all round the island. I have desired general Mercer to have nine or ten flat-bottomed boats built at Newark-bay and Elizabeth-Town, with a design principally to keep up the communication across Hackinsac and Passaic rivers, which I deem a matter of great importance, and extremely necessary to be attended to.

Since I wrote you yesterday, eleven ships more, four brigs, and two sloops, have come into the Hook. I have not yet received intelligence what any of the late arrivals are: but I suppose we shall not long remain in a state of uncertainty.

Having reason to believe that lord Howe will readily come into an exchange of such prisoners as may be more immediately under his command, and that something will be offered on this subject within a day or two, or rather come in answer to the propositions I have made general Howe, I should be glad to have Congress's interpretation of the resolve of the twenty-second instant, empowering the commanders to exchange, &c. whether by the word '*sailor*,' they mean sailors generally, as well those taken in the vessels of private adventurers by the enemy, as those belonging to the continental cruisers, or vessels in the continent's employ; or whether they only design to extend the exchange to the latter,—those in their particular employ.

I would also observe that, heretofore, sailors belonging to merchant ships that have fallen into our hands, and those employed merely as transports, have not generally been considered as prisoners. I submit it to Congress whether it may not be now necessary to pass a resolve declaring their sentiments on this subject, and, in general, who are to be treated as prisoners of war, that are taken on board vessels belonging to the subjects of the British crown, &c.

The

The refult of their opinion upon the firft queftion propofed, you will be pleafed to tranfmit me by the earlieft opportunity.

I have inclofed, for the confideration of Congrefs, a
memorial and petition by captain Holdridge, praying to be
relieved againft the lofs of money ftolen from him,—not
conceiving myfelf authorifed to grant his requeft. The
certificate which attends it proves him a man of charaćter ;
and his cafe is hard, on his ftate of it. Whether making
the lofs good may not open a door to others, and give rife
to applications not fo juft as his may be, I cannot determine. That feems to be the only objećtion to relieving
him.

I am informed by general Putnam that there are fome
of the Stockbridge Indians here (I have not feen them
myfelf) who exprefs great uneafinefs at their not being
employed by us, and have come to inquire into the caufe.
I am fenfible Congrefs had them not in contemplation
when they refolved that Indians might be engaged in our
fervice. However, as they feem fo anxious,—as they
were led to expećt it, from what general Schuyler and the
other commiffioners did,—as we are under difficulties in
getting men, and there may be danger of their (or fome of
them) taking an unfavourable part,—I beg leave to fubmit it as my opinion, under all thefe circumftances, that
they had better be employed.

I have the honour to be, &c.   G. W.

S I R,   *New-York, Auguft* 2, 1776.

YOUR favour of the thirtieth ultimo, with its feveral inclofures, I was honoured with by Wednefday's
poft.

Congrefs having been pleafed to leave with me the
direćtion of colonel Ward's regiment, I have wrote to
governor Trumbull, and requefted him to order their
march to this place, being fully fatisfied that the enemy
mean to make their grand pufh in this quarter, and that
the good of the fervice requires every aid here that can
be obtained. I have alfo wrote to colonel Elmore, and
                                                     directed

directed him to repair hither with his regiment. When it comes, I shall fill up commissions for such officers as appear with their respective companies.

Colonel Holman, with a regiment from the Massachusetts State, is arrived. Colonel Cary from thence is also here, waiting the arrival of his regiment which he hourly expects. He adds, when he left New-London he heard that the third regiment from the Massachusetts was almost ready, and would soon be in motion.

The enemy's force is daily augmenting and becoming stronger by new arrivals. Yesterday, general Greene reports that about forty sail, including tenders, came into the Hook. What they are, or what those have brought that have lately got in, I remain uninformed. However, I think it probable they are part of lord Howe's fleet, with the Hessian troops :—it is time to look for them.

I have the honour to be, &c.   G. W.

P. S. I am extremely sorry to inform Congress our troops are very sickly.

***

SIR,   *New-York, August 5, 1776.*

I WAS honoured with your favour of the thirty-first ultimo on Friday, with its several inclosures ; and return you my thanks for the agreeable intelligence you were pleased to communicate, of the arrival of one of our ships with such valuable articles as arms and ammunition ; also of the capture made by a privateer.

The mode for the exchange of prisoners, resolved on by Congress, is acceded to by general Howe, so far as it comes within his command. A copy of my letter and his answer upon this subject I have the honour to inclose you ; to which I beg leave to refer Congress.

The inclosed copy of a letter from colonel Tupper, who had the general command of the galleys here, will inform Congress of the engagement between them and the ships of war up the North-river on Saturday evening, the damage we sustained. What injury was done ships, I cannot ascertain. It is said they were hi

-eral times by our shot.   All accounts agree that our officers and men, during the whole of the affair, behaved with great spirit and bravery.   The damage done the galleys shews beyond question that they had a warm time of it.   The ships still remain up the river ; and, before any thing further can be attempted against them (should it be thought adviseable) the galleys must be repaired. .

I have also transmitted Congress a copy of a letter I received by Saturday's post from governor Cooke, to which I refer them for the intelligence it contains.   The seizure of our vessels by the Portuguese is, I fear, an event too true.   Their dependence upon the British crown for aid against the Spaniards must force them to comply with every thing required of them.   I wish the Morris may get safe in with her cargo.   As to the ships captain Bachlin saw on the twenty-fifth ultimo, they are probably arrived ; for yesterday twenty-five sail came into the Hook.

By a letter from general Ward, of the twenty-ninth ultimo, he informs me that two of our armed vessels, the day before, had brought into Marblehead a ship bound from Halifax to Staten-Island.   She had in about fifteen hundred and nine pounds' worth of British goods, besides a good many belonging to tories.   A Halifax paper, found on board her, I have inclosed, as also an account sent me by Mr. Hazard, transmitted him by some of his friends, as given by the tories taken in her.   Their intelligence, I dare say, is true respecting the arrival of part of the Hessian troops.   General Ward in his letter mentions, that, the day this prize was taken, captain Burke, in another of our armed vessels, had an engagement with a ship and a schooner which he thought were transports, and would have taken them, had it not been for an unlucky accident in having his quarter-deck blown up. Two of his men were killed, and several more were wounded.

, The hulks and chevaux-de-frise, that have been preparing to obstruct the channel, have got up to the place they are intended for, and will be sunk as soon as pos-

-e transmitted Congress a general return of the ar-
-d about this place on the third instant, by which
erceive the amount of our force.

Before

Before I conclude, I would beg leave to remind Congrefs of the neceffity there is of having fome major-generals appointed for this army, the duties of which are great, extenfive, and impoffible to be difcharged as they ought and the good of the fervice requires, without a competent number of officers of this rank.   I mean to write more fully upon the fubject: and, as things are drawing faft to an iffue, and it is neceffary to make every proper difpofition and arrangement that we poffibly can, I pray that this matter may be taken into confideration, and claim their early attention.   I well know what has prevented appointments of this fort for fome time paft: but the fituation of our affairs will not juftify longer delays in this inftance.   By the firft opportunity, I fhall take the liberty of giving you my fentiments more at large upon the propriety and neceffity of the meafure.

I have the honour to be, &c.   G. W.

SIR,   *New-York, Auguft 7, 1776.*

IN my letter of the fifth which I had the honour of addreffing you, I begged leave to recal the attention of Congrefs to the abfolute neceffity there is for appointing more general officers,—promifing at the fame time, by the firft opportunity, to give my fentiments more at large upon the fubject.

Confident I am that the poftponing this meafure has not proceeded from motives of frugality: otherwife I fhould take the liberty of attempting to prove that we put too much to the hazard by fuch a faving.   I am but too well apprifed of the difficulties that occur in the choice.   They are, I acknowledge, great; but at the fame time it muft be allowed they are of fuch a nature as to prefent themfelves whenever the fubject is thought of.   Time on the one hand does not remove them; on the other, delay may be productive of fatal confequences.

This army, though far fhort as yet of the numbers intended by Congrefs, is by much too unwieldy for the command of any one man, without feveral major-generals to affift.   For it is to be obferved that a brigadier-general at

VOL. I.   S   the

the head of his brigade is no more than a colonel at the head of a regiment, except that he acts upon a larger scale. Officers of more general command are at all times wanted for the good order and government of an army, especially when the army is composed chiefly of raw troops : but in an action they are indispensably necessary. At present there is but one major-general for this whole department and the flying camp ; whereas, at this place alone, less than three cannot discharge the duties with that regularity they ought to be.

If these major-generals are appointed, as undoubtedly they will, out of the present brigadiers, you will want for this place three brigadiers at least. The northern department will require one, if not two (as general Thompson is a prisoner, and the baron Woedtke reported to be dead or in a state not much better) there being at present only one brigadier-general (Arnold) in all that department. For the eastern governments there ought to be one, or a major-general, to superintend the regiments there, and to prevent impositions that might otherwise be practised. These make the number wanted to be six or seven : and who are to be appointed, Congress can best judge.

To make brigadiers of the oldest colonels would be the least exceptionable way : but it is much to be questioned whether by that mode the ablest men would be appointed to office. And I would observe, though the rank of the colonels of the eastern governments was settled at Cambridge last year, it only respected themselves and is still open as to officers of other governments. To pick a colonel here and a colonel there through the army according to the opinion entertained of their abilities, would no doubt be the means of making a better choice, and nominating the fittest persons : but then the senior officers would get disgusted, and, more than probable, with their connexions, quit the service. That might prove fatal at this time. To appoint gentlemen as brigadiers, that had not served in this army, (in this part of it at least) would not wound any one in particular, but hurt the whole equally, and must be considered in a very discouraging light by every officer of merit. View the matter therefore in any point of light you will, there are inconveniences on the one hand, and

difficulties

difficulties on the other, which ought to be avoided. Would they be remedied by appointing the oldest colonels from each State ?—If this mode should be thought expedient, the inclosed list gives the names of the colonels, from New-Hampshire to Pennsylvania inclusive, specifying those who rank first, as I am told, in the several colony lists.

I have transmitted a copy of a letter from Mr. John Glover, setting forth the nature and grounds of a dispute between him and a Mr. Bradford respecting their agency. Not conceiving myself authorised, nor having the smallest inclination to interefere in any degree in the matter, it is referred to Congress, who will determine and give direction upon it in such manner as they shall judge best. I will only observe that Mr. Glover was recommended to me as a proper person for an agent when we first fitted out armed vessels, and was accordingly appointed one ; and, so far as I know, discharged his office with fidelity and industry.

I received yesterday evening a letter from general Schuyler, containing lieutenant M'Michael's report, who had been sent a scout to Ofwego. A copy of the report I have inclosed for the information of Congress, lest general Schuyler should have omitted it in his letter which accompanies this. He was at the German-Flats when he wrote, which was the second instant, and the treaty with the Indians not begun ; nor had the whole expected then arrived. But of these things he will have advised you more fully, I make no doubt.

The pay-master informs me he received a supply of money yesterday. It came very seasonably : for the applications and clamours of the troops had become incessant and distressing beyond measure. There is now two months' pay due to them.

I have the honour to be, &c.   G. W.

SIR,

SINCE closing the letter which I had the honour to write you this morning, two deserters have come in,
who

who left the Solebay man-of-war laſt evening.   One of them is a native of New-York.   Their account is that they were in the engagement with colonel Moultrie at Sullivan's iſland on the ninth of July—(the particulars they give nearly correſpond with the narrative ſent by general Lee)—that they left Carolina three weeks ago as a con-voy to forty-five tranſports having on board general Clin-ton, lord Cornwallis, and the whole ſouthern army con-ſiſting of about three thouſand men, all of whom were landed laſt week on Staten-Iſland in tolerable health ;—that, on Sunday, thirteen tranſports, part of lord Howe's fleet, and having on board Heſſians and Highlanders, came to Staten-Iſland ;—that the remainder of the fleet, which was reported to have, in the whole, twelve thou-ſand men, had parted with theſe troops off the banks of Newfoundland, and were expected to come in every mo-ment ;—that they were getting their heavy carriages and cannon on board, had launched eight gondolas with flat bottoms, and two rafts or ſtages to carry cannon.

Theſe men underſtand that the attack will ſoon be made, if the other troops arrive ;—that they give out they will lay the Jerſies waſte with fire and ſword ;—that the computed ſtrength of their army will be thirty thouſand men.   They further add, that, when they left Carolina, one tranſport got on ſhore, ſo that they were not able to give her relief ; upon which, ſhe ſurrendered, with five com-panies of Highlanders, to general Lee, who, after taking every thing valuable out of her, burnt her ;—that the ad-miral turned general Clinton out of his ſhip after the en-gagement, with a great deal of abuſe ;—great differences between the principal naval and military gentlemen ;—that the ſhips, left in Carolina, are now in ſuch a weakly diſtreſſed condition, they would fall an eaſy prey.

I am, Sir, with great reſpect, &c.   G. W.

Head-Quarters, New-York, Aug. 7, 1776, *one o'clock, P. M.*
The ſhips are changing their poſition, and the men-of-war forming into a line : but I ſtill think they will wait the arrival of the remaining Heſſians before any general attack will be made.   Monday's return will ſhew our ſtrength here.

New-York,

SIR,   *New-York, August* 8, 1776.

By yesterday morning's post, I was honoured with your favour of the second instant, with sundry resolutions of Congress, to which I shall pay strict attention.

As the proposition for employing the Stockbridge Indians has been approved, I have wrote to Mr. Edwards, one of the commissioners, and who lives among them, requesting him to engage them, or, such as are willing, to enter the service. I have directed him to indulge them with liberty to join this or the northern army, or both, as their inclination may lead.

I wish the salutary consequences may result from the regulation respecting seamen taken, that Congress have in view. From the nature of this kind of people, and the privileges granted on their entering into our service, I should suppose many of them will do it. We want them much.

I yesterday transmitted the intelligence I received from the deserters from the Solebay man-of-war. The inclosed copy of a letter by last night's post, from the honourable Mr. Bowdoin, with the information of a captain Kennedy lately taken, corroborate their accounts respecting the Hessian troops. Indeed his report makes the fleet and armament, to be employed against us, greater than what we have heard they would be. However there remains no doubt of their being both large and formidable, and such as will require our most vigorous exertions to oppose them. Persuaded of this, and knowing how much inferior our numbers are and will be to theirs when the whole of their troops arrive,—of the important consequences that may and will flow from the appeal that will soon be made,—I have wrote to Connecticut and New-Jersey, for all the succour they can afford, and also to the convention of this State. What I may receive, and in what time, the event must determine. But I would fain hope, the situation and the exigency of our affairs will call forth the most strenuous efforts and early assistance of those who are friends to the cause. I confess there is but too much occasion for their exertions. I confidently trust they will not be withheld.

S 2

I have

I have inclofed a copy of a letter from Mr. Bowdoin refpecting the eaftern Indians. Congrefs will thereby perceive that they profefs themfelves to be well attached to our intereft,—and the fummary of the meafures taken to engage them in our fervice. I have the treaty at large between the honourable council of the Maffachufetts, on behalf of the United States, with the delegates of the Saint John's and Mickmac tribes. The probability of a copy's being fent already, and its great length, prevent one coming herewith. If Congrefs have not had it forwarded to them, I will fend a copy by the firft opportunity after notice that it has not been received.

Auguft 9.—By a report received from general Greene laft night, at funfet and a little after, about a hundred boats were feen bringing troops from Staten-Ifland to the fhips, three of which had fallen down towards the narrows, having taken in foldiers from thirty of the boats. He adds, that, by the beft obfervations of feveral officers, there appeared to be a general embarkation.

I have wrote to general Mercer for two thoufand men from the flying camp. Colonel Smallwood's battalion, as part of them, I expect this forenoon : but where the reft are to come from, I know not, as, by the general's laft return, not more than three or four hundred of the new levies had got in.

In my letter of the fifth I inclofed a general return of the army under my immediate command; but I imagine the following ftate will give Congrefs a more perfect idea, though not a more agreeable one, of our fituation. For the feveral pofts on New-York, Long and Governor's iflands, and Paulus-Hook, we have, fit for duty, ten thoufand five hundred and fourteen,—fick prefent, three thoufand and thirty-nine,—fick abfent, fix hundred and twenty-nine,—on command, two thoufand nine hundred and forty fix,—on furlough, ninety-feven,—total, feventeen thoufand two hundred and twenty-five. In addition to thefe, we are only certain of colonel Smallwood's battalion in cafe of an immediate attack. Our pofts too are much divided, having waters between many of them, and fome diftant from others fifteen miles. Thefe circumftances, fufficiently diftreffing of themfelves, are much aggravated

by

by the ficknefs that prevails through the army. Every day more or lefs are taken down ; fo that the proportion of men that may come in cannot be confidered as a real and ferviceable augmentation on the whole.

'Thefe things are melancholy ; but they are neverthelefs true. I hope for better. Under every difadvantage, my utmoft exertions fhall be employed to bring about the great end we have in view : and, fo far as I can judge from the profeffions and apparent difpofition of my troops, I fhall have their fupport. The fuperiority of the enemy and the expected attack do not feem to have depreffed their fpirits. Thefe confiderations lead me to think, that, though the appeal may not terminate fo happily in our favour as I could wifh, yet they will not fucceed in their views without confiderable lofs. Any advantage they may get, I truft, will coft them dear.

Eight o'clock, P. M.

By the reverend Mr. Madifon and a Mr. Johnfon, two gentlemen of Virginia, who came from Staten-Ifland yefterday, where they arrived the day before in the packet with colonel Guy Johnfon, I am informed that nothing material had taken place in England when they left it ;— that there had been a change in the French miniftry, which, many people thought, foreboded a war ;—that it feemed to be believed by many that Congrefs would attempt to buy off the foreign troops, and that it might be effected without great difficulty. Their accounts from Staten-Ifland nearly correfpond with what we had before : they fay that every preparation is making for an attack ;—that the force now upon the ifland is about fifteen thoufand ;— that they appear very impatient for the arrival of the foreign troops, but a very fmall part having got in. Whether they would attempt any thing before they come, they are uncertain : but they are fure they will as foon as they arrive, if not before. They fay, from what they could collect from the converfation of officers, &c. they mean to hem us in by getting above us and cutting off all communication with the country.

That this is their plan, feems to be corroborated and confirmed by the circumftance of fome fhips of war going out at different times within a few days paft, and other
veffels.

veſſels.   It is probable that a part are to go round and come up the Sound.

Mr. Madiſon ſays lord Howe's powers were not known when he left England ;—that general Conway moved, before his departure, that they might be laid before the commons ; and had his motion rejeſted by a large majority.

I have the honour to be, &c.   G. W.

—————

SIR,   *New-York, Auguſt* 12, 1776.

I HAVE been duly honoured with your favours of the eighth and tenth inſtant, with their ſeveral incloſures. I ſhall pay attention to the reſolution reſpeſting lieutenant Joſiah, and attempt to relieve him from his rigorous uſage. Your letters to ſuch of the gentlemen as were here have been delivered.   The reſt will be ſent by the firſt opportunity.

Since my laſt, of the eighth and ninth, the enemy have made no movements of conſequence.   They remain nearly in the ſame ſtate ; nor have we any further intelligence of their deſigns.   They have not been yet joined by the remainder of the fleet with the Heſſian troops.

Colonel Smallwood and his battalion got in on Friday ; and colonel Miles is alſo here with two battalions more of Pennſylvania riflemen.

The convention of this State have been exerting themſelves to call forth a portion of their militia to an encampment forming above Kingſbridge, to remain in ſervice for the ſpace of one month after their arrival there ; and alſo half of thoſe in King and Queen's counties, to reinforce the troops on Long-Iſland till the firſt of September, unleſs ſooner diſcharged.   General Morris too is to take poſt with his brigade on the Sound and Hudſon's-river for ten days, to annoy the enemy in caſe they attempt to land ; and others of their militia are direſted to be in readineſs; in caſe their aid ſhould be required.   Upon the whole, from the information I have from the convention, the militia ordered are now in motion, or will be in a little

tle time, and will amount to about three thoufand or more. From Connecticut, I am not certain what fuccours are coming. By one or two gentlemen who have come from thence, I am told fome of the militia were affembling, and, from the intelligence they had, would march this week.

By a letter from governor Trumbull, of the fifth, I am advifed that the troops from that State, deftined for the northern army, had marched for Skenefborough. General Ward too, by a letter of the fourth, informs me that the two regiments would march from Bofton laft week, having been cleanfed and generally recovered from the fmall-pox. I have alfo countermanded my orders to colonel Elmore, and directed him to join the northern army, having heard, after my orders to Connecticut for his marching hither, that he and moft of his regiment were at Albany or within its vicinity. General Ward mentions that the council of the Maffachufetts State will have in from two to three thoufand of their militia to defend their lines and different pofts, in lieu of the regiments ordered from thence agreeable to the refolution of Congrefs.

The inclofed copy of a refolve of this State, paffed the tenth inftant, will difcover the apprehenfion they are under of the defection of the inhabitants of King's county from the common caufe, and of the meafures they have taken thereupon. I have directed general Greene to give the committee fuch affiftance as he can, and they may require, in the execution of their commiffion ; though at the fame time I wifh the information the convention have received upon the fubject may prove groundlefs.

I would beg leave to mention to Congrefs, that, in a letter I received from general Lee, he mentions the valuable confequences that would refult from a number of cavalry being employed in the fouthern department. Without them (to ufe his own expreffions) he can anfwer for nothing :—with one thoufand, he would enfure the fafety of thofe States. I fhould have done myfelf the honour of fubmitting this matter to Congrefs before at his particular requeft, had it not efcaped my mind. From his acquaintance with that country, and the nature of the grounds, I doubt not he has weighed the matter well, and prefume he has fully reprefented the advantages that would arife from the eftablifhment of fuch a corps : all I mean, is, in compliance with his requifition, to mention the matter, that fuch confideration may be had upon it (if not already determined) as it may be deferving of.

I have tranfmitted a general return, whereby Congrefs will perceive the whole of our ftrength, except the two battalions under colonel Miles, which, coming fince it was made out, are not included.

I have inclofed a letter juft come to hand from Martinique. Congrefs will pleafe to confider of the purport, favouring me with their anfwer and a return of the letter.

This moment (ten o'clock) report is made by general Greene that a man-of-war came in yefterday, and that fixty fail of fhips are now ftanding in. No doubt, they are a further part of the Heffian fleet.

I have the honour to be, &c.   G. W.

SIR,   *New-York, Auguft* 12, 1776.

THIS will be handed to you by colonel * * * from the northern army, whom the inclofed letter and proceedings of a general court-martial will fhew to have been in arreft, and tried for fundry matters charged againft him. As the court-martial was by order of the commander in that department, the facts committed there, the trial there,—— I am much at a lofs to know why the proceedings were referred to me to approve or difapprove. As my interfering in the matter would carry much impropriety with it, and fhew a want of regard to the rules and practice in fuch inftances,—and as colonel * * * is going to Philadelphia, I have fubmitted the whole of the proceedings to the confideration of Congrefs for their decifion upon his cafe,— perfectly convinced that fuch determination will be had therein, as will be right and juft.

I have the honour to be, &c.   G. W.

New-York,

SIR,   *New-York, August* 13, 1776.

AS there is reafon to believe that but little time will elapfe before the enemy make their attack, I have thought it advifeable to remove all the papers in my hands, refpecting the affairs of the States, from this place. I hope the event will fhew the precaution 'was unneceffary : but yet prudence required that it fhould be done, left by any accident they might fall into their hands. They are all contained in a large box, nailed up, and committed to the care of lieutenant-colonel Reed, brother of the adjutant-general to be delivered to Congrefs, in whofe cuftody I would beg leave to depofite them until our affairs fhall be fo circumftanced as to admit of their return.

The enemy, fince my letter of yefterday, have received a further augmentation of thirty-fix fhips to their fleet, making the whole that have arrived fince yefterday morning, ninety-fix.

I have the honour to be, &c.   G. W.

P. S. I would obferve that I have fent off the box privately, that it might raife no difagreeable ideas ; and have enjoined colonel Reed to fecrecy.

SIR,   *New-York, August* 14, 1776.

SINCE I had the honour of addreffing you on Monday, nothing of importance has occurred here, except that the enemy have received an augmentation to their fleet, of ninety-fix fhips :—fome reports make them more. In a letter I wrote you yefterday by lieutenant-colonel Reed, I advifed you of this : but prefuming it may not reach you fo foon as this will, I have thought proper to mention the intelligence again.

Inclofed I have the honour to tranfmit a copy of the examination of a deferter fent me this morning by general Mercer, to which I beg leave to refer Congrefs for the lateft accounts I have from the enemy. Whether the intelligence he has given is literally true, I cannot determine : but as to the attack, we daily expect it.

Your .

Your favour of the tenth, with its inclofures, was duly received ; and I have inftructed the feveral officers who were promoted, to act in their ftations as you requefted, though their commiffions were not fent.

As we are in extreme want of tents and covering for this army,—a great part of thofe at the out-pofts having nothing to fhelter them, nor houfes to go into,—I fubmit it to Congrefs whether it may not be prudent to remand thofe that were lately fent to Bofton, where there are no troops at prefent ; and, if there were, the neceffity for them would not be great, as the town, and barracks at feveral of the pofts, would be fufficient to receive them.

The inclofed letter from lieutenant-colonel Henfhaw will difcover to Congrefs his views and wifhes, which they will confider and determine on, in whatever way they think right and conducive to the public good ;—meaning only to lay his letter before them.

I take the liberty of mentioning that colonel Varnum of Rhode-Ifland has been with me this morning to refign his commiffion, conceiving himfelf to be greatly injured in not having been noticed in the late arrangement and promotion of general officers.   I remonftrated againft the impropriety of the meafure at this time ; and he has con- fented to ftay till affairs wear a different afpect from what they do at prefent.

Eleven o'clock.—By a report juft come to hand from general Green, twenty fhips more are coming in.

I have the honour to be, &c.   G. W.

SIR,   *New-York, Auguft* 14, 1776.

THIS will be delivered you by captain Moeballe, a Dutch gentleman from Surrinam, who has come to the con- tinent with a view of entering into the fervice of the States, as you will perceive by the inclofed letters from Mr. Brown, of Providence, and general Greene.   What oth- er letters and credentials he has, I know not ; but, at his requeft, have given him this line to Congrefs, to whom he wifhes to be introduced, and where he will make his pre- tenfions known.

I have

I have ordered the quarter-mafter immediately to write to Mr. Brown for the Ruffia duck he mentions, with directions to have it inftantly made into tents there,—being in great diftrefs for want of a fufficient number to cover our troops.

I have the honour to be, &c.   G. W.

SIR,   *New-York, Auguft* 15, 1776.

AS the fituation of the two armies muft engage the attention of Congrefs, and lead them to expect that each returning day will produce fome important events, this is meant to inform them that nothing of moment has yet caft up. In the evening of yefterday there were great movements among their boats ; and, from the number that appeared to be paffing and repaffing about the Narrows, we were induced to believe they intended to land a part of their force upon Long-Ifland ; but, having no report from general Greene, I prefume they have not done it.

I have the honour to be, &c.   G. W.

P. S. Your favour of the thirteenth was received by yefterday's poft. I wrote on Monday by the return exprefs, as you fuppofed.

SIR,   *New-York, Auguft* 16, 1776.

I BEG leave to inform you, that fince I had the pleafure of addreffing you yefterday, nothing interefting between the two armies has happened. Things remain nearly in the fituation they then were.

It is with peculiar regret and concern that I have an opportunity of mentioning to Congrefs the fickly condition of our troops. In fome regiments there are not any of the field-officers capable of doing duty : in others the duty is extremely difficult for want of a fufficient number. I have been obliged to nominate fome till Congrefs tranfmit the appointments of thofe they wifh to fucceed to the feveral vacancies occafioned by the late promotions. This being a matter of some consequence, I presume will have their early attention, and that they will fill up the several vacancies also mentioned in the list I had the honour of transmitting some few days ago to the board of war.

I am, Sir, with the utmost respect, &c.   G. W.

SIR,   *New-York, August* 17, 1776.

THE circumstances of the two armies having undergone no material alteration since I had the honour of writing to you last, I have nothing particular or important to communicate respecting them.

In my letter of yesterday I forgot to mention the arrival of lord Dunmore here. By the examination of a captain Hunter (who escaped from the enemy, and came to Amboy on the fourteenth) transmitted me by general Roberdeau, I am certainly informed his lordship arrived on the thirteenth. The examination does not say any thing about the ships he brought with him; it only extends to his force, which it mentions to be weak.

I before now expected the enemy would have made their attack; nor can I account for their deferring it, unless the intelligence given by captain Hunter and another person who escaped about the same time, is the cause, to wit, that they are waiting the arrival of another division of the Hessian troops, which (they say) is still out. Whether that is the reason of the delay, I cannot undertake to determine: but I should suppose things will not long remain in their present state. I have inclosed a copy of general Roberdeau's letter, and of the examination of those two persons, which will shew Congress all the information they have given upon these subjects.

I am just now advised by Mr. Aires, who came from Philadelphia to build the row-galleys, that two of our fire-vessels attempted last night to burn the enemy's ships and tenders up the river. He says that they burned one tender, and one of them boarded the Phœnix, and was grappled with her for near ten minutes; but she cleared herself. We lost both of the vessels. His account is not so particular as I could wish; however, I am certain the attempt
                                                        has

has not fucceeded to our wifhes.   In a little time it is probable the matter will be more minutely reported.

I have the honour to be, &c.   G. W.

———————

SIR,   *New-York, Auguft* 18, 1776.

I HAVE been honoured with your favour of the fixteenth with the inclófure, and am forry it is not in my power to tranfmit Congrefs a copy of the treaty as they require, having fent it away with the other papers that were in my hands.

The refolution they have entered into refpecting the foreign troops, I am perfuaded, would produce falutary effects if it could be properly circulated among them.   I fear it will be a matter of difficulty.   However, I will take every meafure that fhall appear probable to facilitate the end.

I have the honour to inclofe you, for the perufal and confideration of Congrefs, fundry papers marked N° 1 to N° 7, inclufive ; the whole of which, except N° 2 and 7, (my anfwers to lord Drummond and general Howe) I received yefterday evening by a flag, and to which I beg leave to refer Congrefs.

I am exceedingly at a lofs to know the motives and caufes inducing a proceeding of fuch a nature at this time, and why lord Howe has not attempted fome plan of negociation before, as he feems fo defirous of it.   If I may be allowed to conjecture and guefs at the caufe, it may be that part of the Heffians have not arrived, as mentioned in the examination tranfmitted yefterday,—or that general Burgoyne has not made fuch progrefs as was expected, to form a junction of their two armies,—or, what I think equally probable, they mean to procraftinate their operations for fome time, trufting that the militias which have come to our fuccour will foon become tired and return home, as is but too ufual with them.   Congrefs will make their obfervations upon thefe feveral matters, and favour me with the refult as foon as they have done.   They will obferve my anfwer to lord Drummond, who (I am pretty confident) has not attended to the terms of his parole, but

has

has violated it in several instances. It is with the rest of the papers; but if my memory serves me, he was not to hold any correspondence directly or indirectly with those in arms against us, or to go into any port or harbour in America, where the enemy themselves were or had a fleet, or to go on board their ships.

The treaty with the Indians is in the box which lieutenant-colonel Reed, I presume, has delivered before this. If Congress are desirous of seeing it, they will be pleased to have the box opened. It contains a variety of papers, and all the affairs of the army, from my first going to Cambridge, till it was sent away.

This morning the Phœnix and Rose men-of-war, with two tenders, availing themselves of a favourable and brisk wind, came down the river, and have joined the fleet. Our several batteries fired at them in their passage, but without any good effect that I could perceive.

I have the honour to be, &c.　　　　G. W.

SIR,　　　　　　　　　　*New-York, August* 19, 1776.

I HAVE nothing of moment to communicate to Congress, as things are in the situation they were when I had last the honour of addressing them.

By a letter from general Ward, of the twelfth, I find that Whitcomb's regiment, on the eighth, and Phinney's, on the ninth, marched from Boston for Ticonderoga.

Governor Trumbull also, in a letter of the thirteenth, advises me that Ward's regiment in the service of the States was on the march to this army, and that he and his council of safety had in the whole ordered fourteen militia regiments to reinforce us. Three of them have arrived, and amount to about a thousand and twenty men. When the whole come in, we shall be on a much more respectable footing than we have been: but I greatly fear, if the enemy defer their attempt for any considerable time, they will be extremely impatient to return home ; and if they should, we shall be reduced to distress again.

He also adds that captain Van Buren, who had been sent for that purpose, had procured a sufficient supply of

sail-cloth

fail-cloth for the veffels to be employed on the Lake, and a part of the cordage, in that State; and had a profpect of getting the remainder.

As there will be a difficulty in all probability to circulate the papers defigned for the foreign troops, and many mifcarriages may happen before it can be effected, it may be proper to furnifh me with a larger quantity than what I already have.

Inclofed I have the honour to tranfmit you a general return of our whole force at this time, in which are comprehended the three regiments of militia above mentioned. I am forry it fhould be fo much weakened by ficknefs. The return will fhew you how it diftreffes us.

I have the honour to be, &c.   G. W.

P. S.   The poft juft now arrived has brought a further fupply of papers for the Heffians, which makes my requifition unneceffary.

New-York, Auguft 20, 1776.-

SIR,

I WAS yefterday morning favoured with yours of the feventeenth, accompanied by feveral refolutions of Congrefs, and commiffions for officers appointed to the late vacancies in this army.

I wrote fome days ago to general Schuyler to propofe to generals Carleton and Burgoyne an exchange of prifoners in confequence of a former refolve of Congrefs authorifing their commanders in each department to negociate one. That of major Meigs for major French, and captain Dearborn's for any officer of equal rank, I fubmitted to general Howe's confideration, by letter, on the feventeenth, underftanding their paroles had been fent him by general Carleton; but have not yet received his anfwer upon the fubject.

In refpect to the exchange of the prifoners in Canada, if a propofition on that head has not been already made, (and I believe it has not) the inclofed copy of general Carleton's orders (tranfmitted me under feal by major Bigelow, who was fent with a flag to general Burgoyne

T 2.

from.

from Ticonderoga, with the proceedings of Congrefs on the breach of capitulation at the Cedars, and the inhuman treatment of our people afterwards) will fhew it is unnec-effary, as he has determined to fend them to their own provinces, there to remain as prifoners ; interdicting at the fame time all kind of intercourfe between us and his army, except fuch as may be for the purpofe of imploring the king's mercy. The affaffination he mentions, of brigadier-general Gordon, is a fact entirely new to me, and what I never heard of before. I fhall not trouble Congrefs with my ftrictures upon this * * * performance, * * * only obferving that its defign is fomewhat artful, and that each boatman with major Bigelow was furnifhed with a copy.

I have alfo tranfmitted Congrefs a copy of the major's journal, to which I beg leave to refer them for the intelli-gence reported by him on his return from the truce.

By a letter from general Greene yefterday evening, he informed me he had received an exprefs from Hog-Ifland inlet, advifing that five of the enemy's fmall veffels had ap-peared at the mouth of the creek, with fome troops on board ;—alfo that he had heard two periaguas were off Oyfter-bay, the whole fuppofed to be after live-ftock ; and to prevent their getting it, he had detached a party of horfe, and two hundred and twenty men, among them twenty riflemen. I have not received further intelligence upon the fubject.

I am alfo advifed by the examination of a captain Button (mafter of a veffel that had been taken) tranfmitted me by general Mercer, that the general report among the ene-my's troops, when he came off, was, that they were to attack Long-Ifland, and to fecure our works there if poffi-ble, at the fame time that another part of their army was to land above this city. This information is corroborated by many other accounts, and is probably true : nor will it be poffible to prevent them landing on the ifland, as its great extent affords a variety of places favourable for that purpofe, and the whole of our works on it are at the end

oppofite

oppofite to the city. However, we fhall attempt to
harafs them as much as poffible, which will be all that
we can do.

I have the honour to be, &c.   G. W.

SIR,   *New-York, Auguft 21, 1776.*

INCLOSED I have the honour to tranfmit you a
copy of my letter to lord Howe (as well on the fubject of
a general exchange of prifoners in the naval line, as that
of lieutenant Jofiah in particular) and of his lordfhip's anfwer, which, for its matter and manner, is very different
from general Carleton's orders which were forwarded yefterday.

The fituation of the armies being the fame as when I
had the pleafure of addreffing you laft, I have nothing
fpecial to communicate on that head, nor more to add,
than that I am, with all poffible refpect, &c.   G. W.

SIR,   *New-York, Auguft 22, 1776.*

I DO myfelf the honour to tranfmit Congrefs a copy
of a letter I received yefterday evening by exprefs from
governor Livingfton, alfo copies of three reports from colonel Hand.

Though the intelligence reported by the fpy on his return to governor Livingfton has not been confirmed by
the event he mentions, (an attack laft night) there is every
reafon to believe that one is fhortly defigned. The falling down of feveral fhips yefterday evening to the Narrows, crowded with men,—thofe fucceeded by many
more this morning, and a great number of boats parading
around them (as I was juft now informed) with troops,
are all circumftances indicating an attack : and it is not
improbable it will be made to-day.   It could not have happened laft night, by reafon of a moft violent guft.

We are making every preparation to receive them ; and
I truft, under the fmiles of Providence, with our own
                                                 exertions,

exertions, that my next, if they do attack, will tranfmit
an account that will be pleafing to every friend of America, and of the rights of humanity.

I have the honour to be, &c.   G. W..

SIR,   *New-York, Auguft 23, 1776.*

I BEG leave to inform Congrefs, that, yefterday
morning and in the courfe of the preceding night, a confiderable body of the enemy, amounting by report to
eight or nine thoufand, and thefe all Britifh, landed from
the tranfport-fhips mentioned in my laft, at Gravefend-
bay on Long-Ifland, and have approached within three
miles of our lines, having marched acrofs the low cleared
grounds near the woods at Flat-bufh, where they are halted, from my laft intelligence.

I have detached from hence fix battalions as a reinforcement to our troops there, which are all that I can
fpare at this time, not knowing but the fleet may move
up with the remainder of their army, and make an attack
here, on the next flood-tide. If they do not, I fhall
fend a further reinforcement, fhould it be neceffary; and
have ordered five battalions more to be in readinefs for
that purpofe.

I have no doubt but a little time will produce fome important events. I hope they will be happy. The reinforcement detached yefterday went off in high fpirits;
and I have the pleafure to inform you that the whole of
the army, that are effective and capable of duty, difcover
the fame, and great cheerfulnefs. I have been obliged to
appoint major-general Sullivan to the command on the
ifland, owing to general Greene's indifpofition :—he has
been extremely ill for feveral days, and ftill continues
bad.

By Wednefday evening's poft I received a letter from
general Ward, inclofing a copy of the invoice of the ordnance ftores taken by captain Manly, with the appraifement
of the fame, (made in purfuance of my direction, founded
on the order of Congrefs) which I do myfelf the honour
                                                    of

of tranfmitting.   You will alfo receiye the treaty between the commiffioners and the Indians of the Six Nations, and others, at the German-Flats, which general
Schuyler requefted me to forward, by his letter of the
eighteenth inftant.

I have the honour to be, &c.   G. W.

S I R,   *New-York, Auguft* 24, 1776.

THE irregularity of the poft prevents your receiving the early and conftant intelligence it is my wifh to
communicate.   This is the third letter which you will
probably receive from me by the fame poft.   The firft was
of little or no confequence : but that of yefterday gave
you the beft information I had been able to obtain of the
enemy's landing and movements upon Long-Ifland.
Having occafion to go over thither yefterday, I fent my
letter to the poft-office at the ufual hour, being informed
that the rider was expected every moment, and would go
out again directly : but in the evening when I fent to inquire, none had come in.

I now inclofe you a report made to me by general
Sullivan after I left Long-Ifland yefterday.   I do not
conceive that the enemy's whole force was in motion, but
a detached party rather.   I have fent over four more regiments, with boats, to be ready either to reinforce the
troops under general Sullivan, or to return to this place,
if the remainder of the fleet at the watering-place fhould
pufh up to the city ; which hitherto (I mean, fince the
landing upon Long-Ifland) they have not had in their
power to do, on account of the wind which has either
been a-head or too fmall when the tide has ferved.   I
have nothing further to trouble the Congrefs with at
prefent, than that I am theirs and your moft obedient
humble fervant,   G. W.

S I R,   *New-York, Auguft* 26, 1776.

I HAVE been duly honoured with your favours of
the twentieth and twenty-fourth, and am happy to find
my

my anfwer to lord Drummond has met the approbation of Congrefs. Whatever his views were, moft certainly his conduct refpecting his parole is highly reprehenfible.

Since my letter of the twenty-fourth, almoft the whole of the enemy's fleet have fallen down to the Narrows; and, from this circumftance, and the ftriking of their tents and their feveral encampments on Staten-Ifland from time to time previous to the departure of the fhips from thence, we are led to think they mean to land the main body of their army on Long-Ifland, and to make their grand pufh there. I have ordered over confiderable reinforcements to our troops there, and fhall continue to fend more as circumftances may require. There has been a little fkir-mifhing and irregular firing kept up between their and our advanced guards, in which colonel Martin of the Jerfey levies has received a wound in his breaft, which, it is ap-prehended, will prove mortal; a private has had his leg broke by a cannon-ball, and another has received a fhot in the groin from their mufketry. This is all the damage they have yet done us :—what they have fuftained, is not known.

The fhifting and changing the regiments have undergone of late has prevented their making proper returns, and of courfe put it out of my power to tranfmit a general one of the army. However, I believe our ftrength is much the fame as it was when the laft was made, with the ad-dition of nine militia regiments come from the State of Connecticut, averaging about three hundred and fifty men each. Thefe are nine of the fourteen regiments mention-ed in my letter of the nineteenth. Our people ftill con-tinue to be very fickly.

The papers defigned for the foreign troops have been put into feveral channels, in order that they might be conveyed to them; and, from the information I had yef-terday, I have reafon to believe many have fallen into their hands.

I have inclofed a copy of lord Drummond's fecond let-ter (in anfwer to mine) which I received fince I tranf-mitted his firft, and which I have thought neceffary to lay before Congrefs, that they may poffefs the whole of the

correfpondence

correfpondence between us, and fee how far he has exculpated himfelf from the charge alleged againft him. The log-book he mentions to have fent colonel Moylan proves nothing in his favour. That fhews he had been at Bermuda, and from thence to fome other ifland, on his paffage from which to this place, the veffel he was in was boarded by a pilot who brought her into the Hook, where he found the Britifh fleet, which his lordfhip avers he did not expect were there, having underftood their deftination was to the fouthward.

I have the honour to be, &c.   G. W.

[The following letter is from one of the General's fecretaries, whofe fignature will alfo appear to a few of the fubfequent letters in this volume.]

S I R,   *New-York, Auguft 17, 1776, 8 o'clock, P. M.*

I THIS minute returned from our lines on Long-Ifland, where I left his excellency the General. From him I have it in command to inform Congrefs, that yefterday he went there, and continued till evening, when, from the enemy's having landed a confiderable part of their forces,—and many of their movements,—there was reafon to apprehend they would make in a little time a general attack. As they would have a wood to pafs through before they could approach the lines, it was thought expedient to place a number of men there on the different roads leading from where they were ftationed, in order to harafs and annoy them in their march. This being done, early this morning a fmart engagement enfued between the enemy and our detachments, which, being unequal to the force they had to contend with, have fuftained a pretty confiderable lofs : at leaft many of our men are miffing. Among thofe that have not returned, are general Sullivan and lord Stirling. The enemy's lofs is not known certainly : but we are told by fuch of our troops as were in the engagement and have come in, that they had many killed and wounded. Our party brought off a lieutenant, ferjeant, and corporal, with twenty privates, prifoners.

While

While thefe detachments were engaged, a column of the enemy defcended from the woods, and marched towards the centre of our lines with a defign to make an impreffion, but were repulfed. This evening they appeared very numerous about the fkirts of the woods, where they have pitched feveral tents : and his excellency inclines to think they mean to attack and force us from our lines by way of regular approaches, rather than in any other manner.

To-day, five fhips of the line came up towards the town, where they feemed defirous of getting, as they turned a long time againft an unfavourable wind : and on my return this evening, I found a deferter from the twenty-third regiment, who informed me that they defign, as foon as the wind will permit them to come up, to give us a fevere cannonade, and to filence our batteries, if poffible.

I have the honour to be, in great hafte, Sir, your moft obedient,   ROBERT H. HARRISON.

S I R,   *Long-Ifland, Aug.* 29, 1776, *half after* 4, *A. M.*

I WAS laft night honoured with your favour of the twenty-feventh, accompanied by fundry refolutions of Congrefs. Thofe refpecting the officers, &c. that may be wounded in the fervice of the States, are founded much in juftice, and (I fhould hope) may be productive of many falutary confequences. As to the encouragement to the Heffian officers, I wifh it may have the defired effect. Perhaps it might have been better had the offer been fooner made.

Before this, you will probably have received a letter from Mr. Harrifon, of the twenty-feventh, advifing of the engagement between a detachment of our men and the enemy on that day. I am forry to inform Congrefs that I have not yet heard either of general Sullivan or lord Stirling, who (they would obferve) were among the miffing after the engagement; nor can I afcertain our lofs. I am hopeful, part of our men will yet get in : feveral did yefterday morning. That of the enemy is alfo uncertain :

certain : the accounts are various. I incline to think they suffered a good deal. Some deserters say five hundred were killed and wounded.

There was some skirmishing, the greatest part of yesterday, between parties from the enemy and our people : in the evening it was pretty smart. The event I have not yet learned.

The weather of late has been extremely wet. Yesterday it rained severely the whole afternoon, which distressed our people much,—not having a sufficiency of tents to cover them, and what we have, not being got over yet. I am in hopes they will all be got to-day, and that they will be more comfortably provided, though the great scarcity of these articles distresses us beyond meafure, not having any thing like a sufficient number to protect our people from the inclemency of the weather ;—which has occafioned much sicknefs, and the men to be almoft broken down.

I have the honour to be, &c.   G. W.

SIR,   *New-York, Auguft 31, 1776.*

INCLINATION as well as duty would have induced me to give Congrefs the earlieft information of my removal and that of the troops, from Long-Ifland and its dependencies, to this city, the night before laft : but the extreme fatigue which myfelf and family have undergone, as much from the weather fince as the engagement on the twenty-feventh, rendered me and them entirely unfit to take pen in hand. Since Monday, fcarce any of us have been out of the lines till our paffage acrofs the Eaft-river was effected yefterday morning ; and, for forty-eight hours preceding that, I had hardly been off my horfe, and never clofed my eyes ; fo that I was quite unfit to write or dictate till this morning.

Our retreat was made without any lofs of men or ammunition, and in better order than I expected from troops in the fituation ours were. We brought off all our cannon and ftores, except a few heavy pieces, which, in the condition the earth was by a long continued rain, we found, upon trial, impracticable. The wheels of the carriages finking up to the hobs rendered it impossible for our whole force to drag them. We left but little provisions on the island, except some cattle which had been driven within our lines, and which, after many attempts to force acrofs the water, we found impossible to effect, circumstanced as we were.

I have inclofed a copy of the council of war held previous to the retreat, to which I beg leave to refer Congrefs for the reafons, or many of them, that led to the adoption of that meafure.

Yefterday evening and laft night, a party of our men were employed in bringing our ftores, cannon, tents, &c. from Governor's-Ifland, which they nearly completed. Some of the heavy cannon remain there ftill, but (I expect) will be got away to-day.

In the engagement on the twenty-feventh, generals Sullivan and Stirling were made prifoners. The former has been permitted, on his parole, to return for a little time. From my lord Stirling I had a letter by general Sullivan (a copy of which I have the honour to tranfmit) that contains his information of the engagement with his brigade. It is not fo full and certain as I could wifh :— he was hurried moft probably, as his letter was unfinifhed : —nor have I been yet able to obtain an exact account of our lofs :—we fuppofe it from feven hundred to a thoufand killed and taken.

General Sullivan fays lord Howe is extremely defirous of feeing fome of the members of Congrefs ; for which purpofe he was allowed to come out and to communicate to them what has paffed between him and his lordfhip. I have confented to his going to Philadelphia, as I do not mean, or conceive it right, to withhold, or prevent him from giving, fuch information as he poffeffes in this inftance.

I am much hurried and engaged in arranging and making new difpofitions of our forces ; the movements of the enemy requiring them to be immediately had ;—and therefore have only time to add, that I am, with my beft regards to Congrefs, their and your moft obedient, &c.

G. W.
New-York.

S I R,   *New-York, September 2, 1776.*

AS my intelligence of late has been rather unfavourable, and would be received with anxiety and concern, peculiarly happy should I esteem myself, were it in my power at this time to transmit such information to Congress, as
would be more pleasing and agreeable to their wishes :—
but, unfortunately for me,—unfortunately for them,—it is
not.

Our situation is truly distressing. The check our detachment sustained on the twenty-seventh ultimo has dif-
pirited too great a proportion of our troops, and filled their
minds with apprehension and despair. The militia, instead
of calling forth their utmost efforts to a brave and manly
opposition in order to repair our losses, are dismayed, in-
tractable, and impatient to return. Great numbers of
them have gone off,—in some instances, almost by whole
regiments, by half ones, and by companies at a time.
This circumstance, of itself, independent of others, when
fronted by a well-appointed enemy superior in number to
our whole collected force, would be sufficiently disagreeable : but,   their example has infected another part
of the arm   their want of discipline, and refusal of
almost eve   _   of restraint and government, have produced a like conduct but too common to the whole, and
an entire disregard of that order and subordination necessary to the well doing of an army, and which had been in-
culcated before, as well as the nature of our military establishment would admit of,—our condition is still more
alarming : and with the deepest concern I am obliged to
confess my want of confidence in the generality of the
troops.

All these circumstances fully confirm the opinion I ever entertained, and which I more than once in my letters
took the liberty of mentioning to Congress, that no dependence could be put in a militia, or other troops than those
enlisted and embodied for a longer period than our regulations heretofore have prescribed. I am persuaded, and as
fully convinced as I am of any one fact that has happened,
that our liberties must of necessity be greatly hazarded if
not entirely lost, if their defence is left to any but a permanent

manent ftanding army,—I mean, one to exift during the
war.   Nor would the expenfe, incident to the fupport of
fuch a body of troops as would be competent to almoft every
exigency, far exceed that which is daily incurred by
calling in fuccour, and new enliftments, which, when effected, are not attended with any good confequences.
Men who have been free, and fubject to no control, cannot
be reduced to order in an inftant : and the privileges and
exemptions they claim and will have, influence the conduct of others ; and the aid derived from them is nearly
counterbalanced by the diforder, irregularity, and confufion
they occafion.

I cannot find that the bounty of ten dollars is likely to
produce the defired effect.   When men can get double
that fum to engage for a month or two in the militia, and
that militia frequently called out, it is hardly to be expected. - The addition of land might have a confiderable influence on a permanent enliftment.

Our number of men at prefent fit for duty is under
twenty thoufand : they were fo by the laft returns and
beft accounts I could get after the enge   ment on Long-
Ifland ; fince which, numbers have de'   d.   I have ordered general Mercer to fend the me   tended for the
flying camp to this place, about a thoufand in number, and
to try with the militia, if practicable, to make a diverfion
upon Staten-Ifland.

Till of late I had no doubt in my own mind, of de-
fending this place : nor fhould I have yet, if the men would
do their duty : but this I defpair of.   It is painful, and extremely grating to me, to give fuch unfavourable accounts:
but it would be criminal to conceal the truth at fo critical
a juncture.   Every power I poffefs fhall be exerted to ferve
the caufe ; and my firft wifh is, that, whatever may be the
event, the Congrefs will do me the juftice to think fo.

If we fhould be obliged to abandon the town, ought it
to ftand as winter quarters for the enemy ? They would
derive great conveniences from it on the one hand ; and
much property would be deftroyed on the other.   It is an
important queftion, but will admit of but little time for de-
liberation.   At prefent I dare fay the enemy mean to preferve it if they can.   If Congrefs therefore fhould refolve
upon

upon the deftruction of it, the refolution fhould be a profound fecret, as the knowledge of it will make a capital
change in their plans.

I have the honour to be, &c.   G. W.

New-York, September 4, 1776.

SIR,

SINCE I had the honour of addreffing you on the
fecond, our affairs have not undergone a change for the
better, nor affumed a more agreeable afpect than what they
then wore.   The militia under various pretences, of ficknefs, &c. are daily diminifhing ; and in a little time, I am
perfuaded, their number will be very inconfiderable.

On Monday night a forty-gun fhip paffed up the Sound
between Governor's and Long-Ifland, and anchored in
Turtle-bay.   In her paffage fhe received a difcharge of
cannon from our batteries, but without any damage ; and,
having a favourable wind and tide, foon got out of their
reach.   Yefterday morning I difpatched major Crane of
the artillery, with two twelve-pounders and a howitzer,
to annoy her ; who, hulling her feveral times, forced her
from that ftation, and to take fhelter behind an ifland,
where fhe ftill continues.   There are feveral other fhips
of war in the Sound, with a good many tranfports or
ftore-fhips which came round Long-Ifland, fo that that
communication is entirely cut off.   The admiral, with the
main body of the fleet, is clofe in with Governor's-Ifland.
Judging it expedient to guard againft every contingency
as far as our peculiar fituation will admit, and that we may
have refources left if obliged to abandon this place, I have
fent away and am removing above Kingfbridge all our
ftores that are unneceffary, and that will not be immediately wanted.

I have inclofed feveral original letters from fome of our
officers prifoners at Quebec, which fell into general Gates's
hands, and were tranfmitted by him to general Schuyler
who fent them to me.   General Gates adds, that the perfons who brought them faid general Burgoyne had fent
meffages to the inhabitants upon the lakes, inviting their

U 2

continuance

continuance on their farms, and affuring them that they
fhould remain in fecurity.

The poft-mafter having removed his office from the city
to Dobbs's ferry, as it is faid, makes it extremely inconvenient, and will be the means of my not giving fuch conftant and regular intelligence as I could wifh. Cannot
fome mode be devifed, by which we may have a pretty
conftant and certain intercourfe and communication kept
up? It is an interefting matter, and of great importance ;
and, as fuch, I am perfuaded, will meet with due attention
from Congrefs.

I have tranfmitted the copy of general Gates's letter as
fent me by general Schuyler, from which Congrefs will
difcover all the information I have refpecting general Burgoyne's meffage, and my lateft intelligence from Ticonderoga, with the returns of the army there. Thofe of the
army here it is impoffible to obtain, till the hurry and buf-
tle we are now in are a little over.

I have the honour to be, &c.   G. W.

P. S.   Congrefs will perceive, by general Gates's letter,
his want of mufket-cartridge paper. It is impoffible to
fupply him from hence. They will therefore be pleafed
to order what he wants (if it can be procured) to be immediately fent him from Philadelphia.

SIR,   *New-York, September* 6, 1776.

I WAS laft night honoured with your favour of the
third, with fundry refolutions of Congrefs ; and perceiving
it to be their opinion and determination that no damage
fhall be done the city in cafe we are obliged to abandon
it, I fhall take every meafure in my power to prevent it.

Since my letter of the fourth, nothing very material has
occurred, unlefs it is that the fleet feem to be drawing
more together, and all getting clofe in with Governor's-
Ifland.   Their defigns we cannot learn ; nor have we
been able to procure the leaft information of late, of any
of their plans or intended operations.

As the enemy's movements are very different from
what we expected,—and, from their large encampments a
                                                    confiderable

confiderable diftance up the Sound, there is reafon to believe they intend to make a landing above or below Kingfbridge, and thereby to hem in our army, and cut off the
communication with the country,—I mean to call a council of general officers to day or to-morrow, and endeavour
to digeft and fix upon fome regular and certain fyftem of
conduct to be purfued in order to baffle their efforts and
counteract their fchemes ; and alfo to determine of the expediency of evacuating or attempting to maintain the city
and the feveral pofts on this ifland. The refult of their
opinion and deliberations I fhall advife Congrefs of by the
earlieft opportunity, which will be by exprefs, having it
not in my power to communicate any intelligence by poft,
as the office is removed to fo great a diftance, and entirely
out of the way.

I have inclofed a lift of the officers who are prifoners,
and from whom letters have been received by a flag. We
know there are others not included in the lift.

General Sullivan having informed me that general Howe
was willing that an exchange of him for general Prefcot
fhould take place, it will be proper to fend general Prefcot
immediately, that it may be effected.

As the militia regiments in all probability will be impatient to return, and become preffing for their pay, I fhall
be glad of the direction of Congrefs whether they are to
receive it here or from the conventions or affemblies of the
refpective States to which they belong. On the one hand,
the fettlement of their abftracts will be attended with trouble and difficulty : on the other they will go away much
better fatisfied, and be more ready to give their aid in future,
if they are paid before their departure.

Before I conclude, I muft take the liberty of mentioning
to Congrefs the great diftrefs we are in for want of money.
Two months' pay (and more to fome battalions) is now
due to the troops here, without any thing in the military
cheft to fatisfy it. This occafions much diffatisfaction,
and almoft a general uneafinefs. Not a day paffes with
complaints and the moft importunate and urgent dem
on this head. As it may injure the fervice greatly, a
want of a regular fupply of cafh produce confeq
the moft fatal tendency, I entreat the attention o

to this fubject, and that we may be provided as foon as can be with a fum equal to every prefent claim.

I have wrote to general Howe, propofing an exchange of general M'Donald for lord Stirling, and fhall be extremely happy to obtain it, as well as that of general Sullivan for general Prefcot, being greatly in want of them, and under the neceffity of appointing, pro tempore, fome of the colonels to command brigades.

I have the honour to be, &c.   G. W.

P. S. As two regiments from North-Carolina and three regiments more from Virginia are ordered here,—if they could embark at Norfolk, &c. and come up the bay with fecurity, it would expedite their arrival, and prevent the men from a long fatiguing march. This however fhould not be attempted if the enemy have veffels in the bay, which might probably intercept them.

———

SIR,   *New-York, September* 7, 1776.

THIS will be delivered you by captain Martindale and lieutenant Turner, who were taken laft fall in the armed brig Wafhington, and who, with Mr. Childs the fecond lieutenant, have lately effected their efcape from Halifax. Captain Martindale and thefe two officers have applied to me for pay from the firft of January till this time : but, not conceiving myfelf authorifed to grant it, however reafonable it may be, as they were only engaged till the laft of December,—at their inftance I have mentioned the matter to Congrefs, and fubmit their cafe to their confideration.

I have the honour to be, &c.   G. W.

———

SIR,   *New-York, Head-Quarters, September* 8, 1776.

SINCE I had the honour of addreffing you on the inftant, I have called a council of the general officers, er to take a full and comprehenfive view of our fitua- thereupon form fuch a plan of future defence as mediately purfued, and fubject to no other alteration

ation than a change of operations on the enemy's side may occasion.

Before the landing of the enemy on Long-Island, the point of attack could not be known, or any satisfactory judgment formed of their intentions. It might be on Long-Island, or Bergen, or directly on the city. This made it necessary to be prepared for each, and has occasioned an expense of labour which now seems useless, and is regretted by those who form a judgment from after-knowledge. But I trust, men of discernment will think differently, and see that by such works and preparations we have not only delayed the operations of the campaign till it is too late to effect any capital incursion into the country, but have drawn the enemy's forces to one point and obliged them to [*disclose*] their plan, so as to enable us to form our defence on some certainty.

It is now extremely obvious from all intelligence,—from their movements and every other circumstance,—that having landed their whole army on Long-Island (except about four thousand on Staten-Island) they mean to inclose us on the island of New-York, by taking post in our rear while the shipping effectually secure the front; and thus, either by cutting off our communication with the country, oblige us to fight them on their own terms, or surrender at discretion,—or by a brilliant stroke endeavour to cut this army in pieces, and secure the collection of arms and stores, which they well know we shall not be able soon to replace.

Having therefore their system unfolded to us, it became an important consideration how it could be most successfully opposed. On every side there is a choice of difficulties; and every measure on our part (however painful the reflection is from experience) to be formed with some apprehension that all our troops will not do their duty. In deliberating on this great question, it was impossible to forget, that history, our own experience, the advice of our ablest friends in Europe, the fears of the enemy, and even the declarations of Congress, demonstrate, that on our side the war should be defensive—(it has ever been called a war of posts)—that we should on all occasions avoid a general action, nor put any thing to the risk, un-

less

lefs compelled by a neceffity into which we ought never
to be drawn.

The arguments on which fuch a fyftem was founded
were deemed unanfwerable ; and experience has given her
fanction. With thefe views, and being fully perfuaded that
it would be prefumption to draw out our young troops
into open ground againft their fuperiors both in number
and difcipline, I have never fpared the fpade and pickaxe.
I confefs I have not found that readinefs to defend even
ftrong pofts at all hazards, which is neceffary to derive the
greateft benefit from them.   The honour of making a brave
defence does not feem to be a fufficient ftimulus when fuccefs is very doubtful, and the falling into the enemy's hands
probable : but I doubt not, this will be gradually attained.
We are now in a ftrong poft, but not an impregnable one,
nay, acknowledged by every man of judgment to be unten-
able, unlefs the enemy will make the attack upon lines
when they can avoid it, and their movements indicate that
they mean to do fo.

To draw the whole army together in order to arrange
the defence proportionate to the extent of lines and works,
would leave the country open for an approach, and put the
fate of this army and its ftores on the hazard of making a
fuccefsful defence in the city, or the iffue of an engagement
out of it.   On the other hand, to abandon a city which
has been by fome deemed defenfible, and on whofe works
much labour has been beftowed, has a tendency to difpirit
the troops and enfeeble our caufe.   It has alfo been confidered as the key to the northern country.   But as to
that, I am fully of opinion that the eftablifhing of ftrong
pofts at Mount-Wafhington on the upper part of this
ifland, and on the Jerfey fide oppofite to it, with the affiftance of the obftructions already made (and which may
be improved) in the water, not only the navigation of
Hudfon's-river, but an eafier and better communication
may be more effectually fecured between the northern and
fouthern States.   This, I believe, every one acquainted
with the fituation of the country will readily agree to ;
and it will appear evident to thofe who have an opportunity of recurring to good maps.

Thefe

Thefe and many other confequences, which will be involved in the determination of our next meafure, have given our minds full employ, and led every one to form a judgment as the various objects prefented themfelves to his view.

The poft at Kingfbridge is naturally ftrong, and is pretty well fortified : the heights about it are commanding, and might foon be made more fo. Thefe are important objects, and I have attended to them accordingly. I have alfo removed from the city all the ftores and ammunition except what was abfolutely neceffary for its defence, and made every other difpofition that did not effentially interfere with that object,—carefully keeping in view, until it fhould be abfolutely determined on full confideration, how far the city was to be defended at all events.

In refolving points of fuch importance, many circumftances peculiar to our own army alfo occur. Being only provided for a fummer's campaign, their clothes, fhoes, and blankets, will foon be unfit for the change of weather which we every day feel. At prefent we have not tents for more than two thirds, many of them old and worn out : but if we had a plentiful fupply, the feafon will not admit of continuing in them long. The cafe of our fick is alfo worthy of much confideration. Their number, by the returns, forms at leaft one fourth of the army. Policy and humanity require they fhould be made as comfortable as poffible.

With thefe and many other circumftances before them, the whole council of general officers met yefterday in order to adopt fome general line of conduct to be purfued at this important crifis. I intended to have procured their feparate opinions on each point ; but time would not admit. I was therefore obliged to collect their fenfe more generally than I could have wifhed. All agreed the town would not be tenable if the enemy refolved to bombard and cannonade it : but the difficulty attending a removal operated fo ftrongly, that a courfe was taken between abandoning it totally and concentring our whole ftrength for its defence : nor were fome a little influenced in their opinion, to whom the determination of Congrefs was known, againft an evacuation

uation totally, as they were led to fufpect Congrefs wifhed
it to be maintained at every hazard.

It was concluded to arrange the army under three divifions ;—five thoufand to remain for the defence of the
city ;—nine thoufand to Kingfbridge and its dependencies,
as well to poffefs and fecure thofe pofts, as to be ready to
attack the enemy who are moving eaftward on Long-Ifl-
and, if they fhould attempt to land on this fide ;—the remainder to occupy the intermediate fpace, and fupport either ;—that the fick fhould be immediately removed to
Orangetown, and barracks prepared at Kingfbridge with
all expedition to cover the troops.

There were fome general officers, in whofe judgment
and opinion much confidence is to be repofed, that were
for a total and immediate removal from the city,—urging
the great danger of one part of the army being cut off before the other can fupport it, the extremities being at leaft
fixteen miles apart ;—that our army, when collected, is
inferior to the enemy ;—that they can move with their
whole force to any point of attack, and confequently muft
fucceed by weight of numbers, if they have only a part to
oppofe them ;—that, by removing from hence, we deprive
the enemy of the advantage of their fhips, which will
make at leaft one half of the force to attack the town ;—
that we fhould keep the enemy at bay, put nothing to the
hazard, but at all events keep the army together, which
may be recruited another year ;—that the unfpent ftores
will alfo be preferved ; and, in this cafe, the heavy artillery can alfo be fecured. But they were overruled by a
majority, who thought for the prefent a part of our force
might be kept here, and attempt to maintain the city a
while longer.

I am fenfible a retreating army is encircled with difficulties ; that the declining an engagement fubjects a general to reproach ; and that the common caufe may be affected by the difcouragement it may throw over the minds of
many. Nor am I infenfible of the contrary effects, if a
brilliant ftroke could be made with any probability of fuccefs, efpecially after our lofs upon Long-Ifland. But,
when the fate of America may be at ftake on the iffue,
when the wifdom of cooler moments and experienced men

have

have decided that we fhould protract the war if poffible, I cannot think it fafe or wife to adopt a different fyftem when the feafon for action draws fo near a clofe.

That the enemy mean to winter in New-York, there can be no doubt :——that, with fuch an armament, they can drive us out, is equally clear. The Congrefs having refolved that it fhould not be deftroyed, nothing feems to remain, but to determine the time of their taking poffeffion. It is our intereft and wifh to prolong it as much as poffible, provided the delay does not affect our future meafures.

The militia of Connecticut is reduced, from fix thoufand, to lefs than two thoufand, and in a few days will be merely nominal. The arrival of fome Maryland troops, &c. from the flying camp, has in a great degree fupplied the lofs of men : but the ammunition they have carried away will be a lofs fenfibly felt. The impulfe for going home was fo irrefiftible, it anfwered no purpofe to oppofe it. Though I would not difcharge, I have been obliged to acquiefce ; and it affords one more melancholy proof, how delufive fuch dependencies are.

Inclofed I have the honour to tranfmit a general return, the firft I have been able to procure for fome time ; alfo a report of captain Newel from our works at Horn's-Hook or Hell-gate. Their fituation is extremely low, and the Sound fo very narrow, that the enemy have them much within their command.

I have the honour to be, &c.   G. W.

P. S. The inclofed information this minute came to hand. I am in hopes we fhall henceforth get regular intelligence of the enemy's movements.

SIR,   *New-York, September* 11, 1776.

I WAS yefterday honoured with your favour of the eighth inftant, accompanied by fundry refolutions of Congrefs, to which I fhall pay the ftricteft attention, and, in the inftances required, make them the future rule of my conduct.

The mode of negociation purfued by lord Howe I did not approve of; but as general Sullivan was fent out upon the bufinefs, and with a meffage to Congrefs, I could not conceive myfelf at liberty to interfere in the matter, as he was in the character of a prifoner, and totally fubject to their power and direction.

The lift of prifoners, before omitted through hurry, is now inclofed; though it will probably have reached Congrefs before this. I fhall write by the firft opportunity for major Hawfackfe to repair to Philadelphia—(he is in the northern army;)—and will alfo mention the feveral appointments in confequence of colonel St. Clair's promotion.

As foon as generals Prefcot and M'Donald arrive, I fhall take meafures to advife general Howe of it, that the propofed exchange for general Sullivan and lord Stirling may be carried into execution.

Since my letter of the eighth, nothing material has occurred, except that the enemy have poffeffed themfelves of Montezore's-ifland, and landed a confiderable number of troops upon it. This ifland lies in the mouth of Haerlem-river, which runs out of the Sound into the North-river, and will give the enemy an eafy opportunity of landing either on the low grounds of Morrifania, if their views are to feize and poffefs the paffes above Kingfbridge, or on the plains of Haerlem, if they defign to intercept and cut off the communication between our feveral pofts. I am making every difpofition and arrangement that the divided ftate of our troops will admit of, and which appear moft likely and the beft calculated to oppofe their attacks; for I prefume there will be feveral. How the event will be, God only knows: but you may be affured that nothing in my power, circumftanced as I am, fhall be wanting, to effect a favourable and happy iffue.

By my letter of the eighth you would perceive that feveral of the council were for holding the town, conceiving it practicable for fome time. Many of them now, upon feeing our divided ftate, have altered their opinion, and allow the expediency and neceffity of concentring our whole force, or drawing it more together. Convinced of the propriety of this meafure, I am ordering our ftores

away,

away, except fuch as may be abfolutely neceffary to keep
as long as any troops remain; that, if an evacuation of
the city becomes inevitable (which certainly muft be the
cafe) there may be as little to remove as poffible.

The inclofed packet contains feveral letters for particular members of Congrefs and for fome gentlemen in Philadelphia. They came to hand yefterday, and were
brought from France by a captain Levez lately arrived at
Bedford in the Maffachufetts State. I muft requeft the
favour of you to open the packet, and to have the letters
put in a proper channel of conveyance to the gentlemen
they are addreffed to.

I have the honour to be, &c. G. W.

SIR, *Head-Quarters, New-York, Sept.* 12, 1776.

HIS excellency being called from Head-Quarters to-
day on bufinefs of importance which prevents his writing,
I therefore do myfelf the honour to inform Congrefs of
what has happened fince his letter of yefterday.

Laft evening the enemy tranfported a number of men
from Buchanan's to Montezore's-ifland, and, by their
feveral movements, more ftrongly indicate their intention
to land fomewhere about Haerlem or Morrifania,—moft
likely, at both at the fame time. This morning one of
the fhips that have been for fome time in the Sound moved down towards Hell-gate; but, the tide leaving her,
fhe could not get near enough to bring her guns to bear
upon our fortification. If fhe means to attack it, it is
probable fhe will warp in the next tide. Their batteries
have kept up a pretty conftant fire againft ours at that
place, but without any confiderable effect. This morning they opened a new one.

I do not recollect any other material occurrence, and
fhall only add, that I have the honour to be, &c.

R. H. HARRISON.

SIR, *New-York, September* 14, 1776.

I HAVE been duly honoured with your favour of the
tenth, with the refolution of Congrefs which accompanied

ed it, and thank them for the confidence they repofe in my judgment refpecting the evacuation of the city. J could wifh to maintain it, becaufe I know it to be of importance : but I am fully convinced that it cannot be done, and that an attempt for that purpofe, if perfevered in, might and moft certainly would be attended with confequences the moft fatal and alarming in their nature.

Senfible of this, feveral of the general officers, fince the determination of the council mentioned in my laft, petitioned that a fecond council might be called to reconfider the propofitions which had been before them upon the fubject. Accordingly I called one on the twelfth, when a large majority not only determined a removal of the army prudent, but abfolutely neceffary,—declaring they were entirely convinced from a full and minute inquiry into our fituation, that it was extremely perilous ; and, from every movement of the enemy, and the intelligence received, their plan of operations was to get in our rear, and, by cutting off the communication with the main, oblige us to force a paffage through them on the terms they wifh, or to become prifoners in fome fhort time for want of neceffary fupplies of provifion.

We are now taking every method in our power to remove the ftores, &c. in which we find almoft infuperable difficulties. They are fo great and fo numerous, that I fear we fhall not effect the whole before we meet with fome interruption. I fully expected that an attack fomewhere would have been made laft night. In that I was difappointed ; and happy fhall I be, if my apprehenfions of one to-night, or in a day or two, are not confirmed by the event. If it is deferred a little while longer, I flatter myfelf all will be got away, and our force be more concentred, and of courfe more likely to refift them with fuccefs.

Yefterday afternoon, four fhips of war, two of forty and two of twenty-eight guns, went up the Eaft-river, paffing between Governor's and Long-Ifland, and anchored about a mile above the city, oppofite Mr. Stivanfent's, where the Rofe man-of-war was lying before. The defign of their going not being certainly known, gives rife to various conjectures,—fome fuppofing they are to cover the landing of

a party

a party of the enemy above the city,—others that they are
to affift in deftroying our battery at Horn's-hook, that they
may have a free and uninterrupted navigation in the Sound.
It is an object of great importance to them, and what they
are induftrioufly trying to effect by a pretty conftant cannonade and bombardment.

Before I conclude, I would beg leave to mention to
Congrefs, that the pay now allowed to nurfes for their attendance on the fick is by no means adequate to their fervices; the confequence of which is, that they are extremely
difficult to procure: indeed they are not to be got; and
we are under the neceffity of fubftituting in their place a
number of men from the refpective regiments, whofe fervice
by that means is entirely loft in the proper line of their duty, and but little benefit rendered to the fick. The officers
I have talked with upon the fubject all agree that they
fhould be allowed a dollar per week, and that for lefs they
cannot be had.

Our fick are extremely numerous, and we find their removal attended with the greateft difficulty. It is a matter
that employs much of our time and care ; and what makes
it more diftreffing is the want of proper and convenient
places for their reception. I fear their fufferings will be
great and many. However, nothing on my part, that
humanity or policy can require, fhall be wanting to make
them comfortable, fo far as the ftate of things will admit of.

I have the honour to be, &c. G. W.

Head-Quarters at Col. Roger Morris's Houfe, Sept. 16, 1776.

SIR,

ON Saturday about funfet, fix more of the enemy's
fhips, one or two of which were men-of-war, paffed between Governor's-ifland and Red-hook, and went up the
Eaft-river to the ftation taken by thofe mentioned in my
laft. In half an hour I received two expreffes,—one from
colonel Serjeant at Horn's-hook [Hell-gate]-giving an
account that the enemy, to the amount of three or four
thoufand, had marched to the river, and were embarking

W 2

for

for Barns's or Montezore's-ifland, where numbers of them were then encamped;—the other from general Mifflin, that uncommon and formidable movements were difcovered among the enemy; which being confirmed by the fcouts I had fent out, I proceeded to Haerlem, where it was fuppofed (or at Morrifania oppofite to it) the principal attempt to land would be made. However, nothing remarkable happened that night: but in the morning they began their operations. Three fhips of war came up the North-river as high as Bloomingdale, which put a total ftop to the removal, by water, of any more of our provifion, &c. and about eleven o'clock thofe in the Eaft-river began a moft fevere and heavy cannonade, to fcour the grounds, and cover the landing of their troops between Turtle-bay and the city, where breaftworks had been thrown up to oppofe them.

As foon as I heard the firing, I rode with all poffible difpatch towards the place of landing, when, to my great furprife and mortification, I found the troops that had been pofted in the lines retreating with the utmoft precipitation, and thofe ordered to fupport them (Parfons's and Fellows's brigades) flying in every direction, and in the greateft confufion,.notwithftanding the exertions of their generals to form them.   I ufed every means in my power to rally and get them into fome order : but my attempts were fruitlefs and ineffectual ; and on the appearance of a fmall party of the enemy, not more than fixty or feventy, their diforder increafed, and they ran away in the greateft confufion, without firing a fingle fhot.

Finding that no confidence was to be placed in thefe brigades, and apprehending that another party of the enemy might pafs over to Haerlem plains and cut off the retreat to this place, I fent orders to fecure the heights in the beft manner with the troops that were ftationed on and near them ; which being done, the retreat was effected with but little or no lofs of men, though, of a confiderable part of our baggage,—occafioned by this difgraceful and daftardly conduct.   Moft of our heavy cannon, and a part of our ftores and provifions which we were about removing, was unavoidably left in the city, though every means (after

it

it had been determined in council to evacuate the poſt)
had been uſed to prevent it.

We are now encamped with the main body of the army
on the heights of Haerlem, where I ſhould hope the enemy would meet with a defeat in caſe of an attack, if the
generality of our troops would behave with tolerable bravery.   But experience to my extreme affliction has convinced me, that this is rather to be wiſhed for than expected.
However, I truſt that there are many who will act like men,
and ſhew themſelves worthy of the bleſſings of freedom.

I have ſent out ſome reconnoitring parties to gain intelligence, if poſſible, of the diſpoſition of the enemy, and
ſhall inform Congreſs of every material event by the earlieſt
opportunity.

I have the honour to be, &c.   G. W.

Head-Quarters at Col. R. Morris's Houſe, Sept. 18, 1776.
SIR,

AS my letter of the ſixteenth contained intelligence of
an important nature, and ſuch as might lead Congreſs to
expect that the evacuation of New-York and retreat to
the heights of Haerlem, in the manner they were made,
would be ſucceeded by ſome other intereſting event, I beg
leave to inform them that as yet nothing has been attempted upon a large and general plan of attack.

About the time of the poſt's departure with my letter,
the enemy appeared in ſeveral large bodies upon the plains
about two and a half miles from hence.   I rode down
to our advanced poſts, to put matters in a proper ſituation
if they ſhould attempt to come on.   When I arrived there
I heard a firing, which, I was informed, was between a
party of our rangers under the command of lieutenant-colonel Knolton, and an advanced party of the enemy.   Our
men came in and told me that the body of the enemy, who
kept themſelves concealed, conſiſted of about three hundred
as near as they could gueſs.   I immediately ordered three
companies of colonel Weeden's regiment from Virginia,
under the command of major Leitch, and colonel Knolton
with his rangers compoſed of volunteers from different

New-England

New-England regiments to try to get in their rear, while a difpofition was making as if to attack them in front, and thereby draw their whole attention that way.

This took effect as I wifhed on the part of the enemy. On the appearance of our party in front, they immediately ran down the hill, took poffeffion of fome fences and bufhes, and a fmart firing began, but at too great a diftance to do much execution on either fide. The parties under colonel Knolton and major Leitch unluckily began their attack too foon, as it was rather in flank than in rear. In a little time major Leitch was brought off wounded, having received three balls through his fide; and in a fhort time after colonel Knolton got a wound which proved mortal. Their men however perfevered, and continued the engagement with the greateft refolution.

Finding that they wanted a fupport, I advanced part of colonel Griffith's and colonel Richardfon's Maryland regiments, with fome detachments from the eaftern regiments who were neareft the place of action. Thefe troops charged the enemy with great intrepidity, and drove them from the wood into the plain, and were pufhing them from thence (having filenced their fire in a great meafure) when I judged it prudent to order a retreat, fearing the enemy (as I have fince found was really the cafe) were fending a large body to fupport their party.

Major Leitch, I am in hopes, will recover : but colonel Knolton's fall is much to be regretted, as that of a brave and good officer. We had about forty wounded : the number of flain is not yet afcertained : but it is very inconfiderable.

By a fergeant who deferted from the enemy and came in this morning, I find that their party was greater than I imagined. It confifted of the fecond battalion of light infantry, a battalion of the royal Highlanders, and three companies of Heffian riflemen, under the command of brigadier-general Leflie. The deferter reports that their lofs in wounded and miffing was eighty-nine, and eight killed. In the latter, his account is too fmall, as our people difcovered and buried double that number. This affair, I am in hopes, will be attended with many falutary confequences, as it feems to have greatly infpirited the

whole

whole of our troops.   The fergeant further adds that a confiderable body of men are now encamped from the Eaft to the North-river, between the feven and eight-mile ftones, under the command of general Clinton.   General Howe, he believes, has his quarters at Mr. Apthorp's houfe.

I have the honour to be, &c.   G. W.

P. S.   I fhould have wrote to Congrefs by exprefs before now, had I not expected the poft every minute ; which, I flatter myfelf, will be a fufficient apology for my delaying it.   The late loffes we have fuftained in our baggage and camp neceffaries have added much to our diftrefs which was very great before.   I muft therefore take the liberty of requefting Congrefs to have forwarded as foon as poffible fuch a fupply of tents, blankets, camp-kettles, and other articles, as can be collected.   We cannot be overftocked.

Head-Quarters at Col. R. Morris's Houfe, Sept. 19, 1776.
SIR,
SINCE I had the honour of addreffing you yefterday, nothing material has occurred.   However, it is probable in a little time the enemy will attempt to force us from hence, as we are informed they are bringing many of their heavy cannon towards the heights and the works we have thrown up.   They have alfo eight or nine fhips of war in the North-river, which (it is faid) are to cannonade our right flank when they open their batteries againft our front.   Every difpofition is making on our part for defence : and Congrefs may be affured that I fhall do every thing in my power to maintain the poft fo long as it fhall appear practicable, and conducive to the general good.

I have the honour to be, &c.   G. W.

SIR,   *Head-Quarters, Heights of Haerlem, Sept.* 20, 1776.
I HAVE been honoured with your favour of the fixteenth with its inclofures.   To prevent the injury and
abufes

abufes which would arife from the militia and other troops carrying away ammunition and continental property, I have publifhed the fubftance of the refolves upon the fubject in general orders.

Since my letter of yefterday, nothing of importance has caft up. The enemy are forming a large and extenfive encampment in the plains mentioned in my laft, and are bufily employed in tranfporting their cannon and ftores from Long-Ifland. As they advance them this way, we may reafonably expect their operations will not long be deferred.

Inclofed are fundry letters, &c. to which Congrefs will be pleafed to pay fuch regard as they may think them deferving of. The letter from monfieur . . . . . came open under cover of one to me. Thofe from colonel Hand and colonel Ward contain a lift of vacancies in their regiments, and of the perfons they efteem proper to fill them. The former, I believe, returned no lift before : the latter fays he never got any commiffions. Generals Howe and Erfkine's proclamations fhew the meafures that have been purfued, to force and feduce the inhabitants of Long-Ifland from their allegiance to the States, and to affift in their deftruction.

As the period will foon arrive, when the troops compofing the prefent army (a few excepted) will be difbanded according to the tenor of their enliftments, and the moft fatal confequences may enfue if a fuitable and timely provifion is not made in this inftance, I take the liberty of fuggefting to Congrefs not only the expediency but the abfolute neceffity there is that their earlieft attention fhould be had to this fubject. In refpect to the time that troops fhould be engaged for, I have frequently given my fentiments ; nor have I omitted to exprefs my opinion of the difficulties that will attend raifing them, nor of the impracticability of effecting it without the allowance of a large and extraordinary bounty.

It is a melancholy and painful confideration to thofe who are concerned in the work and have the command, to be forming armies conftantly, and to be left by troops juft when they begin to deferve the name, or perhaps at a moment when an important blow is expected. This, I

am

am informed, will be the cafe at Ticonderoga with part of the troops there, unlefs fome fyftem is immediately come into, by which they can be induced to ftay. General Schuyler tells me in a letter received yefterday, that De Haas's, Maxwell's, and Wind's regiments ftand engaged only till the beginning of next month, and that the men, he is fearful, will not remain longer than the time of their enliftment.

I would alfo beg leave to mention to Congrefs, that the feafon is faft approaching when clothes of every kind will be wanted for the army. Their diftrefs is already great, and will be increafed as the weather becomes more fevere. Our fituation is now bad, but is much better than that of the militia that are coming to join us from the States of Maffachufetts-Bay and Connecticut in confequence of the requifition of Congrefs. They, I am informed, have not a fingle tent or a neceffary of any kind; nor can I conceive how it will be poffible to fupport them. Thefe circumftances are extremely alarming, and oblige me to wifh Congrefs to have all the tents, clothing of every kind, and camp neceffaries, provided and forwarded, that are to be procured. Thefe eaftern reinforcements have not a fingle neceffary, not a pan or a kettle,—in which we are now greatly deficient. It is with reluctance that I trouble Congrefs with thefe matters: but to whom can I refort for relief unlefs to them? The neceffity therefore, which urges the application, will excufe it, I am perfuaded.

I have not been able to tranfmit Congrefs a general return of the army this week, owing to the peculiar fituation of our affairs, and the great fhifting and changing among the troops. As foon as I can procure one, a copy fhall be forwarded to Congrefs.

I have the honour to be, &c.　　　　G. W.

P. S. *September* 21, 1776. Things with us remain in the fituation they were yefterday.

SIR,　　　　　*Head-Quarters, Haerlem Heights, Sept.* 22, 1776.

I HAVE nothing in particular to communicate to Congrefs refpecting the fituation of our affairs: it is much the fame as when I had the honour of addreffing you laft.

On

On Friday night, about eleven or twelve o'clock, a fire broke out in the city of New-York, near the new or St. Paul's church, as it is said, which continued to burn pretty rapidly till after sunrise the next morning. I have not been informed how the accident happened, nor received any certain account of the damage. Report says many of the houses between the Broadway and the river were consumed.

I have the honour to be, &c.   G. W.

———————

SIR,   *Head-Quarters, Haerlem Heights, Sept.* 24, 1776.

THE post being about to depart, I have only time to add that no event of importance has taken place on this side Hudson's-river since my last of the twenty-second instant.

The inclosed letter, received last night from general Greene who now commands in the Jersies, will give Congress all the information I have respecting the evacuation of Paulus-Hook and the landing of the enemy to possess it.

I this minute obtained a copy of the general return of our force, the first I have been able to procure for some time past, which I do myself the honour of transmitting for the satisfaction of Congress.

I am, Sir, with the greatest respect, &c.   G. W.

P. S.   The thirteen militia regiments from Connecticut being reduced to a little more than seven hundred men rank and file fit for duty, I have thought proper to discharge the whole, to save the States the immense charge that would arise for officers' pay. There are many militia too that have just come in, and on their way from that State, none of whom are provided with a tent, or a single camp utensil. This distresses me beyond measure.

———————

SIR,   *Colonel Morris's on the Heights of Haerlem, Sept.* 24, 1776.

FROM the hours allotted to sleep I will borrow a few moments to convey my thoughts on sundry important matters to Congress. I shall offer them with the sincerity
which

which ought to characterize a man of candour, and with the freedom which may be used in giving useful information without incurring the imputation of presumption.

We are now, as it were, upon the eve of another dissolution of our army. The remembrance of the difficulties which happened upon the occasion last year, the consequences which might have followed the change if proper advantages had been taken by the enemy, added to a knowledge of the present temper and situation of the troops, reflect but a very gloomy prospect upon the appearances of things now, and satisfy me beyond the possibility of doubt, that, unless some speedy and effectual measures are adopted by Congress, our cause will be lost.

It is in vain to expect that any or more than a trifling part of this army will again engage in the service on the encouragement offered by Congress. When men find that their townsmen and companions are receiving twenty, thirty, and more dollars, for a few months' service (which is truly the case,) it cannot be expected, without using compulsion ; and to force them into the service would answer no valuable purpose. When men are irritated, and the passions inflamed, they fly hastily and cheerfully to arms : but after the first emotions are over * * *, a soldier, reasoned with upon the goodness of the cause he is engaged in and the inestimable rights he is contending for, hears you with patience, and acknowledges the truth of your observations, but adds that it is of no more importance to him than others. The officer makes you the same reply, with this further remark, that his pay will not support him, and he cannot ruin himself and family to serve his country, when every member of the community is equally interested and benefited by his labours. * * *

It becomes evidently clear then, that, as this contest is not likely to be the work of a day,—as the war must be carried on systematically,—and to do it you must have good officers,—there are, in my judgment, no other possible means to obtain them but by establishing your army upon a permanent footing, and giving your officers good pay. This will induce gentlemen and men of character to engage : and, till the bulk of your officers are composed of such persons as are actuated by principles of honour and a

spirit of enterprife, you have little to expect from them.
They ought to have fuch allowances as will enable them to
live like and fupport the characters of gentlemen.　＊＊＊
Befides, fomething is due to the man who puts his life in
[*your*] hands, hazards his health, and forfakes the fweets
of domeftic enjoyment.　Why a captain in the continental fervice fhould receive no more than five fhillings currency per day for performing the fame duties that an officer
of the fame rank in the Britifh fervice receives ten fhillings
fterling for, I never could conceive, efpecially when the
latter is provided with every neceffary he requires upon the
beft terms, and the former can fcarce procure them at any
rate.　There is nothing that gives a man confequence and
renders him fit for command, like a fupport that renders
him independent of every body but the State he ferves.

With refpect to the men, nothing but a good bounty can
obtain them upon a permanent eftablifhment : and for no
fhorter time than the continuance of the war, ought they
to be engaged ; as facts inconteftibly prove that the difficulty and coft of enliftments increafe with time.　When
the army was firft raifed at Cambridge, I am perfuaded
the men might have been got, without a bounty, for the
war.　After this, they began to fee that the conteft was
not likely to end fo fpeedily as was imagined, and to feel
their confequence by remarking, that, to get in the militia
in the courfe of the laft year, many towns were induced
to give them a bounty.

Forefeeing the evils refulting from this, and the deftructive confequences which unavoidably would follow
fhort enliftments, I took the liberty in a long letter (date
not now recollected, as my letter-book is not here) to recommend the enliftments for and during the war, affigning
fuch reafons for it as experience has fince convinced me
were well founded.　At that time, twenty dollars would,
I am perfuaded, have engaged the men for this term.　But
it will not do to look back : and, if the prefent opportunity
is flipped, I am perfuaded that twelve months more will
increafe our difficulties four-fold.　I fhall therefore take
the freedom of giving it as my opinion, that a good bounty
be immediately offered, aided by the proffer of at leaft a
hundred or a hundred and fifty acres of land, and a fuit of

clothes

clothes and blanket to each non-commiffioned officer and foldier ; as I have good authority for faying, that, however high the men's pay may appear, it is barely fufficient, in the prefent fcarcity and dearnefs of all kinds of goods, to keep them in clothes, much lefs afford fupport to their families.

If this encouragement then is given to the men, and fuch pay allowed the officers as will induce gentlemen of character and liberal fentiments to engage, and proper care and precaution ufed in the nomination (having more regard to the characters of perfons than the number of men they can enlift,) we fhould in a little time have an army able to cope with any that can be oppofed to it, as there are excellent materials to form one out of. But while the only merit an officer poffeffes is his ability to raife men,— while thofe men confider and treat him as an equal, and (in the character of an officer) regard him no more than a broomftick, being mixed together as one common herd,. no order nor difcipline can prevail ; nor will the officer ever meet with that refpect which is effentially neceffary to due fubordination.

To place any dependence upon militia is affuredly refting upon a broken ftaff,—men juft dragged from the tender fcenes of domeftic life,—unaccuftomed to the din of arms,—totally unacquainted with every kind of military fkill ; which being followed by a want of confidence in themfelves, when oppofed to troops regularly trained, difciplined, and appointed, fuperior in knowledge and fuperior in arms, makes them timid and ready to fly from their own fhadows. Befides, the fudden change in their manner of living (particularly in the lodging) brings on ficknefs in many, impatience in all, and fuch an unconquerable defire of returning to their refpective homes, that it not only produces fhameful and fcandalous defertions among themfelves, but infufes the like fpirit into others.

Again; men accuftomed to unbounded freedom and no control, cannot brook the reftraint which is indifpenfably neceffary to the good order and government of an army ; without which, licentioufnefs and every kind of diforder triumphantly reign. To bring men to a proper degree of fubordination is not the work of a day, a month, or even

a year :

a year : and, unhappily for us and the caufe we are engaged in, the little difcipline I have been labouring to eftablifh in the army under my immediate command is in a
manner done away, by having fuch a mixture of troops as
have been called together within thefe few months.

Relaxed and unfit as our rules and regulations of war
are for the government of an army, the militia (thofe properly fo called ; for of thefe we have two forts, the fix-
months-men, and thofe fent in as a temporary aid) do not
think themfelves fubject to them, and therefore take liberties which the foldier is punifhed for. This creates jealoufy : jealoufy begets diffatisfactions ; and thefe by de-
grees ripen into mutiny, keeping the whole army in a confufed and difordered ftate,—rendering the time of thofe
who wifh to fee regularity and good order prevail, more unhappy than words can defcribe. Befides this, fuch repeated
changes take place, that all arrangement is fet at nought,
and the conftant fluctuation of things deranges every plan
as faft as adopted.

Thefe, Sir, Congrefs may be affured, are but a fmall
part of the inconveniences which might be enumerated,
and attributed to militia : but there is one that merits
particular attention, and that is the expenfe. Certain I
am, that it would be cheaper to keep fifty or a hundred
thoufand in conftant pay, than to depend upon half the
number and fupply the other half occafionally by militia.
The time the latter are in pay before and after they are
in camp, affembling and marching,—the wafte of ammunition, the confumption of ftores, which, in fpite of every
refolution or requifition of Congrefs, they muft be furnifhed with, or fent home,—added to other incidental expenfes confequent upon their coming and conduct in camp,
furpaffes all idea, and deftroys every kind of regularity and
economy which you could eftablifh among fixed and fettled troops, and will, in my opinion, prove (if the fcheme
is adhered to) the ruin of our caufe.

The jealoufies of a ftanding army, and the evils to be
apprehended from one, are remote, and, in my judgment,
fituated and circumftanced as we are, not at all to be
dreaded : but the confequences of wanting one, according
to my ideas formed from the prefent view of things, is
                                                    certain

:ertain and inevitable ruin.   For, if I was called upon to
declare upon oath, whether the militia have been moſt
ſerviceable or hurtful upon the whole, I ſhould ſubſcribe to
the latter.   I do not mean by this, however, to arraign the
conduct of Congreſs : in ſo doing I ſhould equally con-
demn my own meaſures, if I did not my judgment : but
experience, which is the beſt criterion to work by, ſo fully,
clearly and deciſively reprobates the practice of truſting to
militia, that no man who regards order, regularity and
economy, or who has any regard for his own honour, character, or peace of mind, will riſk them upon this iſſue. * * *
    An army formed of good officers moves like clock-
work : but there is no ſituation upon earth leſs enviable
nor more diſtreſſing than that perſon's who is at the head
of troops who are regardleſs of order and diſcipline, and
who are unprovided with almoſt every neceſſary.   In a
word, the difficulties which have forever ſurrounded me
ſince I have been in the ſervice, and kept my mind con-
ſtantly upon the ſtretch,—the wounds which my feelings
(as an officer) have received by a thouſand things which
have happened contrary to my expectation and wiſhes,
* * *—added to a conſciouſneſs of my inability to govern an army compoſed of ſuch diſcordant parts, and under
ſuch a variety of intricate and perplexing circumſtances,—
induce not only a belief, but a thorough conviction in my
mind, that it will be impoſſible (unleſs there is a thorough
change in our military ſyſtem) for me to conduct matters
in ſuch a manner as to give ſatisfaction to the public,
which is all the recompenſe I aim at, or ever wiſhed for.
    Before I conclude, I muſt apologize for the liberties
taken in this letter, and for the blots and ſcratchings therein, not having time to give it more correctly.   With truth I
can add, that, with every ſentiment of reſpect and eſteem,
I am yours and the Congreſs's moſt obedient, &c.

G. W.

Head-Quarters, Haerlem Heights, Sept. 25, 1776.

SIR,

    HAVING wrote you fully on ſundry important
ſubjects this morning, as you will perceive by the letter
which accompanies this, I mean principally now to incloſe

X 2

a copy

a copy of a letter received from general Howe on Sunday morning, with the lifts of the prisoners in his hands,—of those in our possession belonging to the army immediately under his command,—and of my answer, which were omitted to be put in the other. His letter will discover to Congress his refusal to exchange lord Stirling for Mr. M'Donald, considering the latter only as a major. They will be pleased to determine how he is to be ranked in future.

The number of prisoners according to these returns is greater than what we expected. However, I am inclined to believe, that, among those in the lift from Long-Island, are several militia of general Woodhull's party, who were never arranged in this army. As to those taken on the fifteenth, they greatly exceed the number that I supposed fell into their hands in the retreat from the city. At the time that I transmitted an account of that affair, I had not obtained returns, and took the matter upon the officers' reports. They are difficult to get with certainty at any time. In the skirmish of Monday se'nnight, they could have taken but very few.

Before I conclude, I shall take occasion to mention that those returns made with such precision, and the difficulty that will attend the proposed exchange on account of the dispersed and scattered state of the prisoners in our hands, will clearly evince the necessity of appointing commissaries and proper persons to superintend and conduct in such instances. This I took the liberty of urging more than once, as well on account of the propriety of the measure and the saving that would have resulted from it, as that the prisoners might be treated with humanity, and have their wants particularly attended to.

I would also observe (as I esteem it my duty) that this army is in want of almost every necessary,—tents, camp kettles, blankets, and clothes of all kinds. But what is to be done with respect to the two last articles, I know not, as the term of enlistment will be nearly expired by the time they can be provided. This may be exhibited as a further proof of the disadvantages attending the levying of an army upon such a footing as never to know how to keep them without injuring the public or incommoding

the

the men. I have directed the colonel or commanding officer of each corps to ufe his endeavours to procure fuch clothing as is abfolutely neceffary : but at the fame time I confefs, that I do not know how they are to be got.

I have the honour to be, &c.   G. W.

———

Head-Quarters, Heights of Haerlem, September 27, 1776.
SIR,

I HAVE nothing in particular to communicate to Congrefs by this day's poft, as our fituation is the fame as when I laft wrote.

We are now fitting on the bufinefs the committee came upon, which, it is probable, will be finifhed this evening. The refult they will duly report upon their return.

I received yefterday the inclofed declaration by a gentleman from Elizabethtown, who told me many copies were found in the poffeffion of the foldiers from Canada, that were landed there a day or two ago by general Howe's permiffion. I fhall not comment upon it. It feems to be founded on the plan that has been artfully purfued for fome time paft.

I have the honour to be, &c.   G. W.

P. S. The account of the troops, &c. in Canada, comes from a perfon who is among the prifoners fent from Canada. It was anonymous, nor do I know the intelligencer. According to him, the enemy in that quarter are ftronger than we fuppofed, and their naval force much greater on the lakes than we had any idea of. I truft he has taken the matter up on the enemy's report.

———

SIR,   *Head-Quarters, Heights of Haerlem, Sept. 28, 1776.*

BEING about to crofs the North-river this morning in order to view the poft oppofite, and the grounds between that and Paulus-Hook, I fhall not add much more than that I have been honoured with your favour of the twenty-fourth and its feveral inclofures ; and that, fince my letter of yefterday, no important event has taken place.

A 2

As colonel Hugh Stephenson, of the rifle regiment ordered lately to be raised, is dead according to the information I have received, I would beg leave to recommend to the particular notice of Congress captain Daniel Morgan, just returned among the prisoners from Canada, as a fit and proper person to succeed to the vacancy occasioned by his death. The present field-officers of the regiment cannot claim any right in preference to him, because he ranked above them, and as a captain, when he first entered the service. His conduct as an officer, on the expedition with general Arnold last fall,—his intrepid behaviour in the assault upon Quebec, when the brave Montgomery fell,—the inflexible attachment he professed to our cause during his imprisonment, and which he perseveres in,—added to these, his residence in the place colonel Stephenson came from, and his interest and influence in the same circle, and with such men as are to compose such a regiment,—all, in my opinion, entitle him to the favour of Congress, and lead me to believe that in his promotion the States will gain a good and valuable officer for the fort of troops he is particularly recommended to command. * * *

I have the honour to be, &c. G. W.

SIR, *Head-Quarters, Heights of Haerlem, Sept.* 30, 1776.

SINCE I had the honour of addressing you last, nothing of importance has transpired: though, from some movements yesterday on the part of the enemy, it would seem as if something was intended.

The inclosed memorial, from lieutenant-colonel Shephard of the fourth regiment, I beg leave to submit to the consideration of Congress, and shall only add that I could wish they would promote him to the command of the regiment and send him a commission, being a good and valuable officer, and especially as the vacancy is of a pretty long standing, and I have not had (nor has he) any intelligence from colonel Learned himself, (who had the command, and who obtained a discharge on account of his indisposition) of his design to return. I have also inclosed a letter

from

from captain Ballard, which Congress will pleafe to determine on, the fubject being new and not within my authority.

I have the honour to be, &c.   G. W.

P. S. A commiffion was fent for colonel Learned, which is now in my hands, having received no application, or heard from him fince it came.

SIR,   *Head-Quarters, Haerlem Heights, Oct. 2, 1776.*

I DO myfelf the honour of tranfmitting to you the inclofed letter from lieutenant-colonel Livingfton, with fundry copies of general Delancey's orders, which difcover the meafures the enemy are purfuing on Long-Ifland for raifing recruits and obtaining fupplies of provifions. In confequence of the intelligence they contain, and authentic advices through other channels refpecting thefe matters, I have fent brigadier-general George Clinton to meet general Lincoln, who has got as far as Fairfield with part of the troops lately ordered by the Maffachufetts affembly, to concert with him and others an expedition acrofs the Sound with thofe troops, three companies under colonel Livingfton, and fuch further aid as governor Trumbull can afford, in order to prevent if poffible their effecting thofe important objects, and to affift the inhabitants in the removal of their ftock, grain, &c. or in deftroying them, that the enemy may not derive any advantage or benefit from them.

The recruiting fcheme they are profecuting with uncommon induftry; nor is it confined to Long-Ifland alone. Having juft now received a letter from the committee of Weft-Chefter county, advifing that there are feveral companies of men in that and Duchefs county preparing to go off and join the king's army, I have given directions to our guard-boats and the centries at our works at Mount-Wafhington to keep a ftrict look-out in cafe they attempt to come down the North-river; alfo to general Heath at Kingfbridge, that the utmoft vigilance may be obferved by the regiments and troops ftationed above there and down

towards

towards the East-river, that they may intercept them, should they take that route with a view of crossing to Long-Island.   I will use every precaution in my power to prevent those parricides from accomplishing their designs : but I have but little hopes of success, as it will be no difficult matter for them to procure a passage over some part or other of the Sound.

I have been applied to lately by colonel Weedon of Virginia, for permission to recruit the deficiency of men in his regiment out of the troops composing the flying camp,—informing me at the same time that some of those from Maryland had offered to engage.   Colonel Hand of the rifle battalion made a similar application to-day.   If the enlistments could be made, they would have this good consequence,—the securing of so many in the service. However, as the measure might occasion some uneasiness in their own corps, and be considered as a hardship by the States to which they belong, and the means of their furnishing more than the quota extracted from them in the general arrangement, and would make it more difficult for them to complete their own levies, I did not conceive myself at liberty to authorise it without submitting the propriety of it to the consideration of Congress, and obtaining their opinion whether it should be allowed or not.

I have inclosed a list of warrants granted from the second to the thirtieth ultimo inclusive, the only return of the sort that I have been able to make since the resolution for that purpose,—owing to the unsettled state of our affairs, and my having sent my papers away.   You will also receive sundry letters, &c. from general Schuyler, which came under cover to me, and which I have the honour of forwarding.

By a letter just received from the committee of safety of the State of New-Hampshire, I find a thousand of their militia were about to march on the twenty-fourth ultimo to reinforce this army in consequence of the requisition of Congress.   Previous to their march, general Ward writes me he was obliged to furnish them with five hundred pounds of powder and a thousand pounds of musket-ball ; and I have little reason to expect that they are better provided with other articles than they were with ammunition.

In

In fuch cafe they will only add to our prefent diftrefs which is already far too great, and become difgufted with the fervice, though the time they are engaged for is only till the firft of December. This will injure their enlifting for a longer term, if not wholly prevent it.

By three deferters who came from the Galatea man-of-war about five days ago, we are informed that feveral tranf-ports had failed, before they left her, for England, as it was generally reported, in order to return with a fupply of provifions, of which they fay there is a want. General Mercer, in a letter, informed me that general Thompfon faid he had heard they were going to difmifs about a hun-dred of the fhips from the fervice. I am alfo advifed by a letter from Mr. Derby at Bofton, of the twenty-fixth ultimo, that, the day before, a tranfport fnow had been taken and fent into Pifcataqua by a privateer, in her paffage from New-York to the Weft-Indies. She failed with five more under the convoy of a man-of-war, in order to bring from thence the troops that are there, to join general Howe. They were all victualled for four months. From this intelligence it would feem as if they did not apprehend any thing to be meditating againft them by the court of France.

October 3. I have nothing in particular to commu-nicate refpecting our fituation, it being much the fame as when I wrote laft. We had an alarm this morning a lit-tle before four o'clock, from fome of our out-centries, who reported that a large body of the enemy was advan-cing towards our lines. This put us in motion: however, it turned out entirely premature; or at leaft we faw noth-ing of them.

I have the honour to be, &c.   G. W.

SIR,   *Haerlem, October* 4, 1776.

BEFORE I knew of the late refolutions of Con-grefs which you did me the honour to inclofe in your let-ter of the twenty-fourth, and before I was favoured with the vifit of your committee, I took the liberty of giving you my fentiments on feveral points which feemed to be

of

of importance.   I have no doubt but that the committee will make such report of the state and condition of the army, as will induce Congress to believe that nothing but the most vigorous exertions can put matters upon such a footing as to give this continent a fair prospect of success. Give me leave to say, Sir,—I say it with due deference and respect (and my knowledge of the facts, added to the importance of the cause, and the stake I hold in it, must justify the freedom,)—that your affairs are in a more unpromising way than you seem to apprehend.

Your army, as I mentioned in my last, is on the eve of its political dissolution.   True it is, you have voted a larger one in lieu of it : but the season is late ; and there is a material difference between voting of battalions and raising of men.   In the latter there are more difficulties than Congress are aware of ; which makes it my duty (as I have been informed of the prevailing sentiments of this army) to inform them, that, unless the pay of the officers, especially that of the field-officers, is raised, the chief part of those that are worth retaining will leave the service at the expiration of the present term, as the soldiers will also, if some greater encouragement is not offered them than twenty dollars and a hundred acres of land.

Nothing less, in my opinion, than a suit of clothes annually given to each non-commissioned officer and soldier, in addition to the pay and bounty, will avail ; and I question whether that will do, as the enemy (from the information of one John Mash, who, with six others, was taken by our guards) are giving ten pounds bounty for recruits, and have got a battalion under major Rogers nearly completed upon Long-Island.

Nor will less pay, according to my judgment, than I have taken the liberty of mentioning in the inclosed estimate, retain such officers as we could wish to have continued.   The difference per month in each battalion will amount to better than a hundred pounds.   To this may be added the pay of the staff-officers ; for it is presumable they will also require an augmentation : but, being few in number, the sum will not be greatly increased by them, and consequently is a matter of no great moment : but it is a matter of no small importance to make the several of-

fices

&ces defirable. When the pay and eftablifhment of an officer once become objects of interefted attention, the floth, negligence, and even difobedience of orders, which at this time but too generally prevail, will be purged off. But while the fervice is viewed with indifference,—while the officer conceives that he is rather conferring than receiving an obligation,—there will be a total relaxation of all order and difcipline, and every thing will move heavily on, to the great detriment of the fervice, and inexpreffible trouble and vexation of the general.

The critical fituation of our affairs at this time will juftify my faying that no time is to be loft in making of fruitlefs experiments. An unavailing trial of a month to get an army upon the terms propofed may render it impracticable to do it at all, and prove fatal to our caufe ; as I am not fure whether any rubs in the way of our enliftments, or unfavourable turn in our affairs, may not prove the means of the enemy recruiting men fafter than we do. To this may be added the inextricable difficulty of forming one corps out of another, and arranging matters with any degree of order, in the face of an enemy who are watching for advantages.

At Cambridge, laft year, where the officers (and more than a fufficiency of them) were all upon the fpot, we found it a work of fuch extreme difficulty to know their fentiments (each having fome terms to propofe) that I defpaired once of getting the arrangements completed : and I do fuppofe, that at leaft a hundred alterations took place before matters were finally adjufted. What muft it be then under the prefent regulation, where the officer is to negociate this matter with the State he comes from, diftant perhaps two or three hundred miles ?—fome of whom, without leave or licenfe from me, fet out to make perfonal application, the moment the refolve got to their hands. What kind of officers thefe are, I leave Congrefs to judge.

If an officer of reputation (for none other fhould be applied to) is afked to ftay, what anfwer can he give, but in the firft place, that he does not know whether it is at his option to do fo, no provifion being made in the refolution of Congrefs, even recommendatory of this meafure :

confequently, that it refts with the State he comes from (furrounded perhaps with a variety of applications, and influenced probably by local attachments) to determine whether he can be provided for or not ? In the next place, if he is an officer of merit, and knows that the State he comes from is to furnifh more battalions than it at prefent has in the fervice, he will fcarcely, after two years' faithful fervices, think of continuing in the rank he now bears, when new creations are to be made, and men appointed to offices (nowife fuperior in merit, and ignorant perhaps of fervice) over his head. A committee, fent to the army from each State, may upon the fpot fix things with a degree of propriety and certainty, and is the only method I can fee of bringing matters to a decifion with refpect to the officers of the army. But what can be done in the meanwhile towards the arrangement in the country, I know not. In the one cafe you run the hazard of lofing your officers ; in the other, of encountering delay, unlefs fome method could be devifed of forwarding both at the fame inftant.

Upon the prefent plan, I plainly forefee an intervention of time between the old and new army, which muft be filled up with militia (if to be had) with whom no man who has any regard for his own reputation can undertake to be anfwerable for confequences. I fhall alfo be miftaken in my conjectures, if we do not lofe the moft valuable officers in this army, under the prefent mode of appointing them : confequently, if we have an army at all, it will be compofed of materials not only entirely raw, but (if uncommon pains are not taken) entirely unfit : and I fee fuch a diftruft and jealoufy of military power, that the commander in chief has not an opportunity, even by recommendation, to give the leaft affurances of reward for the moft effential fervices. In a word, fuch a cloud of perplexing circumftances appear before me, without one flattering hope, that I am thoroughly convinced, unlefs the moft vigorous and decifive exertions are immediately adopted to remedy thefe evils, that the certain and abfolute lofs of our liberties will be the inevitable confequence ; as one unhappy ftroke will throw a powerful weight into the fcale againft us, enabling general Howe to recruit his

army

army as faft as we fhall ours,—numbers being difpofed [*to join him*] and many actually doing fo already. Some of the moft probable remedies, and fuch as experience has brought to my more intimate knowledge, I have taken the liberty to point out : the reft I beg leave to fubmit to the confideration of Congrefs..

I afk pardon for taking up fo much of their time with my opinions. But I fhould betray that truft which they and my country have repofed in me, were I to be filent upon a matter fo extremely interefting. With the moft perfect efteem, I have the honour to be, &c.   G. W.

SIR,   *Head-Quarters, Haerlem Heights, Oct. 5, 1776.*

I WAS laft night honoured with your favour of the fecond with fundry refolutions of Congrefs. * * *

In refpect to the exchange of prifoners, I fear it will be a work of great difficulty, owing to their difperfed and fcattered fituation throughout the States. In order to effect it, I have wrote to the eaftern governments to have them collected, and to tranfmit me an account of their number, diftinguifhing the names and ranks of the field and commiffioned officers, and the corps they belong to. I have alfo wrote to governor Livingfton of the Jerfeys upon the fubject, and muft take the liberty of requefting Congrefs to give directions that a fimilar return may be made of thofe in Pennfylvania and Maryland, and for their being brought to Brunfwic, that they may be ready to be exchanged for an equal number of thofe of the fame rank.

I obferve, by the refolve of the twenty-fixth ultimo, that the exchange is particularly directed to be made of the officers and foldiers taken on Long-Ifland: But fhould not that follow the exchange of thofe officers and men who have lately returned from Quebec, whofe imprifonment has been much longer, and whofe fervice has not been lefs fevere, and, in many inftances, conducted with great intrepidity ? I have had many applications fince their arrival, by which they claim a kind of preference as far as their number and the circumftances of their rank will allow,

and

and which I thought it my duty to mention, that I may obtain some direction upon the subject.

You will observe by a paragraph of a letter received yesterday from general Howe, a copy of which you have at length, that the non-performance of the agreement between captain Forster and general Arnold, by which the latter stipulated for the return of an equal number of officers and prisoners in our hands for those delivered him, is considered in an unfavourable light, and entirely imputed to me, as having the chief command of the armies of the States, and a controlling power over general Arnold. The pointed manner in which Mr. Howe is pleased to express himself could not personally affect me, supposing there had been no good grounds for the treaty not being ratified, having been nothing more than an instrument of conveying to him the resolutions formed upon the subject. * * *

However, I would beg leave to observe, from the letters from the hostages,—from what has been reported by others respecting captain Forster's having used his endeavours to restrain the savages from exercising their wonted barbarities, though in some instances they did,—his purchasing some of the prisoners for a pretty considerable premium,—but, above all, from the delicate nature of such treaties, and because the non-observance of them must damp the spirits of the officers who make them, and add affliction to the misfortunes of those whom necessity and the nature of the case force into captivity to give them a sanction by a long and irksome confinement,—for these reasons and many more that will readily occur, I could wish Congress to reconsider the matter, and to carry it into execution.

I am sensible the wrong was originally in their employing savages, and that whatever cruelties were committed by them should be esteemed their own acts: yet perhaps, in point of policy, it may not be improper to overlook these infractions on their part, and to pursue that mode which will be the most likely to render the hardships incident to war most tolerable, and the greatest benefits to the State.

I have ventured to say thus much upon the subject from a regard to the service, and because such gentlemen of the

army

army as I have heard mention it feem to wifh the treaty had been ratified rather than difallowed.

Inclofed is a lift of vacancies in the third regiment of Virginia troops, in part occafioned by the death of major Leitch who died of his wounds on Tuefday morning,—and of the gentlemen who ftand next in regimental order, and who are recommended to fucceed to them. You will obferve that captain John Fitzgerald is faid to be appointed to the duty of major. This I have done in order, being the oldeft captain in the regiment, and, I believe, an officer of unexceptionable merit, and as it was highly neceffary at this time to have the corps as well and fully officered as poffible. There is alfo a vacancy in the firft continental battalion by the promotion of lieutenant Clarke to a majority in the flying camp, to which colonel Hand has recommended William Patten to fucceed, as you will perceive by his letter inclofed.

I have taken the liberty to tranfmit a plan for eftablifh-ing a corps of engineers, artificers, &c. fketched out by colonel Putnam, and which is propofed for the confideration of Congrefs. How far they may incline to adopt it, or whether they may choofe to proceed upon fuch an extenfive fcale, they will be pleafed to determine. However, I conceive it a matter well worthy of their confideration, being convinced from experience, and from the reafons fuggefted by colonel Putnam who has acted with great diligence and reputation in the bufinefs, that fome eftablifhment of the fort is highly neceffary, and will be productive of the moft beneficial confequences.

If the propofition is approved by Congrefs, I am informed by good authority that there is a gentleman in Virginia, in the colony fervice, John Stadler, efquire, a native of Germany, whofe abilities in this way are by no means inconfiderable. I am told he was an engineer in the army under general Stanwix, and is reputed to be of fkill and ingenuity in the profeffion. In this capacity I do not know him myfelf, but am intimately acquainted with him in his private character, as a man of underftanding and of good behaviour. I would fubmit his merit to the inquiry of Congrefs; and if he fhould anfwer the report I have

Y 2

had

had of him, I make no doubt but he will be suitably provided for.

The convention of this State have lately seized and had appraised two new ships, valued at six thousand two hundred and twenty-nine pounds York currency, which they have sent down for the purpose of sinking, and obstructing the channel opposite Mount-Washington. The price being high, and the opinions various as to the necessity of the measure, some conceiving the obstruction nearly sufficient already, and others that they would render it secure, I would wish to have the direction of Congress upon the subject by the earliest opportunity, thinking myself, that, if the enemy should attempt to come up, they should be used, sooner than to hazard their passing. I must be governed by circumstances, yet hope for their sentiments before any thing is necessary to be done.

Sundry disputes having arisen of late between officers of different regiments and of the same rank, respecting the right of succession to such vacancies as happen from death or other causes,—some suggesting that it should be in a colonial line and governed by the priority of their commissions; others, that it should be regimentally,—and there being an instance now before me, between the officers of the Virginia regiments, occasioned by the death of major Leitch; it has become absolutely necessary that Congress should determine the mode by which promotions are to be regulated,—whether colonially and by priority of commissions, or regimentally, reserving a right out of the general rule they adopt, to reward for particular merit, or of withholding from office such as may not be worthy to succeed.

I have only proposed two modes for their consideration, being satisfied that promotions through the line (as they are called) can never take place without producing discord, jealousy, distrust, and the most fatal consequences. In some of my letters upon the subject of promotions, and one which I had the honour of addressing to the board of war on the thirtieth ultimo, I advised that the mode should be rather practised than resolved on : but I am fully convinced now of the necessity there is of settling it in one of the two ways I have taken the liberty to point out, and under the restrictions I have mentioned; or the disputes

and

and applications will be endlefs, and attended with great inconveniences.

I have the honour to be, &c.   G. W.

——————

SIR,   *Head-Quarters, Heights of Haerlem, Oct. 7, 1776.*

I DO myfelf the honour of tranfmitting to you a copy of a letter from the comte D'Emery, governor-general of the French part of St. Domingo, which I received yefterday, and alfo my anfwer, which I have inclofed and left open for the confideration of Congrefs, wifhing that it may be fealed if they approve of the fieur De Chambeau's releafement, which I think may be attended with many valuable confequences. If Congrefs concur in fentiment with me, they will be pleafed to give direction for his paffage by the firft opportunity to the French iflands : if they do not, I fhall be obliged by your returning my letter.

I have alfo the pleafure of inclofing a copy of a letter from monfieur P. Pennel, which came to hand laft night, and which contains intelligence of an agreeable and interefting nature, for which I beg leave to refer you to the copy. The polite manner in which monfieur Pennel has requefted to be one of my aides-de-camp demands my acknowledgments. As the appointment will not be attended with any expenfe, and will fhew a proper regard for his complaifance and the attachment he is pleafed to exprefs for the fervice of the American States, I fhall take the liberty of complying with his requifition, and tranfmit him a brevet commiffion, provided the fame fhall be agreeable to Congrefs. Their fentiments upon this fubject you will be kind enough to favour me with by the firft opportunity. The inclofed letter for the fieur De Chambeau you will pleafe to forward to him (if he is to be enlarged) after clofing it.

Before I conclude, I muft take the liberty to obferve that I am under no fmall difficulties on account of the French gentlemen that are here in confequence of the commiffions they have received,—having no means to employ them, or to afford them an opportunity of rendering that fervice they themfelves wifh to give, or which

perhaps

perhaps is expected by the public. Their want of our language is an objection to their being joined to any of the regiments here at this time, were there vacancies, and not other obstacles. These considerations induce me to wish that Congress would adopt and point out some particular mode to be observed respecting them. What it should be, they will be best able to determine. But to me it appears that their being here now can be attended with no valuable consequences, and that, as the power of appointing officers for the new army is vested in the conventions, &c. of the several States, it will be necessary for Congress to direct them to be provided for in the regiments to be raised, according to the ranks they would wish them to bear—(or I am convinced they will never be taken in, let their merit be what it may ;)—or to form them into a distinct corps which may be increased in time. They seem to be genteel, sensible men ; and I have no doubt of their making good officers as soon as they can learn as much of our language as to make themselves well understood : but, unless Congress interfere by their particular direction to the States, they will never be incorporated in any of the regiments to be raised : and, without they are, they will be entirely at a loss, and in the most irksome situation, for something to do, as they now are.

I have the honour to be, &c.   G. W.

SIR,   *Head-Quarters, Haerlem Heights, Oct. 8, 1776.*

SINCE I had the honour of writing you yesterday, I have been favoured with a letter from the honourable council of Massachusetts-Bay, covering one from Richard Derby, esquire, a copy of which is herewith transmitted, as it contains intelligence of an important and interesting nature.

As an exchange of prisoners is about to take place, I am induced, from a question stated in a letter I received from governor Trumbull this morning, to ask the opinion of Congress, in what manner the States that have had the care of them are to be reimbursed the expenses incurred on their account. My want of information in this instance, or whether any account is to be sent in with the prisoners, would not allow me to give him an answer, as nothing that I recollect has ever been said upon the subject. He also mentions another matter, viz. whether such privates as are mechanics, and others who may desire to remain with us, should be obliged to return. In respect to the latter, I conceive there can be no doubt of our being under a necessity of returning the whole, a proposition having been made on our part for a general exchange, and that agreed to : besides, the balance of prisoners is greatly against us ; and I am informed it was particularly stipulated by general Montgomery, that all those that were taken in Canada should be exchanged whenever a cartel was settled for the purpose.

Under these circumstances, I should suppose the several committees having the care of them should be instructed to make the most exact returns of the whole, however willing a part should be to continue with us. At the same time I should think it not improper to inform them of the reasons leading to the measure, and that they should be invited to escape afterwards, which, in all probability, they may effect without much difficulty if they are attached to us, extending their influence to many more, and bringing them away also.

The situation of our affairs and the present establishment of the army requiring our most vigorous exertions to engage a new one, I presume it will be necessary to furnish the pay-master-general as early as possible with money to pay the bounty, lately resolved on, to such men as will enlist. Prompt pay perhaps may have a happy effect, and induce the continuance of some who are here : but, without it, I am certain that nothing can be done ; nor have we time to lose in making the experiment. But then it may be asked, who is to recruit ? or who can consider themselves as officers for that purpose, till the conventions of the different States have made the appointments ?

Yesterday afternoon the exchange between lord Stirling and governor Browne was carried into execution ; and his lordship is now here. He confirms the intelligence mentioned by captain Souther, about the transports he met, by the arrival of the Daphne man-of-war (a twenty-gun ship).

a few

a few days ago, with twelve ships under her convoy, having light-horse on board. They failed with about twenty in each, and lost about eighty in their passage, besides those in the vessel taken by captain Souther. He further adds that he had heard it acknowledged more than once, that, in the action of the sixteenth ultimo, the enemy had a hundred men killed,—about sixty Highlanders of the forty-second regiment, and forty of the light-infantry. This confession coming from themselves, we may reasonably conclude, did not exaggerate the number. * * *

October 9. About eight o'clock this morning, two ships, of forty-four guns each (supposed to be the Roebuck and Phenix,) and a frigate of twenty guns, with three or four tenders, got under way from about Bloomingdale where they had been lying some time, and stood with an easy southerly breeze towards our chevaux-de-frise, which we hoped would have intercepted their passage while our batteries played upon them : but, to our surprise and mortification, they ran through without the least difficulty, and without receiving any apparent damage from our forts, though they kept up a heavy fire from both sides of the river. Their destination or views cannot be known with certainty : but most probably they are sent to stop the navigation, and cut off the supplies of boards, &c. which we should have received, and of which we are in great need. They are standing up, and I have dispatched an express to the convention of this State, that notice may be immediately communicated to general Clinton at the Highland fortifications, to put him on his guard in case they should have any designs against them, and that precautions may be taken to prevent the craft belonging to the river falling into their hands.

I have the honour to be, &c.   G. W.

- - - - - -

SIR,   *Head-Quarters, Haerlem Heights, Oct.* 11, 1776.

I BEG leave to inform you, that, since my letter of the eighth and ninth instant which I had the honour of addressing you, nothing of importance has occurred, except that the ships of war which I then mentioned, in their

passage

paſſage up the river, took a ſloop that was at anchor off the mouth of Spitendevil, and two of our row-gallies which they out-ſailed. The crews, finding that they could not prevent them falling into the enemy's hands, ran them near the ſhore, and effected their own eſcape. From the intelligence I have received, the ſhips are now lying at Tarrytown, without having landed any men (which ſeemed to be apprehended by ſome) or attempted any thing elſe. Their principal views, in all probability, are, to interrupt our navigation, and to receive ſuch diſaffected perſons as incline to take part againſt us. The former they will effect beyond all queſtion ; and I fear that their expectations reſpecting the latter will be but too fully anſwered.

October 12. The incloſed copy of a letter received laſt night from the convention of this State will ſhew you the apprehenſions they are under on account of the diſaffected among them. I have ordered up a part of the militia from Maſſachuſetts under general Lincoln, to prevent, if poſſible, the conſequences which they ſuggeſt may happen, and which there is reaſon to believe the conſpirators have in contemplation. I am perſuaded that they are upon the eve of breaking out, and that they will leave nothing uneſſayed that will diſtreſs us and favour the deſigns of the enemy, as ſoon as their ſchemes are ripe for it.

October 13. Yeſterday the enemy landed at Frog's-Point, about nine miles from hence, further up the Sound. Their number we cannot aſcertain, as they have not advanced from the point,—which is a kind of iſland,—but the water that ſurrounds it is fordable at low tide. I have ordered works to be thrown up at the paſſes from the point to the main. From the great number of ſloops, ſchooners, and nine ſhips, that went up the Sound in the evening, full of men, and from the information of two deſerters who came over laſt night, I have reaſon to believe that the greateſt part of their army has moved upwards or is about to do it, purſuing their original plan of getting in our rear, and cutting off our communication with the country.

The grounds from Frog's-Point are ſtrong and defenſible, being full of ſtone fences, both along the road and acroſs the adjacent fields, which will render it difficult for

artillery,

artillery, or indeed a large body of foot, to advance in any regular order, except through the main road. Our men who are posted on the passes seemed to be in great spirits when I left them last night.

I have the honour to be, &c.   G. W.

SIR,   *Head-Quarters, Haerlem Heights, Oct.* 14, 1776.

HIS excellency having gone this morning to visit our posts beyond Kingsbridge and the several passes leading from Frog's-Point and the necks adjacent, I have the honour to inform you by his command, that no interesting event has taken place since his letter by yesterday's post.

Every day's intelligence from the convention of this State holds forth discoveries of new plots and of new conspiracies. Some of the members seem to apprehend that insurrections are upon the eve of breaking out, and have suggested the necessity of seizing and securing the passes through the Highlands, lest the disaffected should do it. Their preservation being a matter of the greatest importance, his excellency, notwithstanding the situation we are in with respect to troops, has detached colonel Tash with his regiment, lately from New-Hampshire, in addition to the militia mentioned in his last, with directions to receive orders from the convention, as to the station and post he is to occupy.

There are now in our possession several persons, inhabitants of this State, who had engaged to join the enemy, and were intercepted in going to them. There are also two who confess they have been with them, and that they had actually engaged in their service; but, finding the terms (the bounty, pay, &c.) not so advantageous as they expected from the information they had received, they were induced to return. As the affairs of this government are in a precarious situation, and such as, the convention themselves seem to think, forbid their interposition farther than taking measures to apprehend them, his excellency would wish to obtain the sentiments of Congress, and their direction upon a subject so extremely critical and delicate, and

which

which, in the confideration of it, involves many important confequences.

Your favour of the ninth, with its feveral inclofures, his excellency received yefterday morning by the exprefs, who proceeded immediately on his journey.

October 17. I am directed by his excellency to acquaint you that we are again obliged to change our difpofition, to counteract the operations of the enemy. Declining an attack upon our front, they have drawn the main body of their army to Frog's-Point, with a defign of hemming us in, and drawing a line in our rear. To prevent the confequences which would but too probably follow the execution of their fcheme, the general officers determined yefterday that our forces muft be taken from hence, and extended towards Eaft and Weft-Chefter, fo as to outflank them. General Lee, who arrived on Monday, has ftrongly urged the abfolute neceffity of the meafure. It is propofed to leave a garrifon at Fort-Wafhington, and to maintain it if poffible, in order to preferve the communication with the Jerfeys. They are landing their artillery and waggons upon the Point; and there are now feveral boats paffing up the Sound, full of men.

I have the honour to be, &c.   R. H. HARRISON.

P. S. The poft having not come in fince Sunday, till to-day, has been the occafion of not writing to you fince that time. He was expected as ufual; which prevented an exprefs being fent.

SIR,   *Haerlem Heights, October* 18, 1776.

I WAS yefterday morning honoured with your favour of the fifteenth, with the refolutions of the eleventh and fourteenth. The latter, by which Congrefs have authorifed me to appoint monfieur Pennel a brevet aide-decamp, claims a return of my acknowledgments.

Laft night I received a letter from Mr. Varick, fecretary to general Schuyler, inclofing a copy of one from general Arnold to general Gates. The intelligence tranfmitted by general Arnold being of an extremely interefting and important nature, I thought it advifeable to forward the

Vol. I.   Z   fame

fame immediately by exprefs.   You have a copy herewith, which contains the particulars, and to which I beg leave to refer you.

The accounts tranfmitted yefterday by poft will inform you of the movements of the enemy, and of the meafures judged neceffary to be purfued by us, to counteract their defigns.   I have nothing to add on this head, except that ten or eleven fhips, which have been prevented paffing Hell-gate for two or three days for want of wind, are now under way, and proceeding up the Sound.   Amongft them there appear to be two frigates : the reft probably have in ftores, &c.

Inclofed is a copy of the laft general return I have been able to obtain.   It only comes down to the fifth inftant : the fituation of our affairs, and the almoft conftant neceffity of fending detachments from one place to another to watch the enemy's motions, have prevented the officers from making them with regularity.

I have the honour to be, &c.   G. W.

Kingfbridge, October 20, 1776, *half after one o'clock,* P. M.
SIR,

I HAVE it in command from his excellency to tranfmit you the inclofed copies of difpatches which juft now came to hand, and which contain intelligence of the moft interefting and important nature refpecting our affairs in the northern department.   His excellency would have wrote himfelf, but was going to our feveral pofts, when the exprefs arrived.

The enemy are purfuing with great induftry their plan of penetrating the country from the Sound, and of forming a line in our rear.   They are now extended from Frog's-Point to New-Rochelle, from whence it is generally conjectured they mean to take their route by way of the White-Plains, and from thence to draw a line to the North-river.   We on our part have drawn our whole force, except the regiments intended to garrifon Fort-Wafhington, from the ifland of New-York, and have poffeffed ourfelves of the heights, paffes, and advantageous grounds, between

New-Rochelle

New-Rochelle where the van of their army now lies, and the North-river. They will in all probability attempt to effect their purpose by moving higher up. If they do, our forces will move accordingly, it being a principal object to prevent their outflanking us.

On Friday, one of their advanced parties, near East-Chester, fell in with part of colonel Glover's brigade, and a smart and close skirmish ensued, in which, I have the pleasure to inform you, our men behaved with great coolness and intrepidity, and drove the enemy back to their main body.

I have the honour to be, &c.   R. H. HARRISON.

SIR,   *Head-Quarters, Valentine's Hill, Oct. 21, 1776.*

HIS excellency being absent on a visit to the several posts on the left of our lines and at the White-Plains, I have the honour to inform you, by the favour of colonel Whipple, that, since my letter of yesterday, no event of importance has occurred.

I have the honour to be, &c.   R. H. HARRISON.

To the Board of War.

GENTLEMEN,   *Camp on Valentine's Hill, Oct. 22, 1776.*

I AM directed by his excellency, whose business has called him from hence, to acknowledge his receipt of your favours of the twelfth and fifteenth instant, and to inform you in answer to the first, that he will mention the case of the French gentlemen to general Lee, and obtain his opinion as to the best mode of providing for them in a useful way. The horses belonging to the light dragoons who were taken, he thinks, will be very serviceable; and he will write to general Ward or one of the agents to purchase them.

In respect to your requisition for an immediate return of ordnance stores, his excellency says it cannot possibly be complied with in the present unsettled state of the army.

In

In order to effect the good purposes you have in view, he would take the liberty to recommend the establishing of magazines of ammunition and other ordnance stores in proper places of security, from whence supplies could be occasionally drawn.   As large quantities are constantly in demand in time of war, he does not conceive your provision in these instances can be too great.

He will direct the regimental returns in future to include arms and accoutrements, and the commissary-general to transmit monthly lists of rations.   He thinks the regulation extremely proper, though he apprehends the information to be premature respecting the over-quantity suggested to have been drawn, having heard no suspicion of the sort in this army of late.

I have the honour to be, &c.   R. H. Harrison.

SIR,   *Head-Quarters, White-Plains, Oct.* 25, 1776.

THE whole of our army is now here and on the neighbouring heights, except the troops left at Mount-Washington and Kingsbridge, (about fourteen hundred at the former, and six hundred at the latter) and general Lee's division which now forms the rear, and which is on their march.   Our removal, and that of the stores, have been attended with a great deal of trouble, owing to the scarcity and difficulty of procuring waggons.   However, they are nearly effected, and without any loss.   The general officers are now reconnoitring the several passes leading from the enemy, that the most important may be immediately secured.   The situation of their army remains nearly the same as when I had the honour of addressing you on the twenty-first instant.   It differs in nothing unless it is that their main body is more collected about New-Rochelle.   A few of their troops are extended as far as Momarioneck.

On Monday night a detachment of our men, under the command of colonel Hazlet, was sent out to surprise and cut off major Rogers, if possible, with his regiment which was posted there.   By some accident or other the expedition did not succeed so well as I could have wished. However, our advanced party, led on by major Greene of the

the firſt Virginia regiment, fell in with their out-guard, and brought off thirty-ſix priſoners, ſixty muſkets, and ſome blankets.   The number killed is not certainly known : but it is reported by an officer who was there, that he counted about twenty-five.   Our loſs, two killed, and ten or twelve wounded ; among the latter, major Greene, whoſe recovery is very doubtful.

On Wedneſday there was alſo a ſmart ſkirmiſh between a party of colonel Hand's riflemen,— about two hundred and forty,—and nearly the ſame number of Heſſian chaſſeurs, in which the latter were put to the route.   Our men buried ten of them on the field, and took two priſoners, one badly wounded.   We ſuſtained no other loſs than having one lad wounded, ſuppoſed mortally.

The ſhips of war that are in the North river fell down, yeſterday morning or the evening before, to Dobbs's ferry, to prevent our bringing ſtores from below by water, and the removal of thoſe that are landed there.   As ſoon as the waggons, employed in bringing the baggage and ſtores of general Lee's diviſion, are diſengaged, they will be immediately ſent to aſſiſt thoſe already there to remove them.

On Saturday night we had the misfortune to loſe one of the new ſhips intended to be ſunk for obſtructing the channel.   She parted her cables in a ſevere ſquall, when properly ballaſted, and bilged as ſoon as ſhe ſtruck the ſhore. The other ſhip was ſunk well ; and yeſterday morning two brigs, both ready, were ſent down for the ſame purpoſe.

About two o'clock this afternoon, intelligence was brought to Head-Quarters that three or four detachments of the enemy were on their march, and had advanced within about four miles of this place.   It has been fully confirmed ſince by a variety of perſons who have been out to reconnoitre.   Their number cannot be aſcertained : but it is generally conjectured that the detachments are or will be ſucceeded by as many columns compoſing their main body. Our drums have beat to arms, and the men are ordered to their ſeveral poſts.   Moſt probably ſome important event is upon the eve of taking place : I hope it will be victory in favour of our arms.   General Lee, with his diviſion, has not got up ; but I hear he is on his march.

Z 2

Experiment

Experiment having proved it difficult, if not impoſſible, to prevent the enemy from poſſeſſing the navigation of the North-river, and rendering the communication and inter-courſe between the States divided by it extremely hazard-ous and precarious by means of their ſhips of war, it has become a matter of important conſideration how to remedy the evil, and to guard againſt the conſequences which may reſult from it.   I am charged by his excellency to men-tion it to Congreſs as a matter that has employed much of his thought, and that ſeems worthy of their moſt ſerious attention.   He has communicated it to ſeveral of the gen-eral and other officers, and to many gentlemen of ſenſe and diſcernment, who all agree with him, not only upon the propriety but the abſolute neceſſity that two diſtinct armies ſhould be formed,—one to act particularly in the States which lie on the eaſt, the other in thoſe that are on the ſouth of the river ;—the whole however to be raiſed on a general plan, and not to be confined to any particular place by the terms of enliſtment.   Theſe matters,—the apparent difficulty and perhaps impracticability of ſuccours being thrown acroſs the river while the enemy can command it,— have induced his excellency to ſubmit the meaſure to their conſideration, not knowing how their operations may be directed, and foreſeeing that innumerable evils may ariſe if a reſpectable force is not appointed to oppoſe their arms whereſoever they are carried.

I have the honour to be, in great haſte, &c.

R. H. HARRISON.

SIR,   *White-Plains, October 29, 1776.*

THE ſituation of our affairs not permitting his ex-cellency to write himſelf, I have it in charge to inform you, that, on yeſterday morning about ten o'clock, the enemy appeared in ſeveral large columns in our front, and, from their firſt movements, ſeemed as if they meant an at-tack there.   However, halting for a little time, their main body filed off to our left, and preſently began a moſt ſevere and inceſſant cannonade at a part of our troops who had taken poſt on a hill, with a view of throwing up ſome lines. At the ſame time they advanced in two diviſions, and, af-ter a ſmart engagement for about a quarter of an hour, obliged our men to give way.   Our

Our lofs is not certainly known ; but, from conjecture, is between four and five hundred in killed, wounded, and miffing.   What theirs was, we have not heard.

After gaining the hill, (upon which they are entrenching) and leaving a fufficient number of men and artillery to prevent our repoffeffing it, they proceeded to advance by our left ; and, as far as I can difcover, their pofts or encampments now form nearly a femicircle.   It is evident their defign is to get in our rear according to their original plan.   Every meafure is taking to prevent them : but the removal of our baggage, &c. is attended with infinite difficulty and delays.

Our poft, from its fituation, is not fo advantageous as could be wifhed, and was only intended as temporary and occafional, till the ftores belonging to the army, which had been depofited here, could be removed.   The enemy coming on fo fuddenly has diftreffed us much.   They are now clofe at hand, and moft probably will in a little time commence their fecond attack : we expect it every hour :—perhaps it is beginning : I have juft heard the report of fome cannon.   I have the honour to be, &c.

R. H. HARRISON.

———

SIR,   *White-Plains, October 31, 1776.*

SINCE I had the honour of addreffing you on the twenty-ninth inftant, no event of importance has occurred. The enemy are throwing up fome lines and redoubts in our front, with a view of cannonading as foon as they are ready ; and at the fame time are extending their wings farther by our right and left.   It is fuppofed that one of their objects is to advance a part of their troops, and feize on the bridge over Croton river, that the communication may be cut off with the upper country.   To prevent this, a part of our force is detached, with orders to proceed with the utmoft expedition, and to fecure the pafs, if poffible.

We are trying to remove, to guard againft their defigns, but are greatly impeded by reafon of the fcarcity of waggons in proportion to our baggage and ftores.   Every exertion has been employed to obtain a fufficiency ; but they cannot be had in this part of the country.   The quartermafter has fent to Connecticut to get a fupply, if poffible.

Our

Our army is decreasing fast. Several gentlemen, who have come to camp within a few days, have observed large numbers of militia returning home on the different roads; nor are any measures taken as yet to raise the new army, no commissions having come from the States to appoint or signify the nomination of their officers. If this was done, perhaps many who are now here might be induced to engage: but at present there are none authorised to recruit.

His excellency would have wrote himself by the person who carries this (to the care of general Greene ;) but his attention is totally engaged in ordering the affairs of the army, and the best mode for its removal.

I have the honour to be, &c.   R. H. HARRISON.

————

SIR,   *White-Plains, November* 1, 1776.

I AM directed by his excellency to acknowledge his receipt of your favour of the twenty-eighth ultimo which came to hand yesterday evening, and to transmit you a copy of the letter I had the honour of writing you by the Boston express by his command. Had the express been charged with no other letter, the loss would not have been attended with any material injury to us or advantage to the enemy, provided it should come to their hands: but there were others from his excellency, of a very interesting nature, the miscarriage of which gives him much concern. As the bundle was taken away in so sudden and secret a manner, I fear there is but little hope of recovering it,—being done most probably for the express purpose of furnishing the enemy with intelligence, and a state of our army. Besides his excellency's letters, the most material of which was to Mr. Rutledge, there were five or six more from the gentlemen of his family.

My letters of the twenty-ninth and of yesterday, which I had the honour of addressing you, will give a pretty full account of our situation, and of every matter respecting this army antecedent to this date. I only omitted to mention that we have taken thirteen of the Waldeckers, and that, for several days past, our scouting parties have brought in one, two, or three prisoners. In addition to these, we have every day a deserter or two.

About

About six o'clock this morning, a meffenger arrived from lord Stirling (who is with his brigade between two and three miles from White-Plains, on our right, and rather nearer the North-river) with intelligence that the enemy were advancing towards him in two columns. This information has carried his excellency and aides out. The refult of their movement I have not heard : but moft likely they are purfuing their original defign of getting by our flanks and feizing the heights above us. Every precaution is taking to prevent them, and to hurry away our ftores to a more interior part of the country.

I have the honour to be, &c.   R. H. HARRISON.

P. S. His excellency has juft returned, and fays the alarm was premature. It arofe from fome of lord Stirling's advanced guards feeing a body of our men who had been ordered to reinforce him, who were fuppofed to be the enemy. His excellency is very apprehenfive that the army will be greatly diftreffed for want of provifion, particularly in the article of flour, owing to the water conveyance, both in the North and Eaft river, being in the enemy's poffeffion. He has wrote to the convention of this State, and directed Mr. Trumbull, that their utmoft exertions in this inftance may be ufed. There is a good deal of flour on the Jerfey fide : but there is no other way to get it, but by carting and ferrying it over to Peekfkill. This I have wrote to general Greene to have done, by his excellency's direction.

SIR,   *White-Plains, November* 3, 1776.

BY command of his excellency, I have the honour to inform you that our fituation is nearly the fame as when I had the pleafure of writing you laft. It is altered in no inftance, unlefs in the number of our troops, which is every day decreafing by their moft fcandalous defertion and return home. The inclofed letter from general Parfons, who is ftationed near the Saw-pits, and which his excellency directed me to tranfmit, will inform you of the prevalency of this difgraceful practice.

I have the honour to be, &c.   R. H. HARRISON.

To the Board of War.

GENTLEMEN,   *White-Plains, November* 4, 1776.

BY command of his excellency, I have the honour to acknowledge his receipt of your favour of the twenty-fourth ultimo, and to inform you that he esteems the plan you propose to lay before Congress, for preventing more rations being drawn than may be due, well calculated to answer the end. That respecting the sick seems to him not entirely perfect. The captains or commanders of companies are prohibited from drawing pay for such sick as may be discharged from the hospitals as unfit for service. If, during their stay, and before it can be known whether their case will or will not admit of their return, it should become necessary to make up a regimental pay-abstract, in what manner are the officers to make up their rolls? are they to include the sick, or not?

As this is a case which may and must of necessity frequently happen, it appears to his excellency that the intended regulations should be more general, and restrain the officers from including in their pay-abstracts or rolls all the sick they send to the hospitals, and the pay due them previous to their going. In such case, those who are discharged as unfit for service may receive their pay as intended; and those who return to duty can obtain what was due to them when the regiment was paid, by applying to the paymaster with the officer and surgeon's certificates, or be included in a subsequent abstract. The inconveniences and abuses which are designed to be remedied by these regulations, his excellency does not apprehend to arise so much from necessity (as incident to the nature of armies) as from the imperfect institution of the present, and the great mixture and diversity of troops composing it, and also from the inattention of the officers. * * *

The defenceless state of Pennsylvania, as communicated by the committee of safety to your honourable body, is a matter of much concern to his excellency, which is not a little aggravated by the part too many seem ready to take in favour of the enemy. He trusts, however, the defection will be too inconsiderable to threaten any alarming consequences.

Before

Before the receipt of your letter, his excellency had wrote to the commanding officer of the Virginia regiments at Trenton, directing him to march them forward towards general Greene's post, and there remain under his command till further orders, unless special instructions had been or should be given to the contrary by Congress, or for their particular destination.

Agreeable to your request, his excellency has consulted with general Lee upon the best mode for employing the French gentlemen, and making them serviceable. The result is that they should be appointed to regiments by Congress according to the ranks they have been pleased to give them, and with the same pay as is allowed other officers in such cases. Their want of our language is rather an objection : but it is hoped they will attain a sufficient knowledge of it, ere it be long, to be of great service ; and that, in the interim, their advice and assistance in directing of works may be of use where they may be stationed. With great respect, I have the honour to be, &c.

R. H. HARRISON.

SIR,   *White-Plains, November 6, 1776.*

I HAVE the honour to inform you that on yesterday morning the enemy made a sudden and unexpected movement from the several posts they had taken in our front. They broke up their whole encampments the preceding night, and have advanced towards Kingsbridge and the North-river. The design of this manœuvre is a matter of much conjecture and speculation, and cannot be accounted for with any degree of certainty. The grounds we had taken possession of were strong and advantageous, and such as they could not have gained without much loss of blood in case an attempt had been made. I had taken every possible precaution to prevent their outflanking us ;—which may have led to the present measure. They may still have in view their original plan, and, by a sudden wheel, try to accomplish it. Detachments are constantly out to observe their motions, and to harass them as much as possible.

In consequence of this movement I called a council of general officers to-day, to consult of such measures as should

be adopted in cafe they purfued their retreat to New-York ;
the refult of which is herewith tranfmitted.   In refpect to
myfelf, I cannot indulge an idea that general Howe, fuppofing he is going to New-York, means to clofe the campaign, and to fit down without attempting fomething more.
I think it highly probable, and almoft certain, that he will
make a defcent with a part of his troops into Jerfey : and,
as foon as I am fatisfied that the prefent manœuvre is real
and not a feint, I fhall ufe every means in my power to
forward a part of our force to counteract his defigns : nor
fhall I be difappointed if he fends a detachment to the
fouthward for the purpofe of making a winter campaign.

From the information I have received, there is now a
number of tranfports at Red-Hook, with about three
thoufand troops on board.   Their deftination, as given
out, is to Rhode-Ifland : but this feems altogether improbable for various reafons ; among others, the feafon is
much againft it.   In the fouthern States they will find it
milder, and much more favourable for their purpofes.   I
fhall take the liberty of mentioning that it may not be improper to fuggeft the probability of fuch a meafure to the
affemblies and conventions in thofe States, that they may
be on their guard,—and the propriety of their eftablifhing
and laying up magazines of provifions and other neceffaries in fuitable places.   This is a matter of exceeding importance, and what cannot be too much attended to.

From the approaching diffolution of the army, and the
departure of the new levies which is on the eve of taking
place, and the little profpect of levying a new one in time,
I have wrote to the eaftern States by the unanimous advice of the general officers, to forward fupplies of militia
in the room of thofe that are now here, and who, it is feared, will not be prevailed on to ftay any longer than the
time they are engaged for.   The propriety of this application I truft will appear, when it is known that not a
fingle officer is yet commiffioned to recruit, and when it is
confidered how effential it is to keep up fome fhew of
force and fhadow of an army.

I expect the enemy will bend their force againft Fort-
Wafhington, and inveft it immediately.   From fome ad-
vices, it is an object that will attract their earlieft attention.
I am

I am happy to inform you, that, in the engagement on Monday fe'nnight, I have reafon to believe our lofs was by no means fo confiderable as was conjectured at firft. By fome deferters and prifoners we are told, that of the enemy was tolerably great : fome accounts make it about four hundred in killed and wounded : all agree that among the former there was a colonel Carr of the thirty-fifth regiment.

The force that will be fent to Jerfey after I am fatisfied of Mr. Howe's retreat, in addition to thofe now there, according to my prefent opinion, will make it neceffary for me to go with them, to put things in a proper channel, and fuch a way of defence as fhall feem moft probable to check the progrefs of the enemy, in cafe they fhould attempt a defcent there, or a move toward Philadelphia.

I have the honour to be, &c.   G. W.

To the Board of War.

GENTLEMEN,   *White-Plains, November* 8, 1776.

I HAVE been favoured with yours of the thirty-firft ultimo, by monfieur Laytaniac, and muft take the liberty of referring you to my former letters upon the fubject of providing for the French gentlemen who fhall incline to enter the fervice of the States. To me it appears that one of two modes muft be adopted : they muft either be appointed to places in fome of the regiments, or formed into a diftinct corps. The former was advifed as the moft eligible in refpect to the gentlemen who were here before. It requires time to form an accurate opinion of the merits of an officer ; and the prefent fituation of the army will not allow me to pay a particular attention to monfieur Laytaniac, or fuch notice as he may wifh to receive, or I to give : nor is there any way of making his ftay here agreeable.

I have the honour to be, &c.   G. W.

SIR, *White-Plains, November 9, 1776.*

I HAVE the honour to tranfmit you a copy of a letter from general Gates to general Schuyler, and of another paper containing intelligence refpecting the northern army and the fituation of the enemy in that department. They this minute came to hand; and to them I beg leave to refer you for particulars.

By every information I can obtain, and the accounts I had laft night by two deferters who were very intelligent and particular, general Howe ftill has in view an expedition to the Jerfeys, and is preparing for it with the greateft induftry. I have detached the firft divifion of our troops which was thought neceffary to be fent, and which I hope will crofs the river at Peekfkill to-day. The fecond, I expect, will all march this evening; and to-morrow morning I propofe to follow myfelf, in order to put things in the beft train I can, and to give him every poffible oppofition. I hope (when the two divifions arrive, and are joined to fuch other force as I expect to collect) to check his progrefs and prevent him from penetrating any diftance from the river, if not to oblige him to return immediately with fome lofs. Whatever is in my power to effect, fhall be done.

I have the honour to be, &c. G. W.

———

SIR, *Peekfkill, November 11, 1776.*

I HAVE only time to acknowledge the honour of your letter of the fifth inftant, and its feveral inclofures, and to inform you, that, agreeable to the refolves of Congrefs, I fhall ufe every meafure in my power that the moving and prefent confufed ftate of the army will admit of, to appoint officers for recruiting.

You will have been advifed, before this, of the arrival of commiffioners from Maffachufetts. Others have come from Connecticut: but, from the prefent appearance of things, we feem but little if any nearer to levying an army. I had anticipated the refolve refpecting the militia, by writing to the eaftern States and to the Jerfey, by the

advice

advice of my general officers, and from a confcioufnefs of the neceffity of getting in a number of men if poffible, to keep up the appearance of an army. How my applications will fucceed, the event muft determine. I have little or no reafon to expect that the militia now here will remain a day longer than the time they firft engaged for. I have recommended their ftay, and requefted it in general orders. General Lincoln and the Maffachufetts commiffioners are ufing their intereft with thofe from that State : but, as far as I can judge, we cannot rely on their ftaying.

I left White-Plains about eleven o'clock yefterday ;— all peace then. The enemy appeared to be preparing for their expedition to Jerfey according to every information. What their defigns are, or whether their prefent conduct is not a feint, I cannot determine.

The Maryland and Virginia troops under lord Stirling have croffed the river, as have part of thofe from the Jerfey : the remainder are now embarking. The troops, judged neceffary to fecure the feveral pofts through the Highlands, have alfo got up. I am going to examine the paffes, and direct fuch works as may appear neceffary ; after which, and making the beft difpofition I can of things in this quarter, I intend to proceed to Jerfey, which I expect to do to-morrow.

The affemblies of Maffachufetts and Connecticut, to induce their men more readily to engage in the fervice, have voted an advance pay of twenty fhillings per month, in addition to that allowed by Congrefs to privates. It may perhaps be the means of their levying the quotas exacted from them fooner than they could otherwife have been raifed : but I am of opinion, a more fatal and miftaken policy could not have entered their councils, or one more detrimental to the general caufe. The influence of the vote will become continental, and materially affect the other States in making up their levies. If they could do it, I am certain, when the troops come to act together, that jealoufy, impatience and mutiny would neceffarily arife. A different pay cannot exift in the fame army. The reafons are obvious, and experience has proved their force in the cafe of the eaftern and fouthern troops laft fpring. Senfible of this, and of the pernicious confe-

quences

quences that would inevitably refult from the advance, I have prevented the commiffioners from proceeding or publifhing their terms till they could obtain the fenfe of Congrefs upon the fubject, and remonftrated againft it in a letter to governor Trumbull. I am not fingular in opinion: I have the concurrence of all the general officers, of its fatal tendency.

I congratulate you and Congrefs upon the news from Ticonderoga, and that general Carleton and his army have been obliged to return to Canada without attempting any thing.

I have the honour to be, &c. G. W.

SIR, *General Greene's Quarters, Nov.* 14, 1776.

I HAVE the honour to inform you of my arrival here yefterday, and that the whole of the troops belonging to the States, which lay fouth of Hudfon's-river, and which were in New-York government, have paffed over to this fide, except the regiment, lately colonel Smallwood's, which I expect is now on their march.

That they may be ready to check any incurfions the enemy may attempt in this neighbourhood, I intend to quarter them at Brunfwic, Amboy, Elizabethtown, Newark, and about this place, unlefs Congrefs fhould conceive it neceffary for any of them to be ftationed at or more contiguous to Philadelphia. In fuch cafe they will be pleafed to fignify their pleafure. There will be very few of them after the departure of thofe who were engaged for the flying camp, which is faft approaching. The difpofition I have mentioned feems to me well calculated for the end propofed, and alfo for their accommodation.

The movements and defigns of the enemy are not yet underftood. Various are the opinions and reports on this head. From every information, the whole have removed from Dobbs's ferry towards Kingfbridge; and it feems to be generally believed on all hands, that the invefting of Fort-Wafhington is one object they have in view: but that can employ but a fmall part of their force. Whether they intend a fouthern expedition, muft be determined by
time:

time : to me there appears a probability of it, which seems to be favoured by the advices we have that many transports are wooding and watering. General Greene's letter would give you the substance of the intelligence brought by Mr. Mersereau from Staten-Island in this instance, which he received before it came to me.

Inclosed you have copies of two letters from general Howe, and of my answer to the first of them. The letter alluded to, and returned in his last, was one from myself to Mrs. Washington, of the twenty-fifth ultimo, from whence I conclude that all the letters which went by the Bolton express have come to his possession. You will also perceive that general Howe has requested the return of Peter Jack, a servant to major Stewart, to which I have consented, as he was not in the military line, and the requisition agreeable to the custom of war. This servant having been sent to Philadelphia with the Waldeckers and other prisoners, I must request the favour of you to have him conveyed to general Greene by the earliest opportunity, in order that he may be returned to his master.

Before I conclude, I beg leave not only to suggest but to urge the necessity of increasing our field artillery very considerably. Experience has convinced me, as it has every gentleman of discernment in this army, that, while we remain so much inferior to the enemy in this instance, we must carry on the war under infinite disadvantages, and without the smallest probability of success. It has been peculiarly owing to the situation of the country where their operations have been conducted, and to the rough and strong grounds we possessed ourselves of, and over which they had to pass, that they have not carried their arms, by means of their artillery, to a much greater extent. When these difficulties cease by changing the scene of action to a level champaign country, the worst of consequences are to be apprehended. I would therefore, with the concurrence of all the officers whom I have spoken to upon the subject, submit to the consideration of Congress whether immediate measures ought not to be taken for procuring a respect train.

It is agreed on all hands that each battalion should be furnished at least with two pieces, and that a smaller num-

ber

ber than a hundred of three pounds, fifty of fix pounds, and fifty of twelve pounds, fhould not be provided, in addition to thofe we now have.   Befides thefe, if fome eighteen and twenty-four-pounders are ordered, the train will be more ferviceable and complete.   The whole fhould be of brafs, for the moft obvious reafons : they will be much more portable, not half fo liable to burft : and, when they do, no damage is occafioned by it, and they may be caft over again.   The fizes before defcribed fhould be particularly attended to : if they are not, there will be great reafon to expect miftakes and confufion in the charges in time of action, as it has frequently happened in the beft regulated armies.   The difparity between thofe I have mentioned and fuch as are of an intermediate fize is difficult to difcern.

It is alfo agreed that a regiment of artillerifts, with approved and experienced officers, fhould be obtained if poffible, and fome engineers of known reputation and abilities. I am forry to fay, too ready an indulgence has been had to feveral appointments in the latter inftance, and that men have been promoted, who feem to me to know but little if any thing of the bufinefs.

Perhaps this train, &c. may be looked upon by fome as large and expenfive.   True, it will be fo : but when it is confidered that the enemy, having effected but little in the courfe of the prefent campaign, will ufe their utmoft efforts to fubjugate us in the next, every confideration of that fort fhould be difregarded, and every poffible preparation made to fruftrate their * * * attempts. How they are to be procured, is to be inquired into.   That we cannot provide them among ourfelves, or more than a very fmall proportion, fo trifling as not to deferve our notice, is evident.   Therefore I would advife, with all imaginable deference, that, without any abatement of our own internal exertions, application fhould be immediately made to fuch powers as can and may be willing to fupply them.   They cannot be obtained too early, if foon enough : and I am told they be eafily had from France and Holland.

. Trumbull the commiffary-general has frequently mentioned to me of late the inadequacy of his pay to his trouble and the great rifk he is fubject to on account of the

large

large fums of money which pafs through his hands.   He
has ftated his cafe with a view of laying it before Congrefs and
obtaining a more adequate compenfation.   My fentiments
upon the fubject are already known : but yet I fhall take
the liberty to add that I think his complaint to be well
founded, and his pay, confidering the important duties and
rifks of his office, by no means fufficient, and that the footing he feems to think it fhould be upon, himfelf, appears
juft and reafonable.

A propofition having been made long fince to general
Howe and agreed to by him, for an exchange of prifoners
in confequence of the refolutions of Congrefs to that effect,
I fhall be extremely happy if you will give directions to
the committees and thofe having the charge of prifoners in
the feveral States fouth of Jerfey, to tranfmit me proper
lifts of the names of all the commiffioned officers, and of
their ranks and the corps they belong to ; alfo the number
of non-commiffioned and privates, and their refpective regiments.   You will perceive by his letter, he fuppofes me
to have affected fome delay, or to have been unmindful of
the propofition I had made.

I propofe to ftay in this neighbourhood a few days, in
which time I expect the defigns of the enemy will be more
difclofed, and their incurfions be made in this quarter, or
their inveftiture of Fort-Wafhington, if they are intended.

I have the honour to be, &c.   G. W.

***

To the Board of War.

General Greene's Quarters, November 15, 1776.

GENTLEMEN,

ON Wednefday evening I received the favour of your
letter of the eighth inftant, in confequence of which I
ftopped the flag that was going in with the ladies you
mention, pointing out to them the neceffity of the meafure,
and recommending them to write to their hufbands and
connexions to obtain general Howe's affurances for the
releafe of Mrs. Lewis, and Mrs. Robinfon and her children, with their baggage, as the condition on which they

will

will be permitted to go in themfelves.   Thefe terms I can only extend to Mrs. Barrow and Mrs. Kemp who had never obtained my leave : Mrs. Watts had, and my promife that fhe fhould go in.   The whole however were prepared to go, when the letter reached Newark.   The mode I have adopted feems moft likely, and the only proper one, to procure the enlargement of our ladies, which I wifh for much.

I am, gentlemen, with great refpeet, &c.   G. W.

To the Board of War.

GENTLEMEN,   *Hackinfac, November 15, 1776.*
HAVING given my promife to general Howe, on his application, that Peter Jack, a fervant of major Stewart, who was fent to Philadelphia with the Waldeckers and other prifoners, and who has nothing to do in the military line, fhould be returned to his mafter agreeable to the ufage of war in fuch cafes,—I muft take the liberty to requeft the favour of you to have him conveyed to general Greene by the earlieft opportunity, that he may be forwarded to his mafter in compliance with my promife.

I alfo wifh that you would have all the Britifh prifoners collected that you conveniently can, and fent to me as foon as poffible with the Heffian prifoners, that I may exchange them.   The return of the latter I think will be attended with many falutary confequences : but, fhould it be made without that of a large proportion of other troops, it will carry the marks of defign, and occafion precautions to be taken to prevent the ends we have in view.

I have the honour to be, &c.   G. W.

SIR,   *General Greene's Quarters, Nov. 16, 1776.*
SINCE I had the honour of addreffing you laft, an important event has taken place, of which I wifh to give you the earlieft intelligence.

The

The prefervation of the paffage of the North-river was an object of fo much confequence that I thought no pains or expenfe too great for that purpofe : and therefore, after fending off all the valuable ftores except fuch as were neceffary for its defence, I determined, agreeable to the advice of moft of the general officers, to rifk fomething to defend the poft on the eaft fide, called Mount-Wafhington.

When the army moved up in confequence of general Howe's landing at Frog-point, colonel Magaw was left on that command, with about twelve hundred men, and orders given to defend it to the laft. Afterwards, reflecting upon the fmallnefs of the garrifon, and the difficulty of their holding it if general Howe fhould fall down upon it with his whole force, I wrote to general Greene who had the command on the Jerfey fhore, directing him to govern himfelf by circumftances, and to remain or evacuate the poft as he fhould think beft, and revoking the abfolute order to colonel Magaw to defend the poft to the laft extremity. General Greene, ftruck with the importance of the poft, and the difcouragement which our evacuation of pofts muft neceffarily have given, reinforced colonel Magaw with detachments from feveral regiments of the flying camp, but chiefly of Pennfylvania, fo as to make up the number about two thoufand.

In this fituation things were yefterday, when general Howe demanded the furrendry of the garrifon, to which colonel Magaw returned a fpirited refufal. Immediately upon receiving an account of this tranfaction, I came from Hackinfac to this place, and had partly croffed the North-river when I met general Putnam and general Greene, who were juft returning from thence, and informed me that the troops were in high fpirits, and would make a good defence : and it being late at night, I returned..

Early this morning colonel Magaw pofted his troops partly in the lines thrown up by our army on our firft coming thither from New-York, and partly on a commanding hill lying north of Mount-Wafhington,—the lines being all to the fouthward. In this pofition the attack began about ten o'clock, which our troops ftood, and returned the fire in fuch a manner as gave me great hopes the enemy was entirely repulfed. But at this time a body of troops croff-

ed

ed Haerlem-river in boats, and landed infide of the fecond lines, our troops being then engaged in the firft.

Colonel Cadwallader, who commanded in the lines, fent off a detachment to oppofe them : but they, being over-powered by numbers, gave way ; upon which, colonel Cadwallader ordered his troops to retreat in order to gain the fort. It was done with much confufion ; and the enemy croffing over came in upon them in fuch a manner, that a number of them furrendered.

At this time the Heffians advanced on the north fide of the fort in very large bodies. They were received by the troops pofted there, with proper fpirit, and kept back a confiderable time ; but at length they were alfo obliged to fubmit to a fuperiority of numbers, and retire under the cannon of the fort.

The enemy, having advanced thus far, halted ; and immediately a flag went in, with a repetition of the demand of the fortrefs, as I fuppofe. At this time I fent a billet to colonel Magaw, directing him to hold out, and I would endeavour this evening to bring off the garrifon, if the fortrefs could not be maintained, as I did not expect it could, the enemy being poffeffed of the adjacent ground. But, before this reached him, he had entered too far into a treaty to retract : after which, colonel Cadwallader told another meffenger who went over, that they had been able to obtain no other terms than to furrender as prifoners of war. In this fituation matters now ftand. I have ftopped general Beall's and general Heard's brigades, to preferve the poft and ftores here ; which, with the other troops, I hope we fhall be able to effect.

I do not yet know the numbers killed or wounded on either fide : but, from the heavinefs and continuance of the fire in fome places, I imagine there muft have been confiderable execution.

The lofs of fuch a number of officers and men, many of whom have been trained with more than common attention, will, I fear, be feverely felt ; but, when that of the arms and accoutrements is added, much more fo ; and muft be a further incentive to procure as confiderable a fupply as poffible for the new troops, as foon as it can be done.

I have the honour to be, &c.

G. W.
Hackinfac,

SIR,   *Hackinfac, November* 19, 1776.

I HAVE not been yet able to obtain a particular account of the unhappy affair of the fixteenth, nor of the terms on which the garrifon furrendered. The intelligence that has come to hand is not fo full and accurate as I could wifh. One of the artillery, whofe information is moft direct, and who efcaped on Sunday night, fays the enemy's lofs was very confiderable, efpecially in the attack made above the fort by the divifion of Heffians that marched from Kingfbridge, and where lieutenant-colonel Rawlins, of the late colonel Stephenfon's regiment, was pofted.

They burned yefterday one or two houfes on the heights, and contiguous to the fort, and appeared, by advices from general Greene, to be moving in the evening their main body down towards the city. Whether they will clofe the campaign without attempting fomething more, or make an incurfion into Jerfey, muft be determined by the events themfelves.

As Fort-Lee was always confidered as only neceffary in conjunction with that on the eaft fide of the river, to preferve the communication acrofs, and to prevent the enemy from a free navigation, it has become of no importance by the lofs of the other, or not fo material as to employ a force for its defence. Being viewed in this light, and apprehending that the ftores there would be precarioufly fituated, their removal has been determined on to Boundbrook above Brunfwic, Princeton, Springfield, and Acquackenunk bridge, as places that will not be fubject to fudden danger in cafe the enemy fhould pafs the river, and which have been thought proper as repofitories for fome of our ftores of provifion and forage.

The troops belonging to the flying camp under generals Heard and Beall, with what remains of general Ewing's brigade, are now at Fort-Lee, where they will continue till the ftores are got away. By the time that is effected, their term of enliftment will be near expiring; and, if the enemy fhould make a pufh in this quarter, the only troops that there will be to oppofe them, will be Hand's, Hazlett's, the regiments from Virginia, and that, lately Smallwood's,—the latter greatly reduced by the loffes it fuftain-

ed

ed on Long-Island, &c. and sickness: nor are the rest by any means complete. In addition to these, I am told there are a few of the militia of this State, who have been called in by governor Livingston. I shall make such a disposition of the whole at Brunswic and at the intermediate posts, as shall seem most likely to guard against the designs of the enemy, and to prevent them making an irruption or foraging with detached parties.

The inclosed letter from colonels Miles and Atlee will shew Congress the distressed situation of our prisoners in New-York; and their distress will become greater every day by the cold inclement season that is approaching. It will be happy if some expedient can be adopted, by which they may be furnished with necessary blankets and clothing. Humanity and the good of the service require it. I think the mode suggested by these gentlemen, for establishing a credit, appears as likely to succeed, and as eligible, as any that occurs to me. It is probable many articles that may be wanted can be obtained there, and upon better terms than elsewhere. In respect to provision, their allowance perhaps is as good as the situation of general Howe's stores will admit of: it has been said of late by deserters and others that they were rather scant.

By a letter from the paymaster-general, of the seventeenth, he says there will be a necessity that large and early remittances should be made him. The demands, when the troops now in service are dismissed, will be extremely great. Besides, the bounty to recruits will require a large supply; and he adds that the commissary-general has informed him, that, between this and the last of December, he shall have occasion for a million of dollars.

November 21. The unhappy affair of the sixteenth has been succeeded by further misfortunes. Yesterday morning a large body of the enemy landed between Dobbs's ferry and Fort-Lee. Their object was, evidently, to inclose the whole of our troops and stores that lay between the North and Hackinsac rivers, which form a very narrow neck of land. For this purpose, they formed and marched as soon as they had ascended the high grounds towards the fort. Upon the first information of their having landed, and of their movements, our men were ordered

ed to meet them : but finding their numbers greatly fuperior, and that they were extending themfelves to feize on the paffes over the river, it was thought prudent to withdraw our men ; which was effected, and their retreat fecured. We loft the whole of the cannon that was at the fort (except two twelve-pounders) and a great deal of baggage, between two and three hundred tents, about a thoufand barrels of flour, and other ftores in the quartermafter's department. This lofs was inevitable. As many of the ftores had been removed as circumftances and time would admit of. The ammunition had been happily got away.

Our prefent fituation between Hackinfac and Paffaic rivers being exactly fimilar to our late one, and our force here by no means adequate to an oppofition that will promife the fmalleft probability of fuccefs, we are taking meafures to retire over the waters of the latter, when the beft difpofition will be formed that circumftances will admit of.

By colonel Cadwallader, who has been permitted by general Howe to return to his friends, I am informed the furrender of the garrifon on the fixteenth was on the common terms as prifoners of war ; the lofs of the Heffians, about three hundred privates and twenty-feven officers killed and wounded ; about forty of the Britifh troops, and two or three officers ; the lofs on our fide but inconfiderable. I beg leave to refer you to him for a more particular account, and alfo for his relation of the diftreffes of our prifoners. Colonels Miles and Atlee's letter, mentioned above, upon this fubject, was through miftake fent from hence yefterday morning. The mode of relief propofed by them was a credit or fupply of cafh through the means of Mr. Franks. This feems to be doubtful, as he is faid to be in confinement by colonel Cadwallader,—provided it would have been otherwife practicable.

I have the honour to be, &c.   G. W.

P. S. Your favour of the fixteenth was duly received. My letter to the board of war, on the fubject of the return of the Waldeckers, I prefume you will have feen.

SIR,   *Newark, November 23, 1776.*

    I HAVE not yet heard that any provifion is making to fupply the place of the troops compofing the flying camp, whofe departure is now at hand. The fituation of our affairs is truly critical, and fuch as requires uncommon exertions on our part. From the movements of the enemy, and the information we have received, they certainly will make a pufh to poffefs themfelves of this part of the Jerfey. In order that you may be fully apprifed of our weaknefs, and of the neceffity there is of our obtaining early fuccours, I have, by the advice of the general officers here, directed general Mifflin to wait on you. He is intimately acquainted with our circumftances, and will reprefent them better than my hurried ftate will allow.

    I have wrote to general Lee to come over with the continental regiments immediately under his command; thofe with general Heath I have ordered to fecure the paffes through the Highlands. I have alfo wrote to governor Livingfton, requefting of him fuch aid as may be in his power; and would fubmit it to the confideration of Congrefs whether application fhould not be made for part of the Pennfylvania militia to ftep forth at this preffing time.

    Before I conclude, I would mention, if an early and immediate fupply of money could be fent to Mr. Dalham to pay the flying camp troops, it might have a happy effect. They would fubfift themfelves comfortably on their return, provide many neceffaries of which they are in great want; and moreover, it might be the means of inducing many, after feeing their friends, to engage again.

    I expected, on coming here, to have met with many of the militia, but find from inquiry that there are not more than from four to five hundred at the different pofts.

    I have the honour to be, &c.   G. W.

SIR,   *Newark, November 27, 1776.*

    I DO myfelf the honour to acknowledge the receipt of your favours of the twenty-firft and twenty-fourth, with

their

their several inclosures. The execution of the resolves has been and will be attended to as far as in my power.

I have wrote to general Schuyler to send down as early as possible the troops in the northern department from this and the State of Pennsylvania. The proposition for exchanging Mr. Franklin for general Thompson I shall submit to general Howe, as soon as circumstances will allow me.

I have nothing in particular to advise you of, respecting the enemy, more than that they are advancing this way. Part of them have passed the Passaic; and I suppose the main body that they have on this side the North-river would have done the same before now, (as they are coming on) had their progress not been retarded by the weather which has been rainy for several day past. I have scouts and detachments constantly out to harass them and watch their motions, and to gain, if possible, intelligence of their designs.

Colonel Miles, who has been permitted to go to Philadelphia for a few days by general Howe, will deliver you this, and inform you of the distresses of our prisoners, and the necessity of effecting their exchange as far as we have prisoners to give in return.

By a letter from the board of war on the subject of an exchange, they mention that several of the prisoners in our hands have enlisted. It is a measure, I think, that cannot be justified, though the precedent is furnished on the side of the enemy : nor do I conceive it good in point of policy. But, as it has been done, I shall leave it with Congress to order them to be returned or not, as they shall judge fit.

I have the honour to be, &c.   G. W.

SIR,   *Brunswic, November* 30, 1776.

I HAVE been honoured with your favour of the twenty-sixth, and with its inclosures, by which I perceive the measures that have been adopted for forwarding a reinforcement of militia. Their arrival is much to be wished, the situation of our affairs being truly alarming, and

such

such as demands the earlieft aids.   As general Mifflin's prefence may have a happy influence on the difpofition and temper of many of the affociators, I fhall not direct his return fo long as he can be done without, and till it becomes indifpenfably neceffary.

On Thurfday morning I left Newark, and arrived here yefterday with the troops that were there.   It was the opinion of all the generals who were with me, that a retreat to this place was requifite, and founded in neceffity, as our force was by no means fufficient to make a ftand, with the leaft probability of fuccefs, againft an enemy much fuperior in number, and whofe advanced guards were entering the town by the time our rear got out.   It was the wifh of all to have remained there longer, and to have halted before we came thus far ; but, upon due confideration of our ftrength, the circumftances attending the enliftment of a great part of our little force, and the frequent advices that the enemy were embarking or about to embark another detachment for Staten-Ifland with a view of landing at Amboy to co-operate with this, which feemed to be confirmed by the information of fome perfons who came from the ifland, that they were collecting and impreffing all the waggons they could find,—it was judged neceffary to proceed till we came here, not only to prevent their bringing a force to act upon our front and rear, but alfo that we might be more convenient to oppofe any troops they might land at South-Amboy, which many conjectured to be an object they had in view.   This conjecture too had probability and fome advices to fupport it.

I hoped we fhould have met with large and early fuccours by this time : but as yet no great number of the militia of this State has come in ; nor have I much reafon to expect that any confiderable aid will be derived from the counties which lie beyond this river, and in which the enemy are.   Their fituation will prevent it in a great meafure from thofe parts where they are, provided the inclinations of the people were good.   Added to this, I have no affurances that more than a very few of the troops compofing the flying camp will remain after the time of their engagement is out : fo far from it, I am told that fome of general Ewing's brigade, who ftand engaged to

the

the firft of January, are now going away. If thofe go whofe fervice expires this day, our force will be reduced to a mere handful.

From intelligence received this morning, one divifion of the enemy was advanced laft night as far as Elizabeth-town, and fome of their quarter-mafters had proceeded about four or five miles on this fide, to provide barns, &c. for their accommodation. Other accounts fay another divifion, compofed of Heffians, are on the road through Springfield, and are reported to have reached that place laft night. I do not know how far their views extend: but I doubt not, they mean to pufh every advantage refulting from the fmall number and ftate of our troops.

I early began to forward part of the ftores from this place towards Philadelphia. Many are gone: the reft we are removing, and hope to fecure.

I am, Sir, very refpectfully, &c. G. W.

P. S. I have wrote to governor Livingfton, who is exerting himfelf to throw in every affiftance, and to have guards placed at the ferries to prevent the return of the foldiers who are not difcharged.

To the Board of War.

Head-Quarters, Brunfwic, November 30, 1776.

GENTLEMEN,

I AM to acknowledge the receipt of your favours of the eighteenth, nineteenth, and twenty-third inftant, which, from the unfettled fituation of our affairs, I have not been able to anfwer before. That of the eighteenth inclofes a lift of ftores [*imported*] in the Hancock-and-Adams continental fhip, and carried into Dartmouth in New-England, —with a refolve of Congrefs to deliver the mufkets, powder, lead, and flints, to my order. As the other articles of the cargo will be full as ufeful to the army as thofe included in the refolve, I would advife that directions be given to have the whole cargo removed from Dartmouth to fome fecure place in the neighbourhood of Philadelphia, and there depofited till called for. It is by no means prop-

er that so great a quantity of military stores should be lodged with the army, especially at present, as we know not
to-day where we shall be obliged to remove to-morrow:
and that will in all probability be the case while the enemy continue with a light army on this side the North-
river.

In answer to that part of yours of the nineteenth in
which you ask my advice as to the propriety of enlisting
prisoners of war, I would just observe, that, in my opinion,
it is neither consistent with the rules of war, nor politic :
nor can I think, that, because our enemies have committed
an unjustifiable action, by enticing, and, in some instances,
intimidating our men into their service, we ought to follow
their example.   Before I had the honour of yours on this
subject, I had determined to remonstrate to general Howe
on this head.   As to those few who have already enlisted,
I would not have them again withdrawn and sent in, because they might be subjected to punishment : but I would
have the practice discontinued in future.   If you will re-
vert to the capitulation of St. John's and Chamblee, you
will find an express stipulation against the enlisting the prisoners taken there.

I remarked that the enlistment of prisoners was not a
politic step :——my reason is this, that in time of danger I
have always observed such persons most backward, for fear
(I suppose) of falling into the hands of their former masters, from whom they expect no mercy : and this fear they
are apt to communicate to their fellow-soldiers.   They are
also most ready to desert when any action is expected, hoping, by carrying intelligence, to secure their peace.

I met captain Hesketh on the road ; and, as the situation of his family did not admit of delay, I permitted him
to go immediately to New-York, not having the least doubt
but general Howe will make a return of any officer of
equal rank who shall be required.

I have the honour to be, &c.   G. W.

SIR,   *Brunswic, December 1, 1776.*

I YESTERDAY had the honour of writing you,
and to advise you of our arrival here.   I am now to inform

form you that the enemy are ſtill advancing, and that their van-guard had proceeded as far as Bonem, a ſmall town about four miles this ſide of Woodbridge, according to my laſt intelligence.   As to their number, reports are various. Some ſay they were joined yeſterday by a conſiderable reinforcement from Staten-Iſland.   How far this faᆓt may be true, I cannot determine : but, from every information, before, they were between ſix and ſeven thouſand ſtrong.

I have for ſome time paſt ſuppoſed Philadelphia to be the objeᆓt of their movement, and have every reaſon to believe my opinion well founded,—the advices of ſundry perſons who have had an opportunity of mixing and converſing with them on the march, agreeing that ſuch is the report.   I have wrote to governor Livingſton upon the ſubjeᆓt, requeſting his utmoſt exertions to forward on every ſuccour in his power.   The ſame, I truſt, will be attended to in Pennſylvania.   Without a ſufficient number of men and arms, their progreſs cannot be checked :—at preſent our force is totally inadequate to any attempt.

Several officers belonging to the enemy, who were priſoners, have obtained permiſſion to return.   I have not yet ſent in the names of thoſe belonging to us, that are to be exchanged for them.   By a Virginia paper, I perceive that captain Morgan and lieutenant Heath, who were taken priſoners at Quebec, and now on parole, are promoted in the late arrangement of officers in that State—the former to a regiment, the latter to a majority.   It would be well if they were releaſed : but, being Virginians, and not knowing that any gentlemen who were taken at the ſame time are ſo circumſtanced, I have declined claiming their return without the opinion of Congreſs, leſt I ſhould incur the charge of partiality.

I have ſent forward colonel Hampton to colleᆓt proper boats and craft at the ferry for tranſporting our troops : and it will be of infinite importance to have every other craft, beſides what he takes for the above purpoſe, ſecured on the weſt ſide of Delaware : otherwiſe they may fall into the enemy's hands and facilitate their views.

I have the honour to be, &c.   G. W.

P. S. *Half after one o'clock, P. M.* The enemy are faſt advancing : ſome of them are now in ſight.   All the

men

men of the Jerfey flying camp under general Heard, being applied to, have refufed to continue longer in fervice.

- - -

SIR, ·   *December 2, 1776, half after feven, P. M.*

IN a little time after I wrote you this evening, the enemy appeared in feveral parties on the heights oppofite Brunfwic, and were advancing in a large body towards the croffing-place. We had a fmart cannonade whilft we were parading our men, but without any or but little lofs on either fide. It being impoffible to oppofe them with our prefent force with the leaft profpect of fuccefs, we fhall retreat to the weft fide of Delaware (and have advanced about eight miles) where it is hoped we fhall meet a reinforcement fufficient to check their progrefs. I have fent colonel Humpton forward to collect the neceffary boats for our tranfportation, and conceive it proper that the militia from Pennfylvania fhould be ordered towards Trenton, that they may be ready to join us, and act as occafion may require.

I am, Sir, your moft obedient fervant,   G. W.

P. S. I wifh my letters of yefterday may arrive fafe, being informed that the return-exprefs who had them was idling his time, and fhewing them on the road.

- - -

SIR,   *Princeton, December 2, 1776.*

I ARRIVED here this morning with our troops between eight and nine o'clock, when I received the honour of your letter of the firft with its inclofure.

When the enemy firft landed on this fide the North-river, I apprehended that they meant to make a pufh this way; and knowing that the force which I had was not fufficient to oppofe them, I wrote to general Lee to crofs with the feveral continental regiments in his divifion, and hoped he would have arrived before now. By fome means or other he has been delayed. I fuppofe he has paffed the river, as his letter of the twenty-fixth ultimo mentioned that he had marched a brigade the day before, and fhould
follow

follow the next himself. The remainder of the troops I conceived neceffary to guard the feveral paffes through the Highlands ; nor do I think they can be called from thence. Their number is very fmall, being reduced to very few by the departure of the troops who ftood engaged till the thirtieth ultimo.

I underftand there are now at Briftol feveral prifoners. As their exchange at this time cannot be effected with propriety, I think it will be neceffary, under the prefent fituation of affairs, to have them removed immediately to fome more interior place, upon their paroles. If they remain, they may be of infinite difadvantage.

I have the honour to be, &c. G. W.

[On the outfide of the foregoing letter, which is, as ufual, addreffed to the Prefident of Congrefs, appears the following line to Mr. Peters, fecretary to the board of war.]

Sir, difpatch an exprefs immediately, to have the prifoners at Briftol removed. R. H. HARRISON.

SIR, *Head-Quarters, Trenton, Dec.* 3, 1776.

I ARRIVED here myfelf yefterday morning with the main body of the army, having left lord Stirling with two brigades at Princeton and that neighbourhood, to watch the motions of the enemy, and give notice of their approach. I am informed that they had not entered Brunfwic yefterday morning at nine o'clock, but were on the oppofite fide of the Rariton.

Immediately on my arrival here, I ordered the removal of all the military and other ftores and baggage over the Delaware : a great quantity are already got over ; and as foon as the boats come up from Philadelphia, we fhall load them ; by which means I hope to have every thing fecured this night and to-morrow, if we are not difturbed. After being difencumbered of my baggage and ftores, my future fituation will depend entirely upon circumftances.

I have not heard a word from general Lee fince the twenty-fixth of laft month ; which furprifes me not a little, as I have difpatched daily expreffes to him, defiring to know when I might look for him. This makes me fearful

ful that my letters have not reached him.. I am informed
by report that general St. Clair has joined him with three
or four regiments from the northward. To know the
truth of this, and alfo when I may expect him, and with
what numbers, I have this minute difpatched colonel Stew-
ard (general Gates's aide-de-camp) to meet general Lee
and bring me an account.

I look out earneftly for the reinforcement from Philadelphia. I am in hopes, that, if we can draw a good head
of men together, it will give fpirits to the militia of this
State, who have as yet afforded me little or no affiftance;
nor can I find they are likely to do much.

General Heard juft informs me that a perfon, on whofe
veracity he can depend, has reported to him that on Sunday laft he counted a hundred and feventeen fail of fhips
going out of the Hook. You may depend upon being advifed inftantly of any further movement in the enemy's
army or mine.

I have the honour to be, &c.   G. W.

‚ S I R,   *Trenton, December 4, 1776.*

SINCE I had the honour of addreffing you yefterday,
I received a letter from general Lee. On the thirtieth ultimo he was at Peekfkill, and expected to pafs the river
with his divifion two days after. From this intelligence
you will readily conclude that he will not be able to afford
us any aid for feveral days. The report of general St.
Clair's having joined him with three or four regiments, I
believe to be altogether premature, as he mentions nothing
of it. It has arifen, as I am informed, from the return of
fome of the Jerfey and Pennfylvania troops from Ticonderoga, whofe time of fervice is expired. They have
reached Pluckemin, where I have wrote to have them halted and kept together, if they can be prevailed on, till
further orders.

The inclofed is a copy of a letter which came to hand
laft night from major Clark, to which I beg leave to refer
you for the intelligence it contains. The number of the
enemy faid to be embarked is fuppofed to be rather exag-
gerated.

gerated. That there has been an embarkation is not to be doubted, it being confirmed through various channels. By colonel Griffin, who went from Brunfwic on Sunday morning with a captain Sims, to pafs him by our guards, and who was detained by lord Cornwallis till Monday evening on account of his fituation, the amount of general Clinton's force, from what he could collect from the officers, was about fix thoufand : as to their deftination, he could not obtain the leaft information. By him I alfo learn the enemy were in Brunfwic, and that fome of their advanced parties had proceeded two miles on this fide. The heavy rain that has fallen has probably checked their progrefs, and may prevent their further movement for fome time.

I have the honour to be, &c.   G. W.

To Richard Peters, efquire, fecretary to the Board of War.

SIR,   *Head-Quarters, Trenton, Dec.* 4, 1776.

YOURS of the twentieth of laft month was delivered to me by the brigadier La Roche de Fermoy, who is now here, but unable to render me that fervice, which, I dare fay, from his character, he would, were he better acquainted with our language.

I yefterday received a letter from you without a date, mentioning that the prifoners from York-town were directed to halt at Newtown for my orders. On hearing they were there, I fent colonel Moylan to conduct them, and the prifoners from Reading who arrived nearly at the fame time, over towards Brunfwic, and deliver them in.

I hope you have not fent captain Price, lieutenant Peacock, and major Campbell, on to this place, as it is highly improper they fhould fee and know the fituation of our army here and at Princeton. They had better be fent up, under the care of fome perfon, to Newtown or that neighbourhood, and there wait the arrival of fome larger party, who, I imagine, will be foon forwarded from Lancafter, and go in with them.

Lieutenant

Lieutenant Symes came over to me at Brunfwic from Bethlehem without the leaft guard or efcort ; and a lieutenant of the feventh regiment went through our whole army, and was at laft difcovered by a mere accident.   He had a pafs from the council of fafety, and that was all. Such an irregular mode of fuffering prifoners to go in alone muft be put a ftop to, or the enemy will be as well acquainted with our fituation as we are ourfelves.   If they are left at liberty to choofe their own route, they will always take that through our army, for reafons too obvious to mention.

I am, Sir, your moft obedient fervant,   G. W.

I have been obliged to fend down a number of our fick to Philadelphia, to make room for the troops, and to remove them out of the way.   Be pleafed to have fome care taken to have them properly accommodated.   I fhould think part of the houfe-of-employment might be procured for that purpofe.   I have ordered down an officer from each regiment, and a furgeon's mate, if they can be fpared : but I hope they will not want the affiftance of the vifiting phyficians of the hofpital.

S I R,   *Trenton, December 5, 1776.*

AS nothing but neceffity obliged me to retire before the enemy and leave fo much of the Jerfeys unprotected, I conceive it my duty, and it correfponds with my inclination, to make head againft them fo foon as there fhall be the leaft probability of doing it with propriety. That the country might in fome meafure be covered, I left two brigades confifting of the five Virginia regiments and that of Delaware, containing in the whole about twelve hundred men fit for duty, under the command of lord Stirling and general Stephen, at Princeton, till the baggage and ftores could crofs the Delaware, or the troops under their refpective commands fhould be forced from thence. I fhall now, having removed the greateft part of the above articles, face about with fuch troops as are here fit for fervice, and march back to Princeton, and there govern myfelf by circumftances and the movements of general Lee.

At

At any event, the enemy's progress may be retarded by this means if they intend to come on, and the people's fears in some measure quieted, if they do not. Sorry I am to observe, however, that the frequent calls upon the militia of this State, the want of exertion in the principal gentlemen of the country, or a fatal supineness and insensibility of danger till it is too late to prevent an evil that was not only foreseen but foretold, have been the causes of our late disgraces.

If the militia of this State had stepped forth in season (and timely notice they had,) we might have prevented the enemy's crossing the Hackinsac, although without some previous notice of the time and place it was impossible to have done this at the North-river. We might with equal probability of success have made a stand at Brunswic on the Rariton. But as both these rivers were fordable in a variety of places (knee-deep only,) it required many men to defend the passes; and these we had not. At Hackinsac our force was insufficient, because a part was at Elizabeth-town, Amboy, and Brunswic, guarding a coast which I thought most exposed to danger; and at Brunswic, because I was disappointed in my expectation of militia, and because on the day of the enemy's approach (and probably the occasion of it) the term of the Jersey and Maryland brigades' service expired; neither of which would consent to stay an hour longer.

These, among ten thousand other instances, might be adduced to shew the disadvantages of short enlistments, and the little dependence upon militia in times of real danger. But, as yesterday cannot be recalled, I will not dwell upon a subject which, no doubt, has given much uneasiness to Congress, as well as extreme pain and anxiety to myself. My first wish is that Congress may be convinced of the impropriety of relying upon the militia, and of the necessity of raising a larger standing army than what they have voted. The saving in the article of stores, provisions, and in a thousand other things, by having nothing to do with militia unless in cases of extraordinary exigency, and such as could not be expected in the common course of events, would amply support a large army, which, well officered, would be daily improving, instead of continuing a destructive, expensive, and disorderly mob.

I am clear in opinion, that, if forty thousand men had been kept in constant pay since the first commencement of hostilities, and the militia had been excused doing duty during that period, the continent would have saved money. When I reflect on the losses we have sustained for want of good troops, the certainty of this is placed beyond a doubt in my mind. In such case, the militia, who have been harassed and tired by repeated calls upon them (and farming and manufactures in a manner suspended,) would, upon any pressing emergency, have run with alacrity to arms; whereas the cry now is, "they may be as well ruined in one way as another;" and with difficulty they are obtained.

I mention these things to shew, that, in my opinion, if any dependence is placed in the militia another year, Congress will be deceived. When danger is a little removed from them, they will not turn out at all. When it comes home to them, the well-affected, instead of flying to arms to defend themselves, are busily employed in removing their families and effects,—whilst the disaffected are concerting measures to make their submission, and spread terror and dismay all around, to induce others to follow the example. Daily experience and abundant proofs warrant this information.

I shall this day reinforce lord Stirling with about twelve hundred men, which will make his number about two thousand four hundred. To-morrow I mean to repair to Princeton myself, and shall order the Pennsylvania troops (who are not yet arrived, except part of the German battalion and a company of light infantry) to the same place.

By my last advices, the enemy are still at Brunswic; and the account adds that general Howe was expected at Elizabeth-town with a reinforcement, to erect the king's standard, and demand a submission of this State. I can only give this as a report brought from the enemy's camp by some of the country people.

I have the honour to be, &c.   G. W.

Trenton,

SIR,   *Trenton, December* 6, 1776.

I HAVE not received any intelligence of the enemy's movements fince my letter of yefterday. From every information, they ftill remain at Brunfwic, except fome of their parties who are advanced a fmall diftance on this fide. To-day I fhall fet out for Princeton myfelf, unlefs fomething fhould occur to prevent me, which I do not expect.

By a letter of the fourteenth ultimo from a Mr. Caldwell, a clergyman, and a ftaunch friend to the caufe, who has fled from Elizabeth-town, and taken refuge in the mountains about ten miles from hence, I am informed that general or lord Howe was expected in that town to publifh pardon and peace. His words are, " I have not feen his proclamation, but can only fay he gives fixty day of grace, and pardons from the Congrefs down to the committee. No one man in the continent is to be denied his mercy." In the language of this good man, The Lord deliver us from his mercy !

Your letter of the third, by major Livingfton, was duly received. Before it came to hand, I had wrote to general Howe about governor Franklin's exchange, but am not certain whether the letter could not be recovered. I difpatched a meffenger inftantly for that purpofe.

I have the honour to be, &c.   G. W.

SIR,   *Mr. Berkley's Summer Seat, Dec.* 8, 1776.

COLONEL Reed would inform you of the intelligence which I firft met with on the road from Trenton to Princeton yefterday. Before I got to the latter, I received a fecond exprefs informing me, that, as the enemy were advancing by different routes, and attempting by one to get in the rear of our troops which were there, (and whofe numbers were fmall, and the place by no means defenfible) they had judged it prudent to retreat to Trenton. The retreat was accordingly made, and fince to this fide of the river.

This

This information I thought it my duty to communicate as foon as poffible, as there is not a moment's time to be loft in affembling fuch force as can be collected; and as the object of the enemy cannot now be doubted in the fmalleft degree.   Indeed I fhall be out in my conjecture (for it is only conjecture) if the late embarkation at New-York is not for Delaware river, to co-operate with the army under the immediate command of general Howe, who, I am informed from good authority, is with the Britifh troops and his whole force upon this route.

I have no certain intelligence of general Lee, although I have fent frequent expreffes to him, and lately a colonel Humpton to bring me fome accurate accounts of his fituation.   I laft night difpatched another gentleman to him (major Hoops) defiring he would haften his march to the Delaware, in which I would provide boats near a place called Alexandria, for the tranfportation of his troops.   I cannot account for the flownefs of his march.

In the difordered and moving ftate of the army, I cannot get returns: but, from the beft accounts, we had between three thoufand and three thoufand five hundred men, before the Philadelphia militia and German battalion arrived:—they amount to about two thoufand.

I have the honour to be, &c.   G. W.

SIR,   *Head-Quarters, Trenton Falls, Dec.* 9, 1776.

I DID myfelf the honour of writing to you yefterday, and informing you that I had removed the troops to this fide of the Delaware.   Soon after, the enemy made their appearance, and their van entered juft as our rear guard quitted.   We had removed all our ftores, except a few boards.   From the beft information, they are in two bodies, one at and near Trenton, the other fome miles higher up, and inclining towards Delaware; but whether with intent to crofs there, or throw themfelves between general Lee and me, is yet uncertain.

I have this morning detached lord Stirling with his brigade, to take poft at the different landing-places, and prevent them from ftealing a march upon us from above;

for

for I am informed, if they crofs at Coryel's ferry or thereabouts, they are as near to Philadelphia, as we are here. From feveral accounts I am led to think that the enemy are bringing boats with them : if fo, it will be impoffible for our fmall force to give them any confiderable oppofition in the paffage of the river, [*as they may*] make a feint at one place, and, by a fudden removal, carry their boats higher or lower before we can bring our cannon to play upon them.

Under thefe circumftances, the fecurity of Philadelphia fhould be our next object. From my own remembrance, but more from information, (for I never viewed the ground) I fhould think that a communication of lines and redoubts might foon be formed from the Delaware to Schuylkill on the north entrance of the city, the lines to begin on the Schuylkill fide, about the heights of Springatebury, and run eaftward to Delaware, upon the moft advantageous and commanding grounds. If fomething of this kind is not done, the enemy might, in cafe any misfortune fhould befal us, march directly in, and take poffeffion. We have ever found that lines, however flight, are very formidable to them : they would at leaft give a check till people could recover of the fright and confternation that naturally attends the firft appearance of an enemy.

In the mean time every ftep fhould be taken to collect force, not only from Pennfylvania, but from the moft neighbourly States. If we can keep the enemy from entering Philadelphia, and keep the communication by water open for fupplies, we may yet make a ftand, if the country will come to our affiftance till our new levies can be collected.

If the meafure of fortifying the city fhould be adopted, fome fkilful perfon fhould immediately view the grounds, and begin to trace out the lines and works. I am informed there is a French engineer of eminence in Philadelphia at this time : if fo, he will be the moft proper.

I have the honour to be, &c.   G. W.

P. S. I have juft received the inclofed from general Heath. General Mifflin is this moment come up, and tells me that all the military ftores yet remain in Philadelphia. This make the immediate fortifying of the city fo neceffary, that I have defired general Mifflin to return to

take

take charge of the ſtores, and have ordered major-general
Putnam immediately down to ſuperintend the works and
give the neceſſary directions.

———

SIR,   *Head-Quarters, Falls of Delaware, Dec.* 10, 1776.

SINCE I had the honour of addreſſing you yeſterday, nothing of importance has occurred. In reſpect to
the enemy's movements, I have obtained no other information than that they have a number of parties patroling
up and down the river, particularly above. As yet they
have not attempted to paſs ; nor do any of their patroles,
though ſome are exceedingly ſmall, meet with the leaſt interruption from the inhabitants of Jerſey.

By a letter received laſt night from general Lee, of the
eighth inſtant, he was then at Morriſtown, where he entertained thoughts of eſtabliſhing a poſt : but, on receiving
my diſpatches by major Hoops, I ſhould ſuppoſe he would
be convinced of the neceſſity of his proceeding this way
with all the force he can bring.

I have the honour to be, &c.   G. W.

P. S. *Nine o'clock, A. M.* I this minute received information that the enemy were repairing the bridges three
or four miles below Trenton ; which ſeems to indicate an
intention of their paſſing lower down, and ſuggeſts to me
the neceſſity that ſome attention ſhould be had to the fort
at Billingſport, leſt they ſhould poſſeſs themſelves of it ; the
conſideration of which I beg leave to ſubmit to Congreſs.
I have wrote to the council of ſafety on the ſubject.

———

SIR,   *Head-Quarters, Falls of Delaware, Dec.* 11, 1776.

AFTER I had wrote you yeſterday, I received certain information that the enemy, after repairing Croſwix's
bridge, had advanced a party of about five hundred to
Bordentown. By their taking this route, it confirms me
in my opinion, that they have an intention to land between
this and Philadelphia, as well as above, if they can procure boats for that purpoſe.

I laſt

I laſt night directed commodore Seymour to ſtation all his galleys between Bordentown and Philadelphia, to give the earlieſt intelligence of any appearance of the enemy on the Jerſey ſhore.

I yeſterday rode up the river about eleven miles, to lord Stirling's poſt, where I found a priſoner of the forty-ſecond regiment who had been juſt brought in. He informed me that lord Cornwallis was at Pennytown with two battalions of grenadiers, and three of light-infantry, all Britiſh, the Heſſian grenadiers, the forty-ſecond Highland regiment, and two other battalions, the names of which he did not remember. He knew nothing of the reaſons of their being aſſembled there, nor what were their future intentions. But I laſt night received information from my lord Stirling, which had been brought in by his ſcouts, which in ſome meaſure accounted for their being there. They had made a forced march from Trenton on Sunday night, to Coryel's ferry, in hopes of ſurpriſing a ſufficient number of boats to tranſport them; but, finding themſelves diſappointed, had marched back to Pennytown, where they remained yeſterday. From their ſeveral attempts to ſeize boats, it does not look as if they had brought any with them, as I was at one time informed. I laſt night ſent a perſon over to Trenton, to learn whether there was any appearance of building any: but he could not perceive any preparations for a work of that kind; ſo that I am in hopes, if proper care is taken to keep all the craft out of their way, they will find the croſſing of Delaware a matter of conſiderable difficulty.

I received another letter from general Lee laſt evening: it was dated at Chatham (which I take to be near Morriſtown) the eighth of this month. He had then received my letter ſent by major Hoops, but ſeemed ſtill inclined to hang upon the enemy's rear, to which I ſhould have no objection, had I a ſufficient force to oppoſe them in front; but as I have not at preſent, nor do I ſee much probability of further reinforcement, I have wrote to him in the moſt preſſing terms, to join me with all expedition.

Major Sheldon, who commands the volunteer horſe from Connecticut, waits upon Congreſs to eſtabliſh ſome mode of pay. I can only ſay that the ſervice of himſelf

and

and his troop has been such as merits the warmest thanks of the public, and deserves a handsome compensation for their trouble. Whatever is settled now, will serve for a precedent in future. From the experience I have had, this campaign, of the utility of horse, I am convinced there is no carrying on the war without them; and I would therefore recommend the establishment of one or more corps (in proportion to the number of foot) in addition to those already raised in Virginia. If major Sheldon would undertake the command of a regiment of horse on the continental establishment, I believe he could very soon raise them; and I can recommend him as a man of activity and spirit, from what I have seen of him.

I have the honour to be, &c.   G. W.

SIR,   *Trenton Falls, December* 12, 1776.

I LAST night received the favour of Mr. Thompson's letter inclosing the proceedings of Congress of the eleventh instant. As the publication of their resolve, in my opinion, will not lead to any good end, but, on the contrary, may be attended with some bad consequences, I shall take the liberty to decline inserting it in this day's orders. I am persuaded, if the subject is taken up and re-considered, that Congress will concur with me in sentiment. I doubt not but there are some who have propagated the report: but what if they have? Their remaining in or leaving Philadelphia must be governed by circumstances and events. If their departure should become necessary, it will be right: on the other hand, if there should not be a necessity for it, they will remain, and their continuance will shew the report to be the production of calumny and falsehood. In a word, Sir, I conceive it a matter that may be as well disregarded; and that the removal or staying of Congress, depending entirely upon events, should not have been the subject of a resolve.

The intelligence we obtain respecting the movements and situation of the enemy is far from being so certain and satisfactory as I could wish, though every probable means in my power, and that I can devise, are adopted for that purpose.

purpose. The latest I have received was from lord Stirling last night. He says that two grenadiers of the Inniskillen regiment, who were taken and brought in by some countrymen, inform that generals Howe, Cornwallis, Vaughan, &c. with about six thousand of the flying army, were at Pennaytown, waiting for pontoons to come up, with which they mean to pass the river near the Blue Mounts, or at Coryel's ferry,—they believe the latter ;—that the two battalions of guards were at Brunswic, and the Hessian grenadiers, chasseurs, and a regiment or two of British troops, are at Trenton.

Captain Miller of colonel Hand's regiment also informs me, that a body of the enemy were marching to Burlington yesterday morning. He had been sent over with a strong scouting party, and, at day-break, fell in with their advanced guards consisting of about four hundred Hessian troops, who fired upon him before they were discovered, but without any loss, and obliged him to retreat with his party and to take boat. The number of the whole he could not ascertain : but it appeared to be considerable. Captain Miller's account is partly confirmed by commodore Seymour, who reports that four or five hundred of the enemy had entered the town. Upon the whole, there can be no doubt but that Philadelphia is their object, and that they will pass the Delaware as soon as possible. Happy should I be if I could see the means of preventing them : at present, I confess, I do not. All military writers agree that it is a work of great difficulty, nay, impracticable, where there is any extent of coast to guard. This is the case with us ; and we have to do it with a force small and inconsiderable, and much inferior to that of the enemy. Perhaps Congress have some hope and prospect of reinforcements : I have no intelligence of the sort, and wish to be informed on the subject. Our little handful is daily decreasing by sickness and other causes : and, without aid, without considerable succours and exertions on the part of the people, what can we reasonably look for or expect, but an event that will be severely felt by the common cause, and that will wound the heart of every virtuous American, —the loss of Philadelphia ? The subject is disagreeable : but yet it is true. I will leave it, wishing that our situa-

tion

tion may become such as to do away the apprehensions which at this time seem to fill the minds of too many, and with too much justice.

By a letter from general Heath, dated at Peekskill, the eighth, I am advised that lieutenant-colonel Vose was then there with Greaton's, Bonds, and Porter's regiments, amounting in the whole to between five and six hundred men, who were coming this way. He adds that generals Gates and Arnold would be at Goshen that night, with Stark's, Poor's, and Read's regiments; but for what purpose he does not mention.

The inclosed extract of a letter which I received last night contains intelligence of an agreeable nature. I wish to hear its confirmation by the arrival of the several prizes: that with clothing and arms will be an invaluable acquisition.

I shall be glad to be advised of the mode I am to observe in paying the officers; whether they are to be allowed to draw the pay lately established, and from what time, or how long they are to be paid under the old establishment. A pay-roll which was presented yesterday, being made up for the new, has given rise to these propositions. Upon my objecting to it, I was told that Congress or the board of war had established the precedent, by paying the sixth regiment of Virginia troops commanded by colonel Buckner, agreeable to the latter, as they came through Philadelphia.

I have the honour to be, &c.   G. W.

SIR,   *Head-Quarters, Trenton Falls, Dec. 13, 1776.*

THE apparent designs of the enemy being to avoid this ferry, and land their troops above and below us, have induced me to remove from this place the greater part of the troops, and throw them into a different disposition on the river, whereby I hope not only to be more able to impede their passage, but also to avoid the danger of being inclosed in this angle of the river. And notwithstanding the extended appearances of the enemy on the other side, made, at least in part, to divert our attention from any

particular

particular point as well as to harafs us by fatigue, I cannot divest myfelf of the opinion that their principal defign is to ford the river fomewhere above Trenton : to which defign I have had particular refpect in the new arrangement, wherein 1 am fo far happy as to have the concurrence of the general officers at this place.

Four brigades of the army, under generals lord Stirling, Mercer, Stephen and De Fermoy, extend from Yardley's up to Coryel's ferry, pofted in fuch a manner as to guard every fufpicious part of the river, and to afford affiftance to each other in cafe of attack.   General Ewing, with the flying camp of Pennfylvania, and a few Jerfey troops under general Dickinfon, are pofted from Yardley's ferry down to the ferry oppofite Bordentown.   Colonel Cadwallader, with the Pennfylvania militia, occupies the ground above and below the mouth of Nefhaminy river as far down as Dunk's ferry, at which place colonel Nixon is pofted with the third battalion of [*Pennfylvania.*]   A proper quantity of artillery is appointed to each brigade ; and I have ordered fmall redoubts to be thrown up oppofite every place where there is a poffibility of fording.   I fhall remove further up the river to be near the main body of my fmall army, with which every poffible oppofition fhall be given to any further approach of the enemy towards Philadelphia.

As general Armftrong has a good deal of influence in this State, and our prefent force is fmall and inconfiderable, I think he cannot be better employed than to repair to the counties where his intereft lies, to animate the people, promote the recruiting fervice, and encourage the militia to come in.   He will alfo be able to form a proper judgment of the places fuitable for magazines of provifion to be collected.   I have requefted him to wait upon Congrefs on this fubject : and if general Smallwood fhould go to Maryland on the fame bufinefs, I think it would have a happy effect : he is popular and of great influence, and, I am perfuaded, would contribute greatly to that State's furnifhing her quota of men in a little time.   He is now in Philadelphia.

I have the honour to be, &c.   G. W.

Head-Quarters,

S I R,   *Head-Quarters, at Keith's, Dec. 15, 1776.*

ABOUT one o'clock to-day I received a letter from general Sullivan, a copy of which you have inclosed. I will not comment on the melancholy intelligence which it contains, only adding that I sincerely regret general Lee's unhappy fate, and feel much for the loss of my country in his captivity.

In respect to the enemy, they have been induſtrious in their attempts to procure boats and ſmall craft : but as yet their efforts have not ſucceeded. From the lateſt advices that I have of their movements by ſome priſoners and others, they appear to be leaving Trenton, and to be filing off towards Princetown and Allentown. What their deſigns are, whether they mean to retreat, or only a feint, cannot be determined. I have parties out to watch their motions, and to form, if poſſible, an accurate opinion of their plans.

Our force, ſince my laſt, has received no augmentation, —of courſe, by ſickneſs and other cauſes, has diminiſhed: but I am adviſed by a letter from the council of ſafety, which juſt came to hand, that colonels Burd and Gilbreath are marching with their battalions of militia, and alſo that ſome ſmall parties are aſſembling in Cumberland county. * * *

I have the honour to be, &c.   G. W.

S I R,   *Head-Quarters, at Keith's, Dec. 16, 1776.*

IN a late letter which I had the honour of addreſſing you, I took the liberty to recommend that more battalions ſhould be raiſed for the new army than what had been voted. Having fully conſidered the matter, I am more and more convinced not only of the propriety but of the neceſſity of the meaſure. That the enemy will leave nothing un-eſſayed in the courſe of the next campaign to reduce theſe States to the rule of a moſt * * *, muſt be obvious to every one ; and that the militia is not to be depended on, or aid expected from them but in caſes of the moſt preſſing emergency, is not to be doubted. The
firſt

first of thefe propofitions is unqueftionable, and fatal experience has given her fanction to the truth of the latter: indeed their lethargy of late, and backwardnefs to turn out at this alarming crifis, feem to juftify an apprehenfion that nothing can bring them from their homes. For want of their affiftance, a large part of Jerfey has been expofed to ravage and to plunder; nor do I know that Pennfylvania would fhare a better fate, could general Howe effect a paffage acrofs the Delaware with a refpectable force. Thefe confiderations have induced me to wifh that no reliance, except fuch as may arife from neceffity, fhould ever be had in them again; and to make further mention to Congrefs of the expediency of increafing their army. I truft the meafure will meet their earlieft attention.

Had I leifure and were it neceffary, I could fay much upon this head: but, as I have not, and the matter is well underftood, I will not add much. By augmenting the number of your battalions, you will augment your force: the officers of each will have their intereft and influence; and, upon the whole, their numbers will be much greater, though they fhould not be complete. Added to this, from the prefent confufed ftate of Jerfey, and the improper appointment of officers in many inftances, I have little or no expectation that fhe will be able to raife all the troops exacted from her, though I think it might be done, were fuitable fpirited gentlemen commiffioned, who would exert themfelves, and encourage the people, many of whom (for a failure in this inftance, and who are well difpofed) are making their fubmiffions. In a word, the next will be a trying campaign: and as all that is dear and valuable may depend upon the iffue of it, I would advife that nothing fhould be omitted, that fhall feem neceffary to our fuccefs. Let us have a refpectable army, and fuch as will be competent to every exigency.

I will alfo add that the critical fituation of our affairs, and the diffolution of our prefent force, (now at hand) require that every nerve and exertion be employed for recruiting the new battalions. One part of general Howe's movements at this time, I believe, is with a defign to diftract us and prevent this bufinefs. If the inclemency of the weather fhould force him into winter-quarters, he will not remain there longer than neceffity fhall oblige him: he will commence his operations in a fhort fpace of time; and in that time our levies muft be made up, to oppofe him, or I fear the moft melancholy of all events muft take place.

The inclofed extract of a letter from the commiffary-general will fhew his demands for money, and his plans for procuring falted provifions and a quantity of flour from the fouthward. The whole is fubmitted to the confideration of Congrefs; and I wifh the refult of their opinion to be tranfmitted him, with fuch fupplies of money as may be neceffary for himfelf and the departments he mentions.

The clothing of the troops is a matter of infinite import-ance, and, if it could be accomplifhed, would have a hap-py effect. Their diftreffes are extremely great, many of them being entirely naked, and moft fo thinly clad as to be unfit for fervice. I muft entreat Congrefs to write to the agents and contractors upon this fubject, that every poffible fupply may be procured and forwarded with the utmoft expedition. I cannot attend to the bufinefs myfelf, having more than I can poffibly do befides.

I have the honour to be, &c.

G. W.

SIR, *Camp, above Trenton Falls, Dec. 20, 1776.*

I HAVE waited with much impatience to know the determinations of Congrefs on the propofitions made fome time in October laft for augmenting our corps of artillery and eftablifhing a corps of engineers. The time is now come when the firft cannot be delayed without the greateft injury to the fafety of thefe States; and therefore, under the refolution of Congrefs bearing date the twelfth inftant, at the repeated inftances of colonel Knox, and by the preffing advice of all the general officers now here, I have ventured to order three battalions of artillery to be immediately recruited. Thefe are two lefs than colonel Knox recommends, as you will fee by his plan inclofed: but then this fcheme comprehends all the United States, whereas fome of the States have corps already eftablifhed, and thefe three battalions are indifpenfably neceffary for the operations in this quarter, including the northern de-partment.

The

The pay of our artillerifts bearing no proportion with
that in the Englifh or French fervice,—the murmuring and
diffatisfaction thereby occafioned, and the abfolute impoffibility (as I am told) of getting them upon the old terms,
—and the unavoidable neceffity of obtaining them at
all events,—have induced me (alfo by advice) to promife
officers and men that their pay fhould be augmented twenty-five per cent, or that their engagements fhall become
null and void. This may appear to Congrefs premature
and unwarrantable. But, Sir, if they view our fituation in
the light it ftrikes their officers, they will be convinced of
the utility of the meafure, and that the execution could
not be delayed till after their meeting at Baltimore. In
fhort, the prefent exigency of our affairs will not admit of
delay either in council or the field : for well convinced I
am, that, if the enemy go into quarters at all, it will be
for a fhort feafon. But I rather think the defign of general Howe is to poffefs himfelf of Philadelphia this winter,
if poffible ; and in truth I do not fee what is to prevent
him, as ten days more will put an end to the exiftence of
our army. That one great point is to keep us as much
haraffed as poffible, with a view to injure the recruiting
fervice and hinder a collection of ftores and other neceffaries for the next campaign, I am as clear in, as I am of
my exiftence. If therefore,—[*when*] we have to provide
in this fhort interval, and make thefe great and arduous
preparations,—every matter that in its nature is felf-evident
is to be referred to Congrefs at the diftance of a hundred
and thirty or forty miles, fo much time muft neceffarily
elapfe, as to defeat the end in view.

It may be faid that this is an application for powers that
are too dangerous to be entrufted. I can only add that
defperate difeafes require defperate remedies ; and with
truth declare that I have no luft after power, but wifh
with as much fervency as any man upon this wide-extend-
ed continent for an opportunity of turning the fword into
a ploughfhare. But my feelings, as an officer and a man,
have been fuch as to force me to fay that no perfon ever
had a greater choice of difficulties to contend with than I
have. It is needlefs to add that fhort enliftments, and a
miftaken dependence upon militia, have been the origin of
all our misfortunes and the great accumulation of our debt.

We

We find, Sir, that the enemy are daily gathering ftrength from the difaffected. This ftrength, like a fnow-ball, by rolling, will increafe, unlefs fome means can be devifed to check effectually the progrefs of the enemy's arms. Militia may poffibly do it for a little while : but in a little while alfo, the militia of thofe States which have been frequently called upon will not turn out at all ; or, if they do, it will be with fo much reluctance and floth, as to amount to the fame thing :—inftance, New Jerfey !—witnefs, Pennfylvania !—Could any thing but the river Delaware have faved Philadelphia ?—Can any thing (the exigency of the cafe indeed may juftify it) be more deftructive to the recruiting fervice, than giving ten dollars bounty for fix weeks' fervice of the militia, who come in, you cannot tell how,—go, you cannot tell when,—and act, you cannot tell where,—confume your provifions, exhauft your ftores, and leave you at laft at a critical moment ?

Thefe, Sir, are the men I am to depend upon ten days hence : this is the bafis on which your caufe will and muft forever depend, till you get a large ftanding army fufficient of itfelf to oppofe the enemy. I therefore beg leave to give it as my humble opinion, that eighty-eight battalions are by no means equal to the oppofition you are to make, and that a moment's time is not to be loft in raifing a greater number,—not lefs, in my opinion and the opinion of my officers, than a hundred and ten. It may be urged that it will be found difficult enough to complete the firft number. This may be true, and yet the officers of a hundred and ten battalions will recruit many more men, than thofe of eighty-eight. In my judgment this is not a time to ftand upon expenfe : our funds are the only object of confideration. The State of New-York have added one battalion (I wifh they had made it two) to their quota. If any good officers offer to raife men upon continental pay and eftablifhment in this quarter, I fhall encourage them to do fo, and regiment them when they have done it. If Congrefs difapprove of this proceeding, they will pleafe to fignify it, as I mean it for the beft.

It may be thought that I am going a good deal out of the line of my duty, to adopt thefe meafures, or to advife thus freely. A character to lofe,—an eftate to forfeit,—

the

the ineftimable bleffings of liberty at ftake,—and a life devoted,—muft be my excufe.

I have heard nothing of the light-horfe from Virginia,
nor the regiment from the Eaftern-Shore. I wifh to know
what troops are to act in the different departments, and to
have thofe from the fouthward (defigned for this place)
ordered on as faft as they fhall be raifed. The route fhould
be pointed out by which they are to march ; affiftant-com-
miffaries and quarter-mafters upon the communication, to
fupply their wants ; the firft or fecond officer of each battalion to forward them, and the other to come on, receive
and form them at their place of deftination. Unlefs this
is immediately fet about, the campaign, if it fhould be clofed, will be opened in the fpring before we have any men
in the field.

Every exertion fhould be ufed to procure tents : a ·
clothier-general fhould be appointed without lofs of time
for fupplying the army with every article in that way :—he
fhould be a man of bufinefs and abilities. A commiffary
of prifoners muft be appointed to attend the army :—for
want of an officer of this kind, the exchange of prifoners
has been conducted in a moft fhameful and injurious manner. We have had them from all quarters pufhed into
our camps at the moft critical junctures, and without the
leaft previous notice. We have had them travelling through
the different States in all directions by certificates from
committees, without any kind of control ; and have had
inftances of fome going into the enemy's camp without my
privity or knowledge, after paffing in the manner before
mentioned. There may be other officers neceffary which
I do not recollect at this time, and which, when thought
of, muft be provided : for this, Sir, you may rely on, that
the commanding officer, under the prefent eftablifhment, is
obliged to attend to the bufinefs of fo many different departments, as to render it impoffible to conduct that of his
own with the attention neceffary ;—than which, nothing
can be more injurious.

In a former letter, I intimated my opinion of the neceffity of having a brigadier for every three regiments, and a
major-general to every three brigades, at moft. I think
no time is to be loft in making the appointments, that the
arrangements may be confequent. This will not only aid

the

the recruiting fervice, but will be the readieft means of forming and difciplining the army afterwards, which, in the fhort time we have to do it, is of amazing confequence. I have laboured, ever fince I have been in the fervice, to difcourage all kinds of local attachments and diftinctions of country, denominating the whole by the greater name of '*American*:' but I found it impoffible to overcome prejudices; and, under the new eftablifhment, I conceive it beft to ftir up an emulation; in order to do which, would it not be better for each State to furnifh (though not to appoint) their own brigadiers ?—This, if known to be part of the eftablifhment, might prevent a good deal of contention and jealoufy; and would, I believe, be the means of promotions going forward with more fatisfaction, and quiet the higher officers.

Whilft I am fpeaking of promotions, I cannot help giving it as my opinion, that, if Congrefs think proper to confirm what I have done with refpect to the corps of artillery, colonel Knox (at prefent at the head of that department, but who, without promotion, will refign) ought to be appointed to the command of it, with the rank and pay of brigadier. I have alfo to mention, that, for want of fome eftablifhment in the department of engineers agreeable to the plan laid before Congrefs in October laft, colonel Putnam, who was at the head of it, has quitted, and taken a regiment in the State of Maffachufetts. I know of no other man tolerably well qualified for the conducting of that bufinefs. None of the French gentlemen whom I have feen with appointments in that way appear to me to know any thing of the matter. There is one in Philadelphia, who, I am told, is clever: but him I have never feen.

I muft alfo once more beg leave to mention to Congrefs the expediency of letting promotions be in a regimental line. The want of this has already driven fome of the beft officers that were in your army, out of the fervice. From repeated and ftrict inquiry I am convinced you can adopt no mode of promotion that will be better received, or that will give more general fatisfaction. I wifh therefore to have it announced.

The cafting of cannon is a matter that ought not to be one moment delayed: and therefore I fhall fend colonel Knox to put this in a train, as alfo to have travelling carriages
riages

riages and fhot provided,—elaboratories to be eftablifhed, one in Hartford, and another in York. Magazines
of provifions fhould alfo be laid in. Thefe I fhall fix with
the commiffary. As our great lofs laft year proceeded
from a want of teams, I fhall direct the quarter-mafter-general to furnifh a certain number to each regiment to anfwer
the common purpofes thereof, that the army may be enabled to remove from place to place differently from what
we have done, or could do, this campaign. Ammunition
carts, and proper carts for intrenching tools, fhould alfo
be provided, and I fhall direct about them accordingly.
Above all, a ftore of fmall arms fhould be provided, or
men will be of little ufe. The confumption and wafte of
thefe, this year, has been great :—militia, flying-camp men,
&c. coming in without, were obliged to be furnifhed, or
become ufelefs. Many of thefe threw their arms away :
fome loft them, whilft others deferted, and took them away.
In a word, although I ufed every precaution to preferve
them, the lofs has been great ; and this will forever be
the cafe in fuch a mixed and irregular army as ours has
been.

If no part of the troops already embarked at New-York
has appeared in Virginia, their deftination doubtlefs muft
be to fome other quarter ; and that State muft, I fhould
think, be freed from any invafion, if general Howe can be
effectually oppofed in this. I therefore inclofe a memorandum given me by brigadier Stephen of Virginia, which
Congrefs will pleafe to adopt in the whole,—in part,—or
reject,—as may be confiftent with their plans and intelligence.

The divifion of the army, late under the command of
general Lee, now general Sullivan, is juft upon the point
of joining us. A ftrange kind of fatality has attended it.
They had orders on the feventeenth of November to join,
now more than a month. General Gates, with four eaftern regiments, is alfo near at hand : three others from
thofe States were coming on, by his order, by the way of
Peekfkill, and had joined general Heath whom I had ordered on with Parfons's brigade, to join me, leaving Clinton's brigade and fome militia (that were at Forts Montgomery and Conftitution) to guard thofe important paffes
of the Highlands. But the convention of the State of
New-York

New-York feeming to be much alarmed at Heath's coming away,—a fleet appearing off New-London,—and fome part of the enemy's troops retiring towards Brunfwic,—induced me to countermand the order for the march of Parfons's brigade, and to direct the three regiments from Ticonderoga to halt at Morriftown in Jerfey (where I underftand about eight hundred militia had collected,) in order to infpirit the inhabitants, and, as far as poffible, cover that part of the country. I fhall fend general Maxwell this day to take the command of them, and, if to be done, to harafs and annoy the enemy in their quarters, and cut off their convoys.

The care and vigilance, which were ufed in fecuring the boats on this river, have hitherto baffled every attempt of the enemy to crofs : but, from concurring reports and appearances, they are waiting for ice to afford them a paffage.

Since writing the foregoing I have received a letter from governor Cooke of Rhode-Ifland, of which the inclofed is a copy. Previous to this, and immediately upon the firft intelligence obtained of a fleet's going through the Sound, I difpatched orders to generals Spencer and Arnold to proceed without the leaft delay to the eaftward. The firft, I prefume, is gone : the latter, not getting my letter till he came to a place called Eafton, was, by advice of general Gates who alfo met my letter at the fame place, induced to come on hither before he proceeded to the eaftward. Moft of our brigadiers are laid up : not one has come on with the divifion under general Sullivan, but they are left fick at different places on the road.

By accounts from the eaftward, a large body of men had affembled in Rhode-Ifland from the States of Maffachufetts and Connecticut. I prefume (but I have no advice of it) that the militia, ordered from the firft to rendezvous at Danbury (fix thoufand in number) under the command of major general Lincoln, for fupplying the place of the difbanded men of that State in the continental army, will now be ordered to Rhode-Ifland.

In fpeaking of general Lincoln, I fhould not do him juftice, were I not to add that he is a gentleman well worthy of notice in the military line. He commanded the militia from Maffachufetts laft fummer, or fall rather, and much to my fatisfaction,—having proved himfelf on all

occafions

occasions an active, spirited, sensible man.   I do not know
whether it is his wish to remain in the military line, or
whether, if he should, any thing under the rank he now
holds in the State he comes from would satisfy him.   How
far an appointment of this kind might offend the continental brigadiers, I cannot undertake to say : many there are,
over whom he ought not to be placed ; but I know of no
way to discriminate.   Brigadier Reed of New-Hampshire
does not, I presume, mean to continue in service : he
ought not,—as I am told, by the severity of the small-pox,
he is become both blind and deaf.

I have the honour to be, &c.   G. W.

P. S. Generals Gates and Sullivan have this instant
come in.   By them I learn that few or no men are
recruited out of the regiments coming on with them, and
that there is very little reason to expect that these regiments
will be prevailed upon to continue after their term of service expires.   If militia then do not come in, the consequences are but too evident.

SIR,   *Camp above Trenton Falls, Decem. 24, 1776.*

THAT I should dwell upon the subject of our distresses, cannot be more disagreeable to Congress than it is
painful to myself.   The alarming situation to which our
affairs are reduced impels me to the measure.   Inquiry
and investigation,—which in most cases serve to develop
and point out a remedy, in ours, present more and greater
difficulties.   Till of late, I was led to hope from report
that no inconsiderable part of the troops composing the
regiments that were with general Lee, and those from Ticonderoga under general Gates, had enlisted again.   This
intelligence, I confess, gave me reason to expect that I
should have, at the expiration of the present year, a force
somewhat more respectable than what I find will be the case.

Having examined into the state of those regiments, I am
authorised to say from the information of their officers, that
but very few of the men have enlisted.   Those who have are
of the troops from Ticonderoga, and were permitted to visit
their friends and homes, as part of the terms on which
they would re-engage.   In respect to those who marched
                                                    with

with general Lee, I cannot learn that any have. Their refusal, I am told, has not proceeded more from an averfion to the fervice, or any fixed determination not to engage again, than from their wifhes to return home,—the non-appointment of officers in fome inftances,—the turning out of good, and appointing of bad,—and in others, the incomplete or rather no arrangement of them,—a work unhappily committed to the management of their States : nor have I the moft diftant profpect of retaining them a moment longer than the laft of this inftant, notwithftanding the moft preffing folicitations and the obvious neceffity for it.

By the departure of thefe regiments I fhall be left with five from Virginia, Smallwood's from Maryland, a fmall part of Rawlins's, Hand's from Pennfylvania, a part of Ward's from Connecticut, and the German battalion, amounting in the whole at this time from fourteen to fifteen hundred effective men. This handful, and fuch militia as may choofe to join me, will then compofe our army.

When I reflect upon thefe things they fill me with much concern, knowing that general Howe has a number of troops cantoned in the towns bordering on and near the Delaware,—his intentions being to pafs, as foon as the ice is fufficiently formed, to invade Pennfylvania and to poffefs himfelf of Philadelphia if poffible. To guard againft his defigns and the execution of them, fhall employ my every exertion : but how is this to be done ? As yet but few militia have gone to Philadelphia, and they are to be our fupport at this alarming crifis. Had I entertained a doubt of general Howe's intentions to pafs the Delaware on the diffolution of our army, and as foon as the ice is made, it would now be done away. An intercepted letter from a gentleman of Philadelphia (who has joined the enemy) to his friend and partner in the city declares that to be their defign,—that the army would be there in ten or twenty days from the fixteenth inftant, the time of his writing, if the ice fhould be made ;—advifes him by no means to remove their ftores,—that they would be fafe.

The obftacles which have arifen to the raifing of the new army, from the mode of appointing the officers, induce me to hope, if Congrefs refolve on an additional number of battalions to thofe already voted, that they will devife fome other rule by which the officers, efpecially the

field-officers,

field-officers, should be appointed. In case an augmentation should be made to the eastern regiments, a deviation from the former mode will operate more strongly as to them than to other battalions, because there have been many more officers in service from those States, than the regiments voted to be raised would admit of; by which means several deserving men could not have been provided for, had the utmost pains been used for the purpose; and many others of merit have been neglected in the late appointments, and those of little worth and less experience put in their places or promoted over their heads. This has been the case with many of the best officers.

The inclosed letter from the paymaster-general will shew the state of the military chest, and the necessity of a large and immediate supply of cash. The advances to the officers, for bounty and the recruiting service, are great: besides, the regiments, at the expiration of this month, will require pay of their claims. * * *

I have the honour to be, &c. G. W.

P. S. If the public papers have been removed from Philadelphia, I hope those which I sent by lieutenant-colonel Reed before we left New-York have not been forgot. If they have not, I beg the favour of you to break open the chest, and send me the several letter-books sealed up, having frequent occasion to refer to them.

***

To ROBERT MORRIS, *esquire.*

DEAR SIR, *Head-Quarters, Dec. 25, 1776.*

I HAVE your obliging favours of the twenty-first and twenty-third. The blankets are come to hand; but I would not have any of the other goods sent on till you hear again from me.

I agree with you that it is in vain to ruminate upon, or even reflect upon the authors or causes of, our present misfortunes: we should rather exert ourselves, and look forward with hopes that some lucky chance may yet turn up in our favour. Bad as our prospects are, I should not have the least doubt of success in the end, did not the late treachery and defection of those who stood foremost in the op-

poſition

position while fortune smiled upon us, make me fearful that many more will follow their example, who, by using their influence with some and working upon the fears of others, may extend the circle so as to take in whole towns, counties, nay, provinces.   Of this we have a recent instance in Jersey ; and I wish many parts of Pennsylvania may not be ready to receive the yoke.

The security of the continental ships of war in Delaware is certainly a capital object ; and yet to draught the many hands, necessary to fit them out, from the militia, might be dangerous just now : perhaps in a little time hence their places may be supplied with country militia ; and then, if the exigency of affairs requires it, they certainly ought to be spared.   I will just hint to you a proposition that was made, or rather talked of, a few days ago by the officers of two New-England regiments whose time of service will expire on the first of January.   They are most of them water men : and they said their men would willingly go on board the frigates, and navigate them round to any of the ports in New-England, if it was thought they would be safer there than in Delaware.   You may think of this, and let me hear from you on the subject, if the proposition pleases you.

Lieutenant Boger of the navy is already gone in, and I have made a demand of lieutenant Josiah in exchange ; but I have not heard whether lord Howe accedes to it.   I will procure the release of doctor Hodge as soon as it can be done without injuring others by giving him the preference, as I have always made it a rule to demand those first who have been longest in captivity.   I will take the same steps in regard to Mr. Jones, commander of the sloop taken by the Andrew Doria.

I shall take the earliest opportunity of sending in your letter to general Lee, with the bill drawn upon major Small.

From an intercepted letter from a person in the secrets of the enemy, I find their intentions are to cross Delaware as soon as the ice is sufficiently strong.   I mention this, that you may take the necessary steps for the security of such public and private property as ought not to fall into their hands should they make themselves masters of Philadelphia, of which they do not seem to entertain the least doubt.

I hope

I hope the next Chriftmas will prove happier than the prefent, to you, and to, dear Sir, your fincere friend and humble fervant,   G. W.

P. S.   I would juft afk whether you think Chriftiana a fafe place for our ftores ?   Do not you think they would be fafer at Lancafter, or fomewhere more inland ?

———

SIR,   *Head-Quarters, Morriftown, Dec.* 27, 1776.

I HAVE the pleafure of congratulating you upon the fuccefs of an enterprife which I had formed againft a detachment of the enemy lying in Trenton, and which was executed yefterday morning.

The evening of the twenty-fifth I ordered the troops intended for this fervice to parade back of M'Konkey's ferry, that they might begin to pafs as foon as it grew dark, imagining we fhould be able to throw them all over, with the neceffary artillery, by twelve o'clock, and that we might eafily arrive at Trenton by five in the morning, the diftance being about nine miles.   But the quantity of ice, made that night, impeded the paffage of the boats fo much, that it was three o'clock before the artillery could all be got over ; and near four, before the troops took up their line of march.

This made me defpair of furprifing the town, as I well knew we could not reach it before the day was fairly broke. But as I was certain there was no making a retreat without being difcovered, and haraffed on re-paffing the river, I determined to pufh on at all events.   I formed my detachment into two divifions, one to march by the lower or river road, the other by the upper or Pennington road. As the divifions had nearly the fame diftance to march, I ordered each of them, immediately upon forcing the out-guards, to pufh directly into the town, that they might charge the enemy before they had time to form.

The upper divifion arrived at the enemy's advanced poft exactly at eight o'clock ; and in three minutes after, I found, from the fire on the lower road, that that divifion had alfo got up.   The out-guards made but fmall oppofition, though, for their numbers, they behaved very well, keeping up a conftant retreating fire from behind houfes.

VOL. I.   E e   We

We prefently faw their main body formed : but, from their motions, they feemed undetermined how to act.

Being hard preffed by our troops, who had already got poffeffion of their artillery, they attempted to file off by a road on their right, leading to Princeton. But, perceiving their intention, I threw a body of troops in their way ; which immediately checked them. Finding from our dif-pofition, that they were furrounded, and that they muft inevitably be cut to pieces if they made any further refift-ance, they agreed to lay down their arms. The number that fubmitted in this manner was twenty-three officers and eight hundred and eighty-fix men. Colonel Rahl the commanding officer, and feven others, were found wound-ed in the town. I do not exactly know how many they had killed ; but I fancy not above twenty or thirty, as they never made any regular ftand. Our lofs is very trifling indeed,—only two officers and one or two privates wounded.

I find that the detachment of the enemy confifted of the three Heffian regiments of Lanfpach, Kniphaufen, and Rahl, amounting to about fifteen hundred men, and a troop of Britifh light horfe : but, immediately upon the begin-ning of the attack, all thofe who were not killed or taken pufhed directly down the road towards Bordentown. Thefe would likewife have fallen into our hands, could my plan have been completely carried into execution. Gen-eral Ewing was to have croffed before day at Trenton fer-ry, and taken poffeffion of the bridge leading out of town : but the quantity of ice was fo great, that, though he did every thing in his power to effect it, he could not get over. This difficulty alfo hindered general Cadwallader from croffing with the Pennfylvania militia from Briftol. He got part of his foot over : but finding it impoffible to em-bark his artillery, he was obliged to defift.

I am fully confident, that, could the troops under gen-erals Ewing and Cadwallader have paffed the river, I fhould have been able with their affiftance to have driven the ene-my from all their pofts below Trenton. But the numbers I had with me being inferior to theirs below me, and a ftrong battalion of light infantry being at Princeton above me, I thought it moft prudent to return the fame evening

with

with the prifoners and the artillery we had taken. We found no ftores of any confequence in the town.

In juftice to the officers and men, I muft add that their behaviour upon this occafion reflects the higheft honour upon them.   The difficulty of paffing the river in a very fevere night, and their march through a violent ftorm of fnow and hail, did not in the leaft abate their ardour : but, when they came to the charge, each feemed to vie with the other in preffing forward : and were I to give a preference to any particular corps, I fhould do great injuftice to the others.

Colonel Baylor, my firft aide-de-camp, will have the honour of delivering this to you ; and from him you may be made acquainted with many other particulars.   His fpirited behaviour upon every occafion requires me to recommend him to your particular notice.

I have the honour to be, &c.   G. W.

Inclofed you have a prrticular lift of the prifoners, artillery and other ftores.

* * *

SIR,   *Newtown, December* 29, 1776.

I AM juft fetting out to attempt a fecond paffage over the Delaware with the troops that were with me on the morning of the twenty-fixth.   I am determined to effect it if poffible ; but know that it will be attended with much fatigue and difficulty on account of the ice, which will neither allow us to crofs on foot, nor give us an eafy paffage with boats.   General Cadwallader croffed from Briftol on the twenty-feventh, and, by his letter of yefterday, was at Bordentown with about eighteen hundred men. In addition to thefe, general Mifflin fent over five hundred from Philadelphia on Friday, three hundred yefterday evening from Burlington, and will follow to-day with feven or eight hundred more.   I have taken every precaution in my power for fubfifting the troops, and fhall, without lofs of time, and as foon as circumftances will admit of it, purfue the enemy in their retreat,—try to beat up more of their quarters,—and, in a word, in every inftance, adopt fuch meafures as the exigency of our affairs requires, and our fituation will juftify.

Had

Had it not been for the unhappy failure of generals Ewing and Cadwallader in their attempts to pass on the night of the twenty-fifth,—and if the several concerted attacks could have been made,—I have no doubt but that our views would have succeeded to our warmest expectations. What was done occasioned the enemy to leave their several posts on the Delaware with great precipitation. The peculiar distresses to which the troops who were with me were reduced by the severities of cold, rain, snow, and storm,—the charge of the prisoners they had taken,—and another reason that might be mentioned,—and the little prospect of receiving succours on account of the season and situation of the river,—would not authorize a further pursuit at that time.

Since transmitting the list of prisoners, a few more have been discovered and taken in Trenton,—among them a lieutenant-colonel, and a deputy-adjutant-general,—the whole amounting to about a thousand.

I have been honoured wtth your letter of the twenty-third and its several inclosures, to which I shall pay due attention. A flag goes in this morning with a letter to general Howe, and another to general Lee. For the latter, Robert Morris, esquire, has transmitted a bill of exchange, drawn by two British officers, for a hundred and sixteen pounds nine shillings and three pence, on major Small, for money furnished them in South-Carolina, which I trust will be paid. This supply is exclusive of the sum you have resolved to be sent him, and which Mr. Morris will procure in time.

I have the honour to be, &c.　　　　　　　G. W.

P. S. I am under great apprehensions about obtaining proper supplies of provision for our troops : I fear it will be extremely difficult, if not impracticable, as the enemy, from every account, have taken and collected every thing they could find.

END OF THE FIRST VOLUME.